abigail AND THE SNOWMAN

ROGER LANGRIDGE

WITH FRED STRESING

kaboom!™

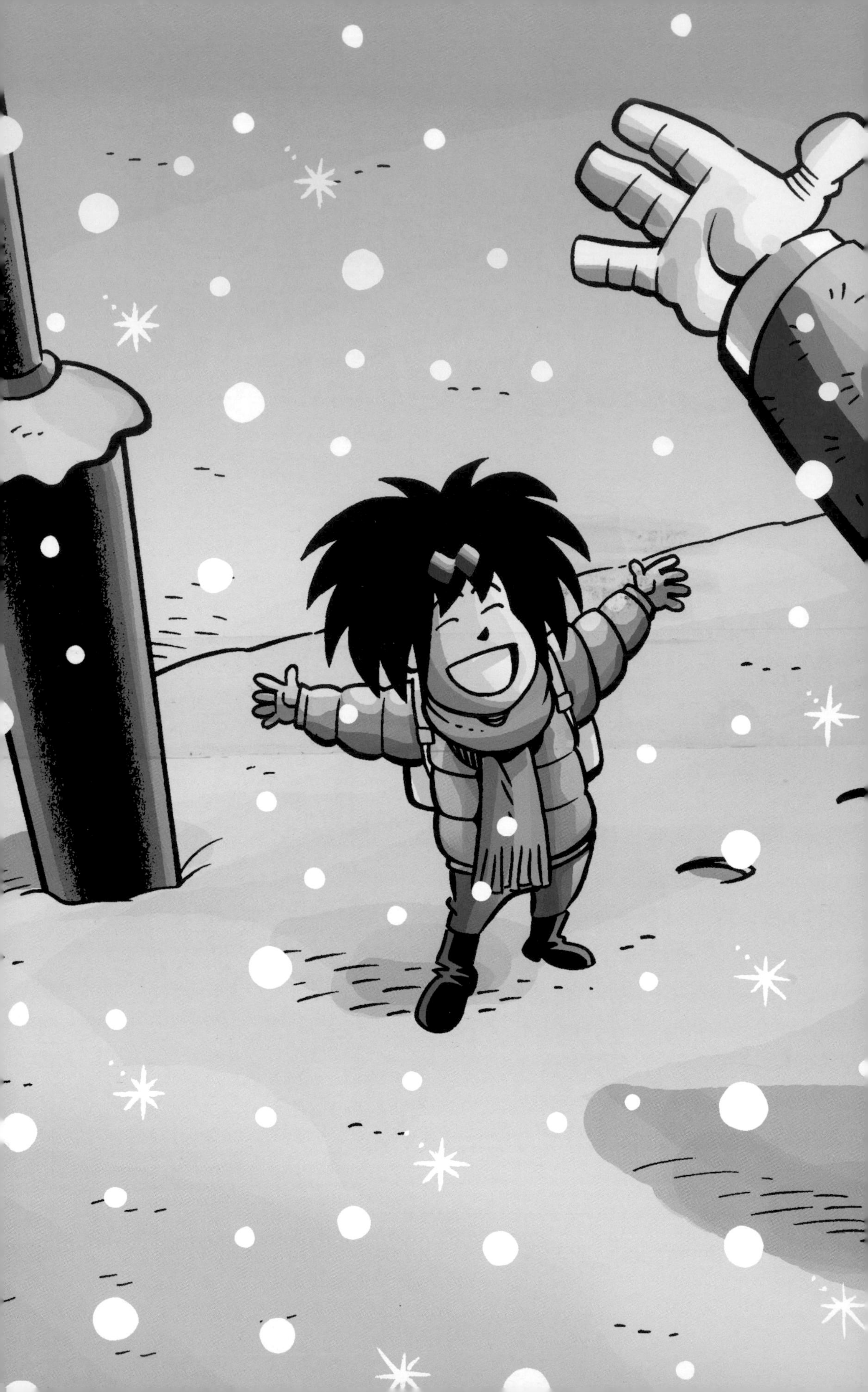

kaBOOM!™
WWW.**BOOM-STUDIOS**.COM

ABIGAIL AND THE SNOWMAN, October 2016. Published by KaBOOM!, a division of Boom Entertainment, Inc. Abigail and the Snowman is ™ & © 2016 Roger Langridge. Originally published in single magazine form as ABIGAIL AND THE SNOWMAN No. 1-4. ™ & © 2014, 2015 Roger Langridge. All rights reserved. KaBOOM!™ and the KaBOOM! logo are trademarks of Boom Entertainment, Inc., registered in various countries and categories. All characters, events, and institutions depicted herein are fictional. Any similarity between any of the names, characters, persons, events, and/or institutions in this publication to actual names, characters, and persons, whether living or dead, events, and/or institutions is unintended and purely coincidental. KaBOOM! does not read or accept unsolicited submissions of ideas, stories, or artwork.

A catalog record of this book is available from OCLC and from the BOOM! Studios website, www.boom-studios.com, on the Librarians Page.

BOOM! Studios, 5670 Wilshire Boulevard, Suite 450, Los Angeles, CA 90036-5679.
Printed in China. First Printing.

ISBN: 978-1-60886-900-8, eISBN: 978-1-61398-571-7

By
Roger Langridge

Colors by
Fred Stresing

Designer Jillian Crab
Assistant Editor Cameron Chittock
Original Series Editor Rebecca Taylor
Collection Editor Sierra Hahn

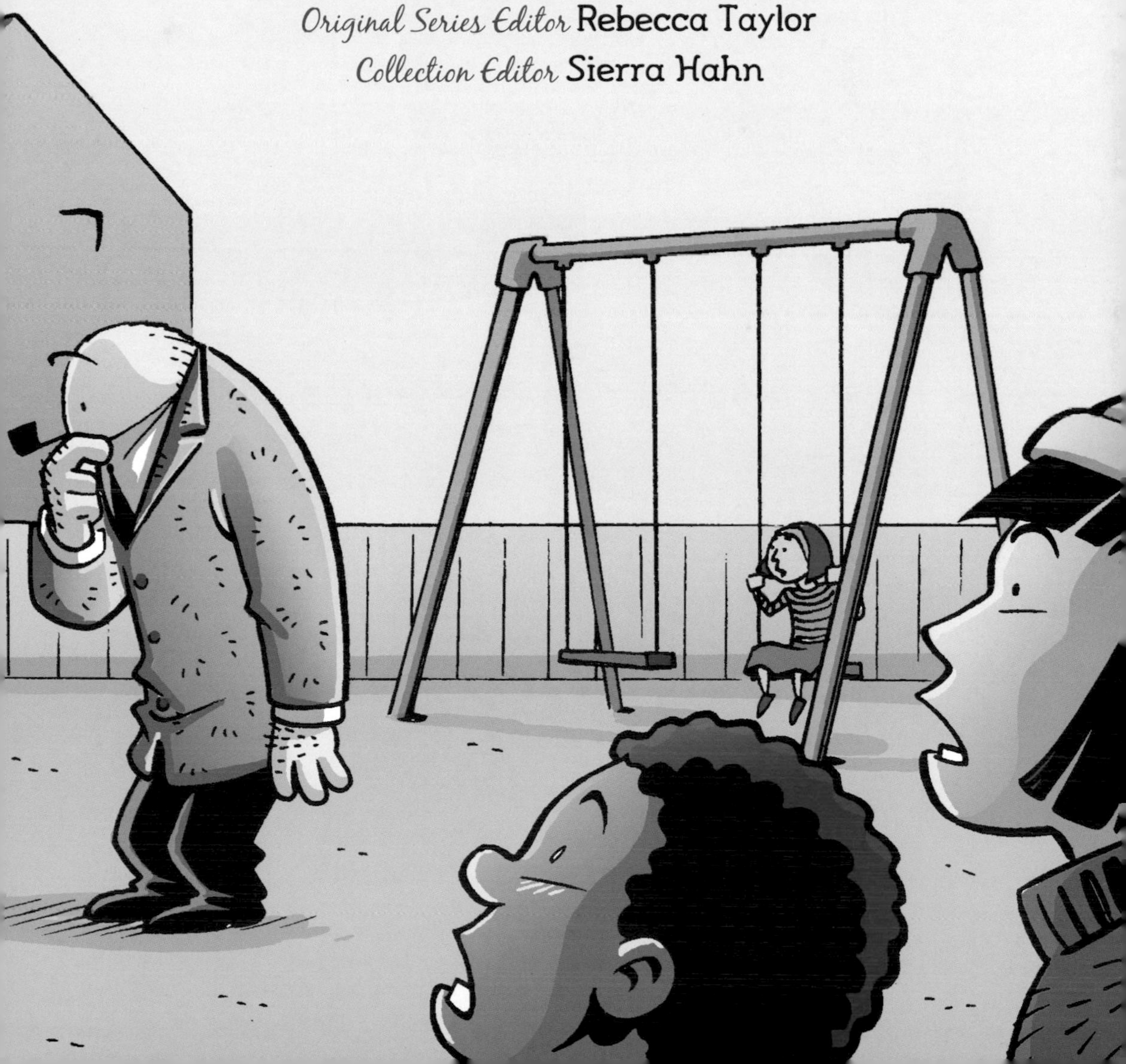

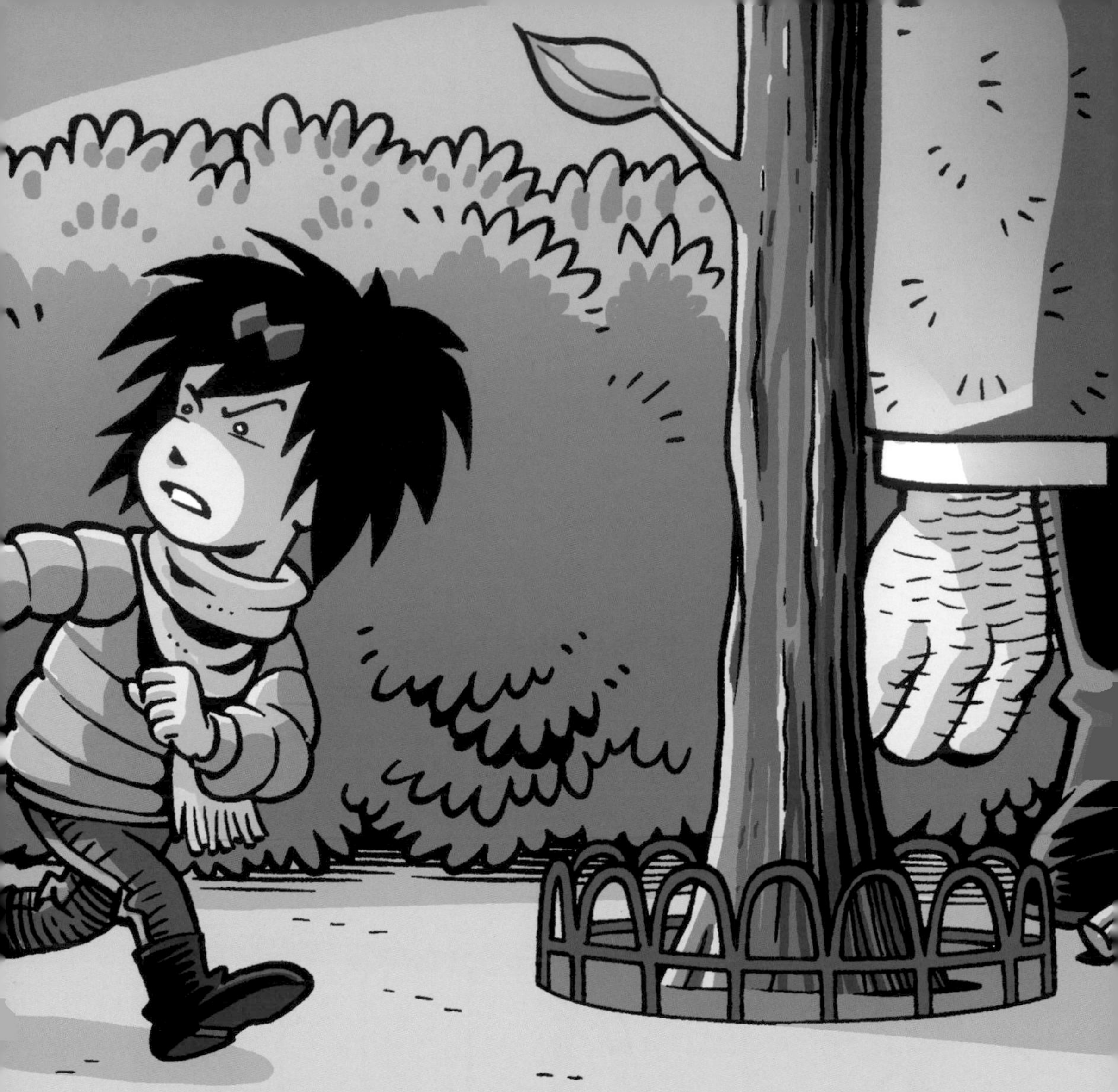

chapter one

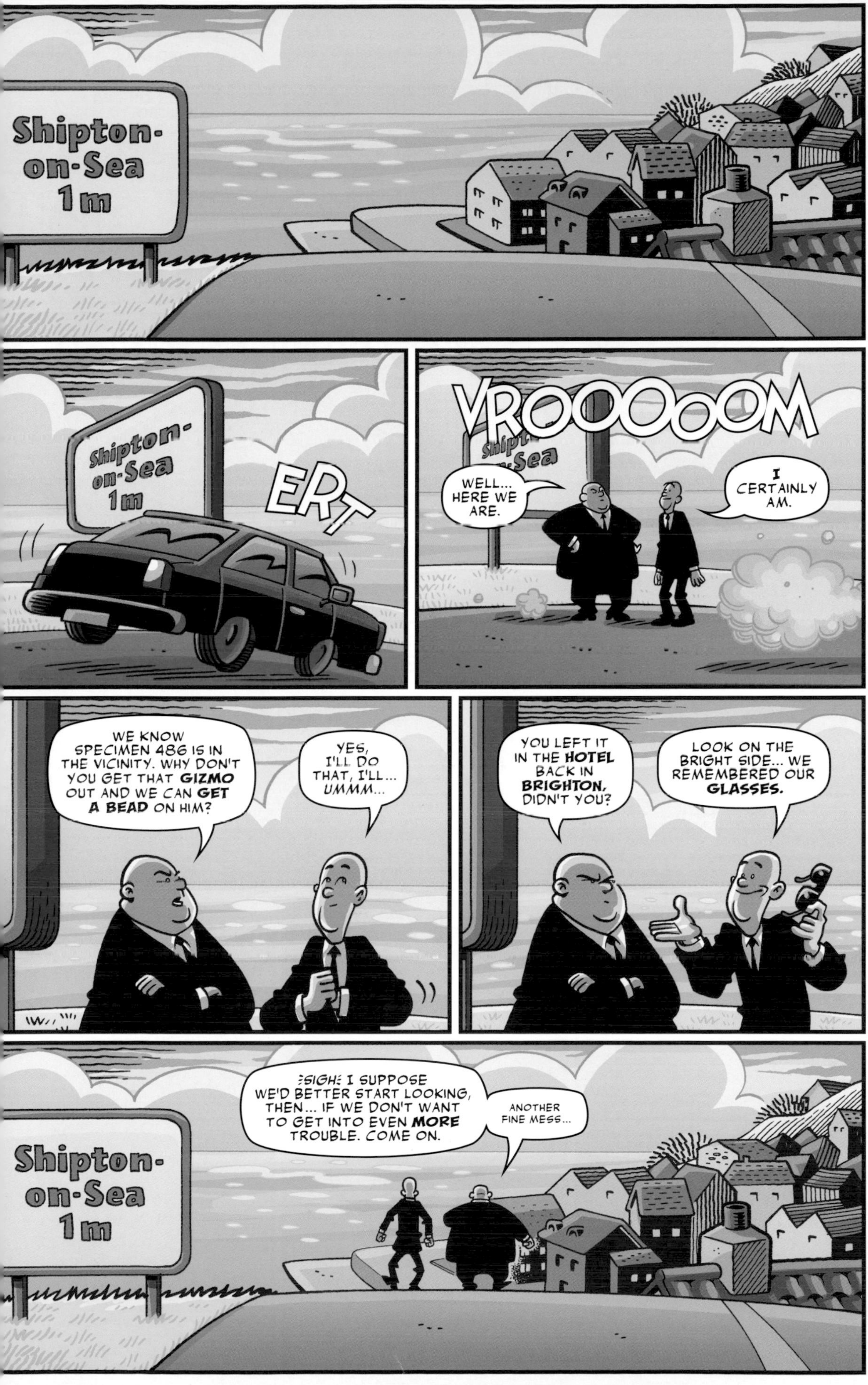
Shipton-on-Sea 1m
Shipton-on-Sea 1m
ERT
VROOOOOOM
WELL... HERE WE ARE.
I CERTAINLY AM.
WE KNOW SPECIMEN 486 IS IN THE VICINITY. WHY DON'T YOU GET THAT GIZMO OUT AND WE CAN GET A BEAD ON HIM?
YES, I'LL DO THAT, I'LL... UMMM...
YOU LEFT IT IN THE HOTEL BACK IN BRIGHTON, DIDN'T YOU?
LOOK ON THE BRIGHT SIDE... WE REMEMBERED OUR GLASSES.
Shipton-on-Sea 1m
:SIGH: I SUPPOSE WE'D BETTER START LOOKING, THEN... IF WE DON'T WANT TO GET INTO EVEN MORE TROUBLE. COME ON.
ANOTHER FINE MESS...

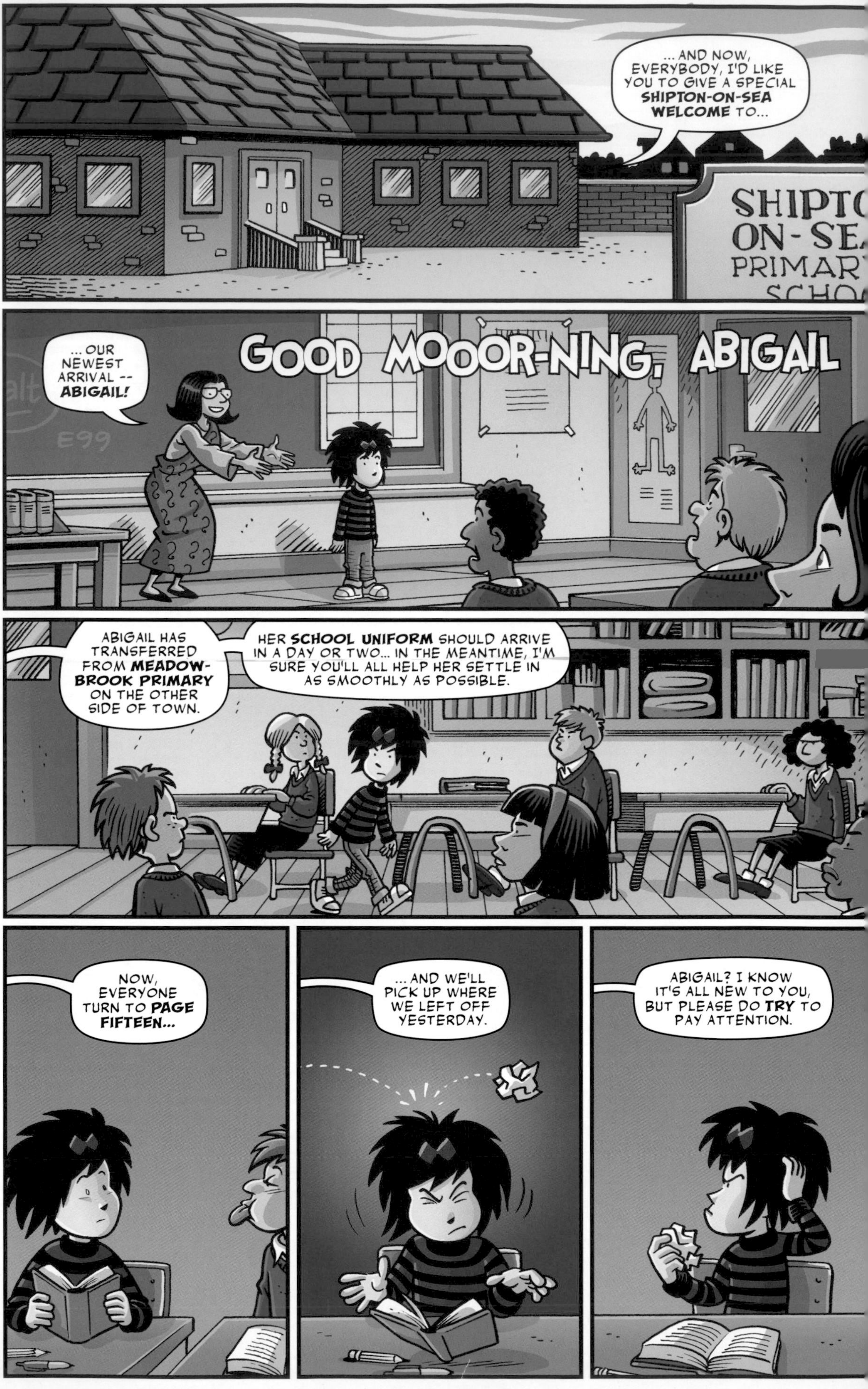
... AND NOW, EVERYBODY, I'D LIKE YOU TO GIVE A SPECIAL **SHIPTON-ON-SEA WELCOME** TO...
SHIPTO ON-SEA PRIMARY SCHO
... OUR NEWEST ARRIVAL -- **ABIGAIL!**
GOOD MOOOR-NING, ABIGAIL
ABIGAIL HAS TRANSFERRED FROM **MEADOW-BROOK PRIMARY** ON THE OTHER SIDE OF TOWN.
HER **SCHOOL UNIFORM** SHOULD ARRIVE IN A DAY OR TWO... IN THE MEANTIME, I'M SURE YOU'LL ALL HELP HER SETTLE IN AS SMOOTHLY AS POSSIBLE.
NOW, EVERYONE TURN TO **PAGE FIFTEEN...**
... AND WE'LL PICK UP WHERE WE LEFT OFF YESTERDAY.
ABIGAIL? I KNOW IT'S ALL NEW TO YOU, BUT PLEASE DO **TRY** TO PAY ATTENTION.

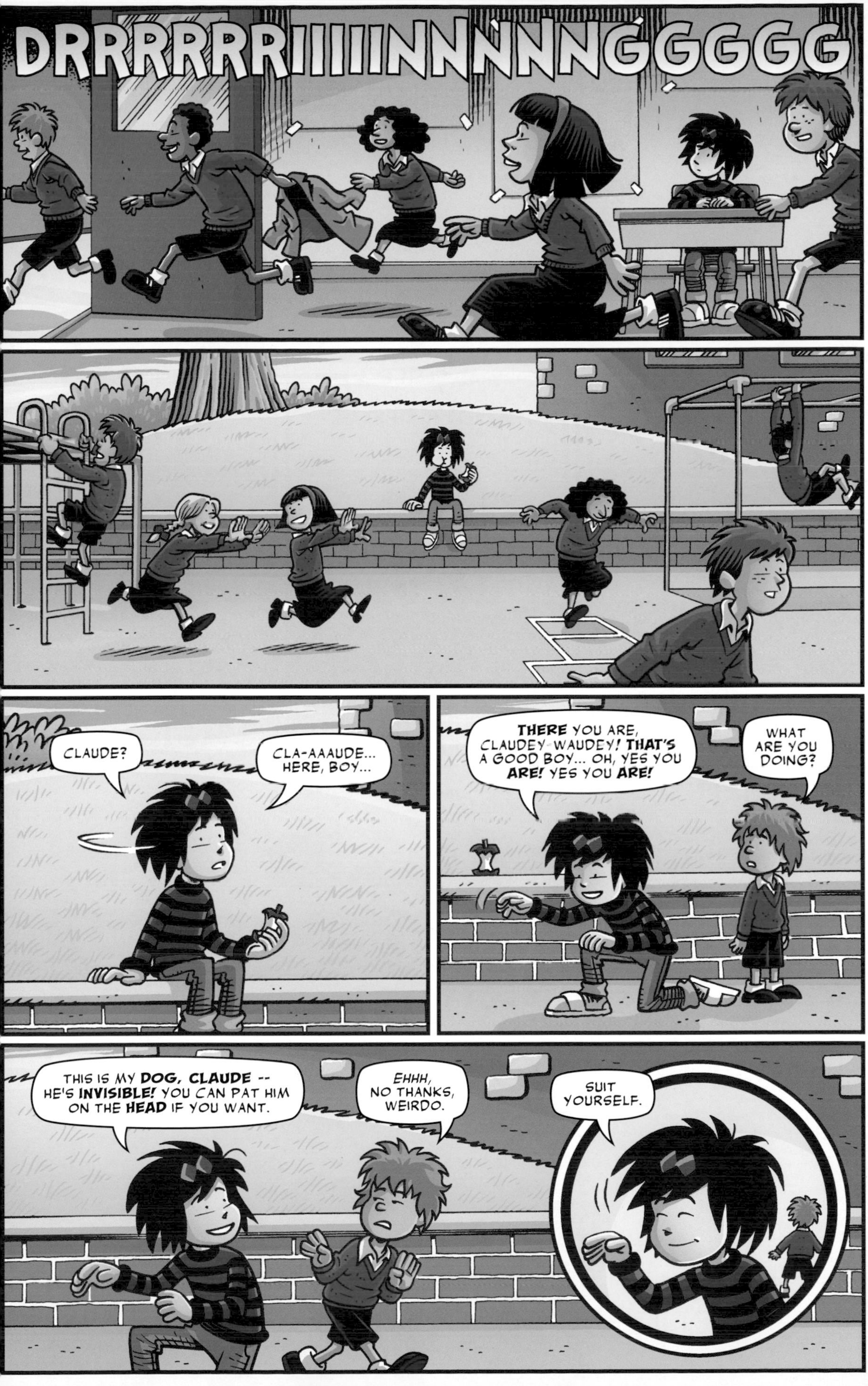
DRRRRRRIIIIINNNNNGGGGG
CLAUDE?
CLA-AAAUDE... HERE, BOY...
THERE YOU ARE, CLAUDEY-WAUDEY! THAT'S A GOOD BOY... OH, YES YOU ARE! YES YOU ARE!
WHAT ARE YOU DOING?
THIS IS MY DOG, CLAUDE -- HE'S INVISIBLE! YOU CAN PAT HIM ON THE HEAD IF YOU WANT.
EHHH, NO THANKS, WEIRDO.
SUIT YOURSELF.

BLAH BLAH BLAH
POST-WAR AUSTERITY
BLAH BLAH

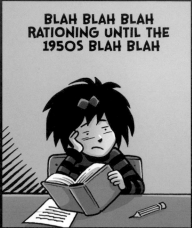

BLAH BLAH BLAH
RATIONING UNTIL THE
1950S BLAH BLAH

BLAH BLAH
DISMANTLING THE
EMPIRE BLAH
BLAH BLAH

DRRRRRRRRIIIIIIIIIIINNNNNGGGGG

ALL RIGHT, YOU'VE GOT ALL
WEEKEND. LET'S HAVE THOSE
ESSAYS WRITTEN UP BY
MONDAY, EVERYBODY!

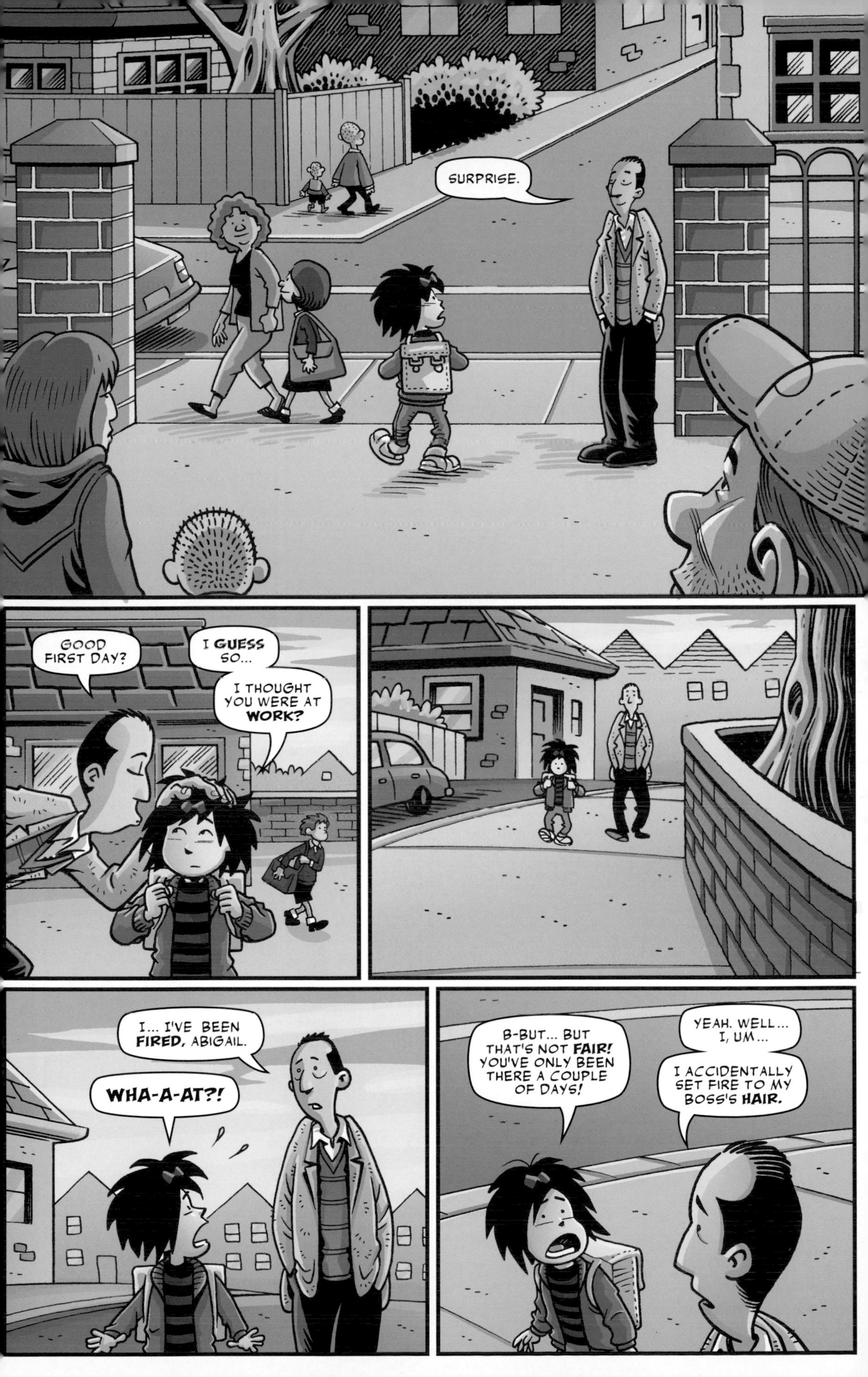
SURPRISE.
GOOD FIRST DAY?
I GUESS SO...
I THOUGHT YOU WERE AT WORK?
I... I'VE BEEN FIRED, ABIGAIL.
WHA-A-AT?!
B-BUT... BUT THAT'S NOT FAIR! YOU'VE ONLY BEEN THERE A COUPLE OF DAYS!
YEAH. WELL... I, UM...
I ACCIDENTALLY SET FIRE TO MY BOSS'S HAIR.

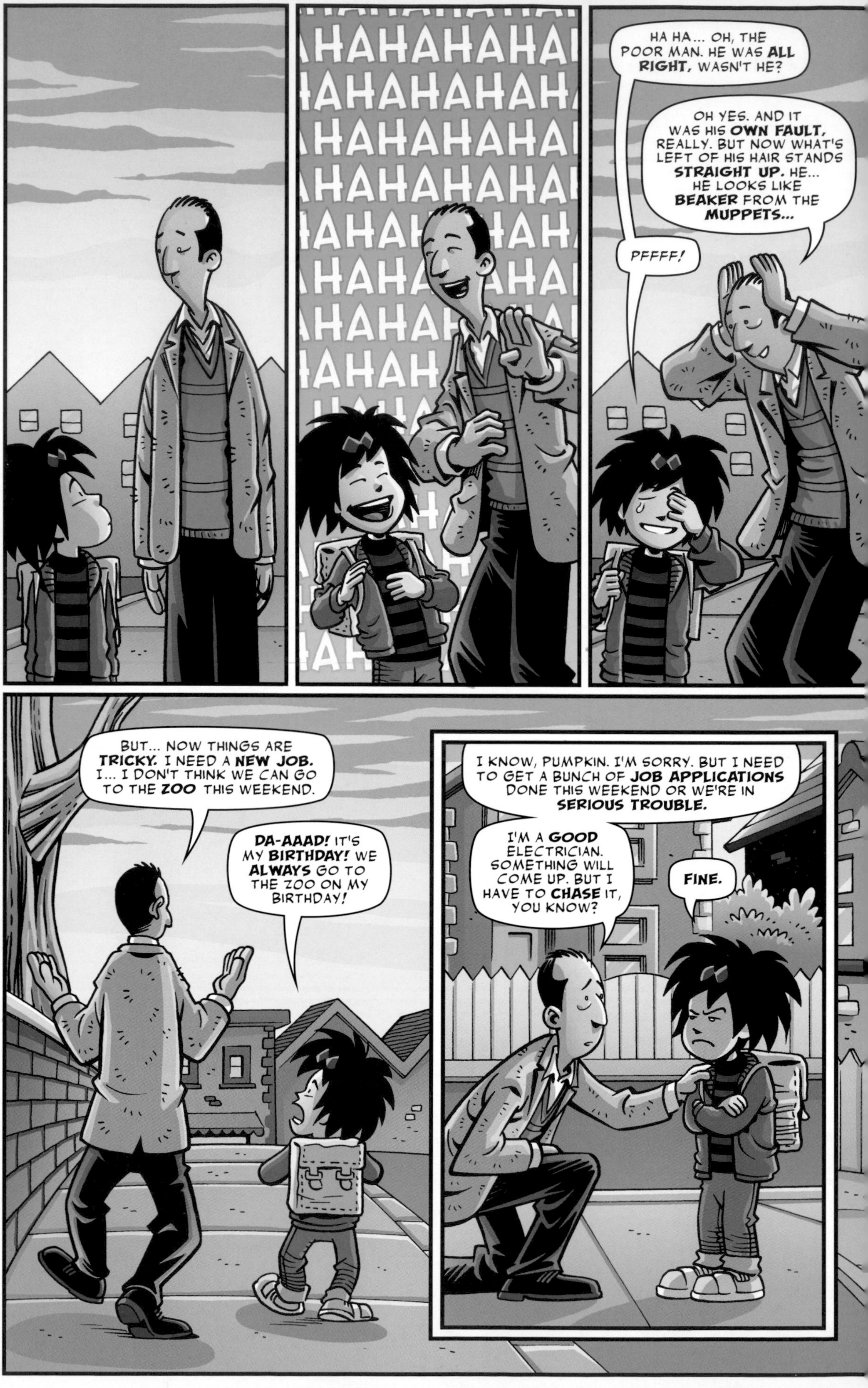

HAHAHAHAHAHAHAHAHA
HA HA... OH, THE POOR MAN. HE WAS ALL RIGHT, WASN'T HE?
OH YES. AND IT WAS HIS OWN FAULT, REALLY. BUT NOW WHAT'S LEFT OF HIS HAIR STANDS STRAIGHT UP. HE... HE LOOKS LIKE BEAKER FROM THE MUPPETS...
PFFFF!
BUT... NOW THINGS ARE TRICKY. I NEED A NEW JOB. I... I DON'T THINK WE CAN GO TO THE ZOO THIS WEEKEND.
DA-AAAD! IT'S MY BIRTHDAY! WE ALWAYS GO TO THE ZOO ON MY BIRTHDAY!
I KNOW, PUMPKIN. I'M SORRY. BUT I NEED TO GET A BUNCH OF JOB APPLICATIONS DONE THIS WEEKEND OR WE'RE IN SERIOUS TROUBLE.
I'M A GOOD ELECTRICIAN. SOMETHING WILL COME UP. BUT I HAVE TO CHASE IT, YOU KNOW?
FINE.

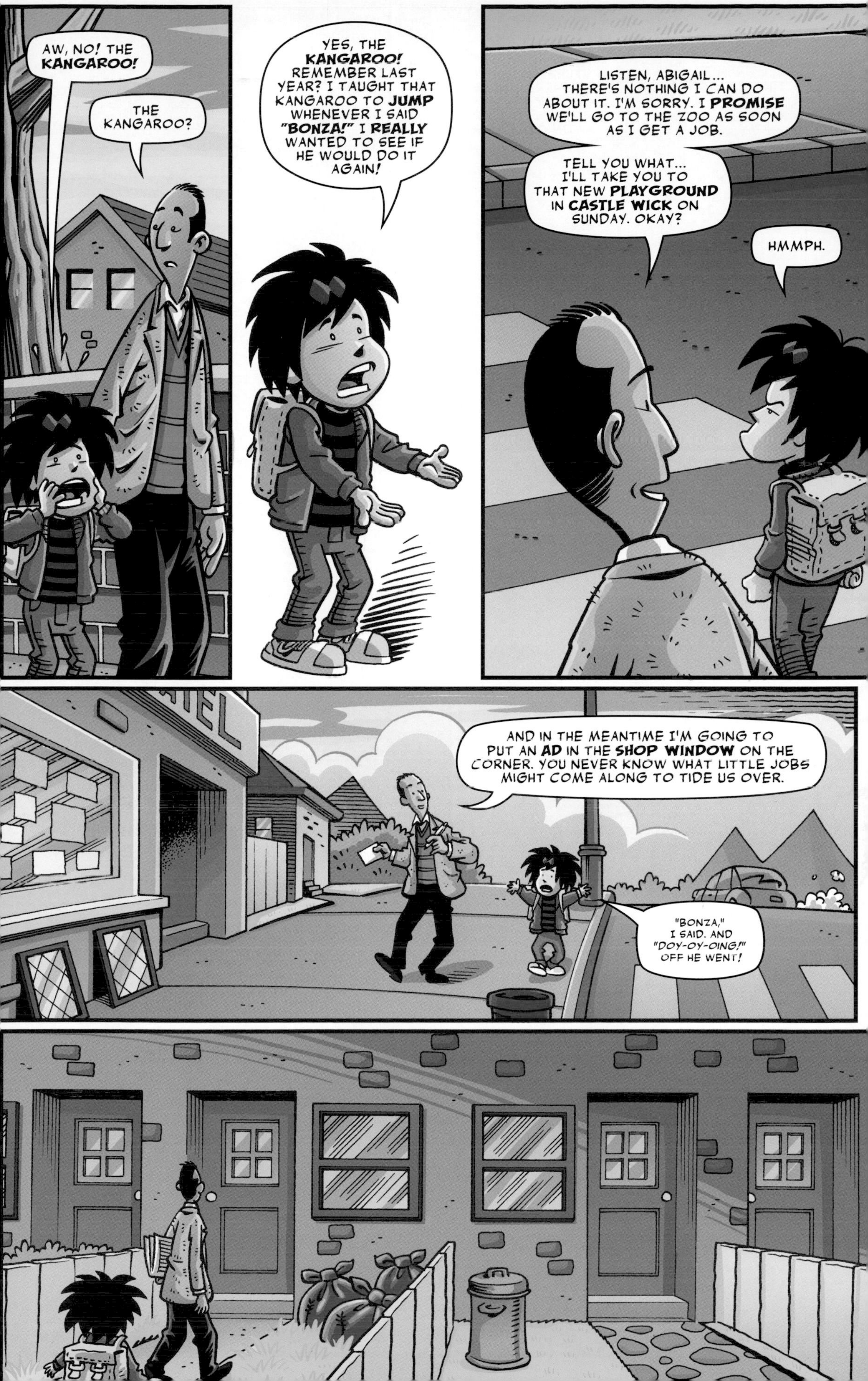
AW, NO! THE KANGAROO!
THE KANGAROO?
YES, THE KANGAROO! REMEMBER LAST YEAR? I TAUGHT THAT KANGAROO TO JUMP WHENEVER I SAID "BONZA!" I REALLY WANTED TO SEE IF HE WOULD DO IT AGAIN!
LISTEN, ABIGAIL... THERE'S NOTHING I CAN DO ABOUT IT. I'M SORRY. I PROMISE WE'LL GO TO THE ZOO AS SOON AS I GET A JOB.
TELL YOU WHAT... I'LL TAKE YOU TO THAT NEW PLAYGROUND IN CASTLE WICK ON SUNDAY. OKAY?
HMMPH.
AND IN THE MEANTIME I'M GOING TO PUT AN AD IN THE SHOP WINDOW ON THE CORNER. YOU NEVER KNOW WHAT LITTLE JOBS MIGHT COME ALONG TO TIDE US OVER.
"BONZA," I SAID. AND "DOY-OY-OING!" OFF HE WENT!

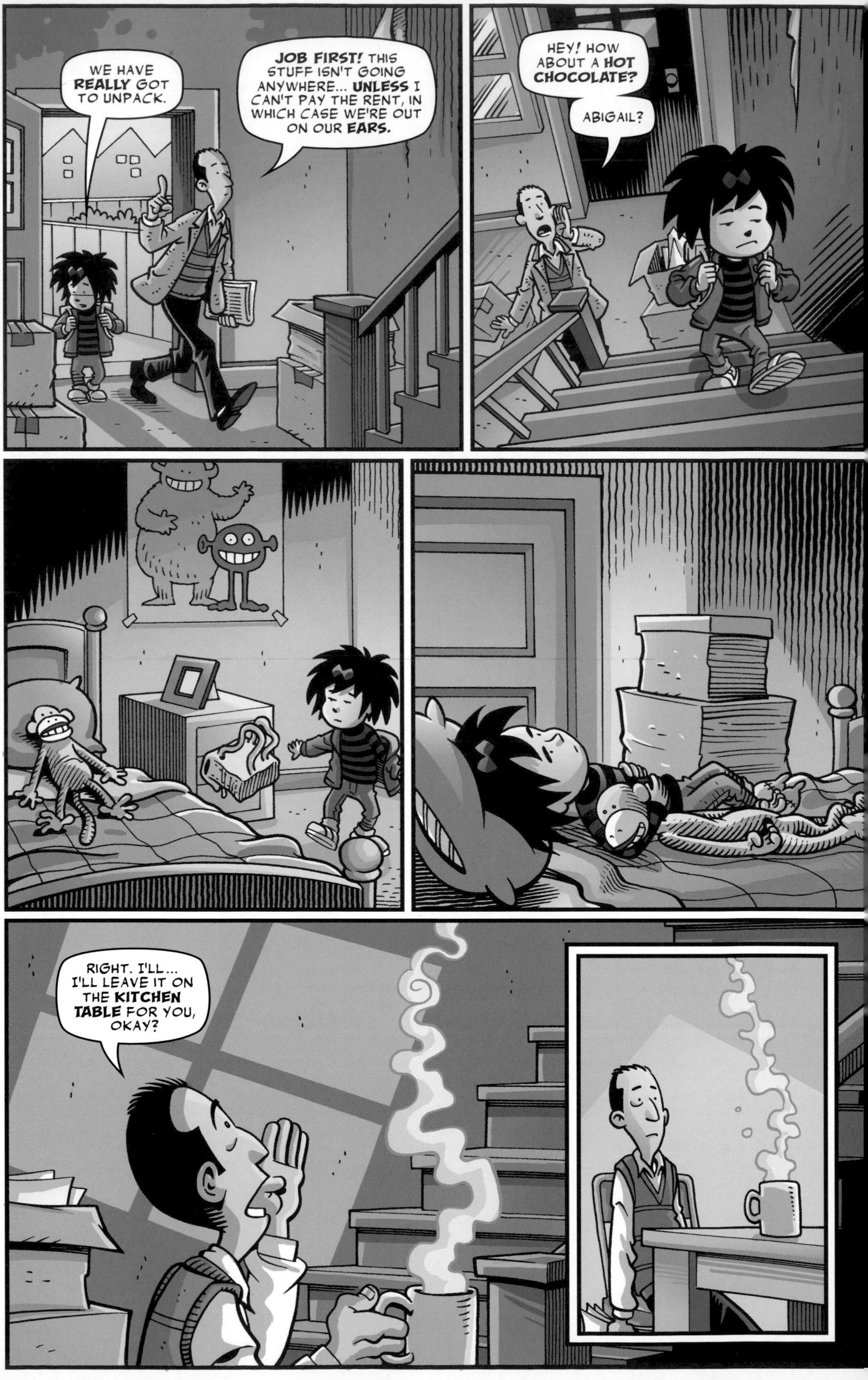
WE HAVE REALLY GOT TO UNPACK.
JOB FIRST! THIS STUFF ISN'T GOING ANYWHERE... UNLESS I CAN'T PAY THE RENT, IN WHICH CASE WE'RE OUT ON OUR EARS.
HEY! HOW ABOUT A HOT CHOCOLATE?
ABIGAIL?
RIGHT. I'LL... I'LL LEAVE IT ON THE KITCHEN TABLE FOR YOU, OKAY?

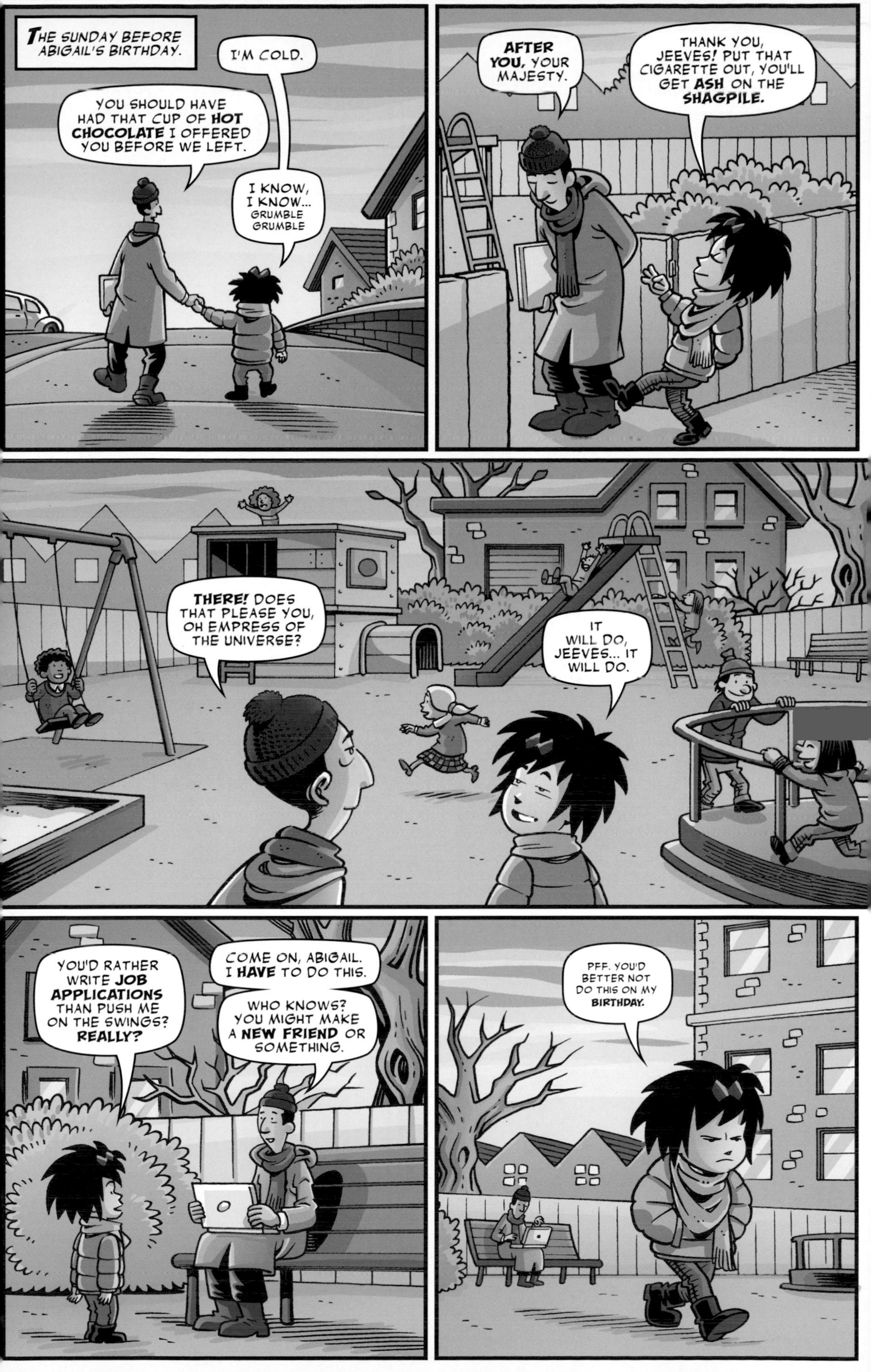
THE SUNDAY BEFORE ABIGAIL'S BIRTHDAY.
YOU SHOULD HAVE HAD THAT CUP OF HOT CHOCOLATE I OFFERED YOU BEFORE WE LEFT.
I'M COLD.
I KNOW, I KNOW... GRUMBLE GRUMBLE
AFTER YOU, YOUR MAJESTY.
THANK YOU, JEEVES! PUT THAT CIGARETTE OUT, YOU'LL GET ASH ON THE SHAGPILE.
THERE! DOES THAT PLEASE YOU, OH EMPRESS OF THE UNIVERSE?
IT WILL DO, JEEVES... IT WILL DO.
YOU'D RATHER WRITE JOB APPLICATIONS THAN PUSH ME ON THE SWINGS? REALLY?
COME ON, ABIGAIL. I HAVE TO DO THIS.
WHO KNOWS? YOU MIGHT MAKE A NEW FRIEND OR SOMETHING.
PFF. YOU'D BETTER NOT DO THIS ON MY BIRTHDAY.

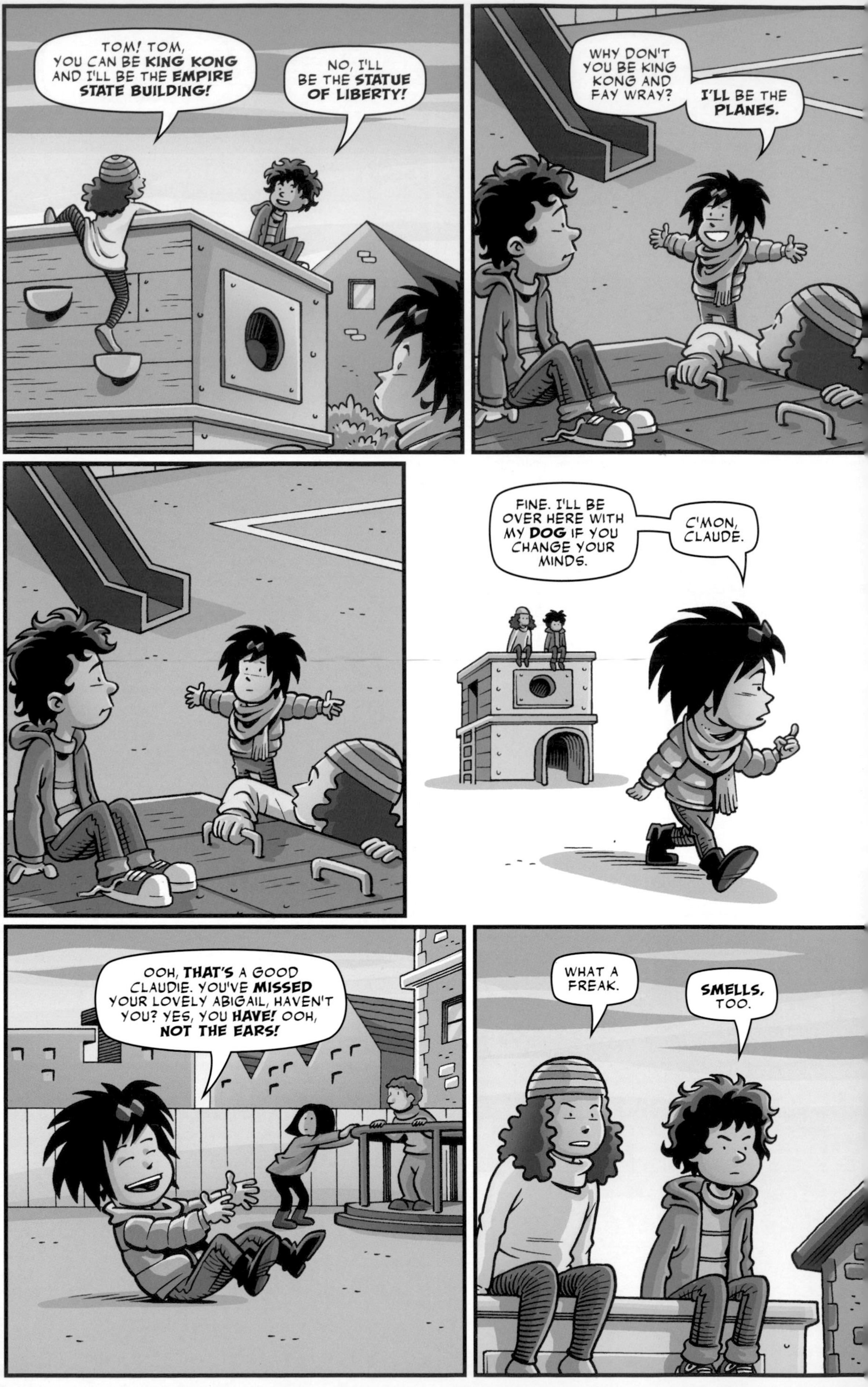
TOM! TOM, YOU CAN BE KING KONG AND I'LL BE THE EMPIRE STATE BUILDING!
NO, I'LL BE THE STATUE OF LIBERTY!
WHY DON'T YOU BE KING KONG AND FAY WRAY?
I'LL BE THE PLANES.
FINE. I'LL BE OVER HERE WITH MY DOG IF YOU CHANGE YOUR MINDS.
C'MON, CLAUDE.
OOH, THAT'S A GOOD CLAUDIE. YOU'VE MISSED YOUR LOVELY ABIGAIL, HAVEN'T YOU? YES, YOU HAVE! OOH, NOT THE EARS!
WHAT A FREAK.
SMELLS, TOO.

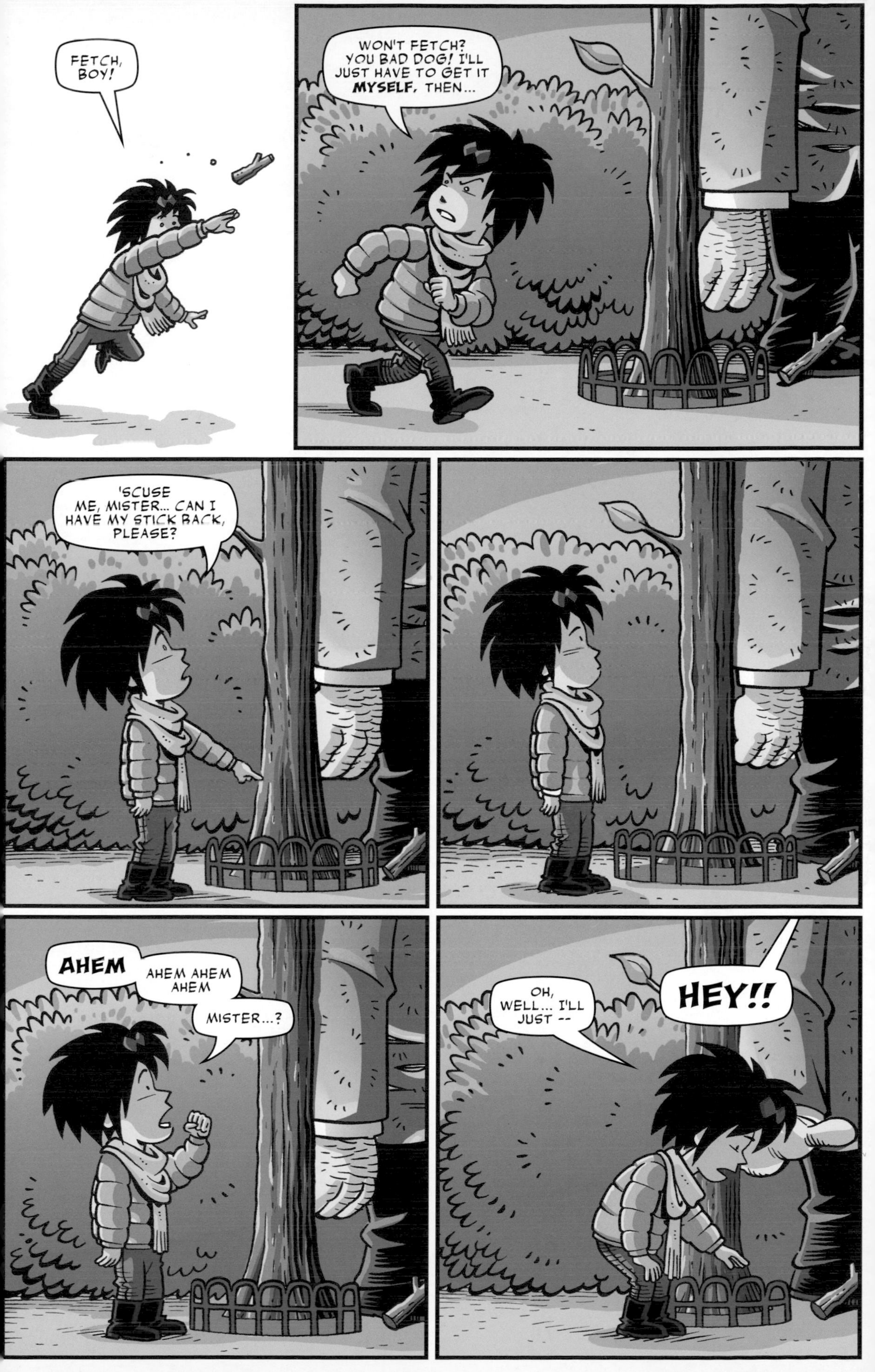
FETCH, BOY!
WON'T FETCH? YOU BAD DOG! I'LL JUST HAVE TO GET IT MYSELF, THEN...
'SCUSE ME, MISTER... CAN I HAVE MY STICK BACK, PLEASE?
AHEM
AHEM AHEM AHEM
MISTER...?
OH, WELL... I'LL JUST --
HEY!!

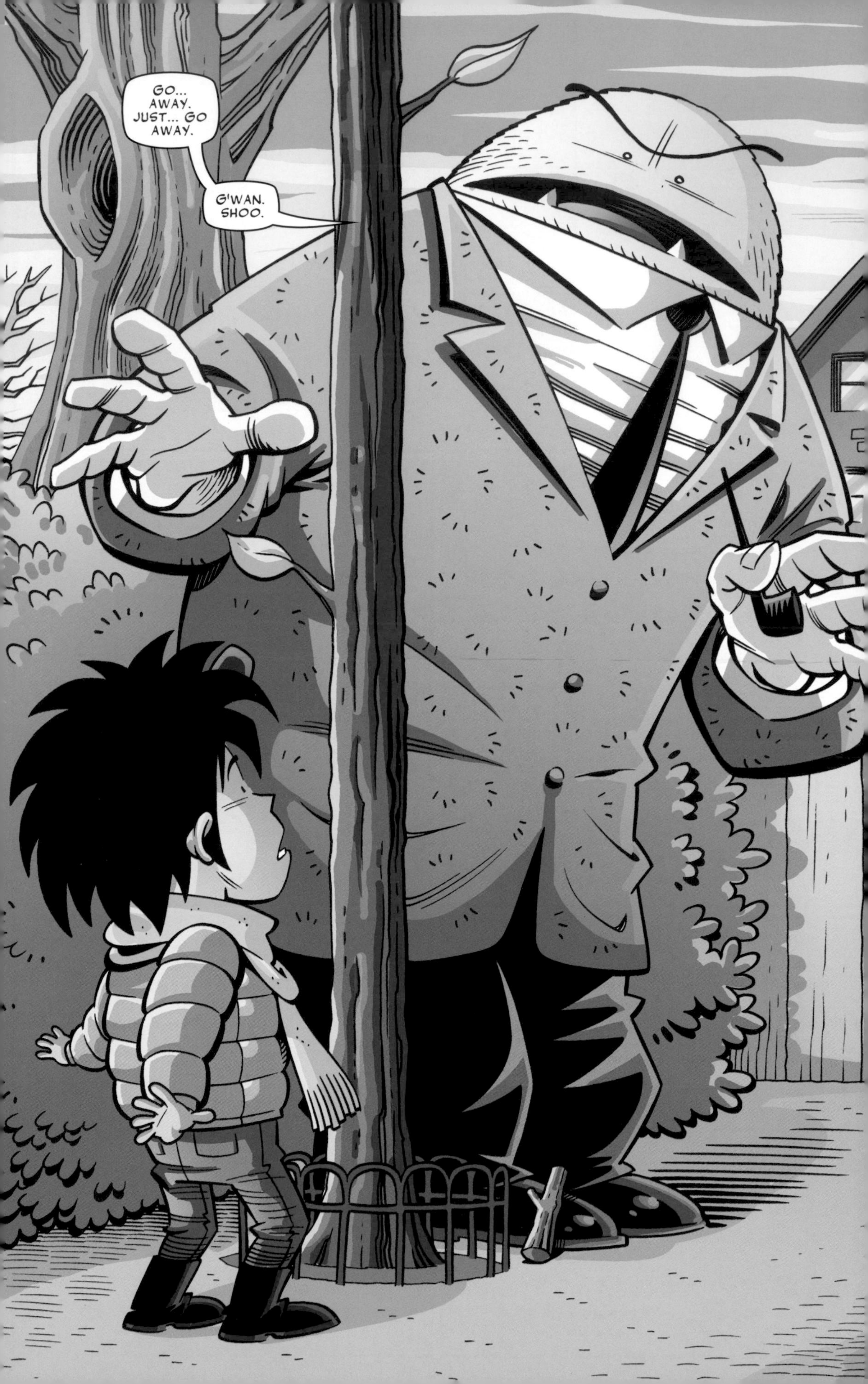
GO... AWAY. JUST... GO AWAY.
G'WAN. SHOO.

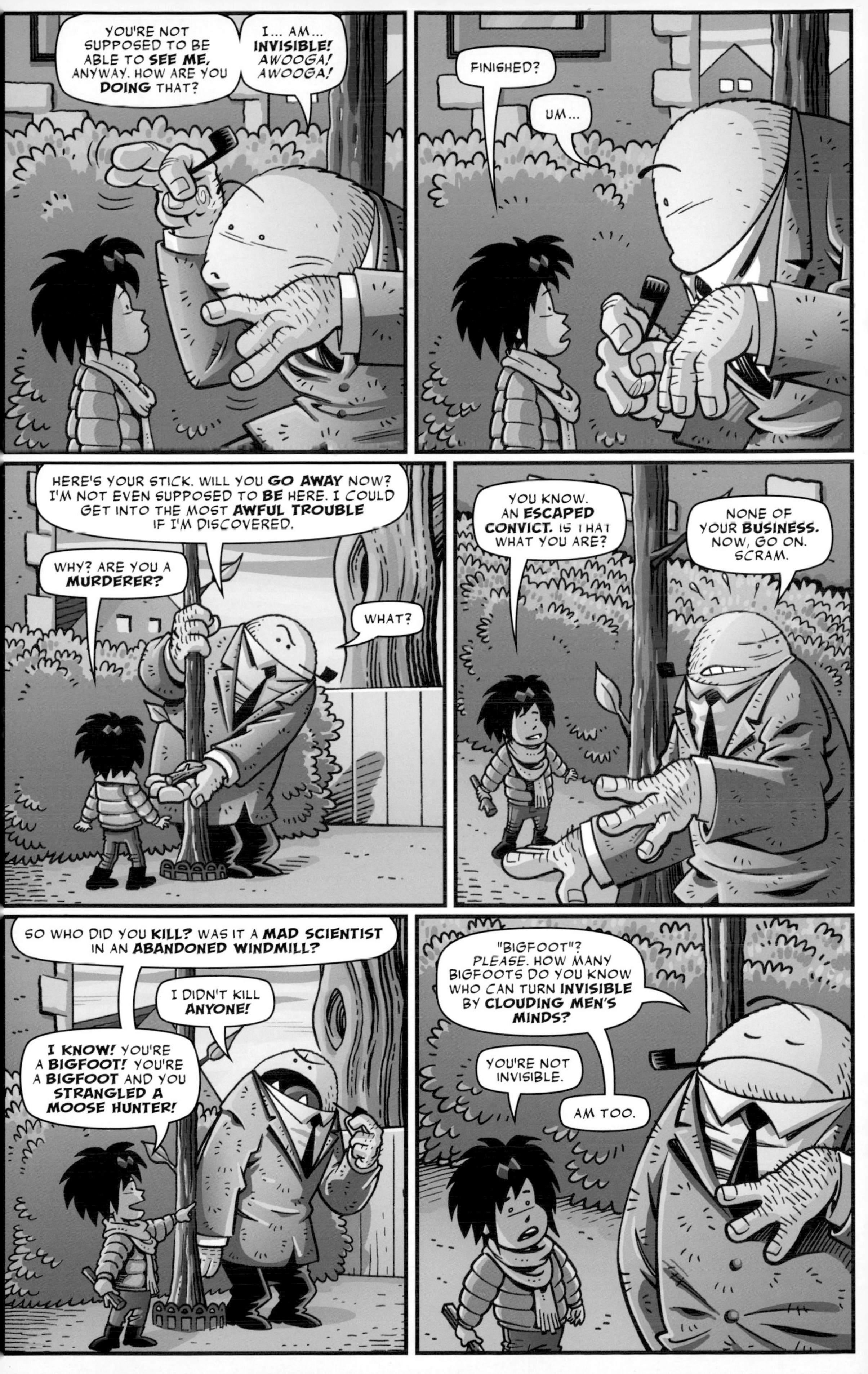
YOU'RE NOT SUPPOSED TO BE ABLE TO SEE ME, ANYWAY. HOW ARE YOU DOING THAT?
I... AM... INVISIBLE! AWOOGA! AWOOGA!
FINISHED?
UM...
HERE'S YOUR STICK. WILL YOU GO AWAY NOW? I'M NOT EVEN SUPPOSED TO BE HERE. I COULD GET INTO THE MOST AWFUL TROUBLE IF I'M DISCOVERED.
WHY? ARE YOU A MURDERER?
WHAT?
YOU KNOW. AN ESCAPED CONVICT. IS THAT WHAT YOU ARE?
NONE OF YOUR BUSINESS. NOW, GO ON. SCRAM.
SO WHO DID YOU KILL? WAS IT A MAD SCIENTIST IN AN ABANDONED WINDMILL?
I DIDN'T KILL ANYONE!
I KNOW! YOU'RE A BIGFOOT! YOU'RE A BIGFOOT AND YOU STRANGLED A MOOSE HUNTER!
"BIGFOOT"? PLEASE. HOW MANY BIGFOOTS DO YOU KNOW WHO CAN TURN INVISIBLE BY CLOUDING MEN'S MINDS?
YOU'RE NOT INVISIBLE.
AM TOO.

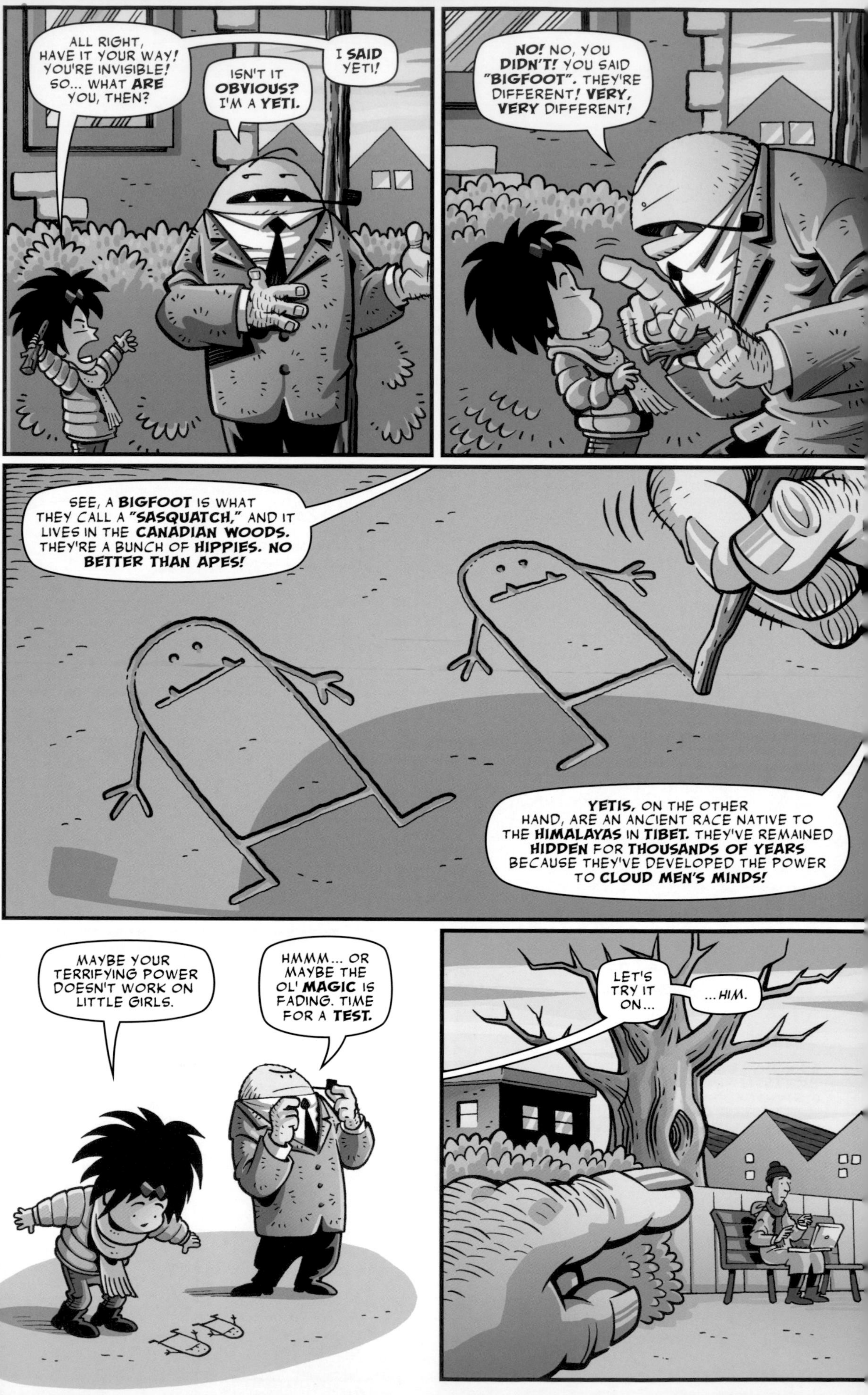
ALL RIGHT, HAVE IT YOUR WAY! YOU'RE INVISIBLE! SO... WHAT ARE YOU, THEN?
ISN'T IT OBVIOUS? I'M A YETI.
I SAID YETI!
NO! NO, YOU DIDN'T! YOU SAID "BIGFOOT". THEY'RE DIFFERENT! VERY, VERY DIFFERENT!
SEE, A BIGFOOT IS WHAT THEY CALL A "SASQUATCH," AND IT LIVES IN THE CANADIAN WOODS. THEY'RE A BUNCH OF HIPPIES. NO BETTER THAN APES!
YETIS, ON THE OTHER HAND, ARE AN ANCIENT RACE NATIVE TO THE HIMALAYAS IN TIBET. THEY'VE REMAINED HIDDEN FOR THOUSANDS OF YEARS BECAUSE THEY'VE DEVELOPED THE POWER TO CLOUD MEN'S MINDS!
MAYBE YOUR TERRIFYING POWER DOESN'T WORK ON LITTLE GIRLS.
HMMM... OR MAYBE THE OL' MAGIC IS FADING. TIME FOR A TEST.
LET'S TRY IT ON...
...HIM.

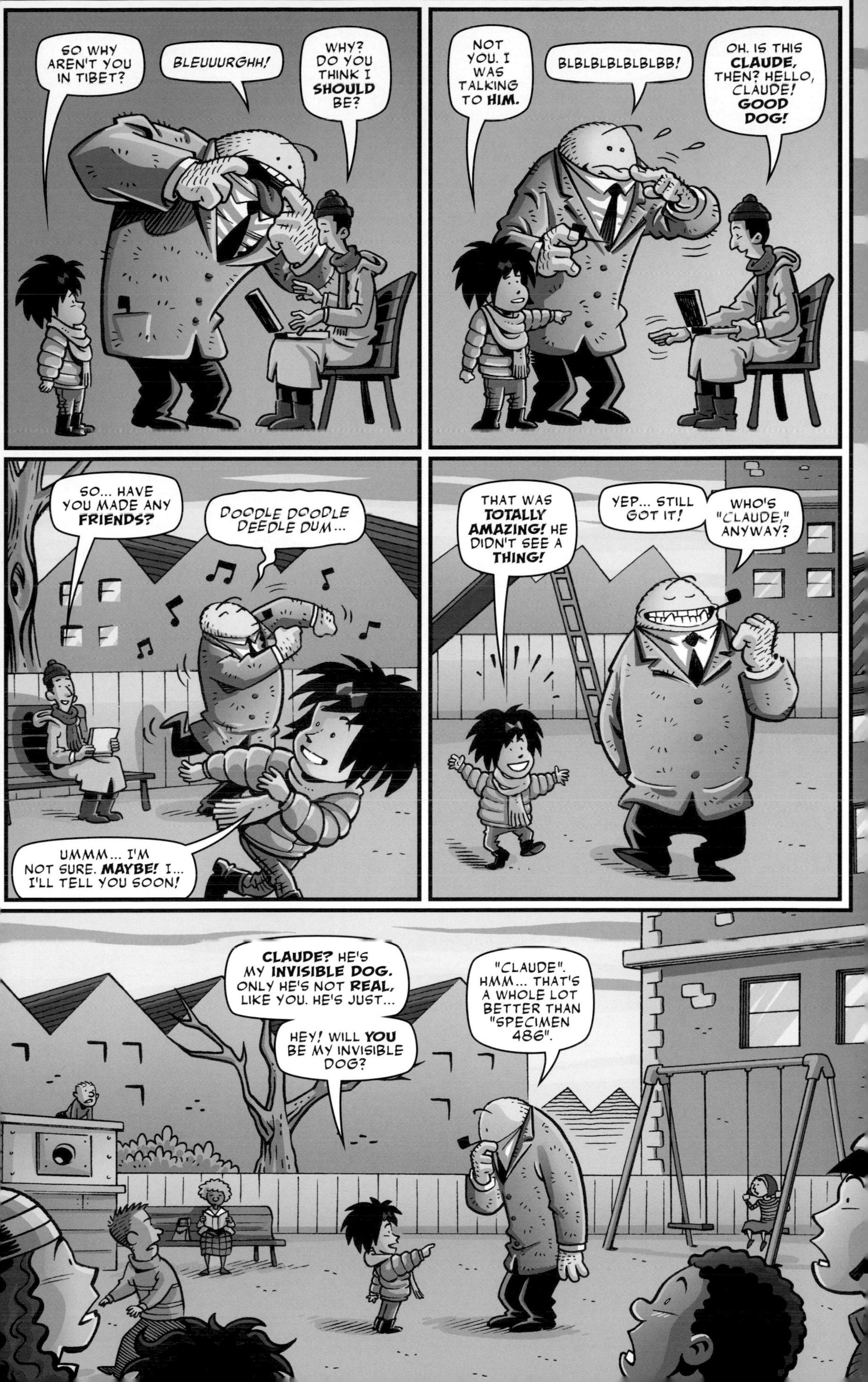
SO WHY AREN'T YOU IN TIBET?
BLEUUURGHH!
WHY? DO YOU THINK I SHOULD BE?
NOT YOU. I WAS TALKING TO HIM.
BLBLBLBLBLBLBB!
OH. IS THIS CLAUDE, THEN? HELLO, CLAUDE! GOOD DOG!
SO... HAVE YOU MADE ANY FRIENDS?
DOODLE DOODLE DEEDLE DUM...
UMMM... I'M NOT SURE. MAYBE! I... I'LL TELL YOU SOON!
THAT WAS TOTALLY AMAZING! HE DIDN'T SEE A THING!
YEP... STILL GOT IT!
WHO'S "CLAUDE," ANYWAY?
CLAUDE? HE'S MY INVISIBLE DOG. ONLY HE'S NOT REAL, LIKE YOU. HE'S JUST...
HEY! WILL YOU BE MY INVISIBLE DOG?
"CLAUDE". HMM... THAT'S A WHOLE LOT BETTER THAN "SPECIMEN 486".

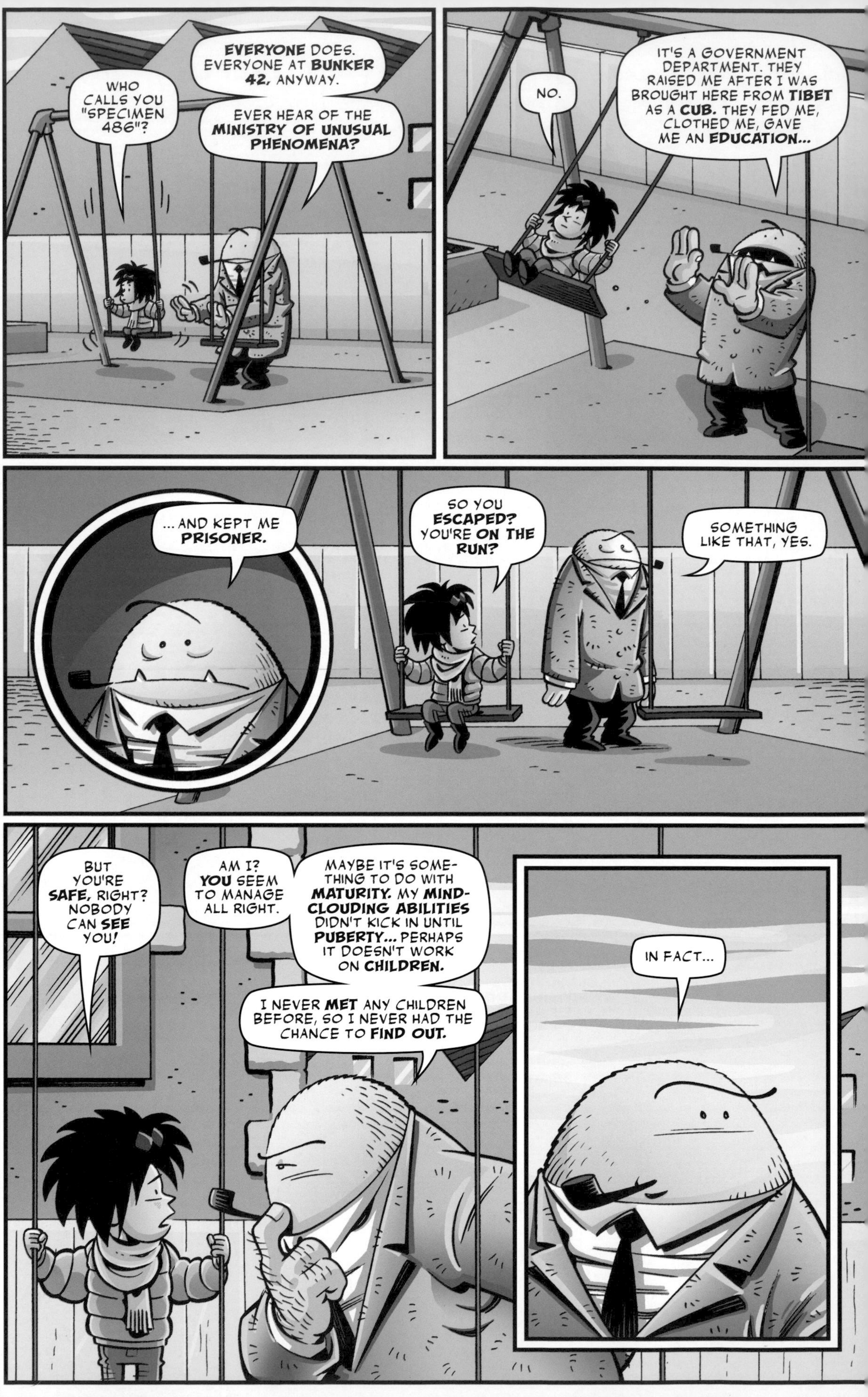
WHO CALLS YOU "SPECIMEN 486"?
EVERYONE DOES. EVERYONE AT BUNKER 42, ANYWAY.
EVER HEAR OF THE MINISTRY OF UNUSUAL PHENOMENA?
NO.
IT'S A GOVERNMENT DEPARTMENT. THEY RAISED ME AFTER I WAS BROUGHT HERE FROM TIBET AS A CUB. THEY FED ME, CLOTHED ME, GAVE ME AN EDUCATION...
...AND KEPT ME PRISONER.
SO YOU ESCAPED? YOU'RE ON THE RUN?
SOMETHING LIKE THAT, YES.
BUT YOU'RE SAFE, RIGHT? NOBODY CAN SEE YOU!
AM I? YOU SEEM TO MANAGE ALL RIGHT.
MAYBE IT'S SOMETHING TO DO WITH MATURITY. MY MIND-CLOUDING ABILITIES DIDN'T KICK IN UNTIL PUBERTY... PERHAPS IT DOESN'T WORK ON CHILDREN.
I NEVER MET ANY CHILDREN BEFORE, SO I NEVER HAD THE CHANCE TO FIND OUT.
IN FACT...

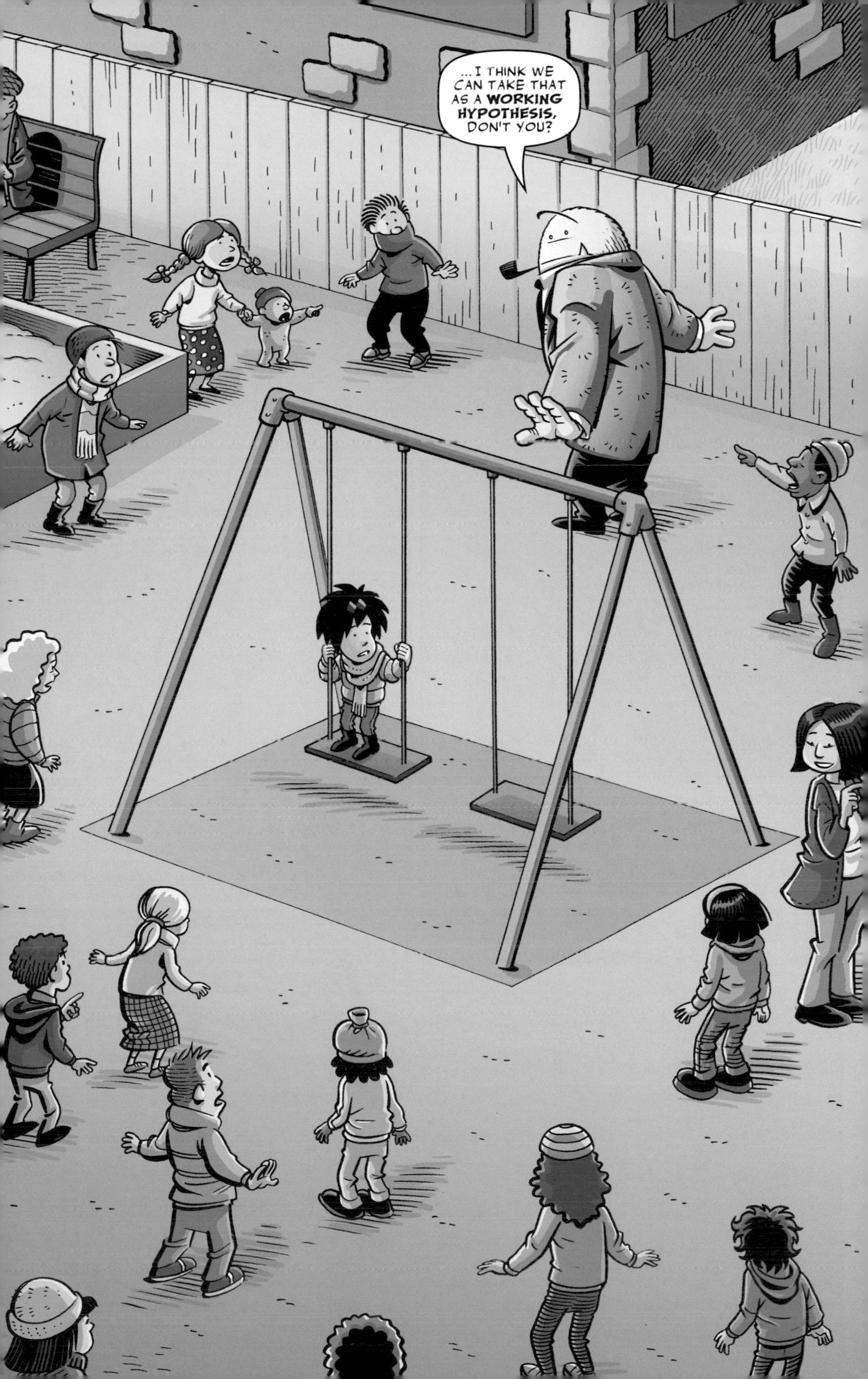
...I THINK WE CAN TAKE THAT AS A **WORKING HYPOTHESIS,** DON'T YOU?

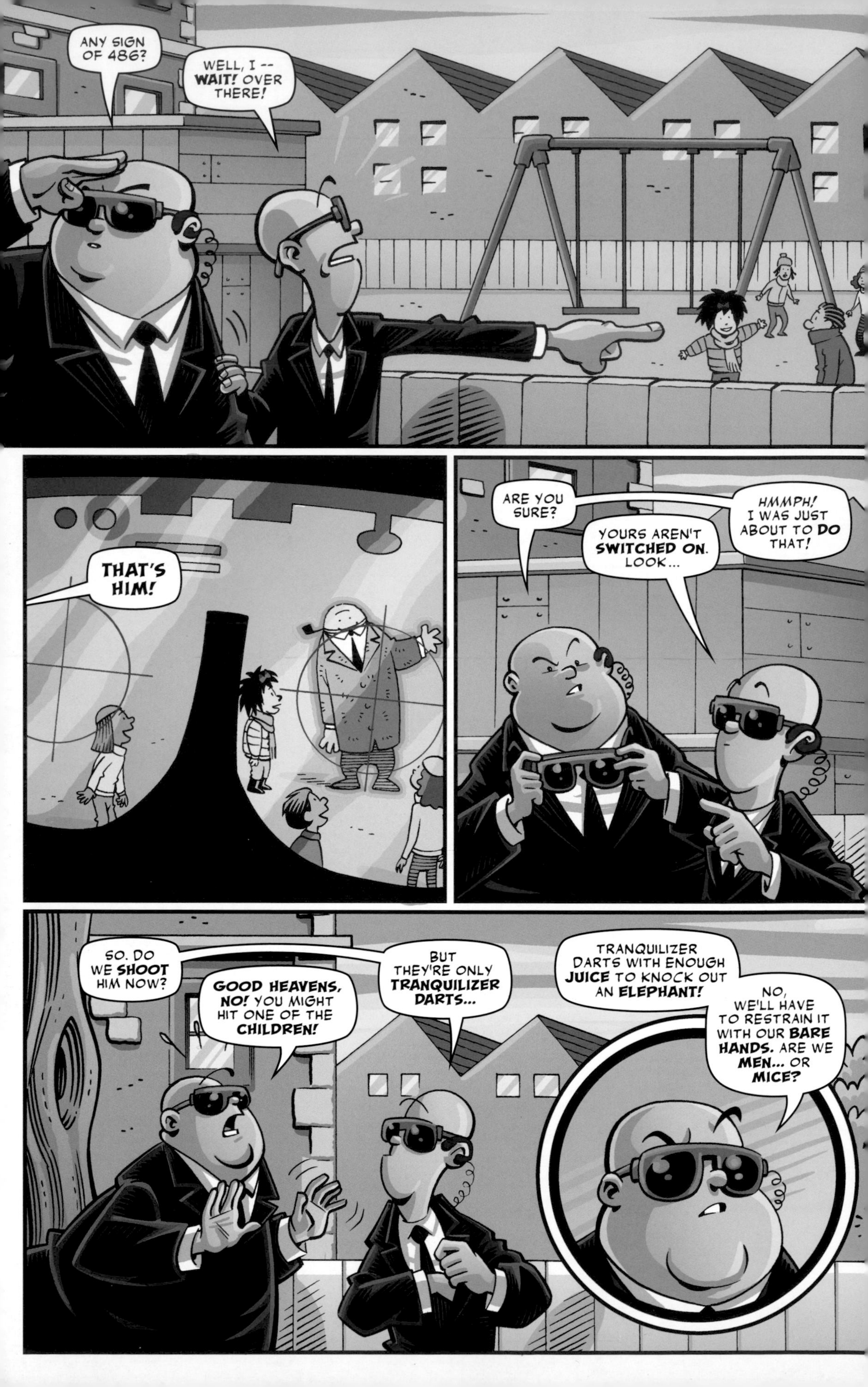
ANY SIGN OF 486?
WELL, I -- WAIT! OVER THERE!
THAT'S HIM!
ARE YOU SURE?
YOURS AREN'T SWITCHED ON. LOOK...
HMMPH! I WAS JUST ABOUT TO DO THAT!
SO. DO WE SHOOT HIM NOW?
GOOD HEAVENS, NO! YOU MIGHT HIT ONE OF THE CHILDREN!
BUT THEY'RE ONLY TRANQUILIZER DARTS...
TRANQUILIZER DARTS WITH ENOUGH JUICE TO KNOCK OUT AN ELEPHANT!
NO, WE'LL HAVE TO RESTRAIN IT WITH OUR BARE HANDS. ARE WE MEN... OR MICE?

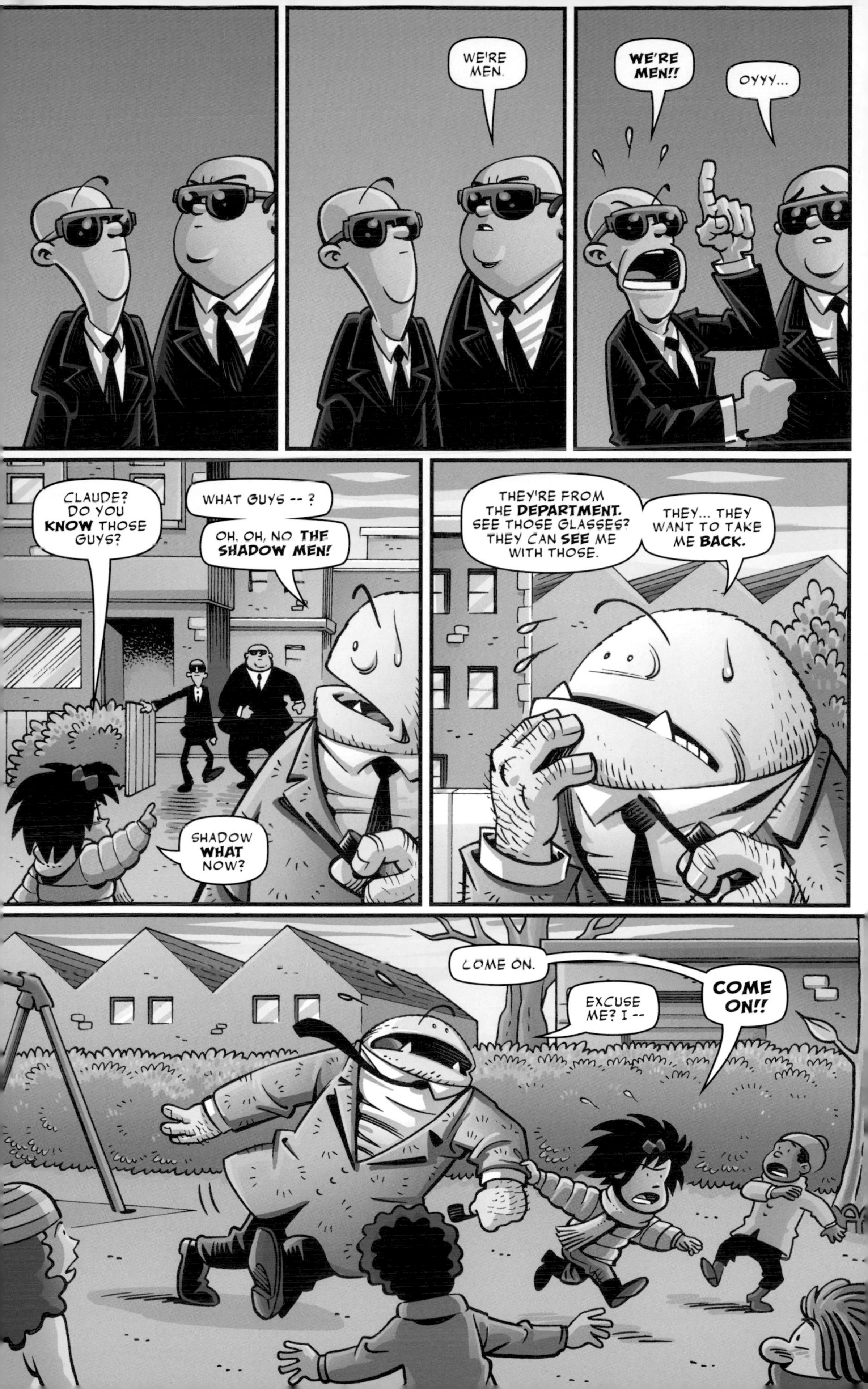
WE'RE MEN.
WE'RE MEN!!
OYYY...
CLAUDE? DO YOU KNOW THOSE GUYS?
WHAT GUYS -- ?
OH, OH, NO THE SHADOW MEN!
SHADOW WHAT NOW?
THEY'RE FROM THE DEPARTMENT. SEE THOSE GLASSES? THEY CAN SEE ME WITH THOSE.
THEY... THEY WANT TO TAKE ME BACK.
COME ON.
COME ON!!
EXCUSE ME? I --

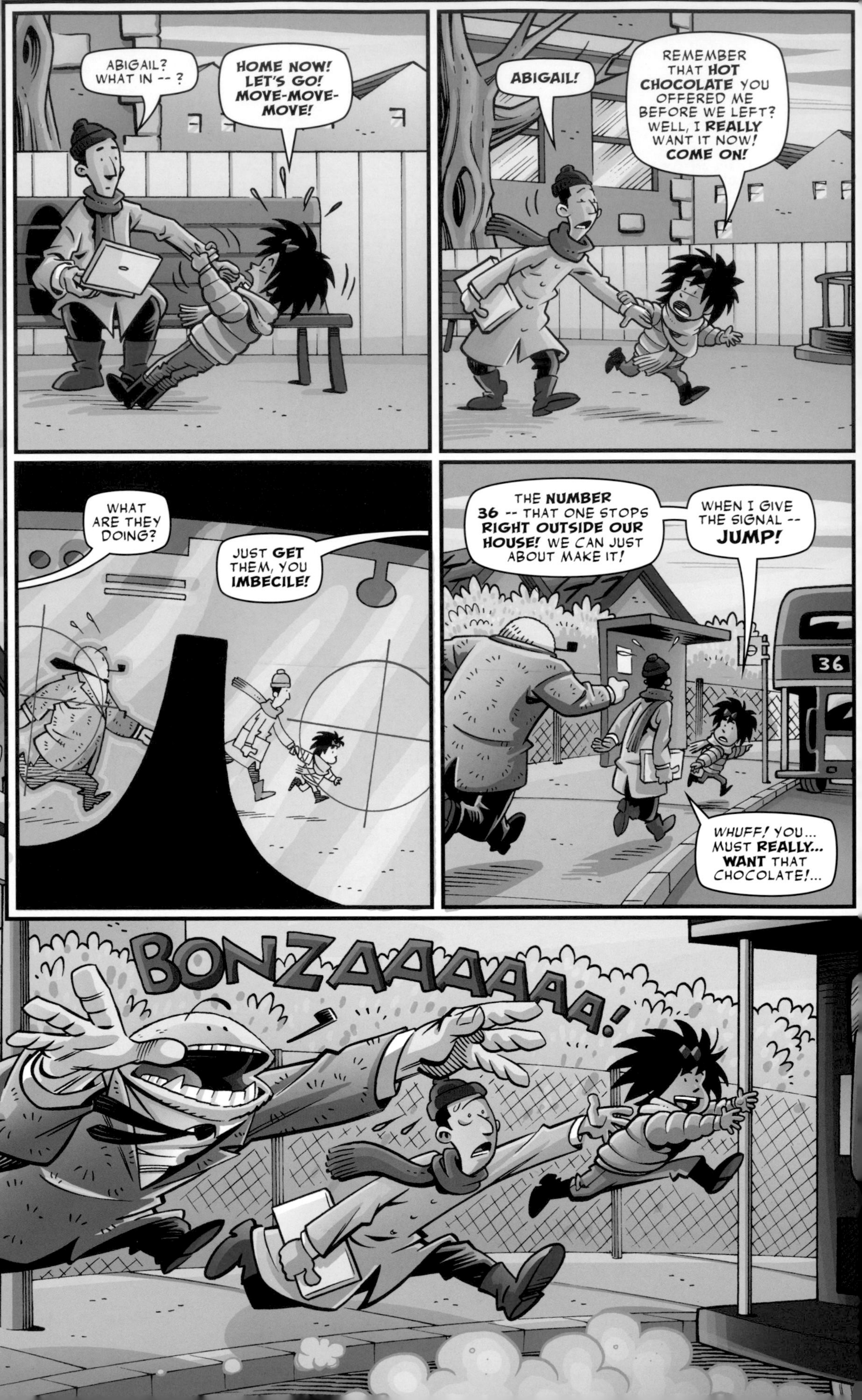
ABIGAIL? WHAT IN -- ?
HOME NOW! LET'S GO! MOVE-MOVE-MOVE!
ABIGAIL!
REMEMBER THAT HOT CHOCOLATE YOU OFFERED ME BEFORE WE LEFT? WELL, I REALLY WANT IT NOW! COME ON!
WHAT ARE THEY DOING?
JUST GET THEM, YOU IMBECILE!
THE NUMBER 36 -- THAT ONE STOPS RIGHT OUTSIDE OUR HOUSE! WE CAN JUST ABOUT MAKE IT!
WHEN I GIVE THE SIGNAL -- JUMP!
36
WHUFF! YOU... MUST REALLY... WANT THAT CHOCOLATE!...
BONZAAAAAAA!

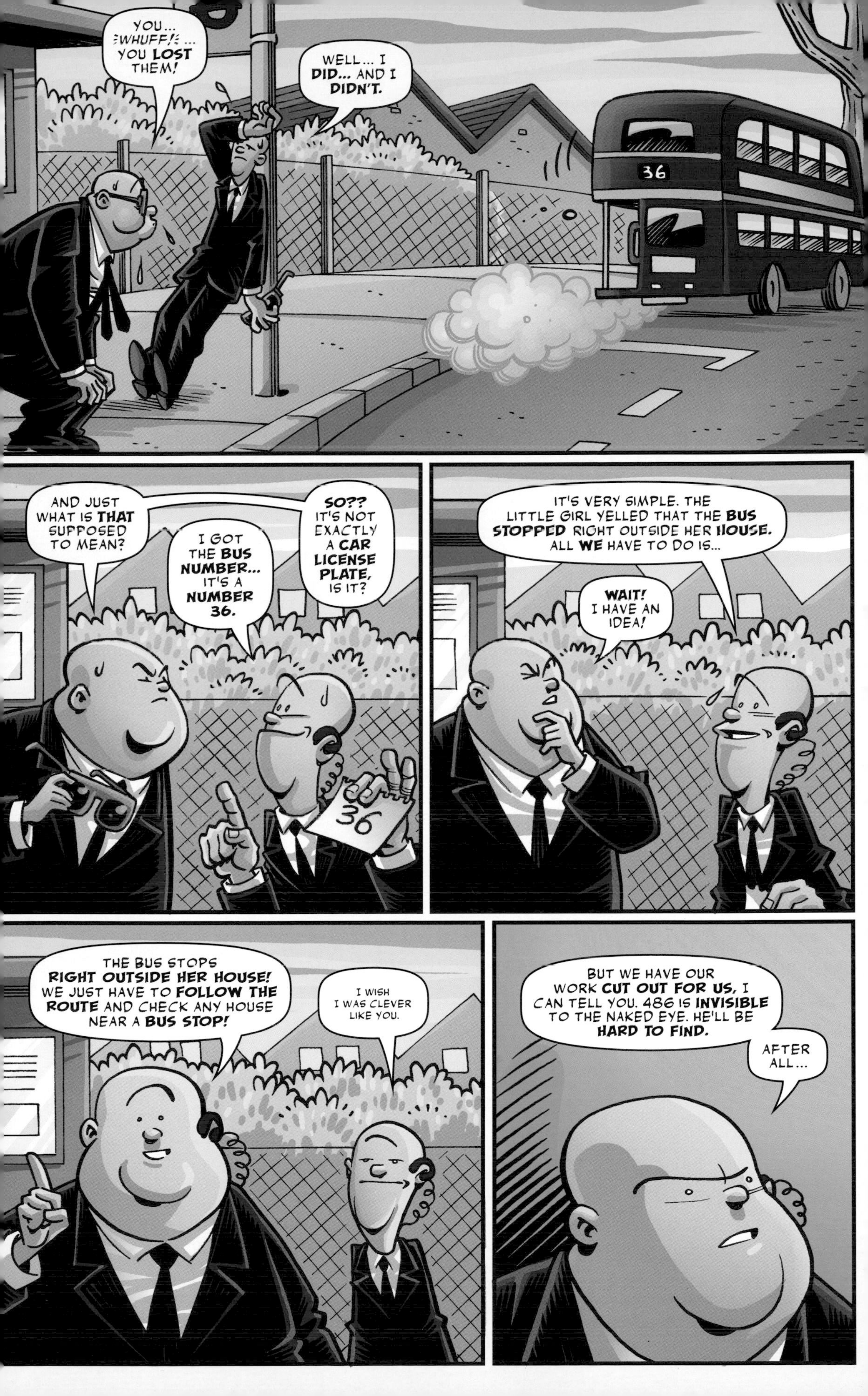
YOU... ≈WHUFF!≈ ... YOU LOST THEM!
WELL... I DID... AND I DIDN'T.
36
AND JUST WHAT IS THAT SUPPOSED TO MEAN?
I GOT THE BUS NUMBER... IT'S A NUMBER 36.
SO?? IT'S NOT EXACTLY A CAR LICENSE PLATE, IS IT?
36
IT'S VERY SIMPLE. THE LITTLE GIRL YELLED THAT THE BUS STOPPED RIGHT OUTSIDE HER HOUSE. ALL WE HAVE TO DO IS...
WAIT! I HAVE AN IDEA!
THE BUS STOPS RIGHT OUTSIDE HER HOUSE! WE JUST HAVE TO FOLLOW THE ROUTE AND CHECK ANY HOUSE NEAR A BUS STOP!
I WISH I WAS CLEVER LIKE YOU.
BUT WE HAVE OUR WORK CUT OUT FOR US, I CAN TELL YOU. 486 IS INVISIBLE TO THE NAKED EYE. HE'LL BE HARD TO FIND.
AFTER ALL...

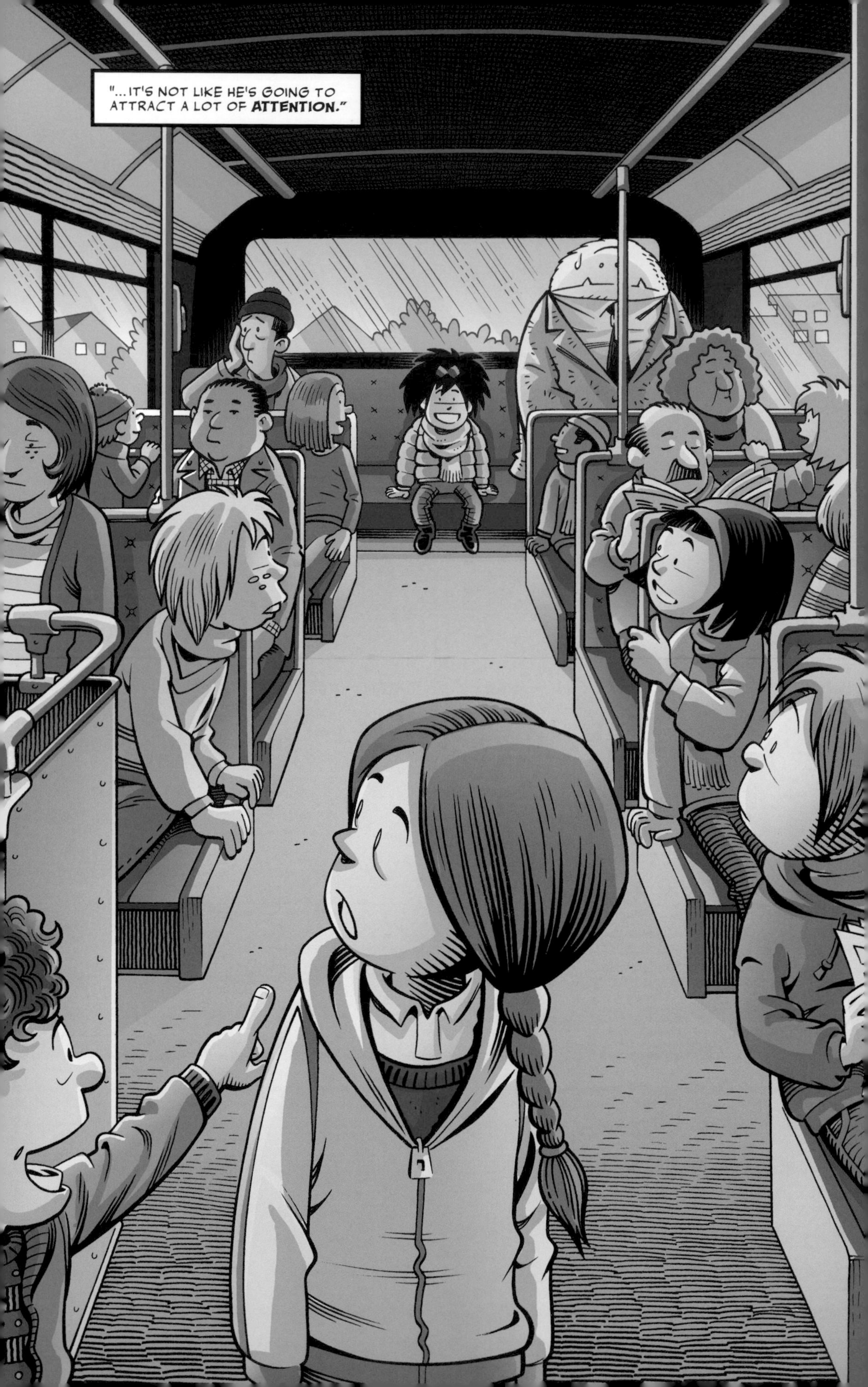
"...IT'S NOT LIKE HE'S GOING TO ATTRACT A LOT OF **ATTENTION.**"

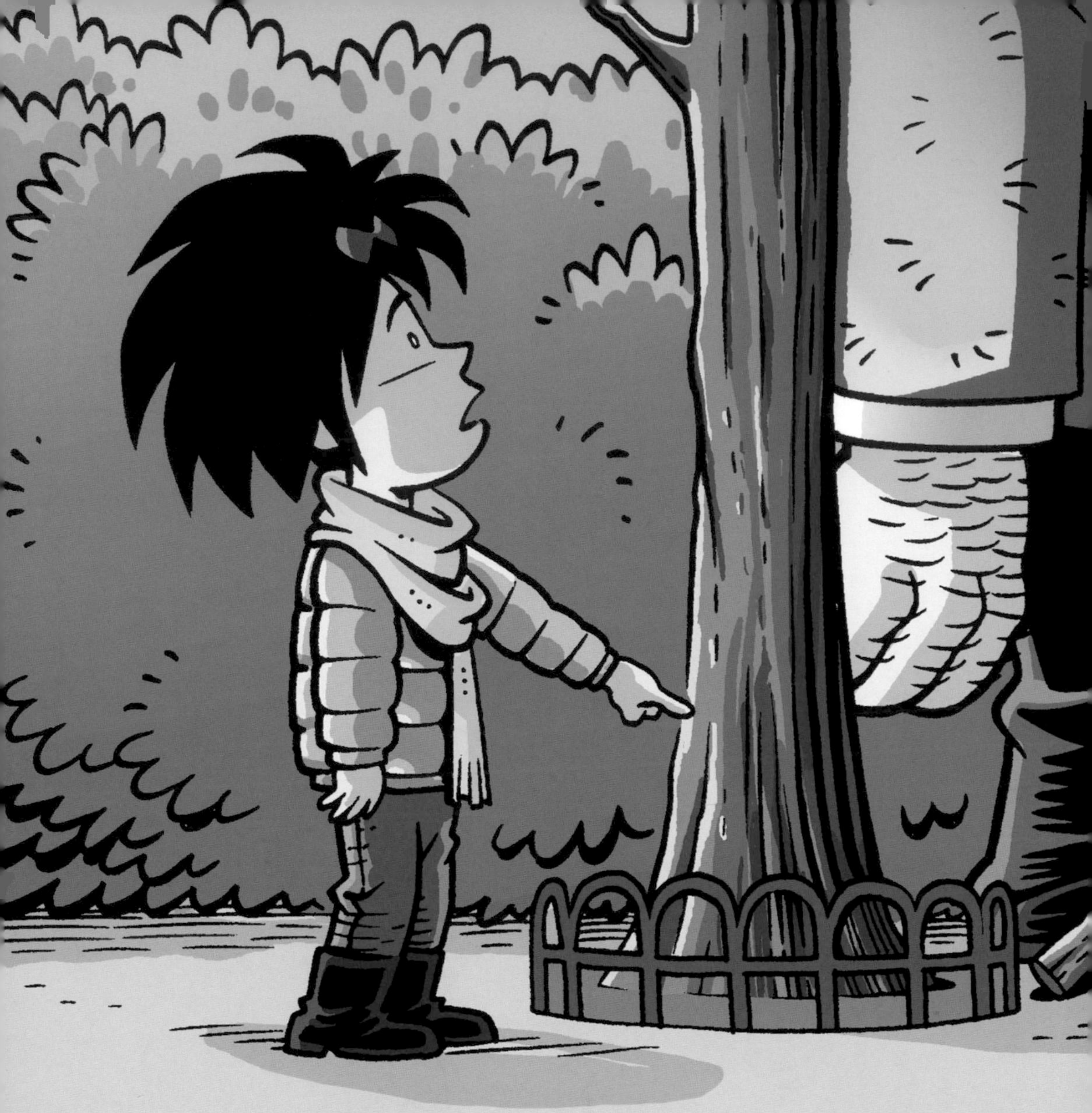

chapter two

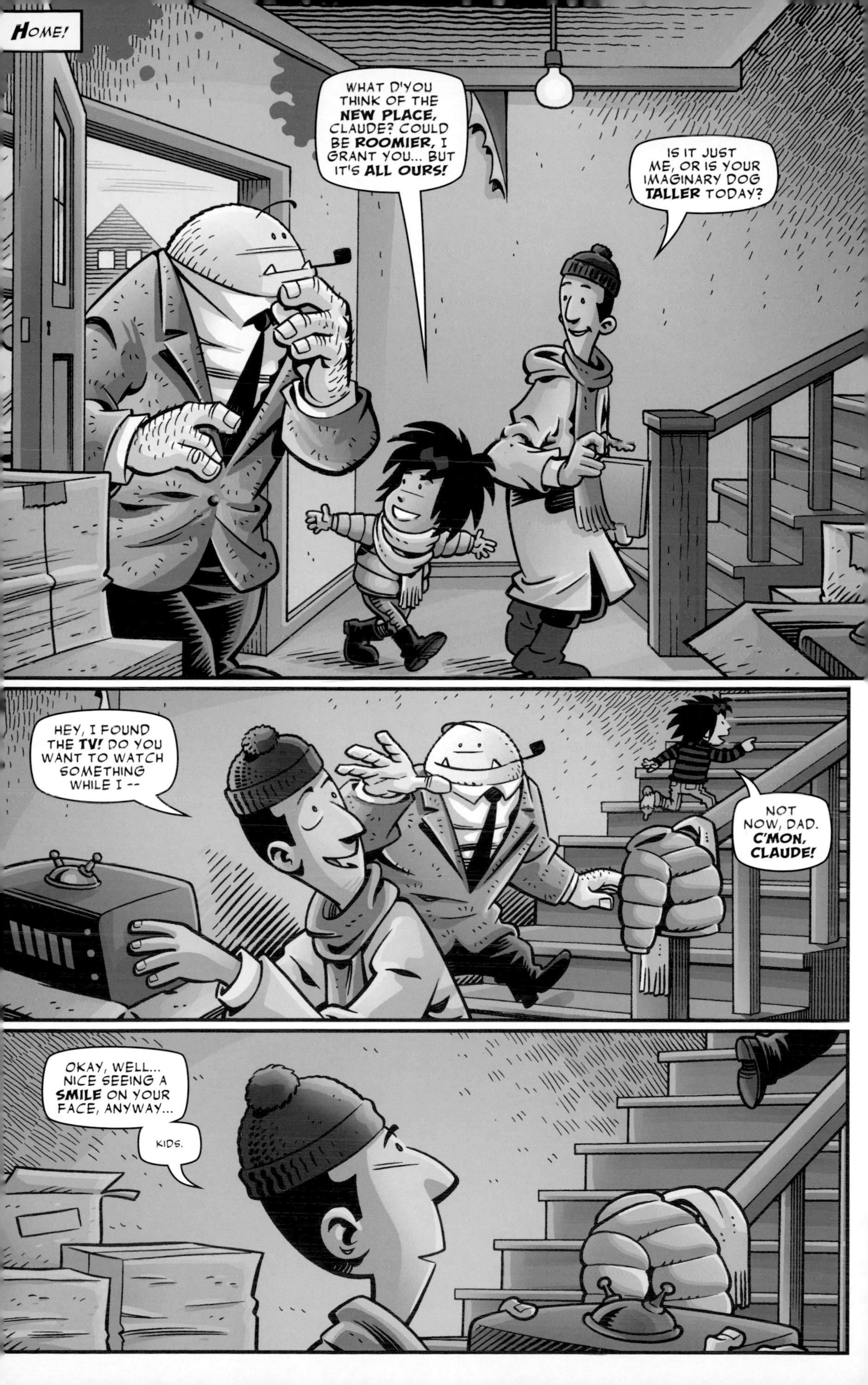
HOME!
WHAT D'YOU THINK OF THE NEW PLACE, CLAUDE? COULD BE ROOMIER, I GRANT YOU... BUT IT'S ALL OURS!
IS IT JUST ME, OR IS YOUR IMAGINARY DOG TALLER TODAY?
HEY, I FOUND THE TV! DO YOU WANT TO WATCH SOMETHING WHILE I --
NOT NOW, DAD. C'MON, CLAUDE!
OKAY, WELL... NICE SEEING A SMILE ON YOUR FACE, ANYWAY...
KIDS.

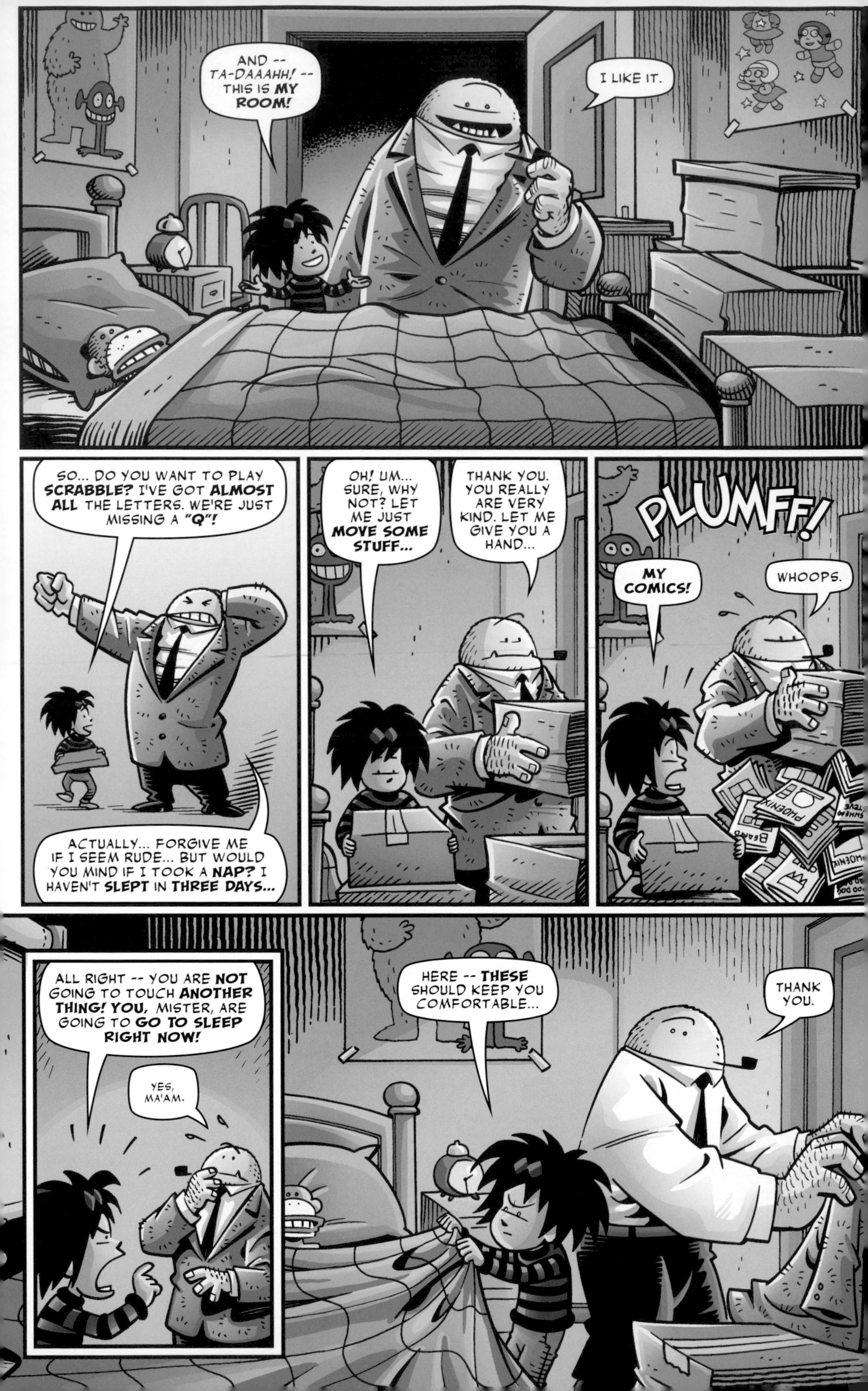
AND -- TA-DAAAHH! -- THIS IS MY ROOM!
I LIKE IT.
SO... DO YOU WANT TO PLAY SCRABBLE? I'VE GOT ALMOST ALL THE LETTERS. WE'RE JUST MISSING A "Q"!
ACTUALLY... FORGIVE ME IF I SEEM RUDE... BUT WOULD YOU MIND IF I TOOK A NAP? I HAVEN'T SLEPT IN THREE DAYS...
OH! UM... SURE, WHY NOT? LET ME JUST MOVE SOME STUFF...
THANK YOU. YOU REALLY ARE VERY KIND. LET ME GIVE YOU A HAND...
PLUMFF!
MY COMICS!
WHOOPS.
ALL RIGHT -- YOU ARE NOT GOING TO TOUCH ANOTHER THING! YOU, MISTER, ARE GOING TO GO TO SLEEP RIGHT NOW!
YES, MA'AM.
HERE -- THESE SHOULD KEEP YOU COMFORTABLE...
THANK YOU.

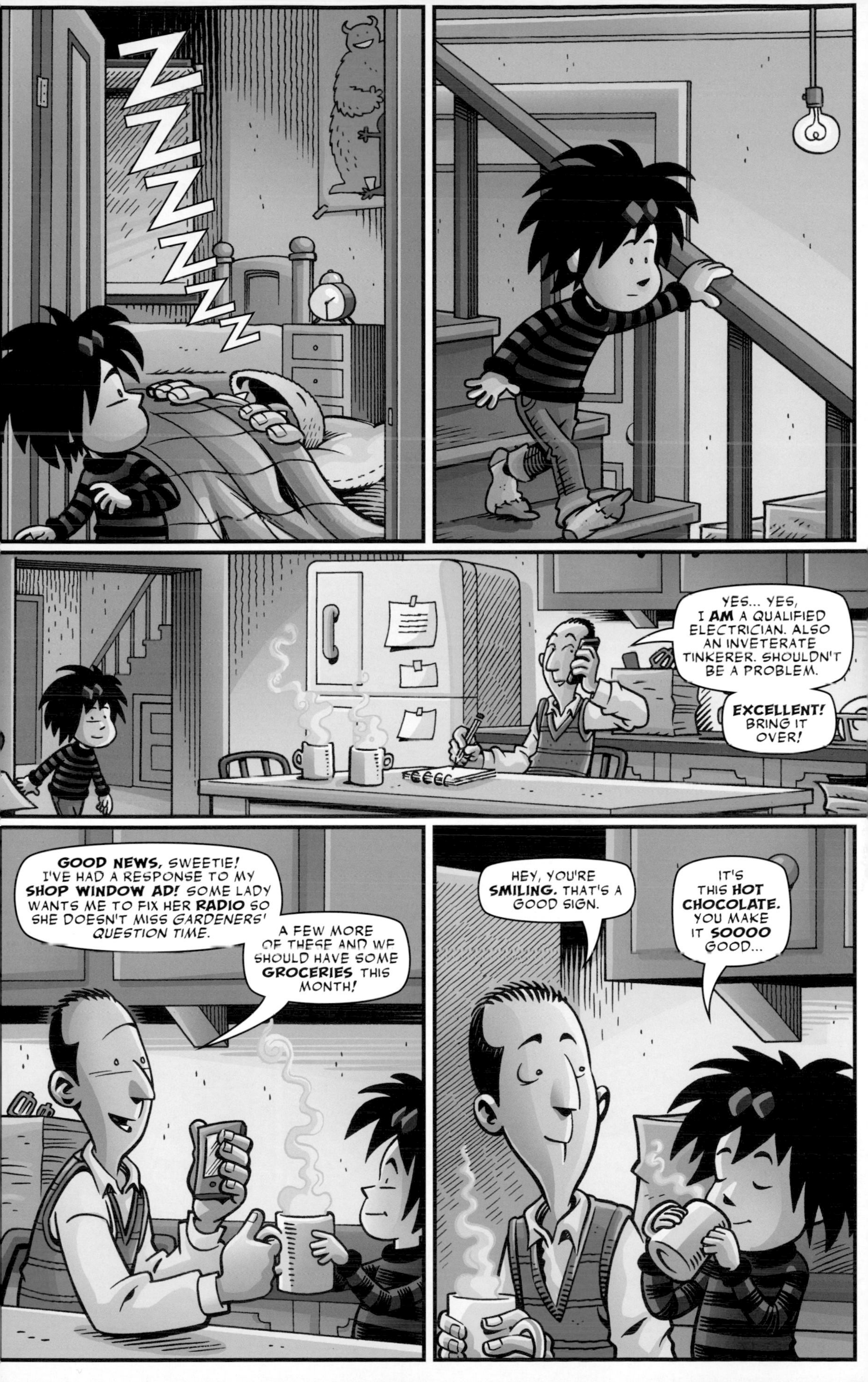
ZZZZZZ
YES... YES, I AM A QUALIFIED ELECTRICIAN. ALSO AN INVETERATE TINKERER. SHOULDN'T BE A PROBLEM.
EXCELLENT! BRING IT OVER!
GOOD NEWS, SWEETIE! I'VE HAD A RESPONSE TO MY SHOP WINDOW AD! SOME LADY WANTS ME TO FIX HER RADIO SO SHE DOESN'T MISS GARDENERS' QUESTION TIME.
A FEW MORE OF THESE AND WE SHOULD HAVE SOME GROCERIES THIS MONTH!
HEY, YOU'RE SMILING. THAT'S A GOOD SIGN.
IT'S THIS HOT CHOCOLATE. YOU MAKE IT SOOOO GOOD...

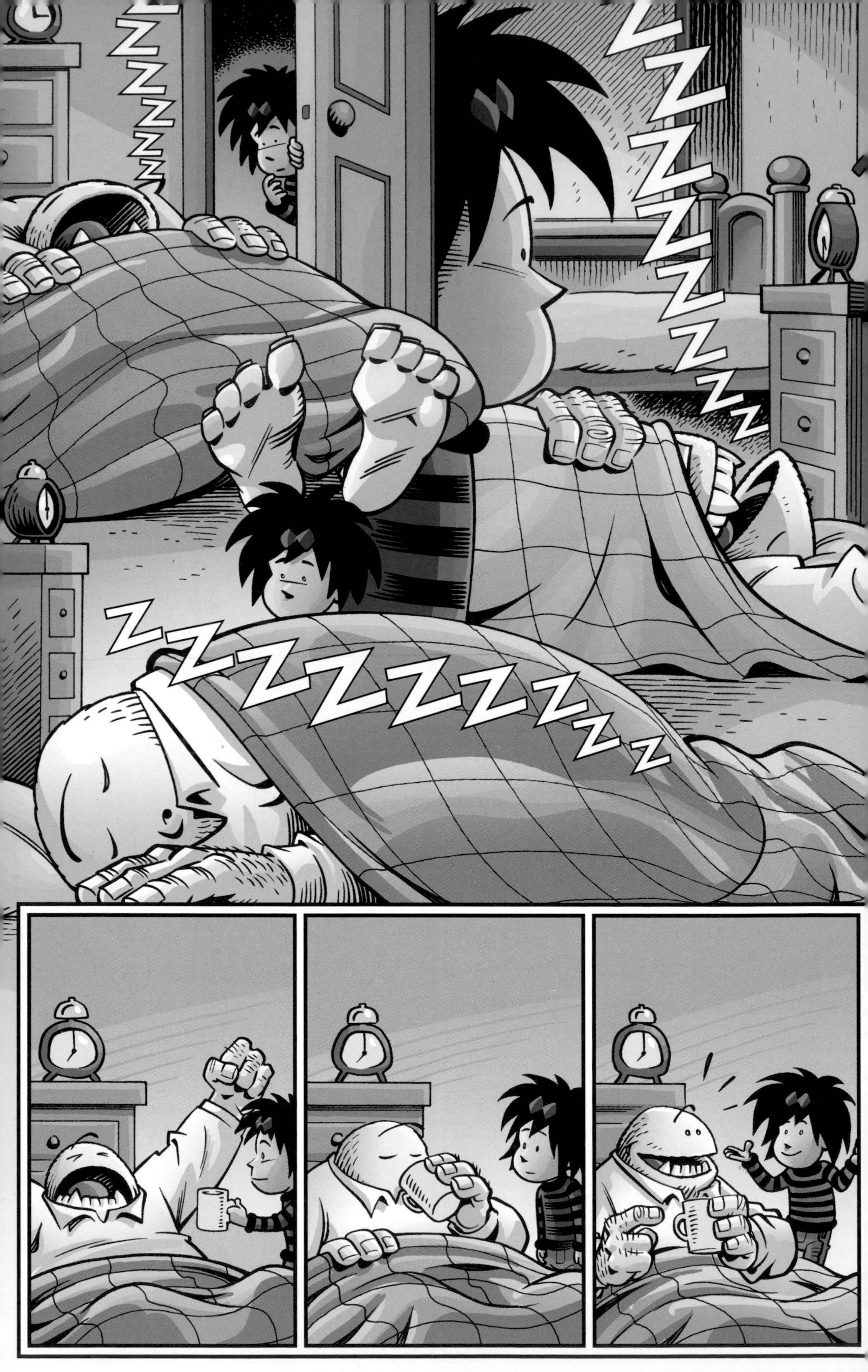
ZZZZZZ
ZZZZZZZZZZ
ZZZZZZZZZZZ

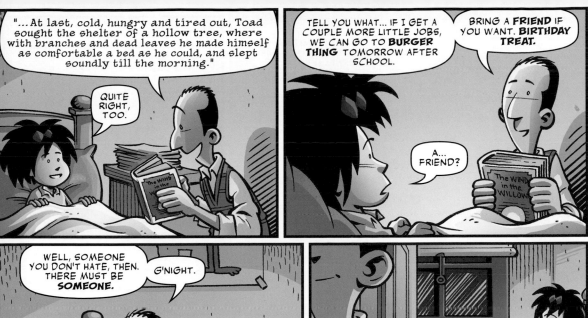

"...At last, cold, hungry and tired out, Toad sought the shelter of a hollow tree, where with branches and dead leaves he made himself as comfortable a bed as he could, and slept soundly till the morning."
QUITE RIGHT, TOO.
TELL YOU WHAT... IF I GET A COUPLE MORE LITTLE JOBS, WE CAN GO TO BURGER THING TOMORROW AFTER SCHOOL.
BRING A FRIEND IF YOU WANT. BIRTHDAY TREAT.
A... FRIEND?
The WIND in the WILLOWS
WELL, SOMEONE YOU DON'T HATE, THEN. THERE MUST BE SOMEONE.
G'NIGHT.
G'NIGHT, DAD.
The WIND in the WILLOWS
HEY, MUM... IT'S BEEN A LITTLE WHILE, I KNOW... BUT I JUST WANTED TO THANK YOU FOR WHATEVER YOU DID... UP THERE... THAT BROUGHT CLAUDE INTO MY LIFE.
I PROMISE I'LL LOOK AFTER HIM.
WERE YOU TALKING TO YOUR MOTHER?
HEYYY! THAT'S PRIVATE!
I WON'T TELL. WAS SHE NICE?
I... DON'T KNOW. I WAS REALLY LITTLE WHEN SHE DIED. BUT... I STILL LIKE TO TALK TO HER. OKAY?
OKAY.
ABIGAIL?
MM?
WHY WAS THE TOAD WEARING A DRESS AGAIN? I NODDED OFF DURING THAT PART...

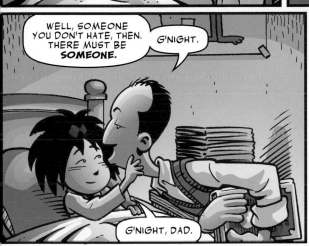

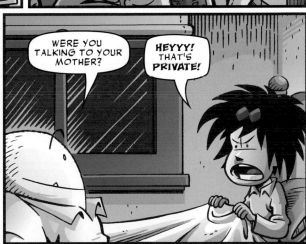

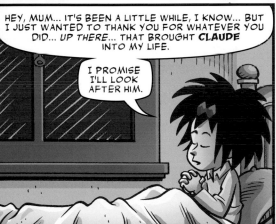

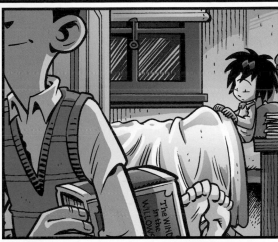

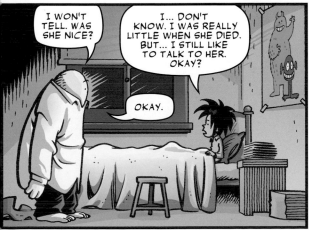

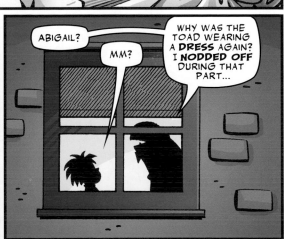

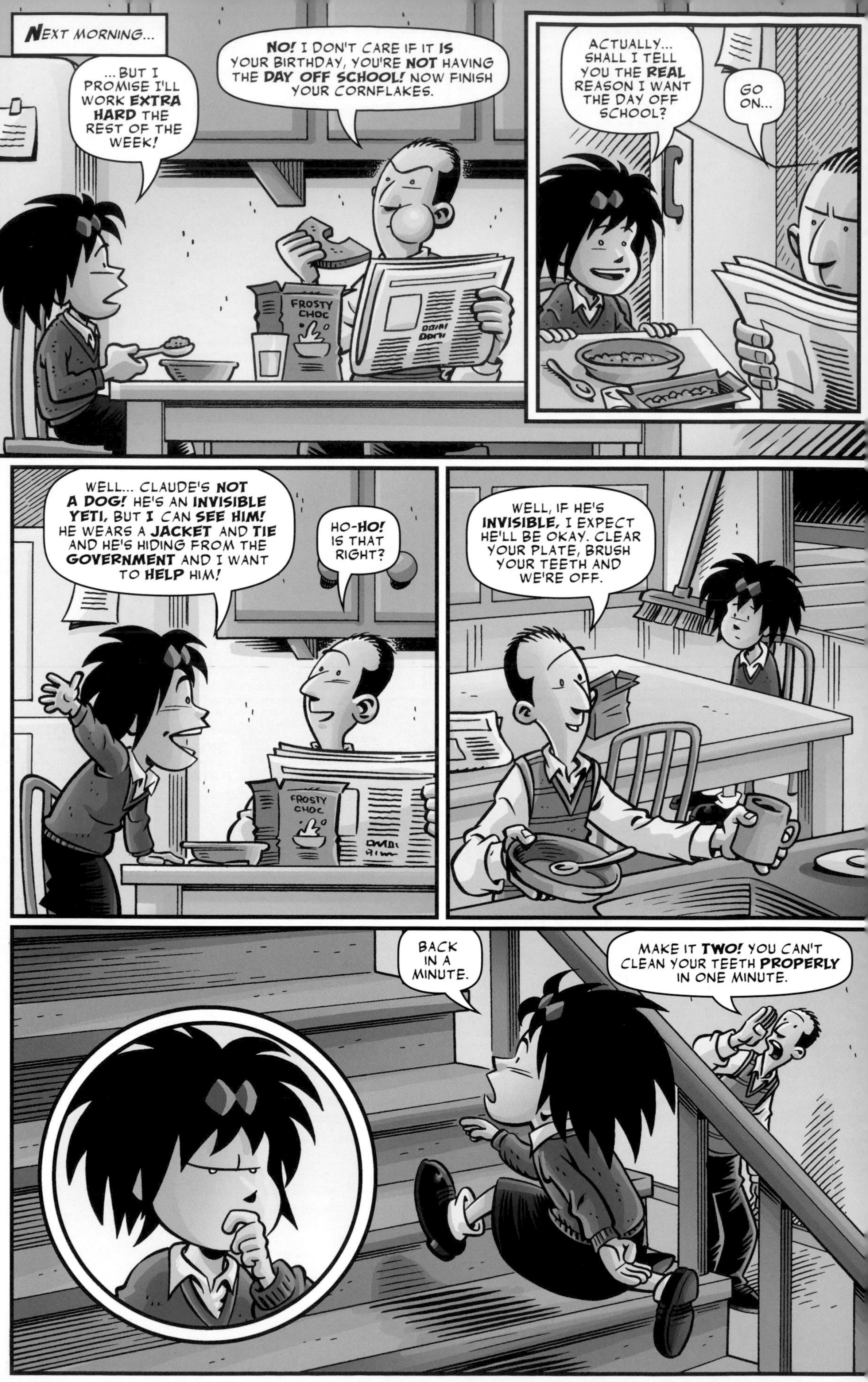
NEXT MORNING...
...BUT I PROMISE I'LL WORK EXTRA HARD THE REST OF THE WEEK!
NO! I DON'T CARE IF IT IS YOUR BIRTHDAY, YOU'RE NOT HAVING THE DAY OFF SCHOOL! NOW FINISH YOUR CORNFLAKES.
FROSTY CHOC
ACTUALLY... SHALL I TELL YOU THE REAL REASON I WANT THE DAY OFF SCHOOL?
GO ON...
WELL... CLAUDE'S NOT A DOG! HE'S AN INVISIBLE YETI, BUT I CAN SEE HIM! HE WEARS A JACKET AND TIE AND HE'S HIDING FROM THE GOVERNMENT AND I WANT TO HELP HIM!
HO-HO! IS THAT RIGHT?
FROSTY CHOC
WELL, IF HE'S INVISIBLE, I EXPECT HE'LL BE OKAY. CLEAR YOUR PLATE, BRUSH YOUR TEETH AND WE'RE OFF.
BACK IN A MINUTE.
MAKE IT TWO! YOU CAN'T CLEAN YOUR TEETH PROPERLY IN ONE MINUTE.

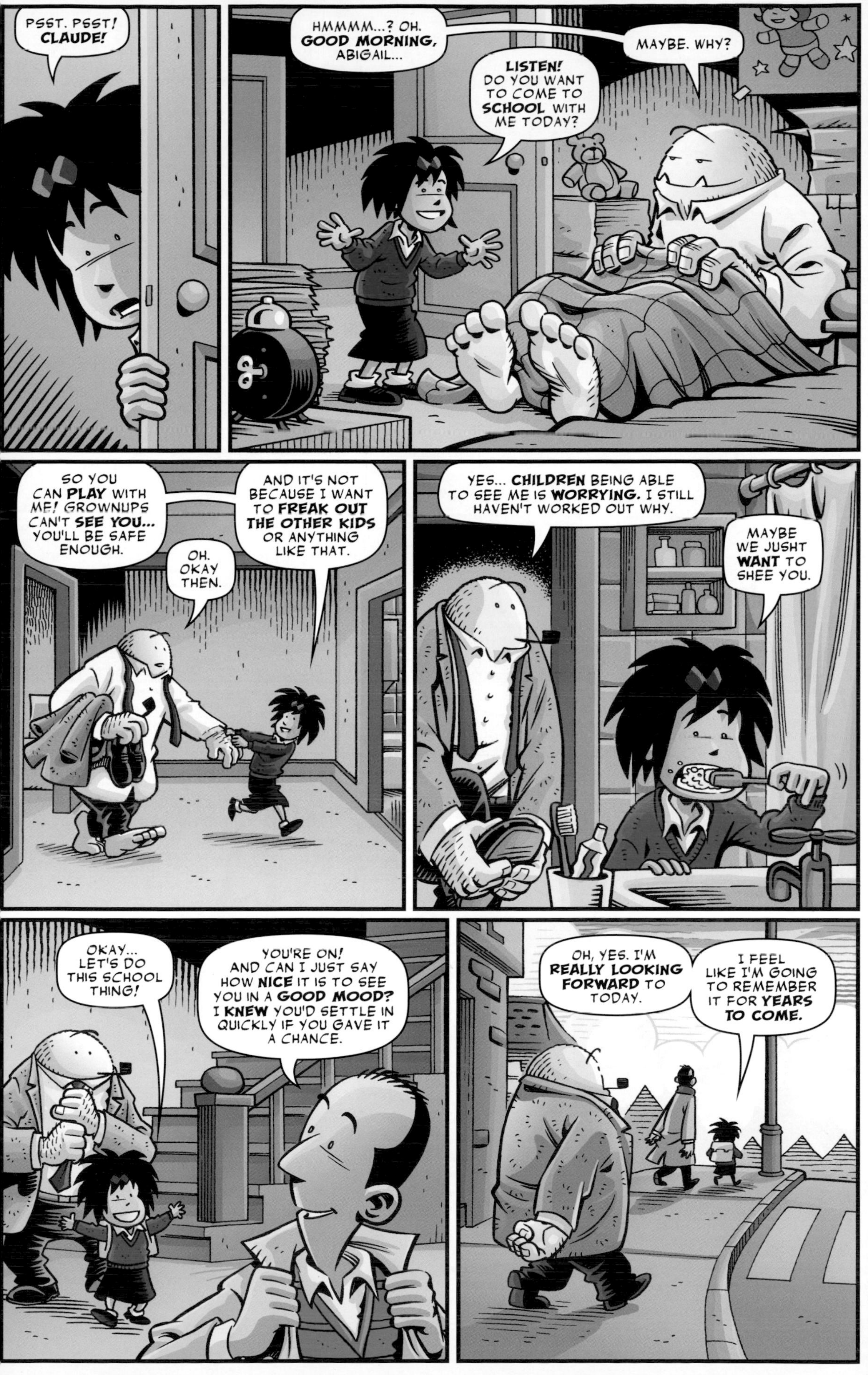
PSST. PSST! CLAUDE!
HMMMM...? OH. GOOD MORNING, ABIGAIL...
LISTEN! DO YOU WANT TO COME TO SCHOOL WITH ME TODAY?
MAYBE. WHY?
SO YOU CAN PLAY WITH ME! GROWNUPS CAN'T SEE YOU... YOU'LL BE SAFE ENOUGH.
AND IT'S NOT BECAUSE I WANT TO FREAK OUT THE OTHER KIDS OR ANYTHING LIKE THAT.
OH. OKAY THEN.
YES... CHILDREN BEING ABLE TO SEE ME IS WORRYING. I STILL HAVEN'T WORKED OUT WHY.
MAYBE WE JUSHT WANT TO SHEE YOU.
OKAY... LET'S DO THIS SCHOOL THING!
YOU'RE ON! AND CAN I JUST SAY HOW NICE IT IS TO SEE YOU IN A GOOD MOOD? I KNEW YOU'D SETTLE IN QUICKLY IF YOU GAVE IT A CHANCE.
OH, YES. I'M REALLY LOOKING FORWARD TO TODAY.
I FEEL LIKE I'M GOING TO REMEMBER IT FOR YEARS TO COME.

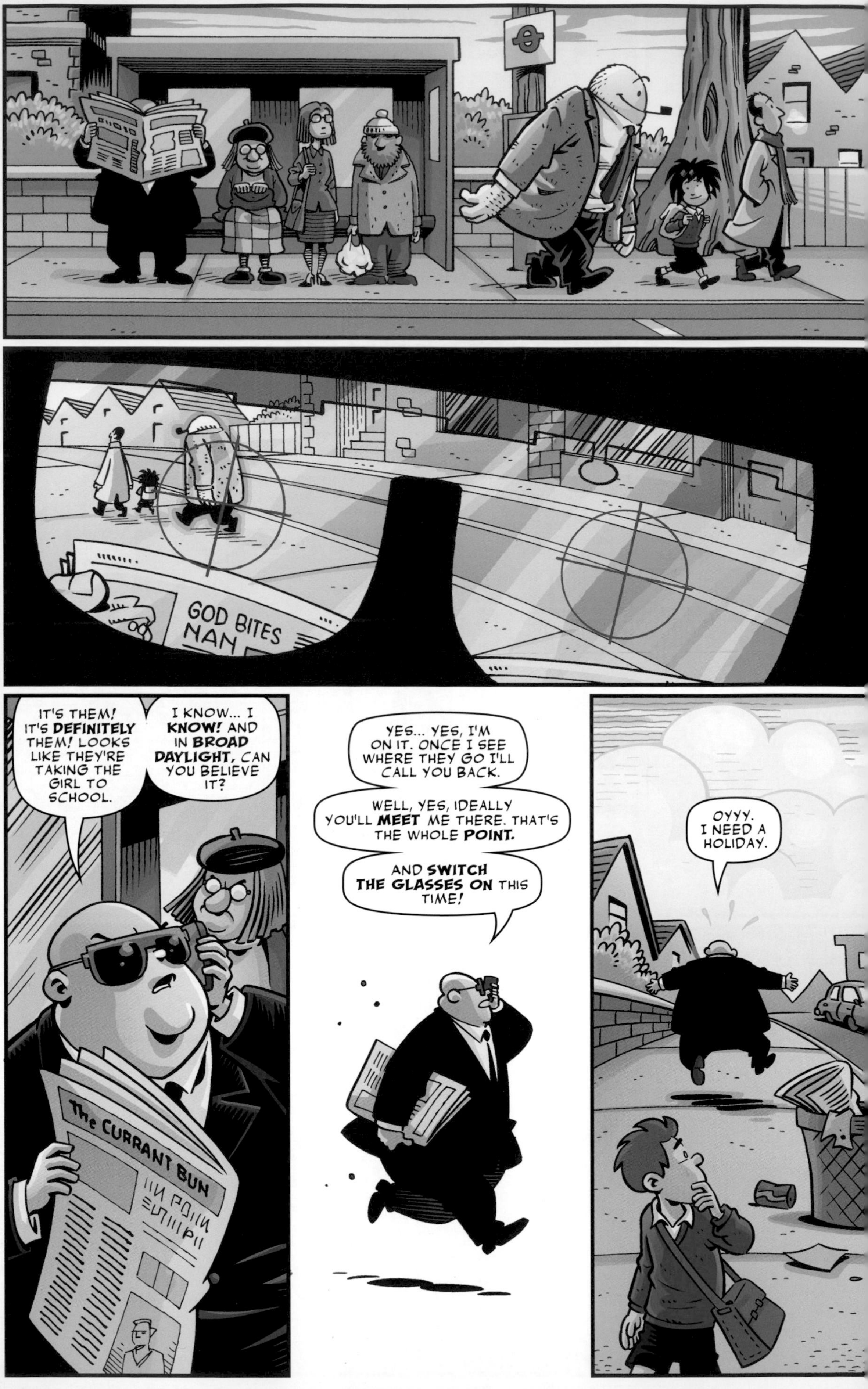
GOD BITES NAN
IT'S THEM! IT'S DEFINITELY THEM! LOOKS LIKE THEY'RE TAKING THE GIRL TO SCHOOL.
I KNOW... I KNOW! AND IN BROAD DAYLIGHT, CAN YOU BELIEVE IT?
The CURRANT BUN
YES... YES, I'M ON IT. ONCE I SEE WHERE THEY GO I'LL CALL YOU BACK.
WELL, YES, IDEALLY YOU'LL MEET ME THERE. THAT'S THE WHOLE POINT.
AND SWITCH THE GLASSES ON THIS TIME!
OYYY. I NEED A HOLIDAY.

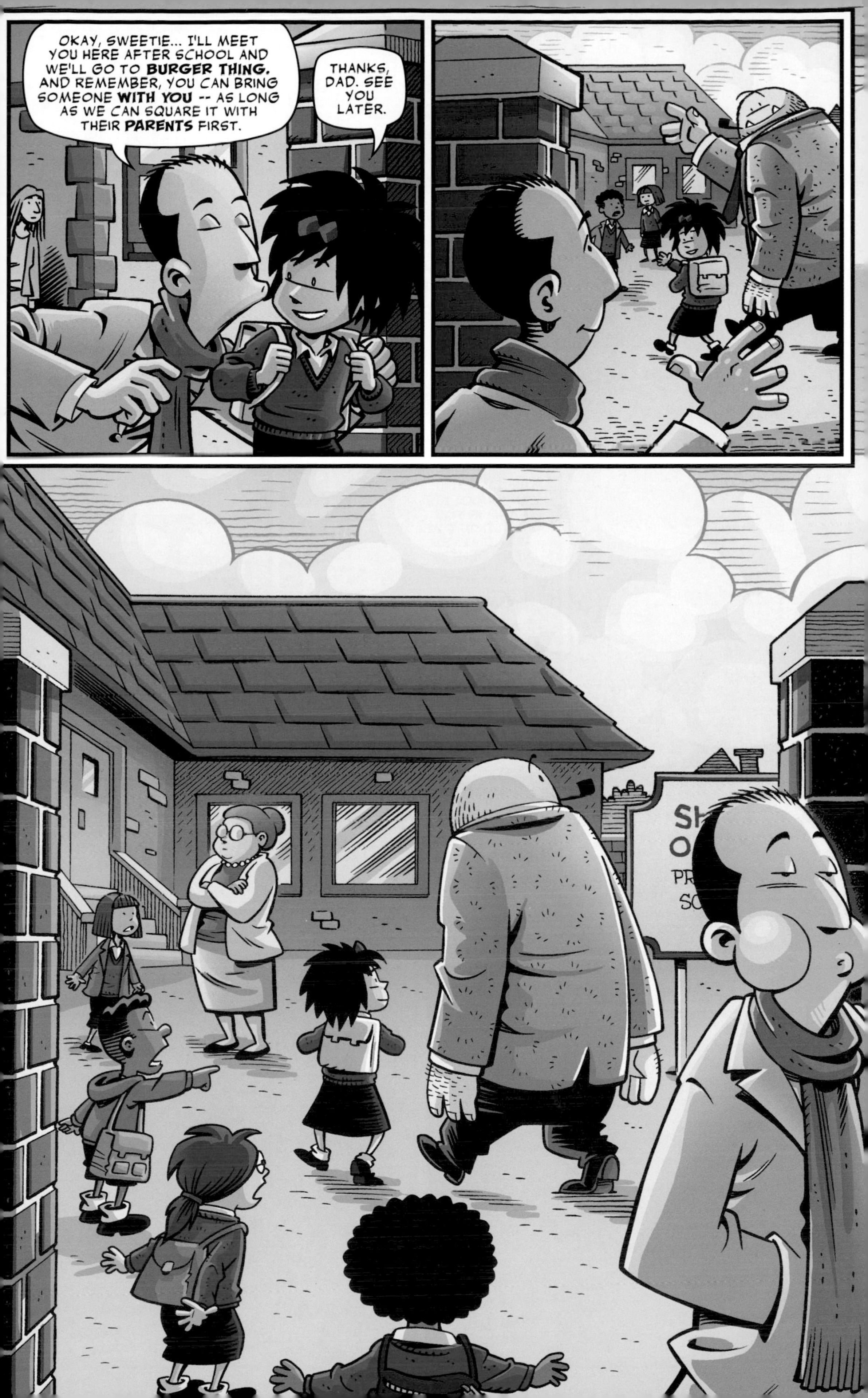
OKAY, SWEETIE... I'LL MEET YOU HERE AFTER SCHOOL AND WE'LL GO TO **BURGER THING.** AND REMEMBER, YOU CAN BRING SOMEONE **WITH YOU** -- AS LONG AS WE CAN SQUARE IT WITH THEIR **PARENTS** FIRST.
THANKS, DAD. SEE YOU LATER.

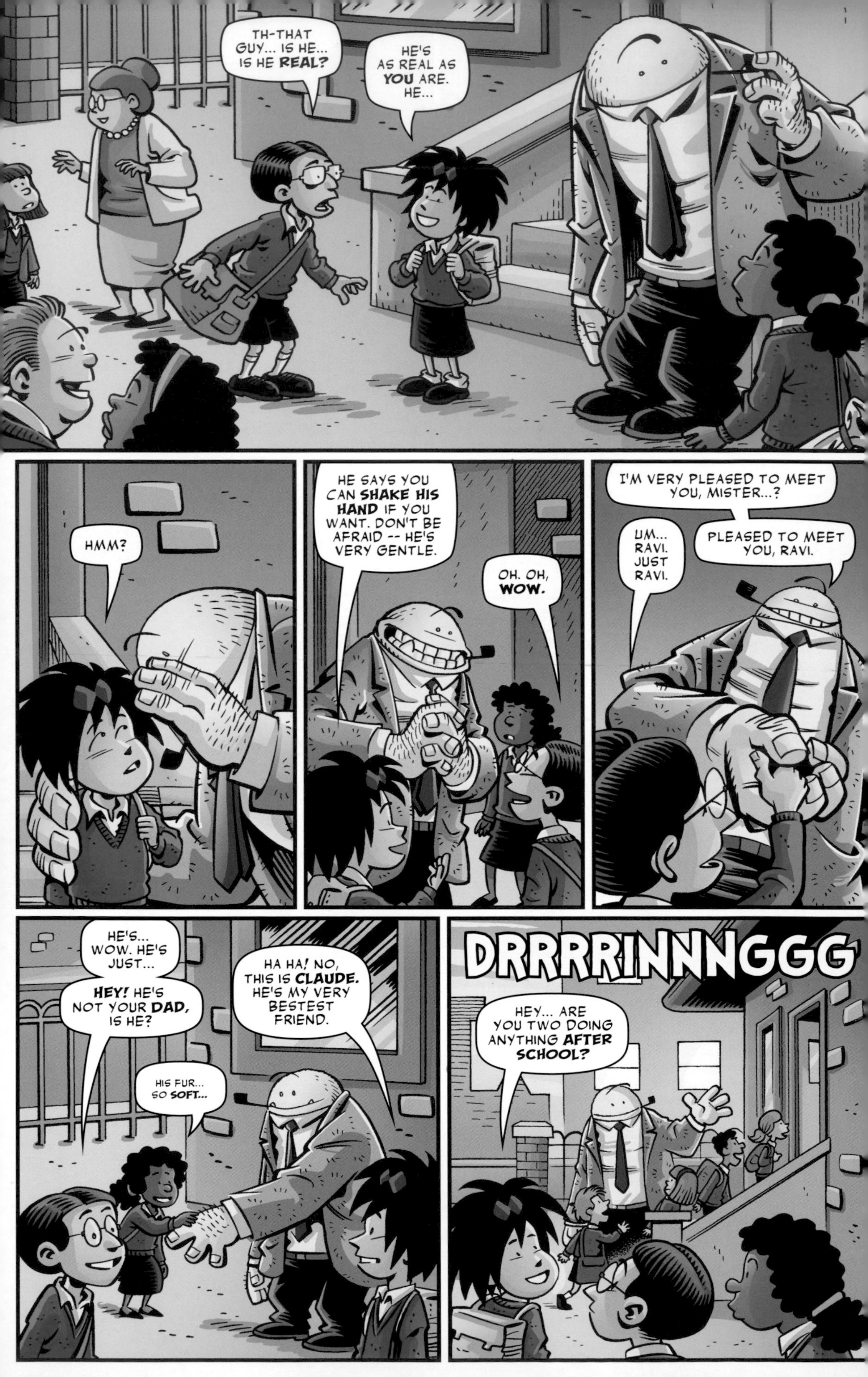

TH-THAT GUY... IS HE... IS HE **REAL?**
HE'S AS REAL AS **YOU** ARE. HE...
HMM?
HE SAYS YOU CAN **SHAKE HIS HAND** IF YOU WANT. DON'T BE AFRAID -- HE'S VERY GENTLE.
OH. OH, **WOW.**
I'M VERY PLEASED TO MEET YOU, MISTER...?
UM... RAVI. JUST RAVI.
PLEASED TO MEET YOU, RAVI.
HE'S... WOW. HE'S JUST...
HEY! HE'S NOT YOUR **DAD,** IS HE?
HA HA! NO, THIS IS **CLAUDE.** HE'S MY VERY BESTEST FRIEND.
HIS FUR... SO **SOFT...**
DRRRRINNNGGG
HEY... ARE YOU TWO DOING ANYTHING **AFTER SCHOOL?**

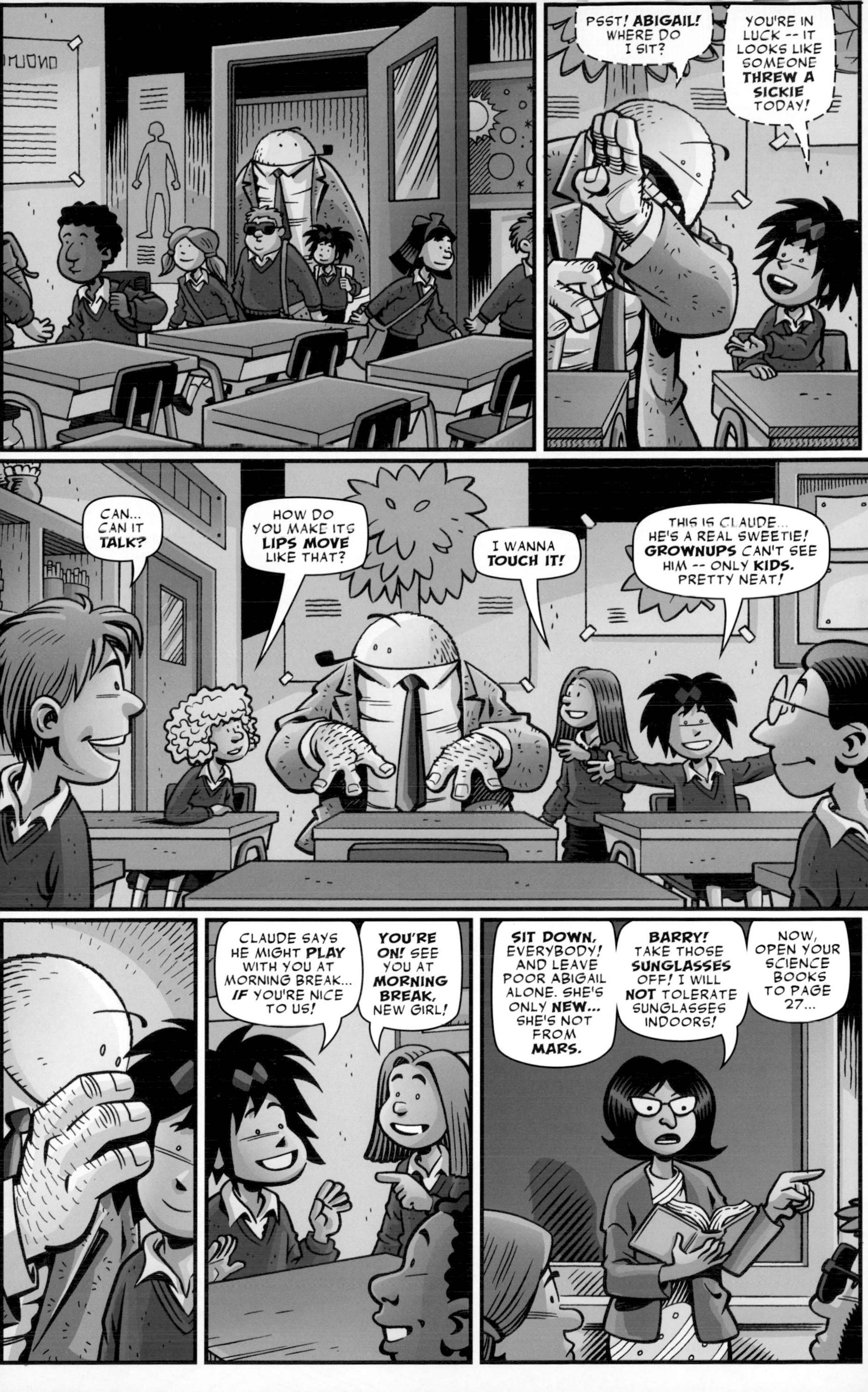
PSST! ABIGAIL! WHERE DO I SIT?
YOU'RE IN LUCK -- IT LOOKS LIKE SOMEONE THREW A SICKIE TODAY!
CAN... CAN IT TALK?
HOW DO YOU MAKE ITS LIPS MOVE LIKE THAT?
I WANNA TOUCH IT!
THIS IS CLAUDE... HE'S A REAL SWEETIE! GROWNUPS CAN'T SEE HIM -- ONLY KIDS. PRETTY NEAT!
CLAUDE SAYS HE MIGHT PLAY WITH YOU AT MORNING BREAK... IF YOU'RE NICE TO US!
YOU'RE ON! SEE YOU AT MORNING BREAK, NEW GIRL!
SIT DOWN, EVERYBODY! AND LEAVE POOR ABIGAIL ALONE. SHE'S ONLY NEW... SHE'S NOT FROM MARS.
BARRY! TAKE THOSE SUNGLASSES OFF! I WILL NOT TOLERATE SUNGLASSES INDOORS!
NOW, OPEN YOUR SCIENCE BOOKS TO PAGE 27...

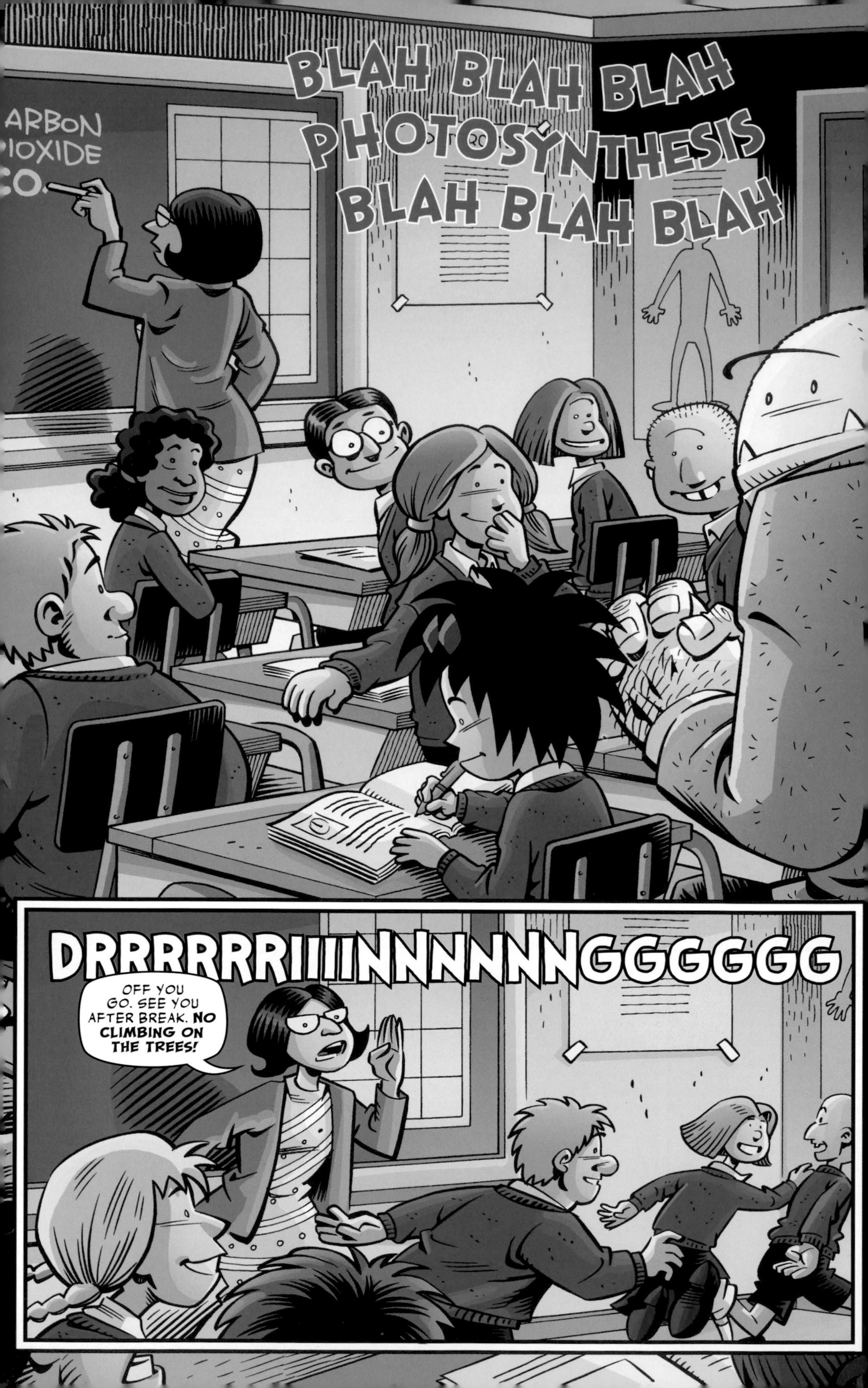
ARBON
IOXIDE
CO
BLAH BLAH BLAH
PHOTOSYNTHESIS
BLAH BLAH BLAH
DRRRRRRIIIINNNNNNGGGGGG
OFF YOU GO. SEE YOU AFTER BREAK. **NO CLIMBING ON THE TREES!**

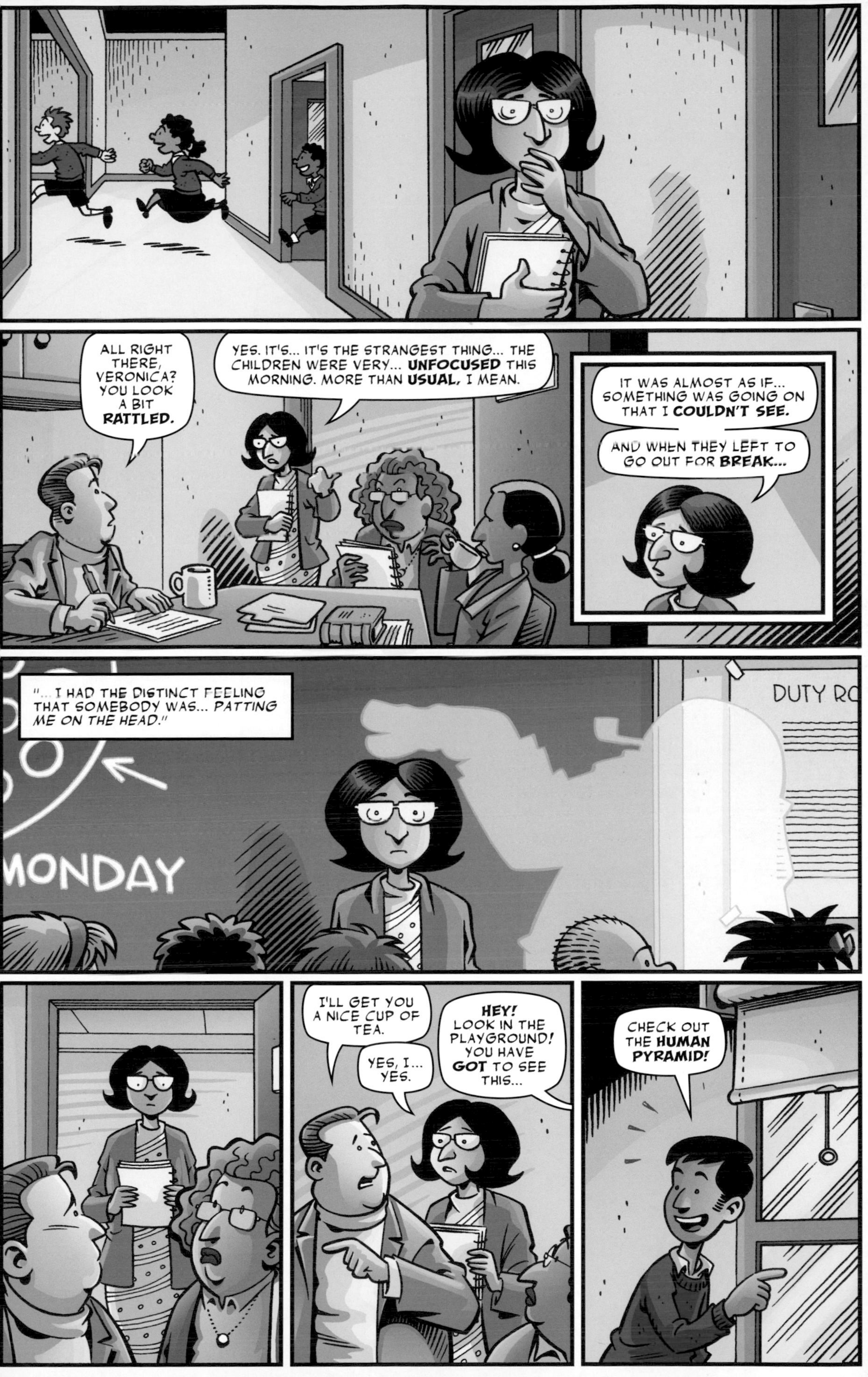
ALL RIGHT THERE, VERONICA? YOU LOOK A BIT **RATTLED.**
YES. IT'S... IT'S THE STRANGEST THING... THE CHILDREN WERE VERY... **UNFOCUSED** THIS MORNING. MORE THAN **USUAL**, I MEAN.
IT WAS ALMOST AS IF... SOMETHING WAS GOING ON THAT I **COULDN'T SEE.**
AND WHEN THEY LEFT TO GO OUT FOR **BREAK...**
"... I HAD THE DISTINCT FEELING THAT SOMEBODY WAS... *PATTING ME ON THE HEAD.*"
DUTY RO
MONDAY
I'LL GET YOU A NICE CUP OF TEA.
YES, I... YES.
HEY! LOOK IN THE PLAYGROUND! YOU HAVE **GOT** TO SEE THIS...
CHECK OUT THE **HUMAN PYRAMID!**

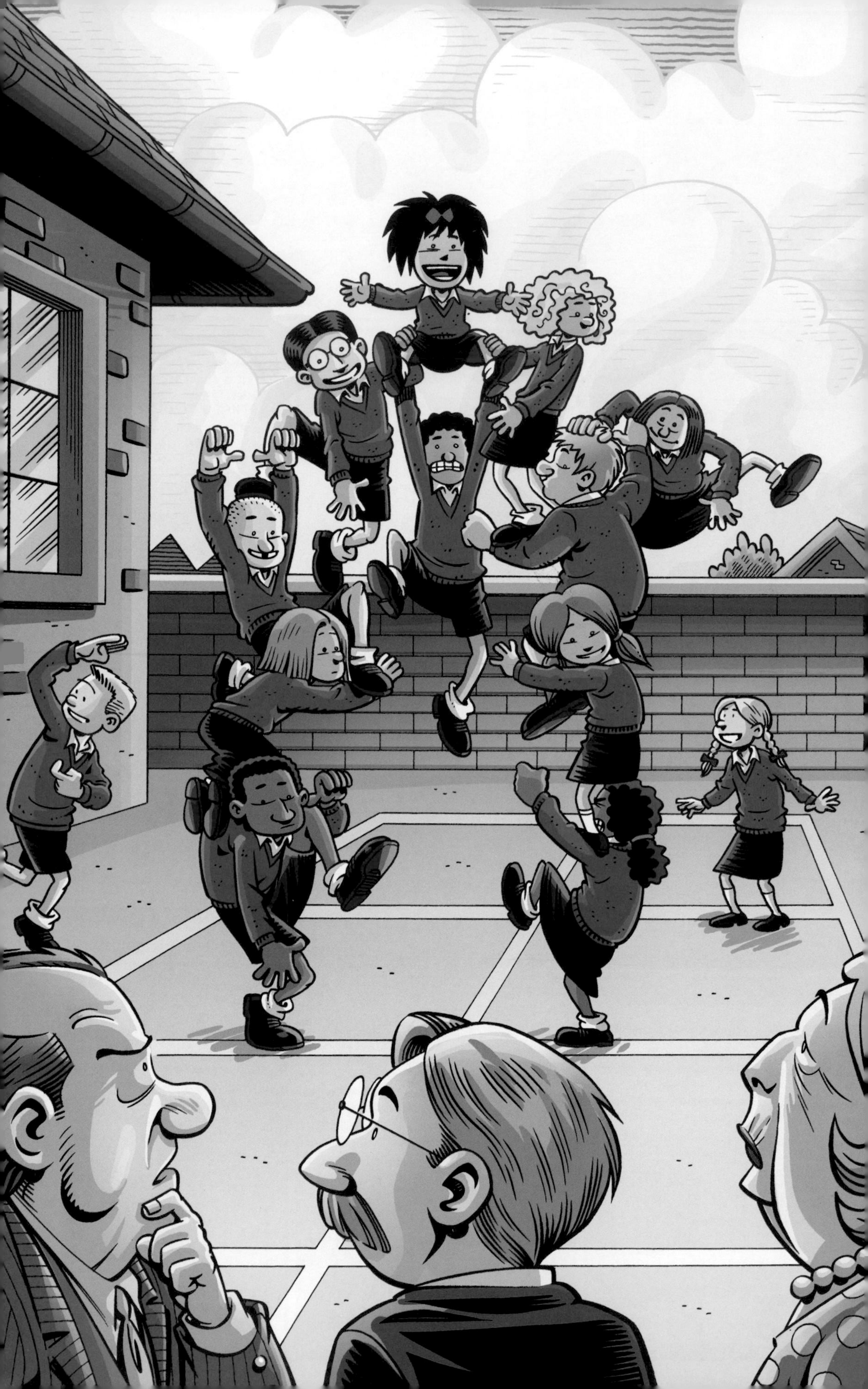

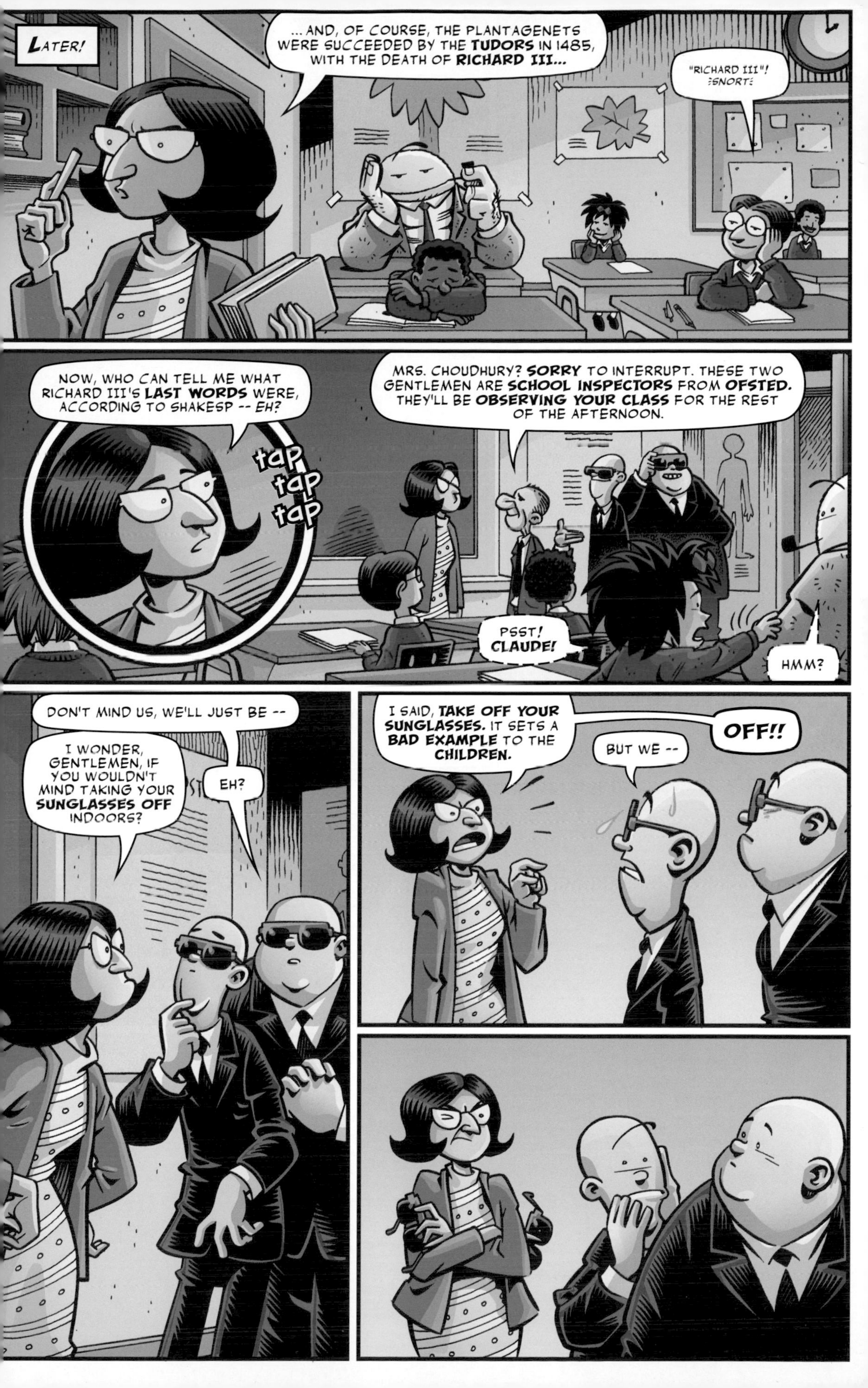
LATER!
... AND, OF COURSE, THE PLANTAGENETS WERE SUCCEEDED BY THE **TUDORS** IN 1485, WITH THE DEATH OF **RICHARD III...**
"RICHARD III"! ≥SNORT≤
NOW, WHO CAN TELL ME WHAT RICHARD III'S **LAST WORDS** WERE, ACCORDING TO SHAKESP -- *EH?*
tap tap tap
MRS. CHOUDHURY? **SORRY** TO INTERRUPT. THESE TWO GENTLEMEN ARE **SCHOOL INSPECTORS** FROM **OFSTED.** THEY'LL BE **OBSERVING YOUR CLASS** FOR THE REST OF THE AFTERNOON.
PSST! **CLAUDE!**
HMM?
DON'T MIND US, WE'LL JUST BE --
I WONDER, GENTLEMEN, IF YOU WOULDN'T MIND TAKING YOUR **SUNGLASSES OFF** INDOORS?
EH?
I SAID, **TAKE OFF YOUR SUNGLASSES.** IT SETS A **BAD EXAMPLE** TO THE **CHILDREN.**
BUT WE --
OFF!!

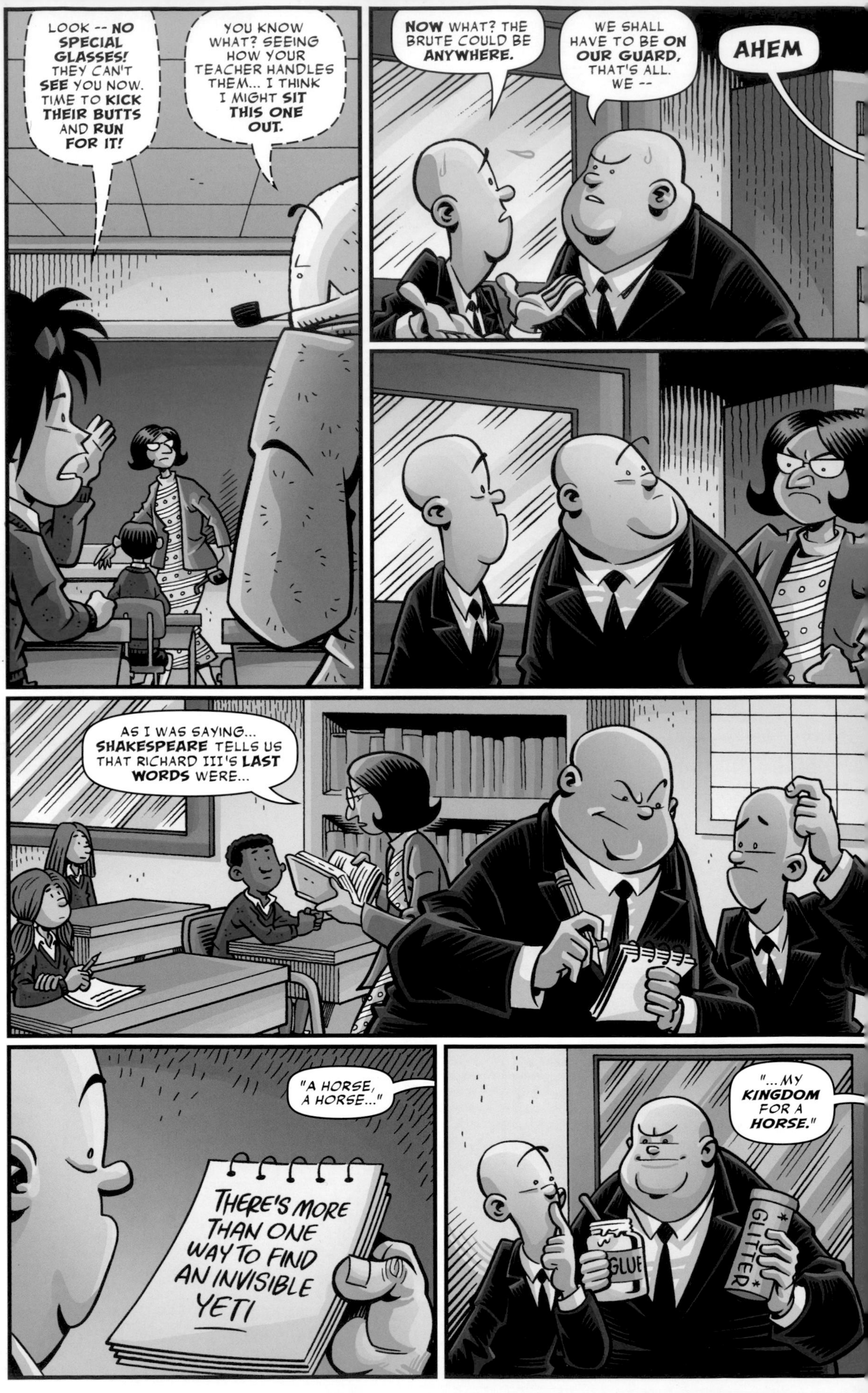
LOOK -- NO SPECIAL GLASSES! THEY CAN'T SEE YOU NOW. TIME TO KICK THEIR BUTTS AND RUN FOR IT!
YOU KNOW WHAT? SEEING HOW YOUR TEACHER HANDLES THEM... I THINK I MIGHT SIT THIS ONE OUT.
NOW WHAT? THE BRUTE COULD BE ANYWHERE.
WE SHALL HAVE TO BE ON OUR GUARD, THAT'S ALL. WE --
AHEM
AS I WAS SAYING... SHAKESPEARE TELLS US THAT RICHARD III'S LAST WORDS WERE...
"A HORSE, A HORSE..."
THERE'S MORE THAN ONE WAY TO FIND AN INVISIBLE YETI
"...MY KINGDOM FOR A HORSE."
GLUE
GLITTER

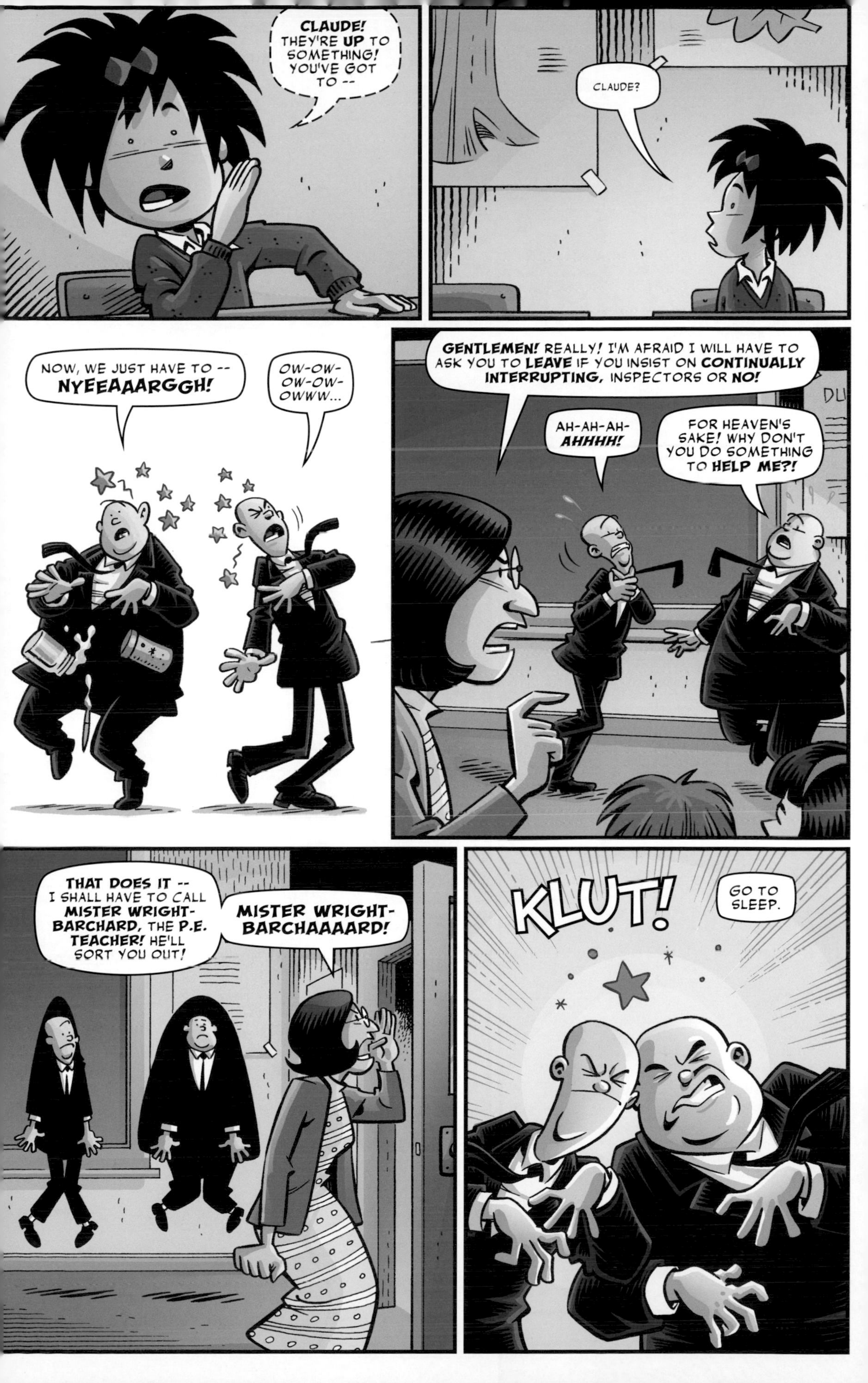
CLAUDE! THEY'RE UP TO SOMETHING! YOU'VE GOT TO --
CLAUDE?
NOW, WE JUST HAVE TO -- NYEEAAARGGH!
OW-OW-OW-OW-OWWW...
GENTLEMEN! REALLY! I'M AFRAID I WILL HAVE TO ASK YOU TO LEAVE IF YOU INSIST ON CONTINUALLY INTERRUPTING, INSPECTORS OR NO!
AH-AH-AH-AHHHH!
FOR HEAVEN'S SAKE! WHY DON'T YOU DO SOMETHING TO HELP ME?!
THAT DOES IT -- I SHALL HAVE TO CALL MISTER WRIGHT-BARCHARD, THE P.E. TEACHER! HE'LL SORT YOU OUT!
MISTER WRIGHT-BARCHAAAARD!
KLUT!
GO TO SLEEP.

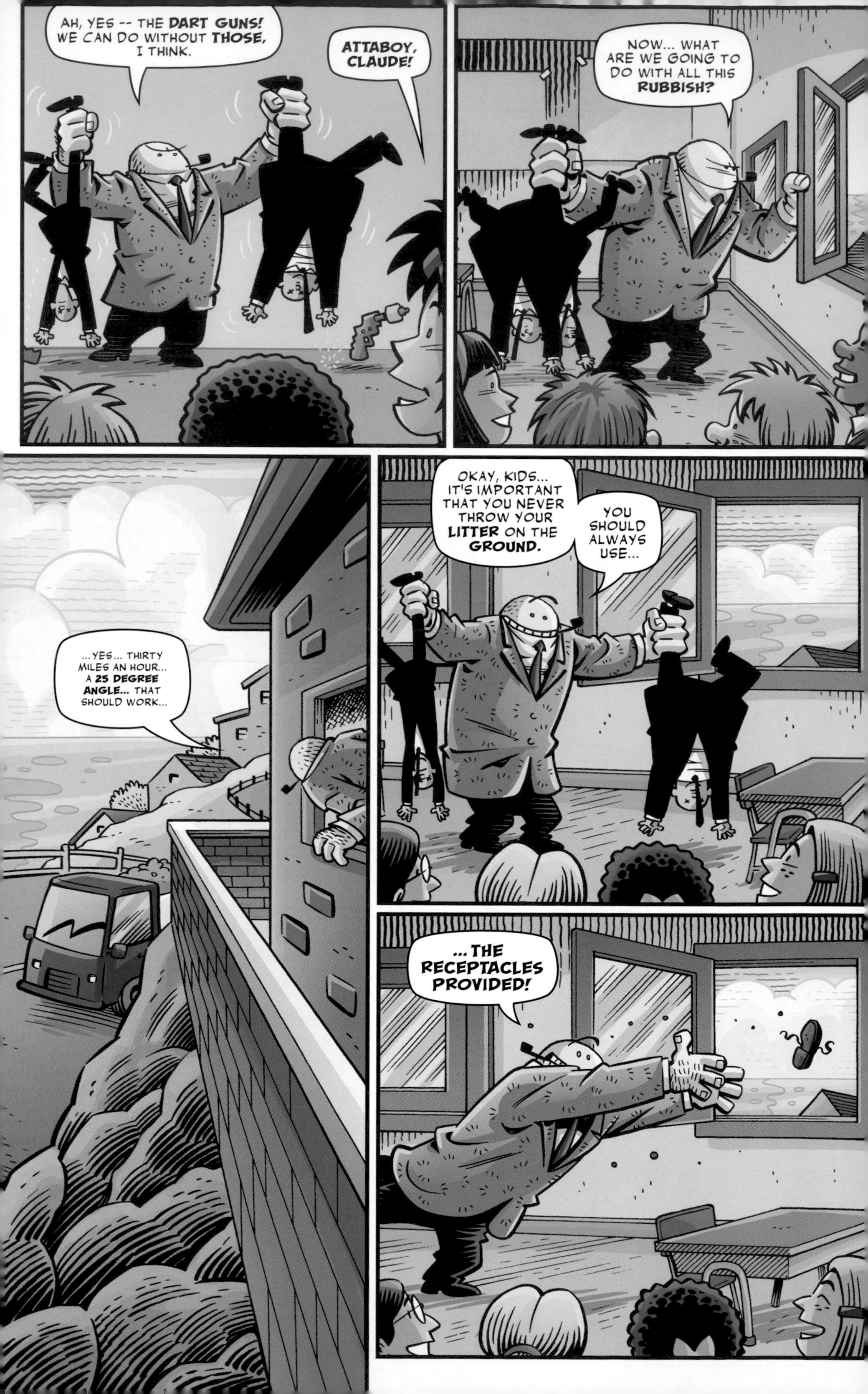

AH, YES -- THE DART GUNS! WE CAN DO WITHOUT THOSE, I THINK.
ATTABOY, CLAUDE!
NOW... WHAT ARE WE GOING TO DO WITH ALL THIS RUBBISH?
...YES... THIRTY MILES AN HOUR... A 25 DEGREE ANGLE... THAT SHOULD WORK...
OKAY, KIDS... IT'S IMPORTANT THAT YOU NEVER THROW YOUR LITTER ON THE GROUND.
YOU SHOULD ALWAYS USE...
...THE RECEPTACLES PROVIDED!

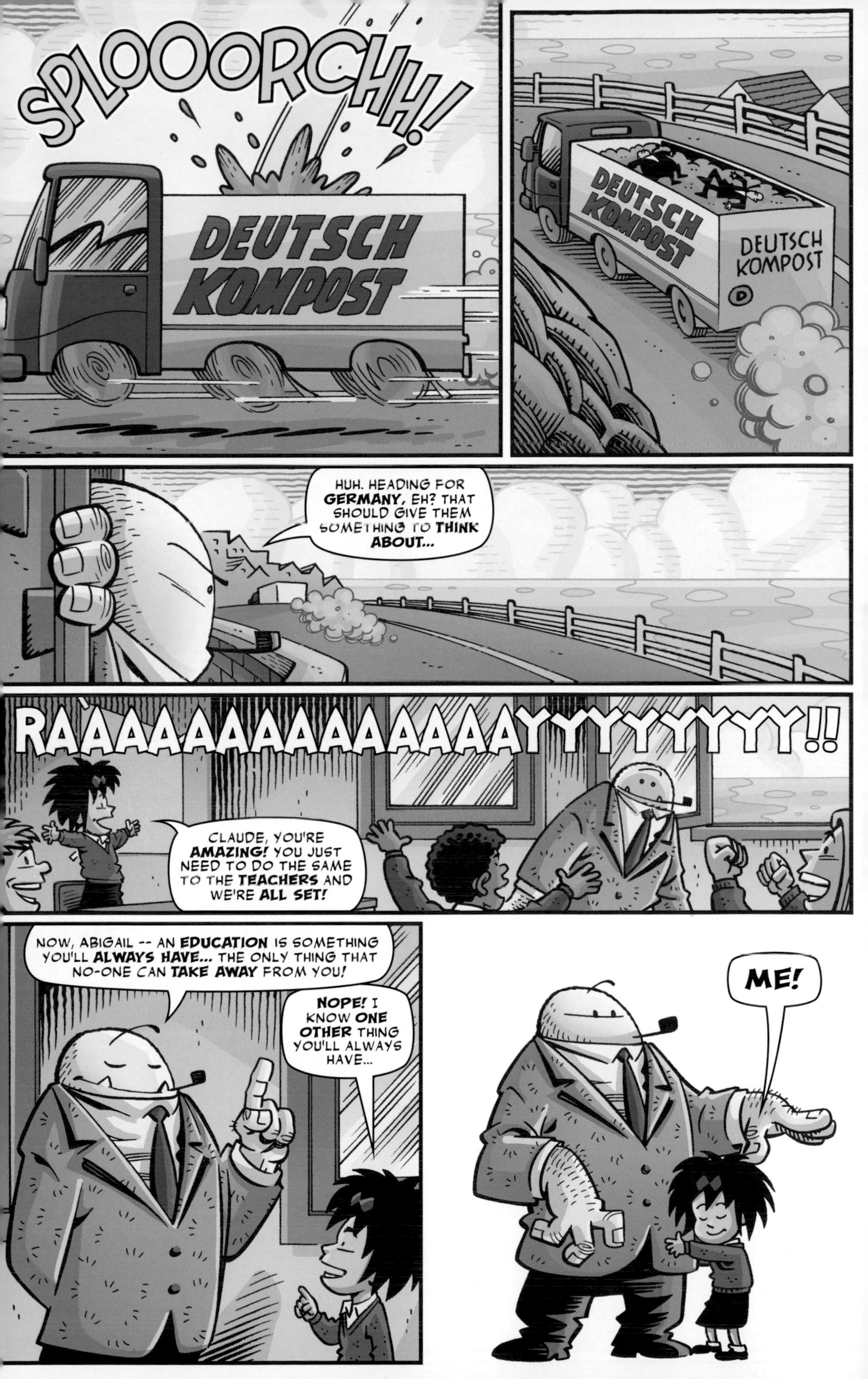
SPLOOORCHH!
DEUTSCH KOMPOST
DEUTSCH KOMPOST
DEUTSCH KOMPOST
HUH. HEADING FOR GERMANY, EH? THAT SHOULD GIVE THEM SOMETHING TO THINK ABOUT...
RAAAAAAAAAAAAAYYYYYYYY!!
CLAUDE, YOU'RE AMAZING! YOU JUST NEED TO DO THE SAME TO THE TEACHERS AND WE'RE ALL SET!
NOW, ABIGAIL -- AN EDUCATION IS SOMETHING YOU'LL ALWAYS HAVE... THE ONLY THING THAT NO-ONE CAN TAKE AWAY FROM YOU!
NOPE! I KNOW ONE OTHER THING YOU'LL ALWAYS HAVE...
ME!

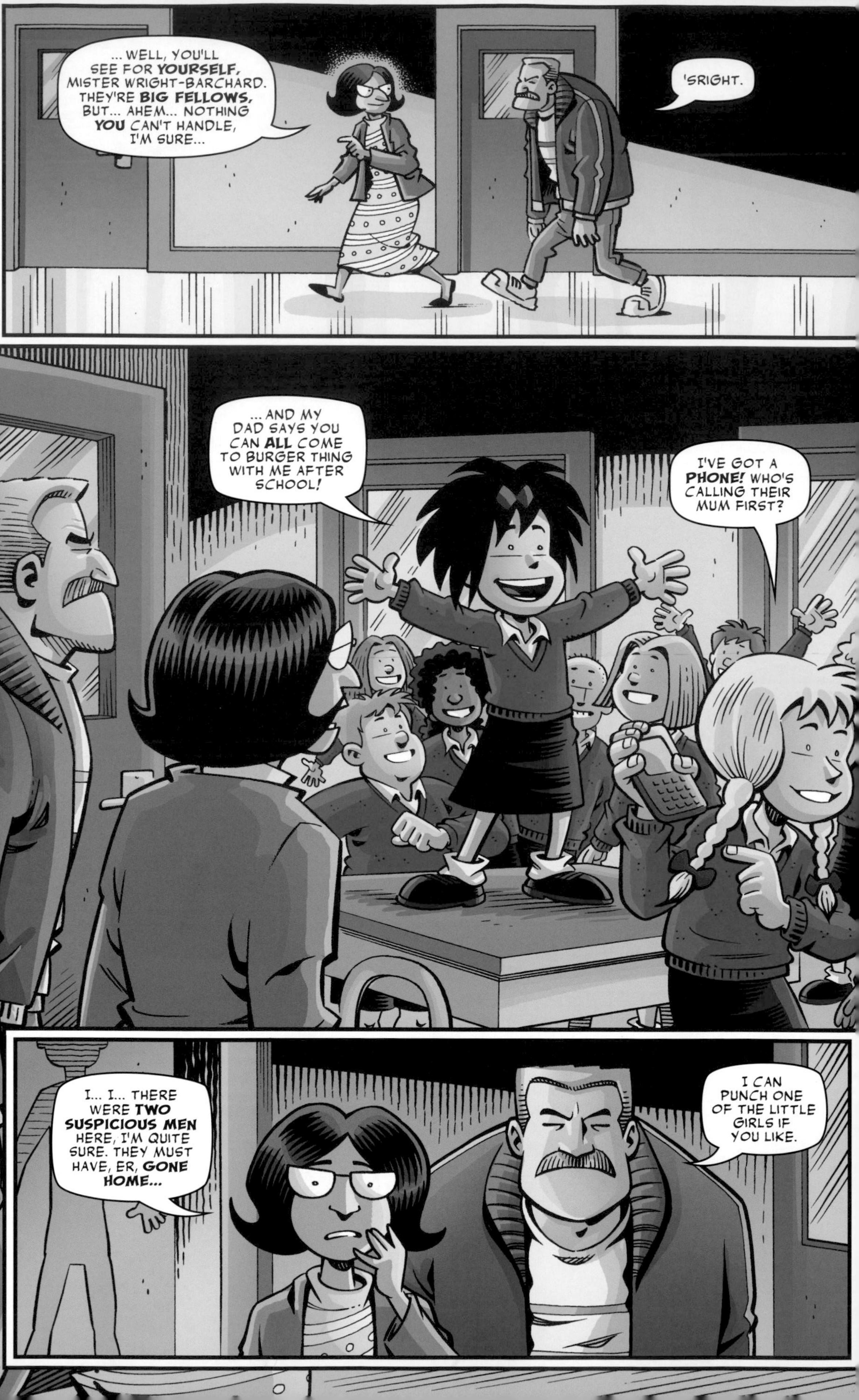
... WELL, YOU'LL SEE FOR **YOURSELF,** MISTER WRIGHT-BARCHARD. THEY'RE **BIG FELLOWS,** BUT... AHEM... NOTHING **YOU** CAN'T HANDLE, I'M SURE...
'SRIGHT.
... AND MY DAD SAYS YOU CAN **ALL** COME TO BURGER THING WITH ME AFTER SCHOOL!
I'VE GOT A **PHONE!** WHO'S CALLING THEIR MUM FIRST?
I... I... THERE WERE **TWO SUSPICIOUS MEN** HERE, I'M QUITE SURE. THEY MUST HAVE, ER, **GONE HOME...**
I CAN PUNCH ONE OF THE LITTLE GIRLS IF YOU LIKE.

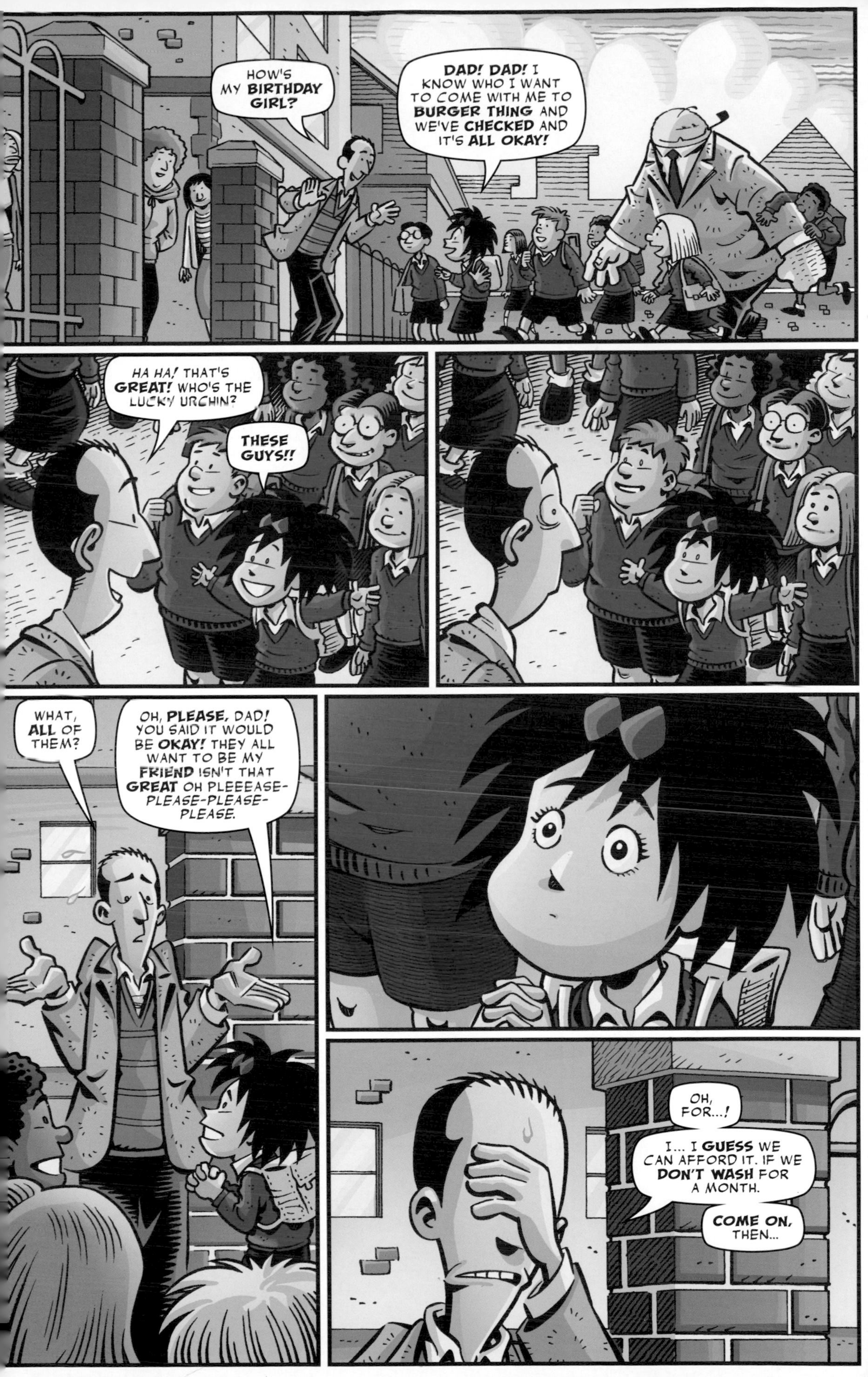
HOW'S MY BIRTHDAY GIRL?
DAD! DAD! I KNOW WHO I WANT TO COME WITH ME TO BURGER THING AND WE'VE CHECKED AND IT'S ALL OKAY!
HA HA! THAT'S GREAT! WHO'S THE LUCKY URCHIN?
THESE GUYS!!
WHAT, ALL OF THEM?
OH, PLEASE, DAD! YOU SAID IT WOULD BE OKAY! THEY ALL WANT TO BE MY FRIEND ISN'T THAT GREAT OH PLEEEASE-PLEASE-PLEASE-PLEASE.
OH, FOR...!
I... I GUESS WE CAN AFFORD IT. IF WE DON'T WASH FOR A MONTH.
COME ON, THEN...

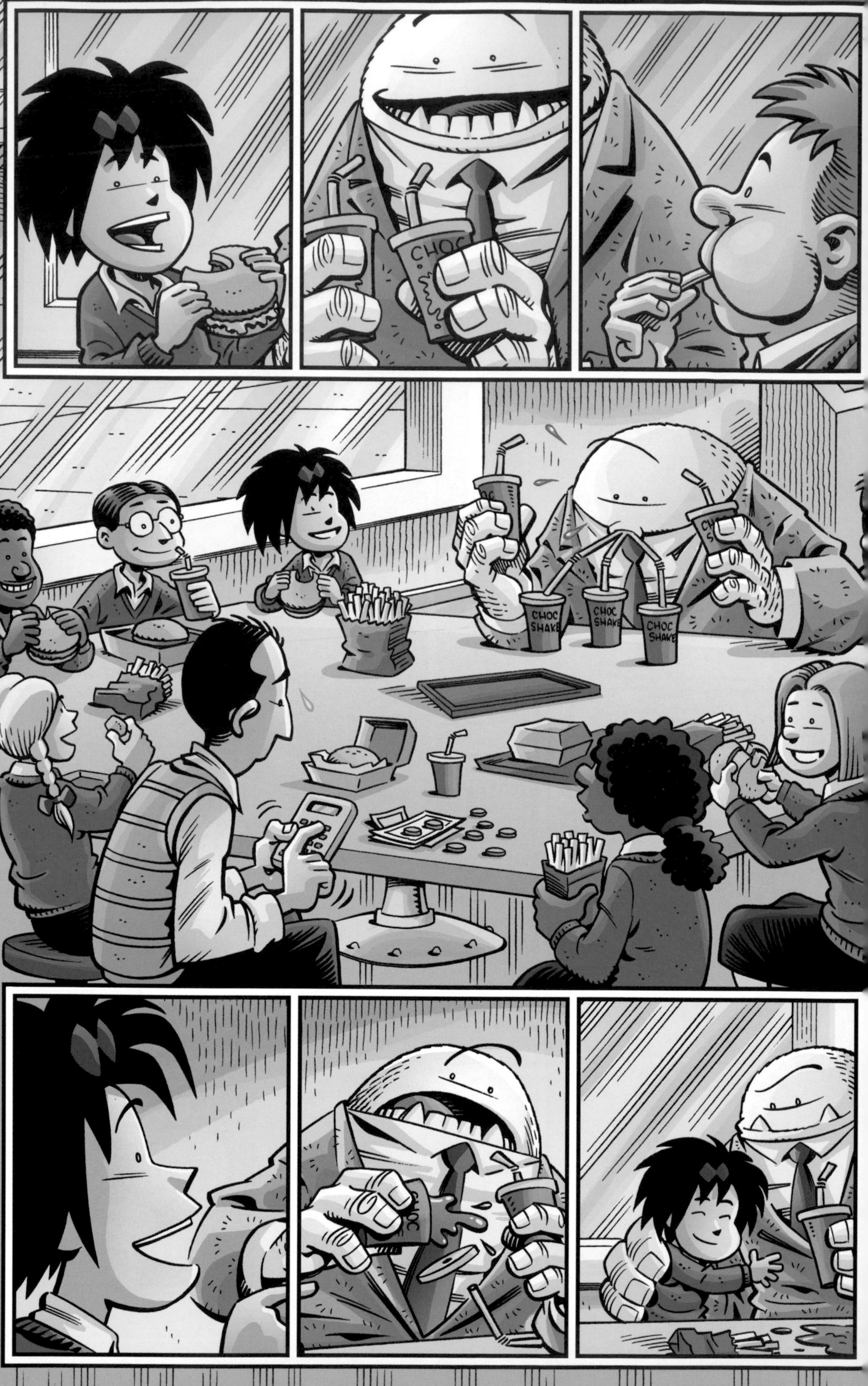
CHOC
CHOC SHAKE
CHOC SHAKE
CHOC SHAKE

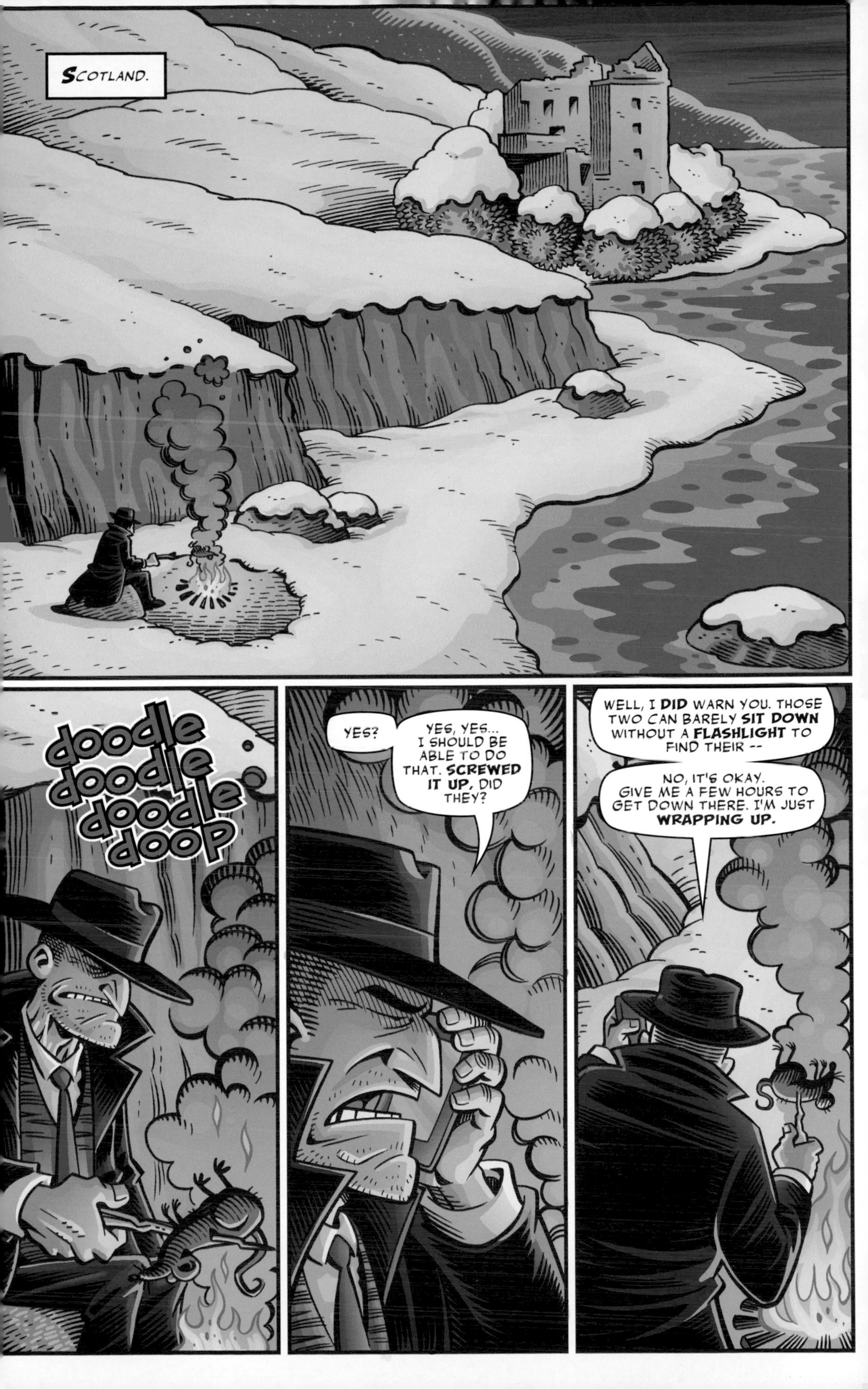
SCOTLAND.
doodle doodle doodle doodle doop
YES?
YES, YES... I SHOULD BE ABLE TO DO THAT. SCREWED IT UP, DID THEY?
WELL, I DID WARN YOU. THOSE TWO CAN BARELY SIT DOWN WITHOUT A FLASHLIGHT TO FIND THEIR --
NO, IT'S OKAY. GIVE ME A FEW HOURS TO GET DOWN THERE. I'M JUST WRAPPING UP.

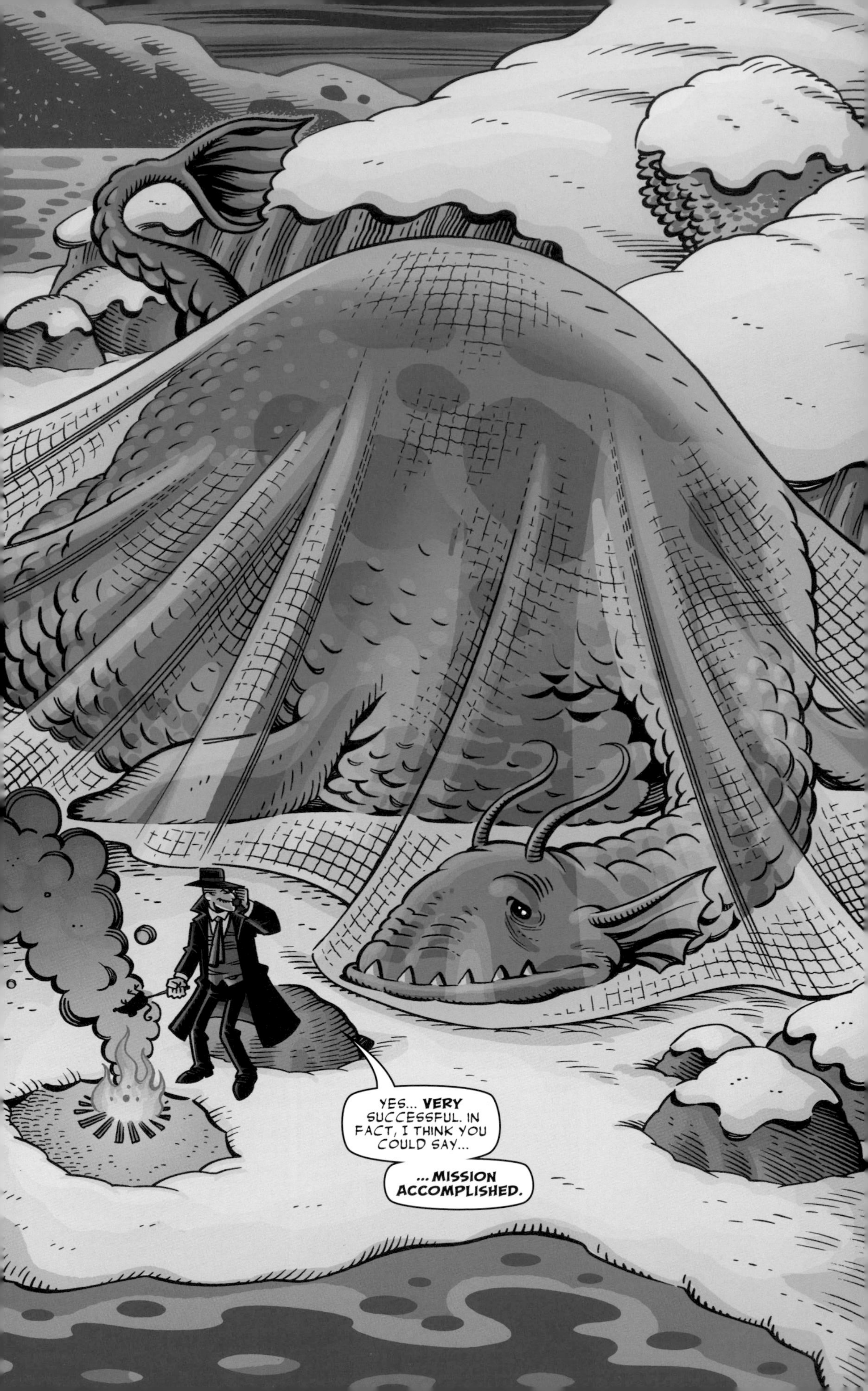
YES... **VERY** SUCCESSFUL. IN FACT, I THINK YOU COULD SAY...
...MISSION ACCOMPLISHED.

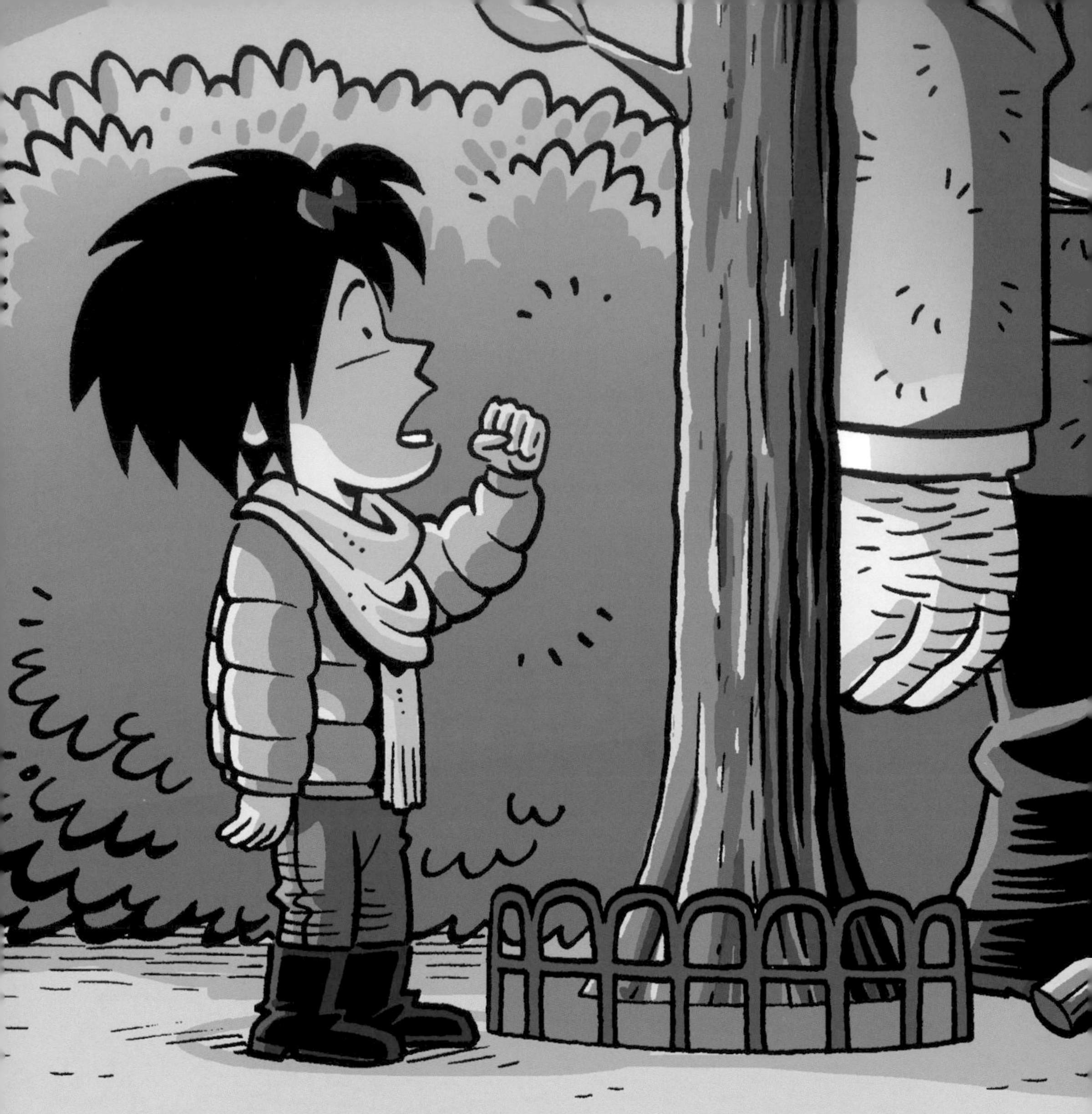

chapter three

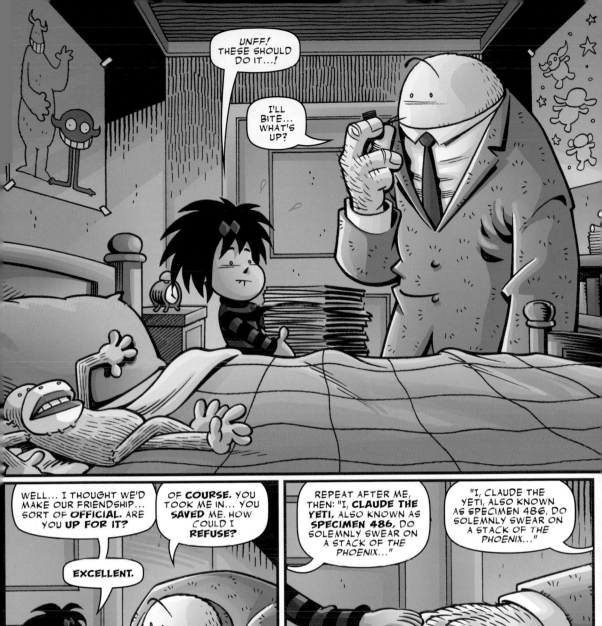

UNFF! THESE SHOULD DO IT...!

I'LL BITE... WHAT'S UP?

WELL... I THOUGHT WE'D MAKE OUR FRIENDSHIP... SORT OF **OFFICIAL**. ARE YOU **UP FOR IT**?

OF **COURSE**. YOU TOOK ME IN... YOU **SAVED** ME. HOW COULD I **REFUSE**?

EXCELLENT.

REPEAT AFTER ME, THEN: "I, **CLAUDE THE YETI**, ALSO KNOWN AS **SPECIMEN 486**, DO SOLEMNLY SWEAR ON A STACK OF THE **PHOENIX**..."

"I, **CLAUDE THE YETI**, ALSO KNOWN AS SPECIMEN 486, DO SOLEMNLY SWEAR ON A STACK OF THE **PHOENIX**..."

"...THAT I WILL BE ABIGAIL'S **BESTEST FRIEND** FOR EVER AND EVER."

"...THAT I WILL BE ABIGAIL'S **BESTEST FRIEND** FOR EVER AND EVER."

AND THAT GOES **DOUBLE** FOR ME.

ALL **RIGHT**, THEN.

TIME TO GO OUTSIDE AND **PLAY**, I THINK...

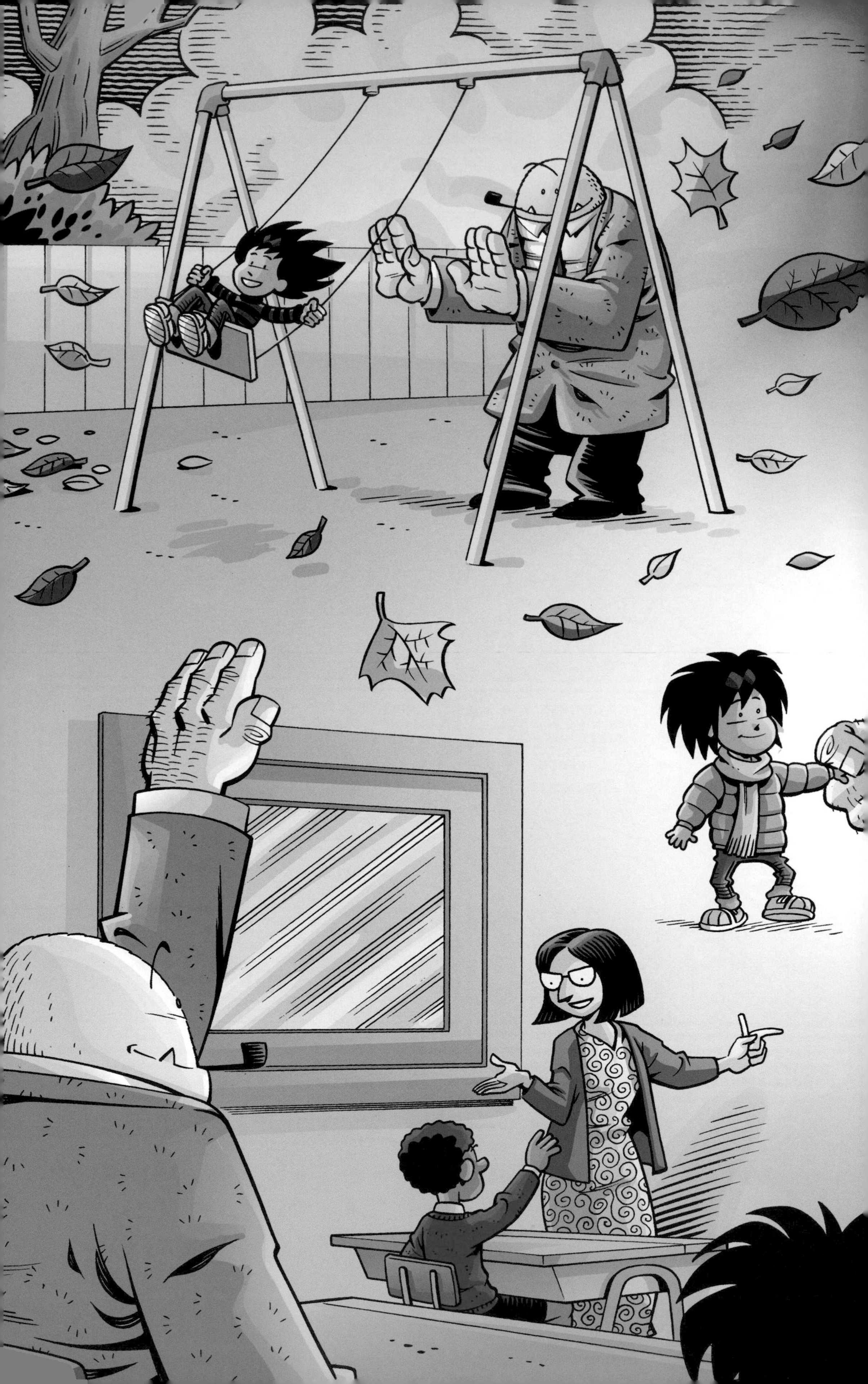

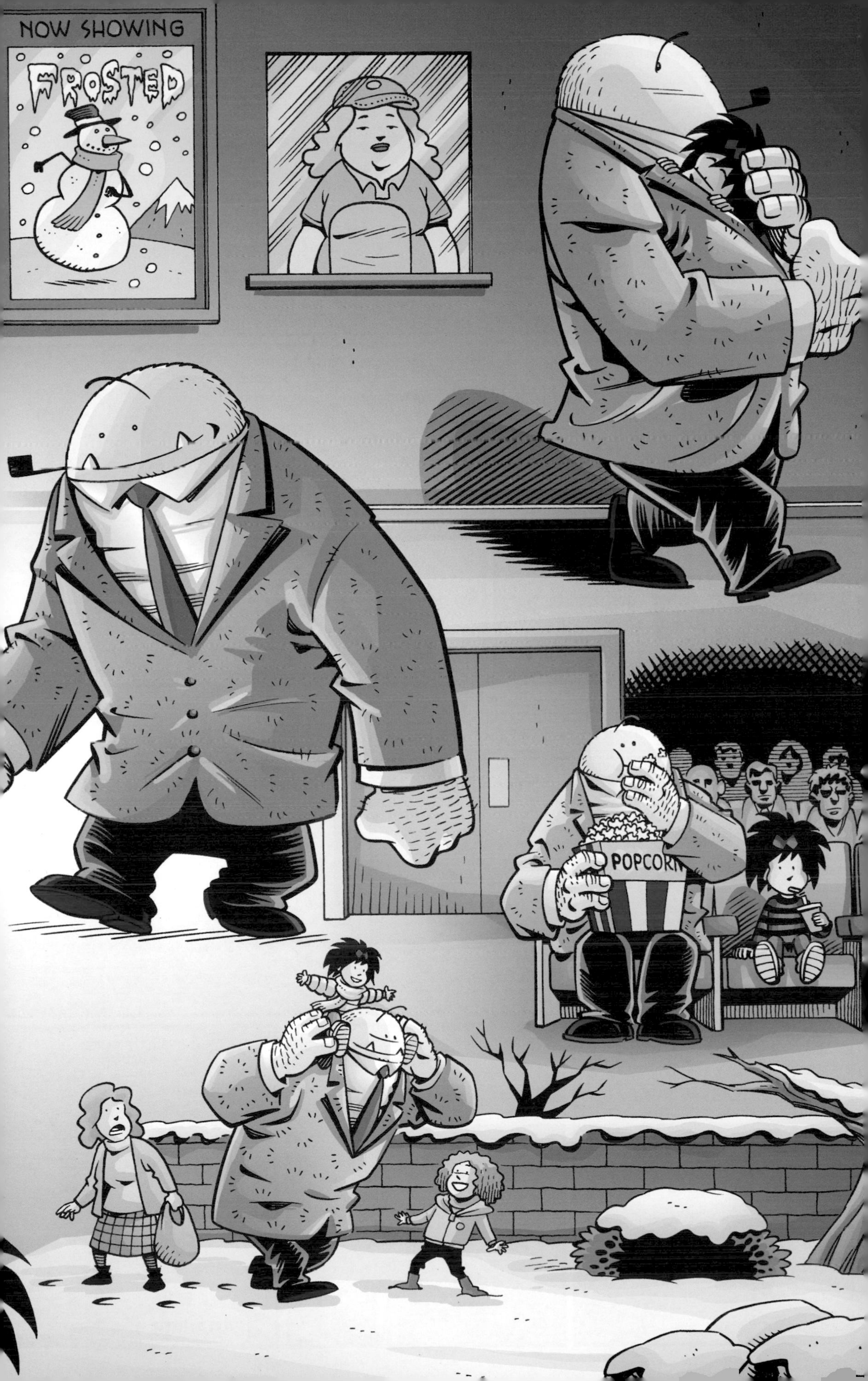
NOW SHOWING
FROSTED
POPCORN

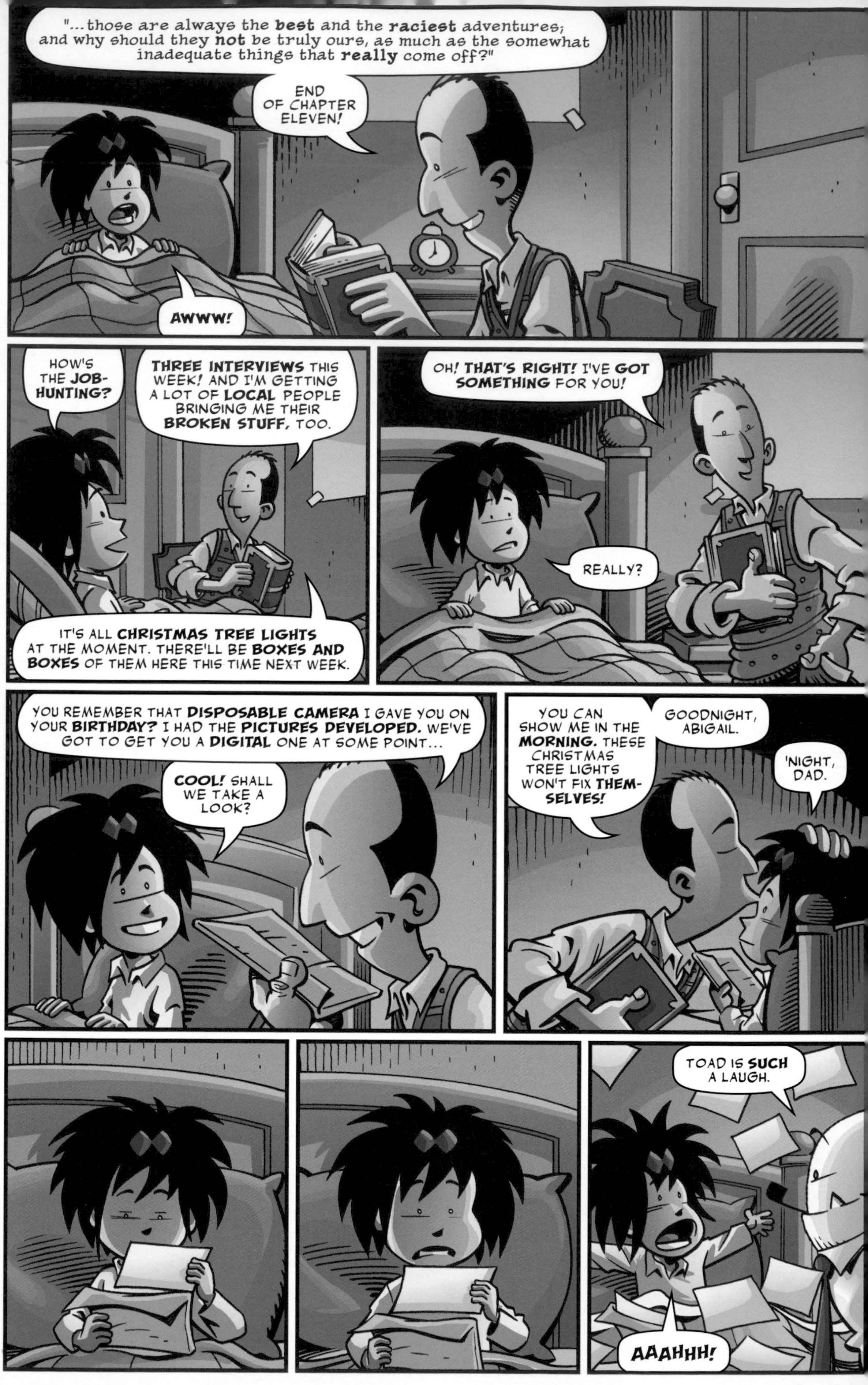
"...those are always the best and the raciest adventures; and why should they not be truly ours, as much as the somewhat inadequate things that really come off?"
END OF CHAPTER ELEVEN!
AWWW!
HOW'S THE JOB-HUNTING?
THREE INTERVIEWS THIS WEEK! AND I'M GETTING A LOT OF LOCAL PEOPLE BRINGING ME THEIR BROKEN STUFF, TOO.
IT'S ALL CHRISTMAS TREE LIGHTS AT THE MOMENT. THERE'LL BE BOXES AND BOXES OF THEM HERE THIS TIME NEXT WEEK.
OH! THAT'S RIGHT! I'VE GOT SOMETHING FOR YOU!
REALLY?
YOU REMEMBER THAT DISPOSABLE CAMERA I GAVE YOU ON YOUR BIRTHDAY? I HAD THE PICTURES DEVELOPED. WE'VE GOT TO GET YOU A DIGITAL ONE AT SOME POINT...
COOL! SHALL WE TAKE A LOOK?
YOU CAN SHOW ME IN THE MORNING. THESE CHRISTMAS TREE LIGHTS WON'T FIX THEMSELVES!
GOODNIGHT, ABIGAIL.
'NIGHT, DAD.
TOAD IS SUCH A LAUGH.
AAAHHH!

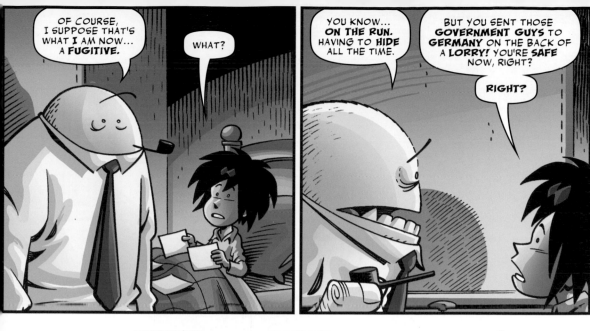

OF COURSE, I SUPPOSE THAT'S WHAT *I* AM NOW... A **FUGITIVE**.

WHAT?

YOU KNOW... **ON THE RUN**. HAVING TO **HIDE** ALL THE TIME.

BUT YOU SENT THOSE **GOVERNMENT GUYS** TO **GERMANY** ON THE BACK OF A **LORRY!** YOU'RE **SAFE** NOW, RIGHT?

RIGHT?

ABIGAIL... YOU HAVE TO UNDERSTAND... THIS IS THE **GOVERNMENT**. THEY CAN THROW THE RESOURCES OF THE **ENTIRE COUNTRY** AT ME IF THEY FEEL LIKE IT.

THOSE GUYS ARE **GONE** FOR NOW... BUT THEY'LL BE **BACK**. OR OTHERS **LIKE** THEM.

BUT... BUT IT WASN'T REALLY ANY DIFFERENT BACK IN THE **HIMALAYAS,** WAS IT? DIDN'T YOU CONSTANTLY HAVE TO DODGE MOUNTAINEERS... EXPLORERS... **SCIENTISTS**?

THE SCIENTISTS **GOT** YOU, AFTER ALL.

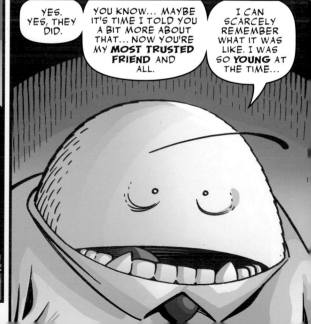

YES. YES, THEY DID.

YOU KNOW... MAYBE IT'S TIME I TOLD YOU A BIT MORE ABOUT THAT... NOW YOU'RE MY **MOST TRUSTED FRIEND** AND ALL.

I CAN SCARCELY REMEMBER WHAT IT WAS LIKE. I WAS SO **YOUNG** AT THE TIME...

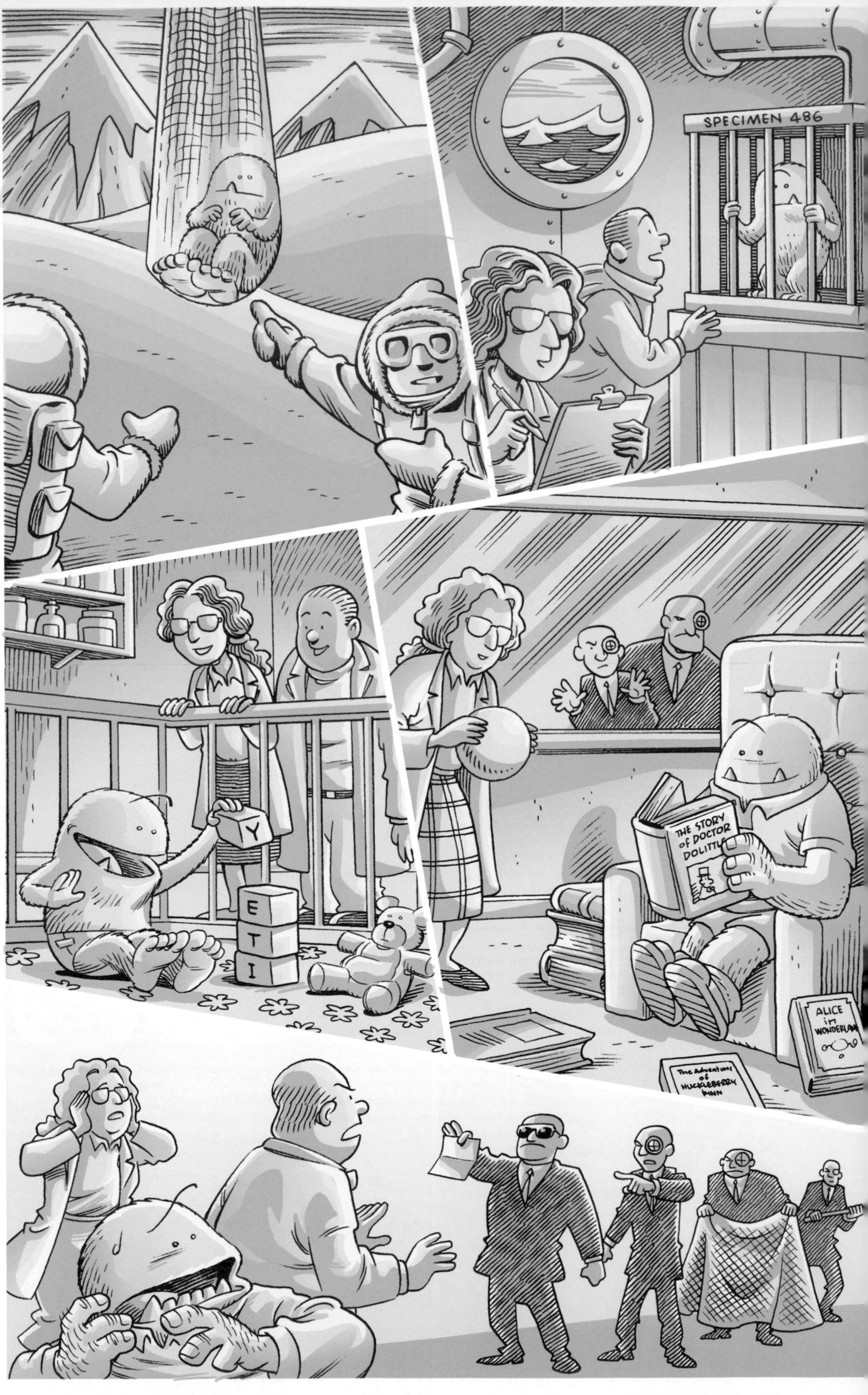
SPECIMEN 486
Y
E
T
I
THE STORY of DOCTOR DOLITTL
ALICE in
The Adventures of HUCKLEBERRY FINN

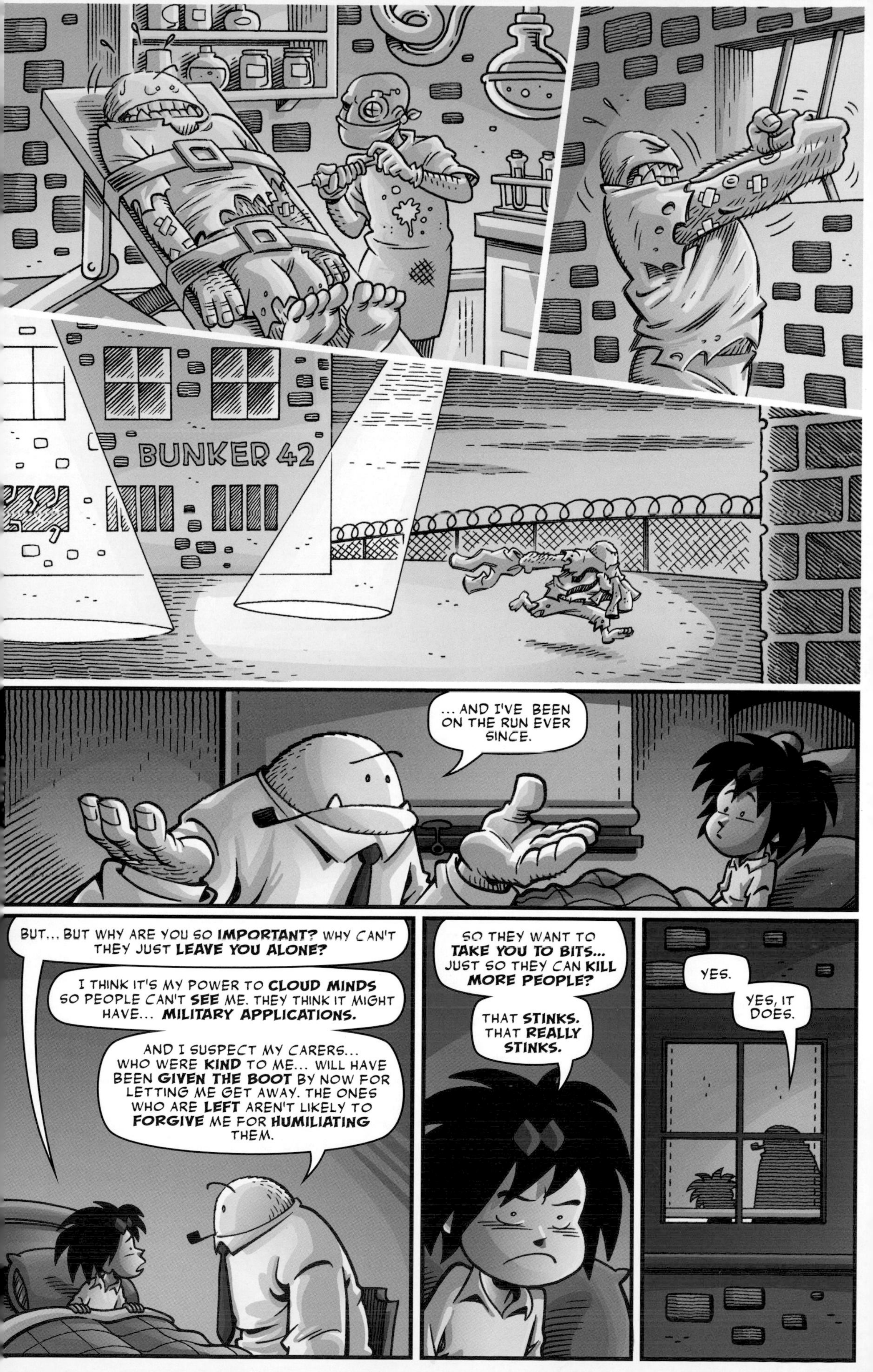
BUNKER 42
... AND I'VE BEEN ON THE RUN EVER SINCE.
BUT... BUT WHY ARE YOU SO IMPORTANT? WHY CAN'T THEY JUST LEAVE YOU ALONE?
I THINK IT'S MY POWER TO CLOUD MINDS SO PEOPLE CAN'T SEE ME. THEY THINK IT MIGHT HAVE... MILITARY APPLICATIONS.
AND I SUSPECT MY CARERS... WHO WERE KIND TO ME... WILL HAVE BEEN GIVEN THE BOOT BY NOW FOR LETTING ME GET AWAY. THE ONES WHO ARE LEFT AREN'T LIKELY TO FORGIVE ME FOR HUMILIATING THEM.
SO THEY WANT TO TAKE YOU TO BITS... JUST SO THEY CAN KILL MORE PEOPLE?
THAT STINKS. THAT REALLY STINKS.
YES.
YES, IT DOES.

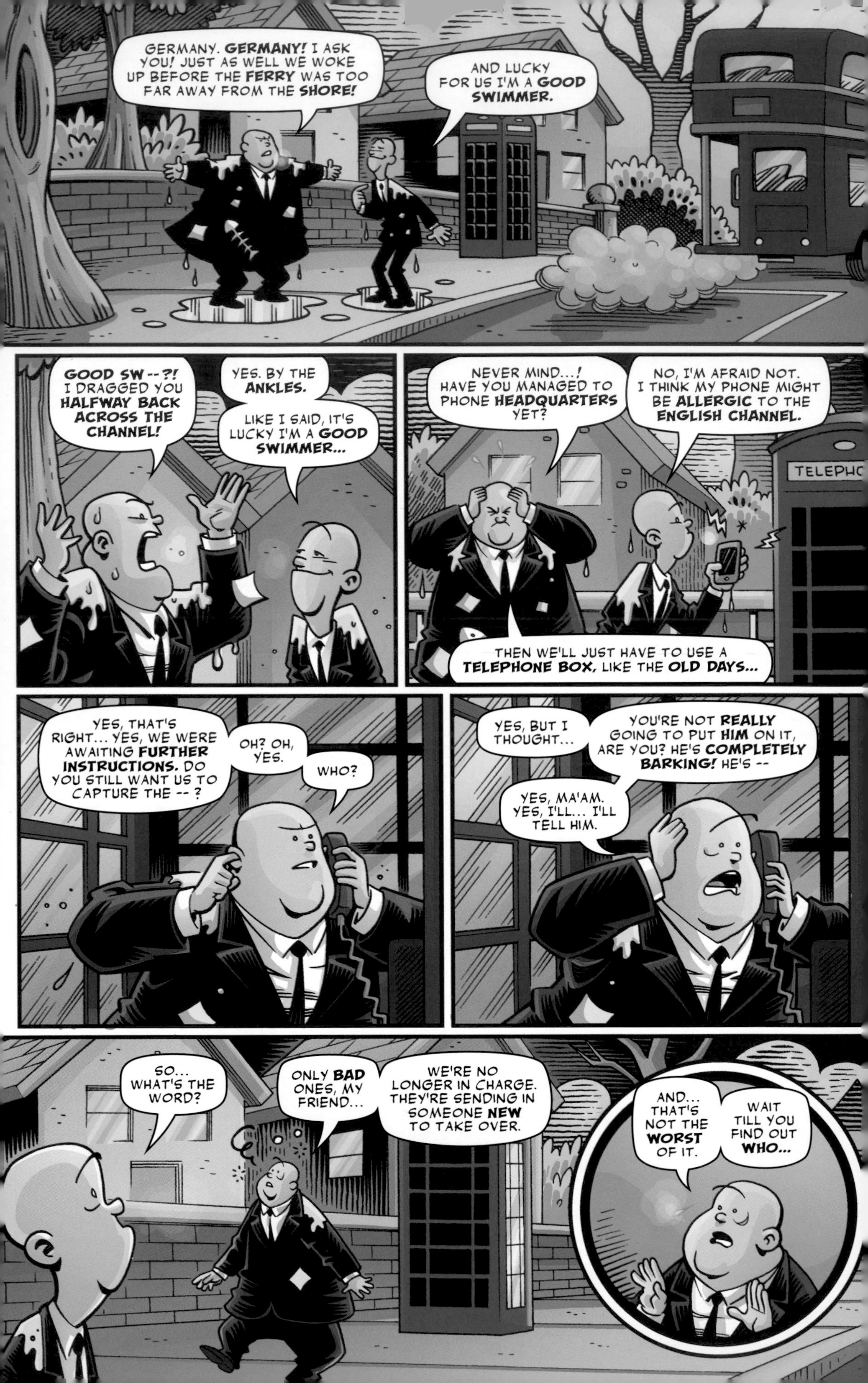
GERMANY. **GERMANY!** I ASK YOU! JUST AS WELL WE WOKE UP BEFORE THE **FERRY** WAS TOO FAR AWAY FROM THE **SHORE!**
AND LUCKY FOR US I'M A **GOOD SWIMMER.**
GOOD SW--?! I DRAGGED YOU **HALFWAY BACK ACROSS THE CHANNEL!**
YES. BY THE **ANKLES.**
LIKE I SAID, IT'S LUCKY I'M A **GOOD SWIMMER...**
NEVER MIND...! HAVE YOU MANAGED TO PHONE **HEADQUARTERS** YET?
NO, I'M AFRAID NOT. I THINK MY PHONE MIGHT BE **ALLERGIC** TO THE **ENGLISH CHANNEL.**
TELEPHO
THEN WE'LL JUST HAVE TO USE A **TELEPHONE BOX,** LIKE THE **OLD DAYS...**
YES, THAT'S RIGHT... YES, WE WERE AWAITING **FURTHER INSTRUCTIONS.** DO YOU STILL WANT US TO CAPTURE THE -- ?
OH? OH, YES.
WHO?
YES, BUT I THOUGHT...
YOU'RE NOT **REALLY** GOING TO PUT **HIM** ON IT, ARE YOU? HE'S **COMPLETELY BARKING!** HE'S --
YES, MA'AM. YES, I'LL... I'LL TELL HIM.
SO... WHAT'S THE WORD?
ONLY **BAD** ONES, MY FRIEND...
WE'RE NO LONGER IN CHARGE. THEY'RE SENDING IN SOMEONE **NEW** TO TAKE OVER.
AND... THAT'S NOT THE **WORST** OF IT.
WAIT TILL YOU FIND OUT **WHO...**

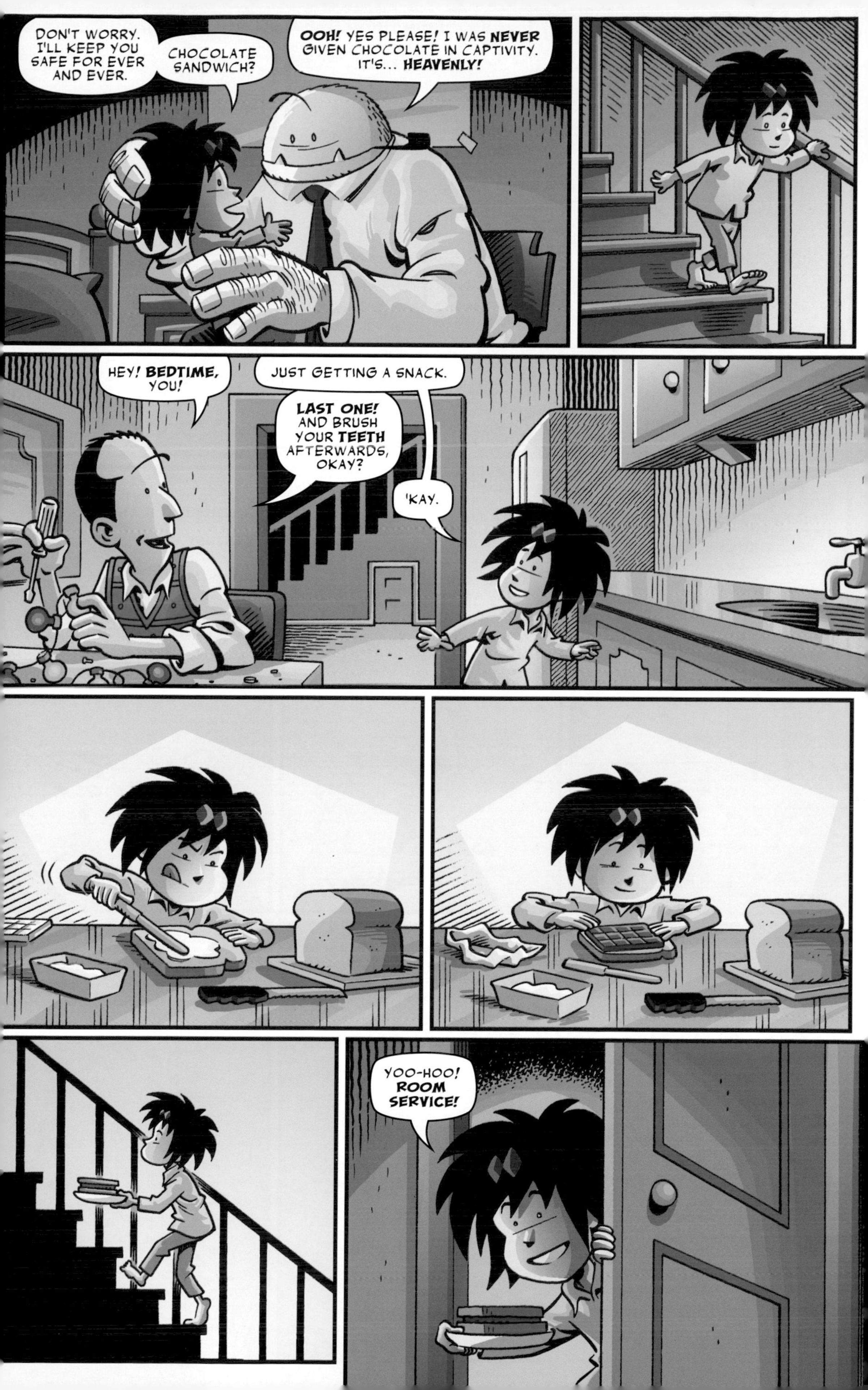
DON'T WORRY. I'LL KEEP YOU SAFE FOR EVER AND EVER.
CHOCOLATE SANDWICH?
OOH! YES PLEASE! I WAS NEVER GIVEN CHOCOLATE IN CAPTIVITY. IT'S... HEAVENLY!
HEY! BEDTIME, YOU!
JUST GETTING A SNACK.
LAST ONE! AND BRUSH YOUR TEETH AFTERWARDS, OKAY?
'KAY.
YOO-HOO! ROOM SERVICE!

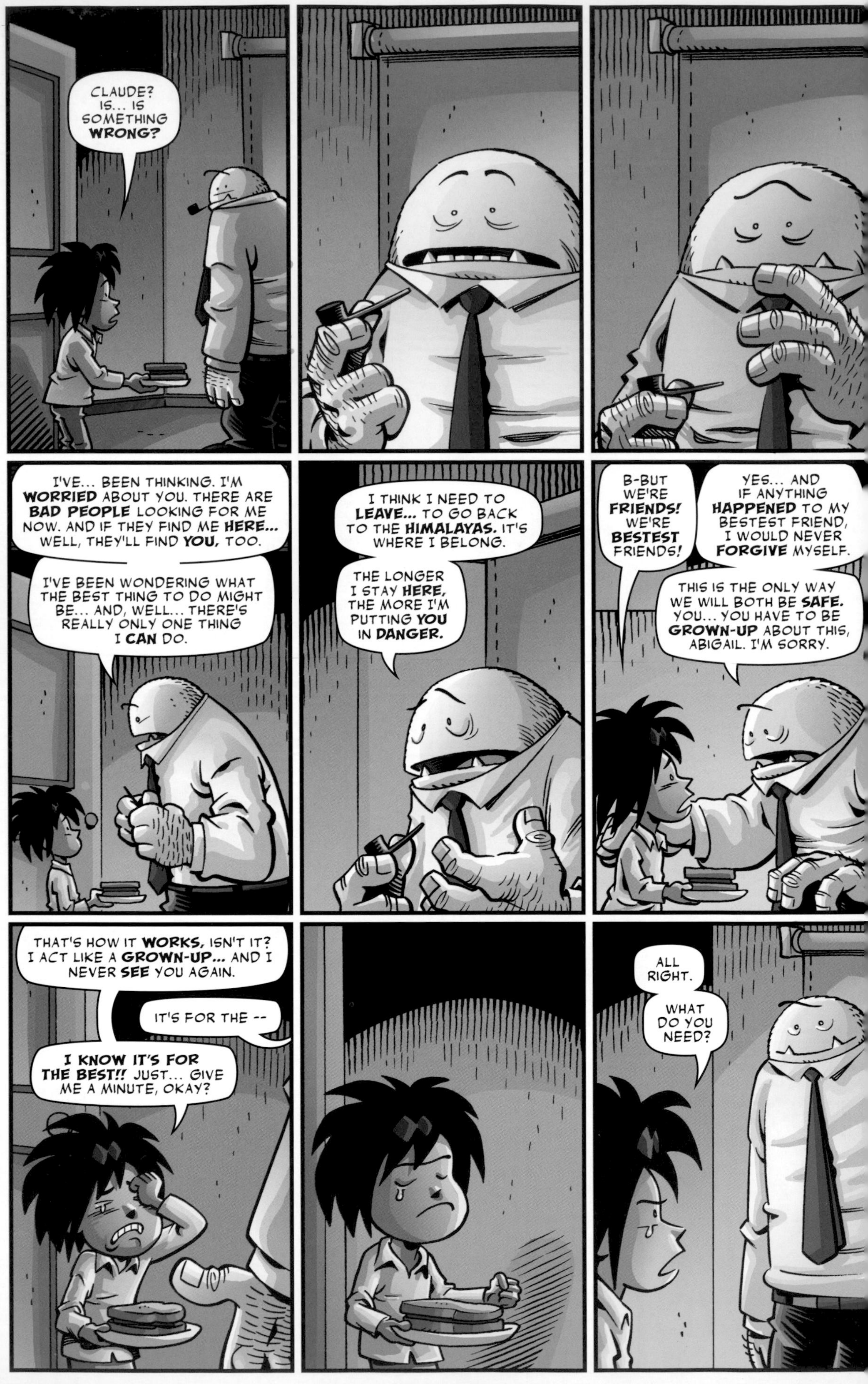
CLAUDE? IS... IS SOMETHING WRONG?
I'VE... BEEN THINKING. I'M WORRIED ABOUT YOU. THERE ARE BAD PEOPLE LOOKING FOR ME NOW. AND IF THEY FIND ME HERE... WELL, THEY'LL FIND YOU, TOO.
I'VE BEEN WONDERING WHAT THE BEST THING TO DO MIGHT BE... AND, WELL... THERE'S REALLY ONLY ONE THING I CAN DO.
I THINK I NEED TO LEAVE... TO GO BACK TO THE HIMALAYAS. IT'S WHERE I BELONG.
THE LONGER I STAY HERE, THE MORE I'M PUTTING YOU IN DANGER.
B-BUT WE'RE FRIENDS! WE'RE BESTEST FRIENDS!
YES... AND IF ANYTHING HAPPENED TO MY BESTEST FRIEND, I WOULD NEVER FORGIVE MYSELF.
THIS IS THE ONLY WAY WE WILL BOTH BE SAFE. YOU... YOU HAVE TO BE GROWN-UP ABOUT THIS, ABIGAIL. I'M SORRY.
THAT'S HOW IT WORKS, ISN'T IT? I ACT LIKE A GROWN-UP... AND I NEVER SEE YOU AGAIN.
IT'S FOR THE --
I KNOW IT'S FOR THE BEST!! JUST... GIVE ME A MINUTE, OKAY?
ALL RIGHT.
WHAT DO YOU NEED?

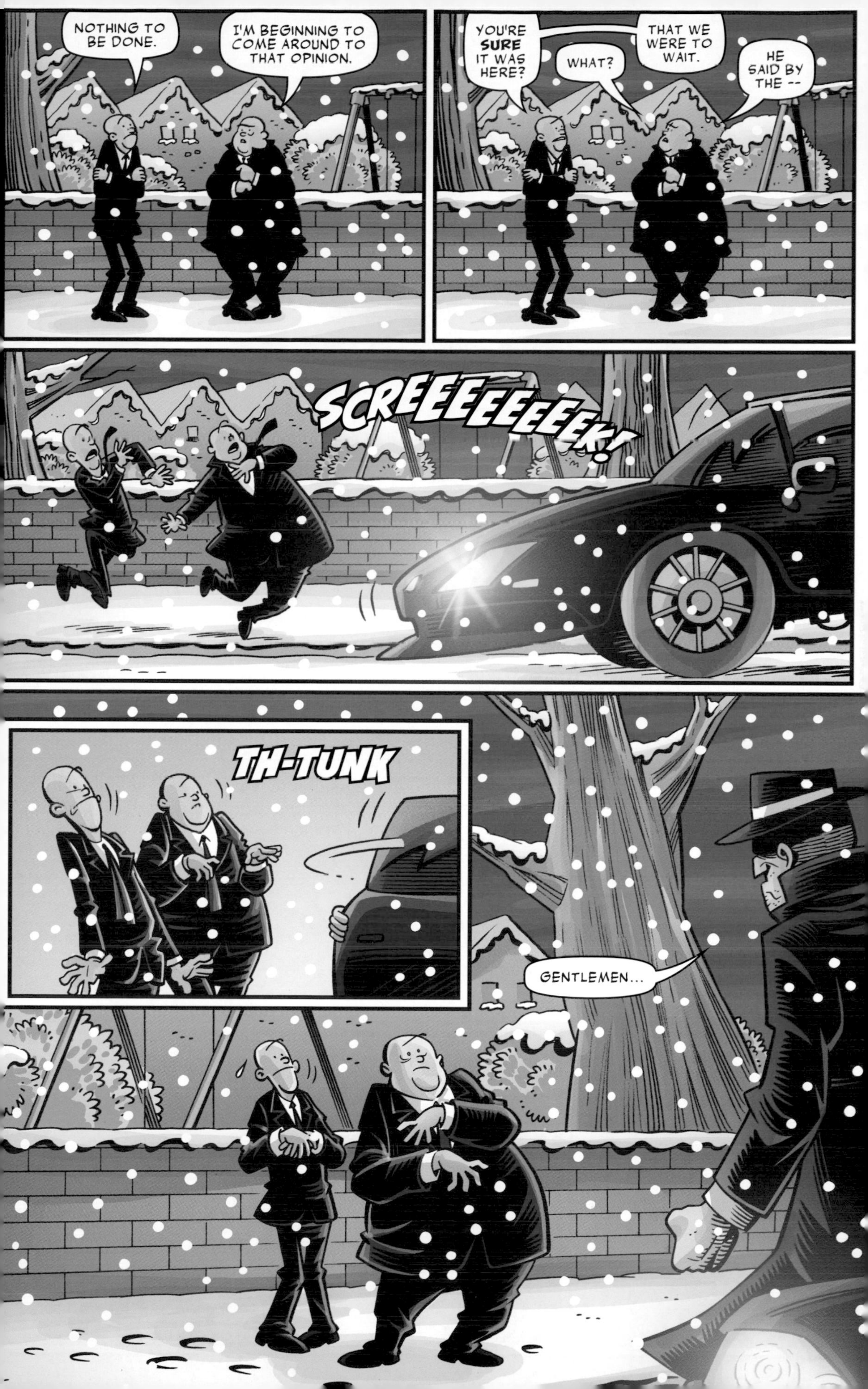
NOTHING TO BE DONE.
I'M BEGINNING TO COME AROUND TO THAT OPINION.
YOU'RE **SURE** IT WAS HERE?
WHAT?
THAT WE WERE TO WAIT.
HE SAID BY THE --
SCREEEEEEEEEK!
TH-TUNK
GENTLEMEN...

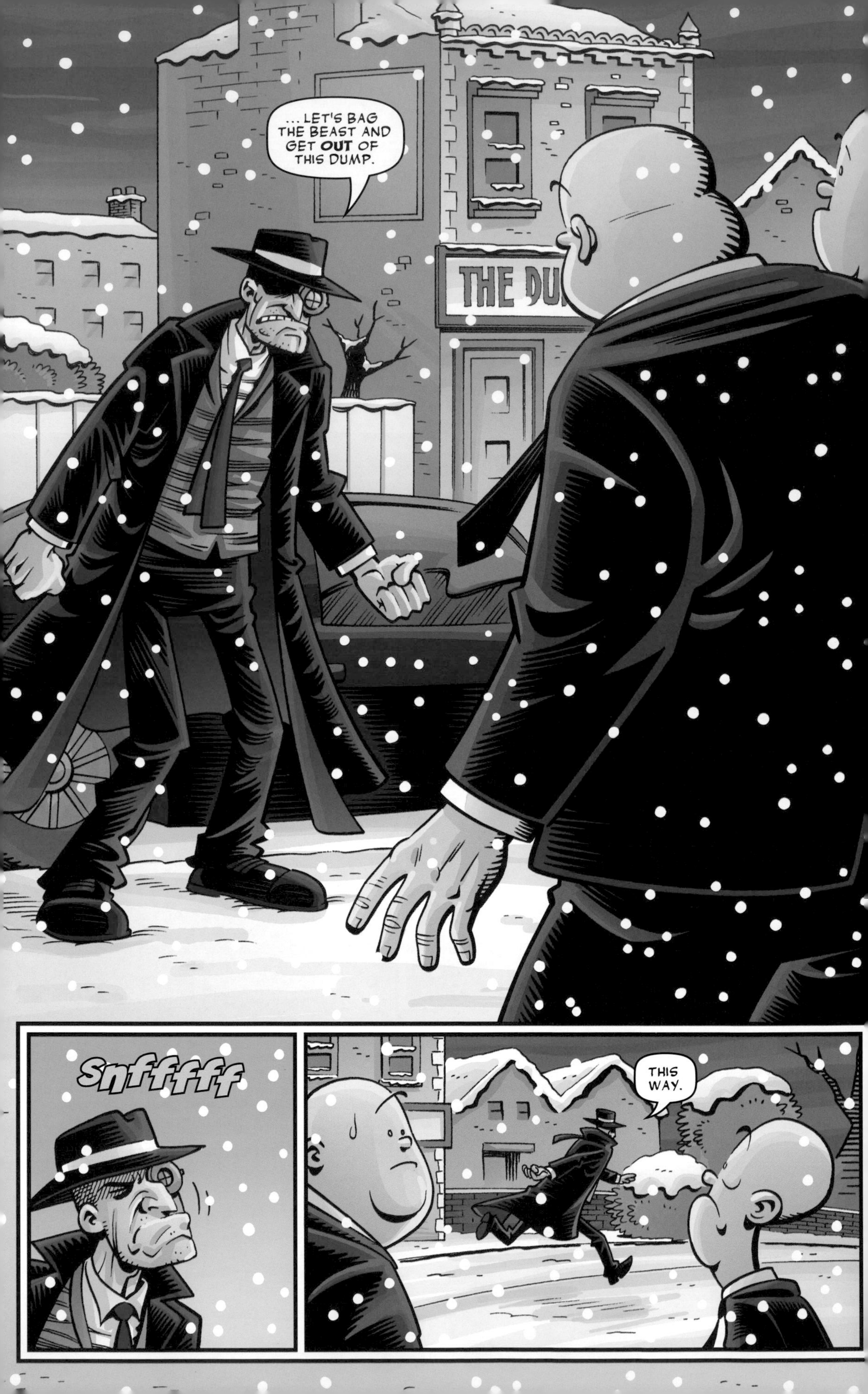
...LET'S BAG THE BEAST AND GET **OUT** OF THIS DUMP.
THE DU
SNFFFFF
THIS WAY.

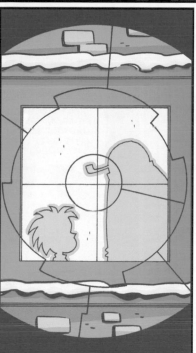

WAIT OUTSIDE.

YOU'LL ONLY GET IN THE WAY.

THE COMPUTER'S IN MY **DAD'S** ROOM. HE'S GOING TO BE **WORKING DOWN-STAIRS** FOR AGES, SO WE SHOULD BE **OKAY...**

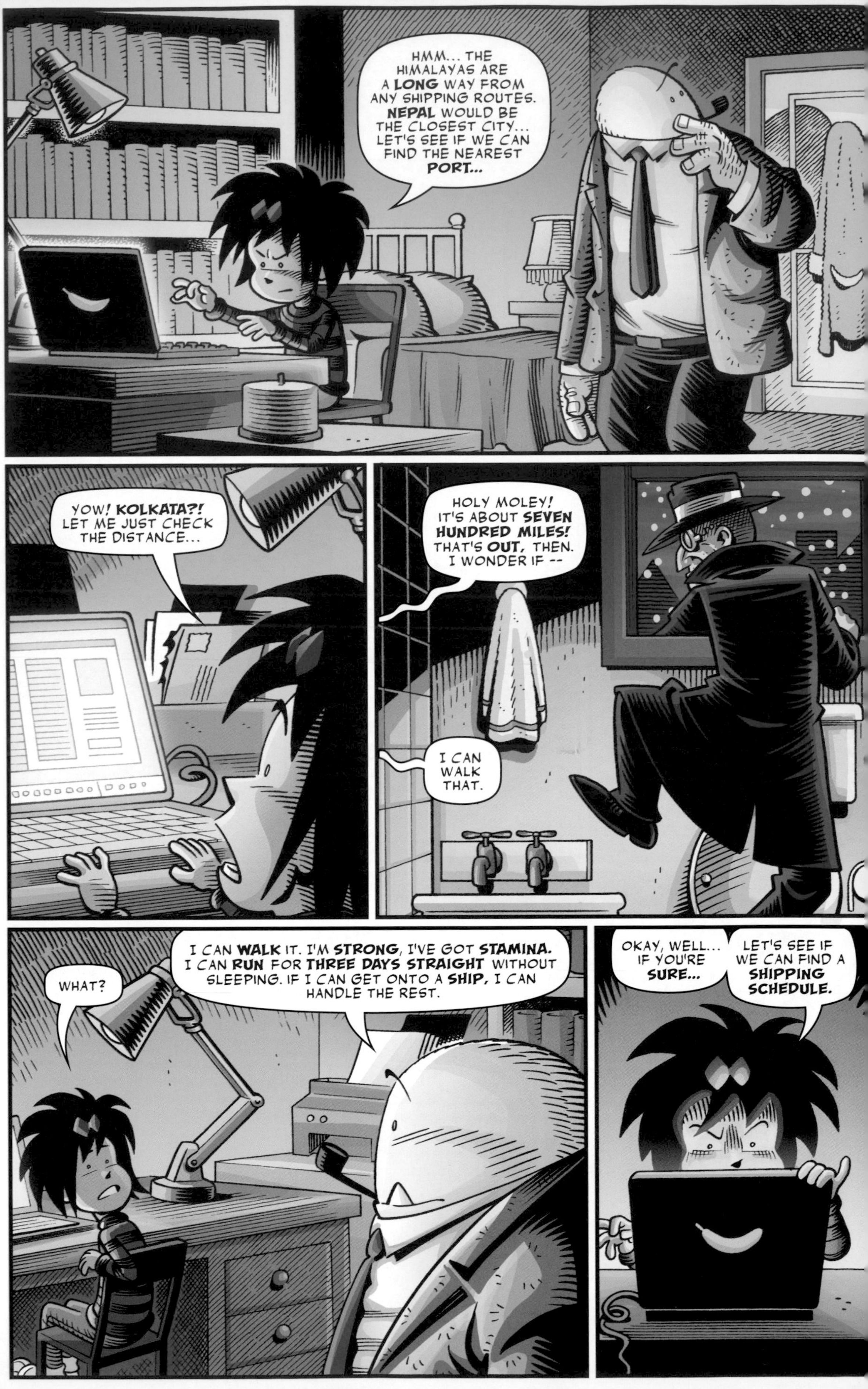
HMM... THE HIMALAYAS ARE A LONG WAY FROM ANY SHIPPING ROUTES. NEPAL WOULD BE THE CLOSEST CITY... LET'S SEE IF WE CAN FIND THE NEAREST PORT...
YOW! KOLKATA?! LET ME JUST CHECK THE DISTANCE...
HOLY MOLEY! IT'S ABOUT SEVEN HUNDRED MILES! THAT'S OUT, THEN. I WONDER IF --
I CAN WALK THAT.
WHAT?
I CAN WALK IT. I'M STRONG, I'VE GOT STAMINA. I CAN RUN FOR THREE DAYS STRAIGHT WITHOUT SLEEPING. IF I CAN GET ONTO A SHIP, I CAN HANDLE THE REST.
OKAY, WELL... IF YOU'RE SURE...
LET'S SEE IF WE CAN FIND A SHIPPING SCHEDULE.

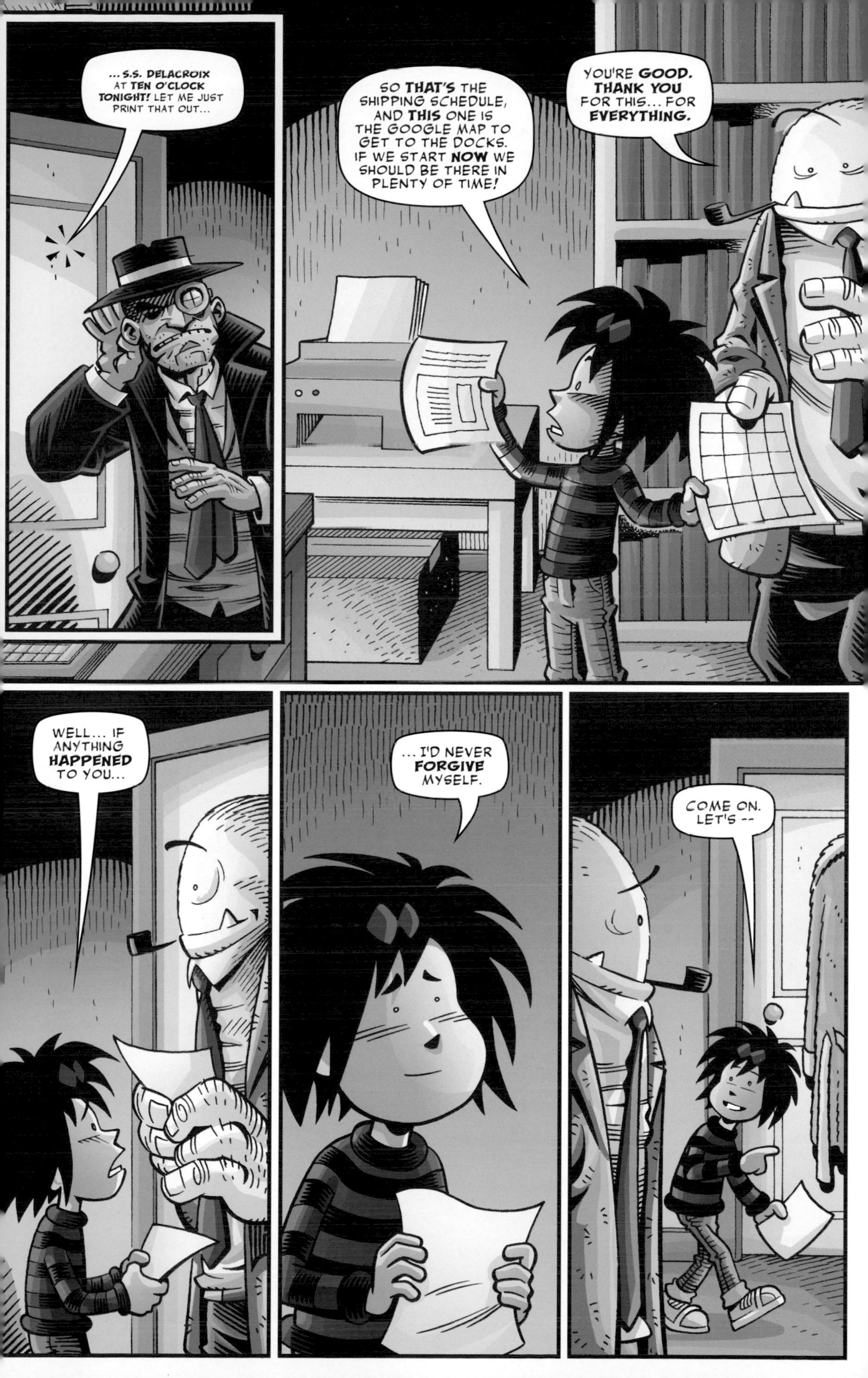
...S.S. DELACROIX AT TEN O'CLOCK TONIGHT! LET ME JUST PRINT THAT OUT...
SO THAT'S THE SHIPPING SCHEDULE, AND THIS ONE IS THE GOOGLE MAP TO GET TO THE DOCKS. IF WE START NOW WE SHOULD BE THERE IN PLENTY OF TIME!
YOU'RE GOOD. THANK YOU FOR THIS... FOR EVERYTHING.
WELL... IF ANYTHING HAPPENED TO YOU...
...I'D NEVER FORGIVE MYSELF.
COME ON. LET'S --

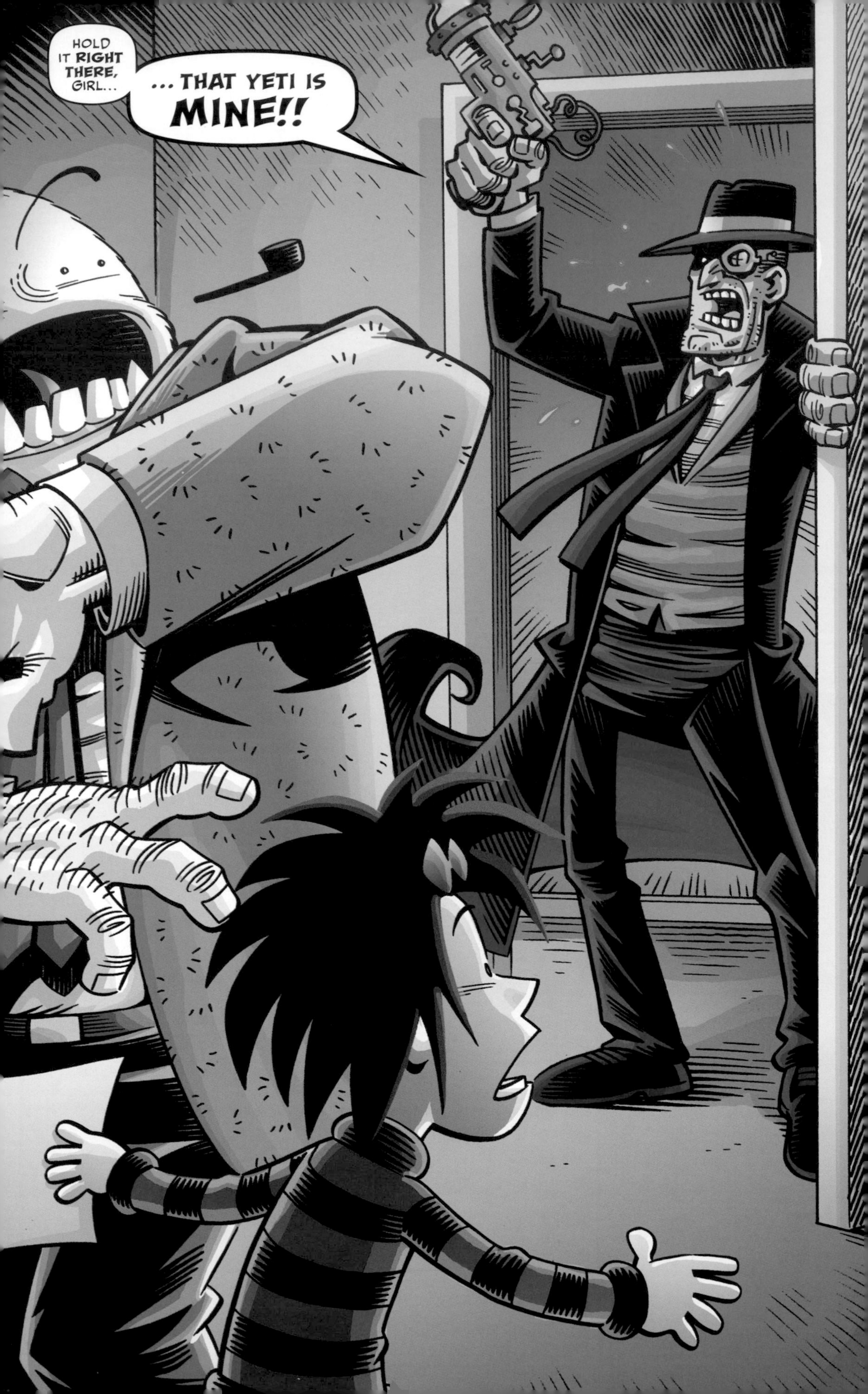
HOLD IT RIGHT THERE, GIRL...
... THAT YETI IS MINE!!

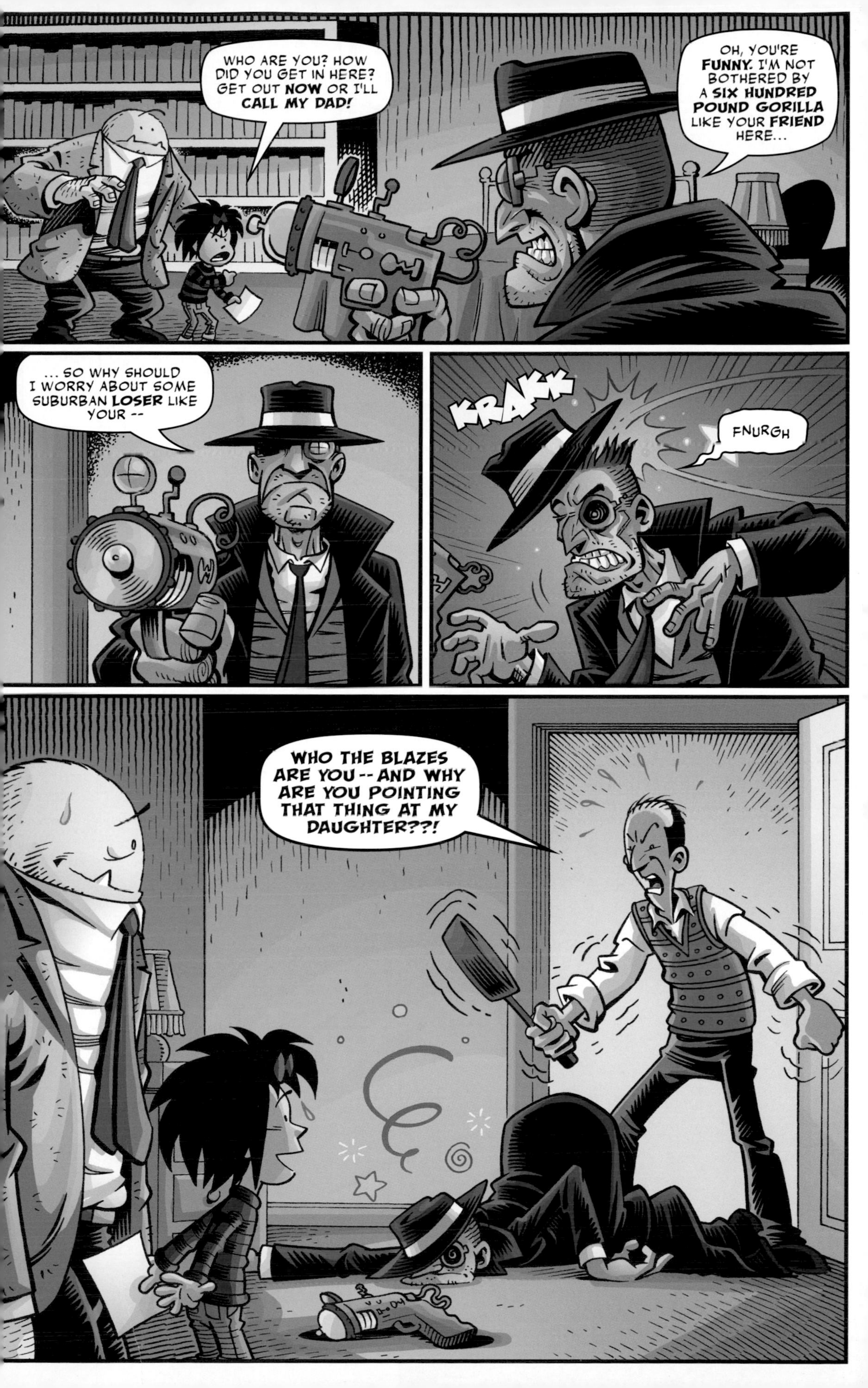
WHO ARE YOU? HOW DID YOU GET IN HERE? GET OUT NOW OR I'LL CALL MY DAD!
OH, YOU'RE FUNNY. I'M NOT BOTHERED BY A SIX HUNDRED POUND GORILLA LIKE YOUR FRIEND HERE...
... SO WHY SHOULD I WORRY ABOUT SOME SUBURBAN LOSER LIKE YOUR --
KRAKK
FNURGH
WHO THE BLAZES ARE YOU -- AND WHY ARE YOU POINTING THAT THING AT MY DAUGHTER??!

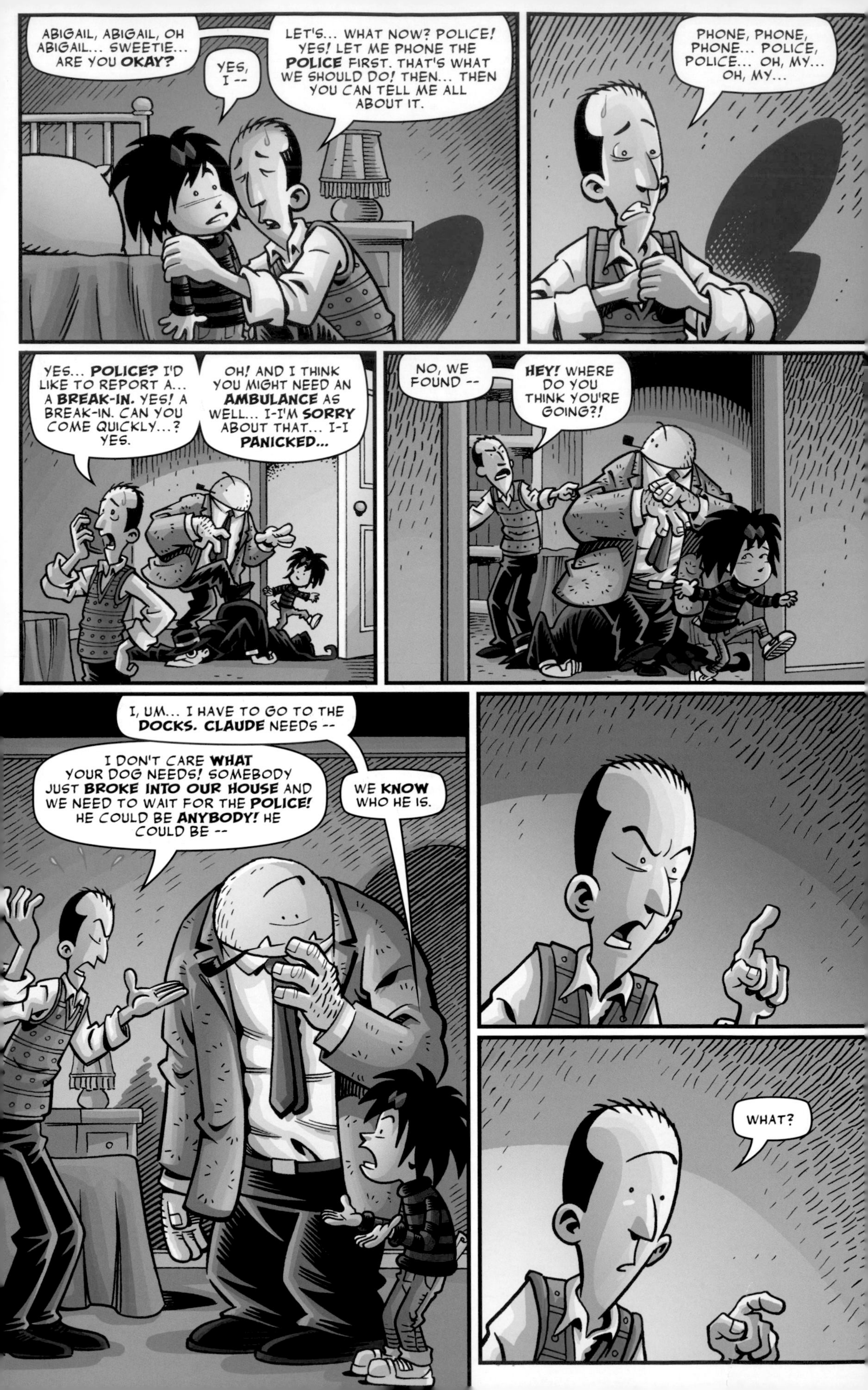

ABIGAIL, ABIGAIL, OH ABIGAIL... SWEETIE... ARE YOU OKAY?
YES, I --
LET'S... WHAT NOW? POLICE! YES! LET ME PHONE THE POLICE FIRST. THAT'S WHAT WE SHOULD DO! THEN... THEN YOU CAN TELL ME ALL ABOUT IT.
PHONE, PHONE, PHONE... POLICE, POLICE... OH, MY... OH, MY...
YES... POLICE? I'D LIKE TO REPORT A... A BREAK-IN. YES! A BREAK-IN. CAN YOU COME QUICKLY...? YES.
OH! AND I THINK YOU MIGHT NEED AN AMBULANCE AS WELL... I-I'M SORRY ABOUT THAT... I-I PANICKED...
NO, WE FOUND --
HEY! WHERE DO YOU THINK YOU'RE GOING?!
I, UM... I HAVE TO GO TO THE DOCKS. CLAUDE NEEDS --
I DON'T CARE WHAT YOUR DOG NEEDS! SOMEBODY JUST BROKE INTO OUR HOUSE AND WE NEED TO WAIT FOR THE POLICE! HE COULD BE ANYBODY! HE COULD BE --
WE KNOW WHO HE IS.
WHAT?

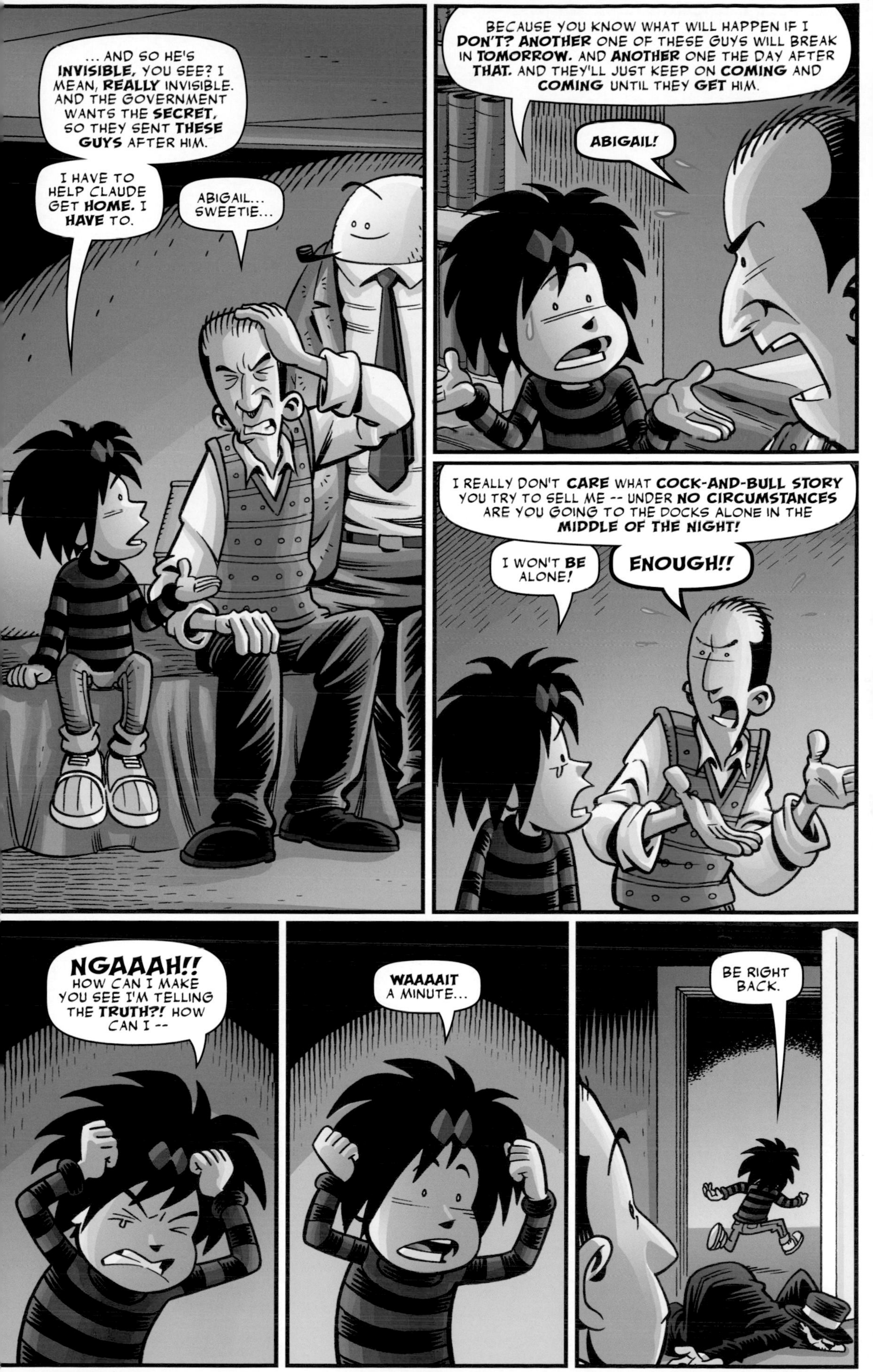
... AND SO HE'S INVISIBLE, YOU SEE? I MEAN, REALLY INVISIBLE. AND THE GOVERNMENT WANTS THE SECRET, SO THEY SENT THESE GUYS AFTER HIM.
I HAVE TO HELP CLAUDE GET HOME. I HAVE TO.
ABIGAIL... SWEETIE...
BECAUSE YOU KNOW WHAT WILL HAPPEN IF I DON'T? ANOTHER ONE OF THESE GUYS WILL BREAK IN TOMORROW. AND ANOTHER ONE THE DAY AFTER THAT. AND THEY'LL JUST KEEP ON COMING AND COMING UNTIL THEY GET HIM.
ABIGAIL!
I REALLY DON'T CARE WHAT COCK-AND-BULL STORY YOU TRY TO SELL ME -- UNDER NO CIRCUMSTANCES ARE YOU GOING TO THE DOCKS ALONE IN THE MIDDLE OF THE NIGHT!
I WON'T BE ALONE!
ENOUGH!!
NGAAAH!! HOW CAN I MAKE YOU SEE I'M TELLING THE TRUTH?! HOW CAN I --
WAAAAIT A MINUTE...
BE RIGHT BACK.

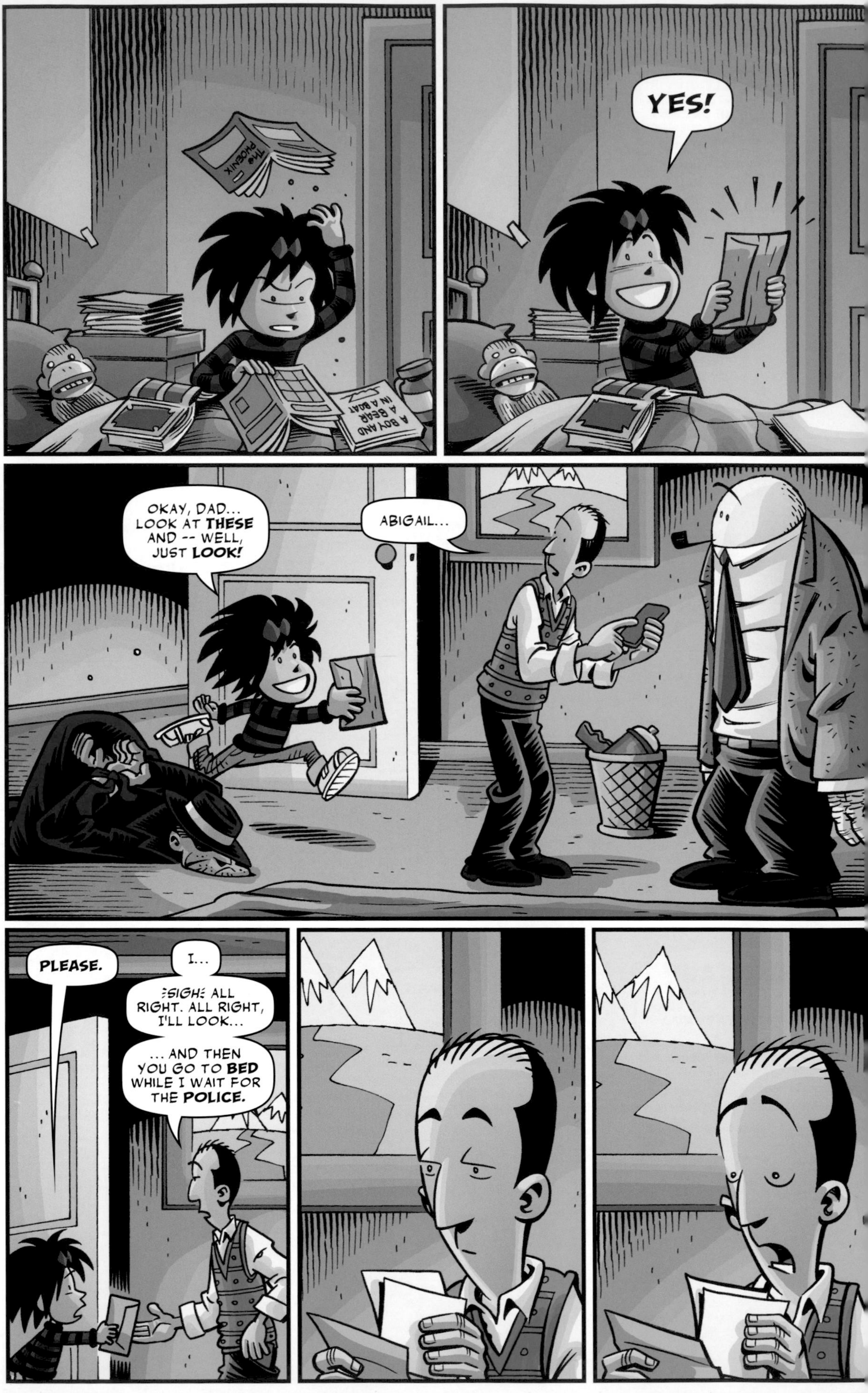
THE PHOENIX
A BOY AND A BEAR IN A BOAT
YES!
OKAY, DAD... LOOK AT THESE AND -- WELL, JUST LOOK!
ABIGAIL...
PLEASE.
I...
SIGH ALL RIGHT. ALL RIGHT, I'LL LOOK...
... AND THEN YOU GO TO BED WHILE I WAIT FOR THE POLICE.

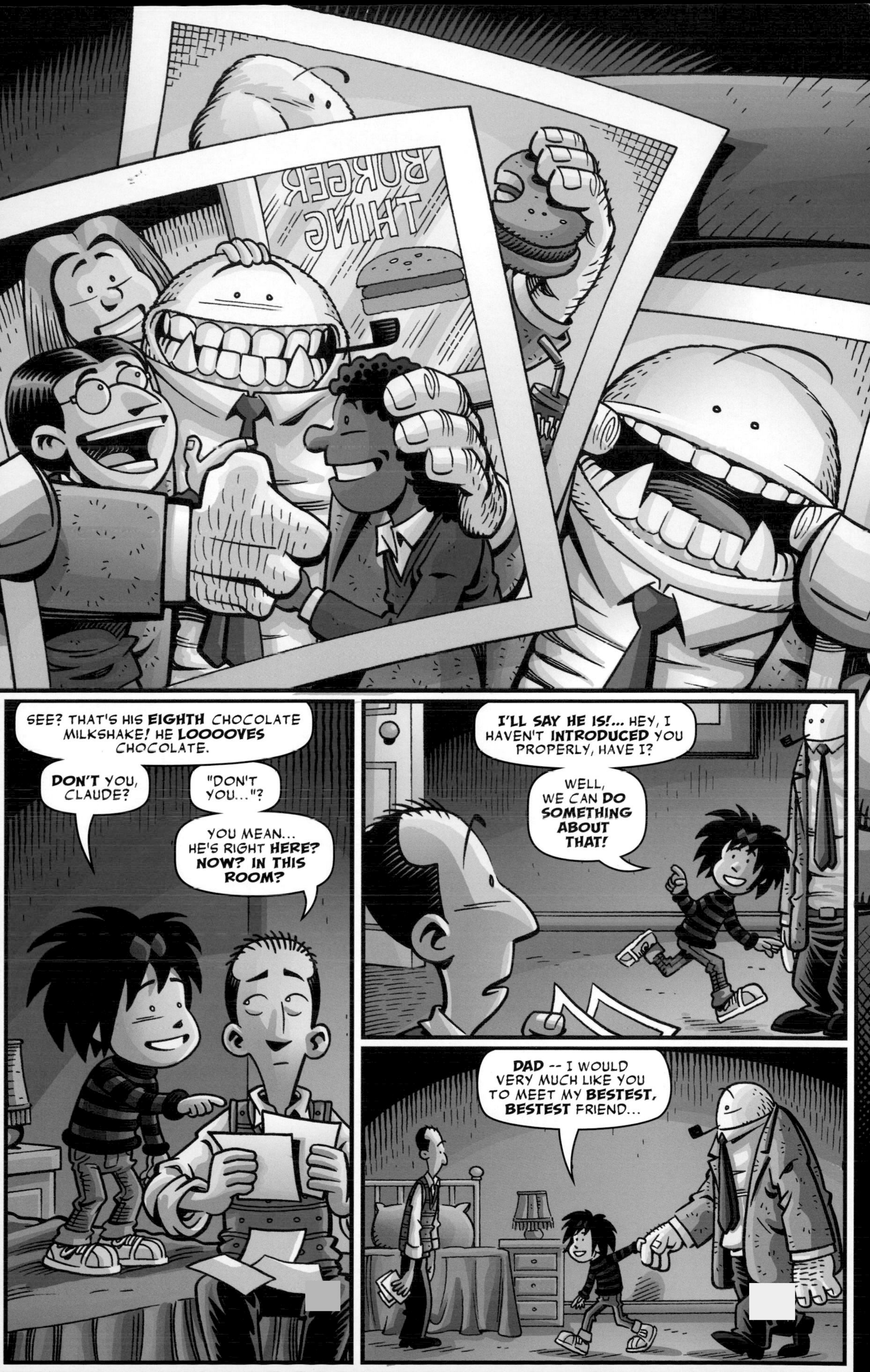
BURGER THING
SEE? THAT'S HIS EIGHTH CHOCOLATE MILKSHAKE! HE LOOOOVES CHOCOLATE.
DON'T YOU, CLAUDE?
"DON'T YOU..."?
YOU MEAN... HE'S RIGHT HERE? NOW? IN THIS ROOM?
I'LL SAY HE IS!... HEY, I HAVEN'T INTRODUCED YOU PROPERLY, HAVE I?
WELL, WE CAN DO SOMETHING ABOUT THAT!
DAD -- I WOULD VERY MUCH LIKE YOU TO MEET MY BESTEST, BESTEST FRIEND...

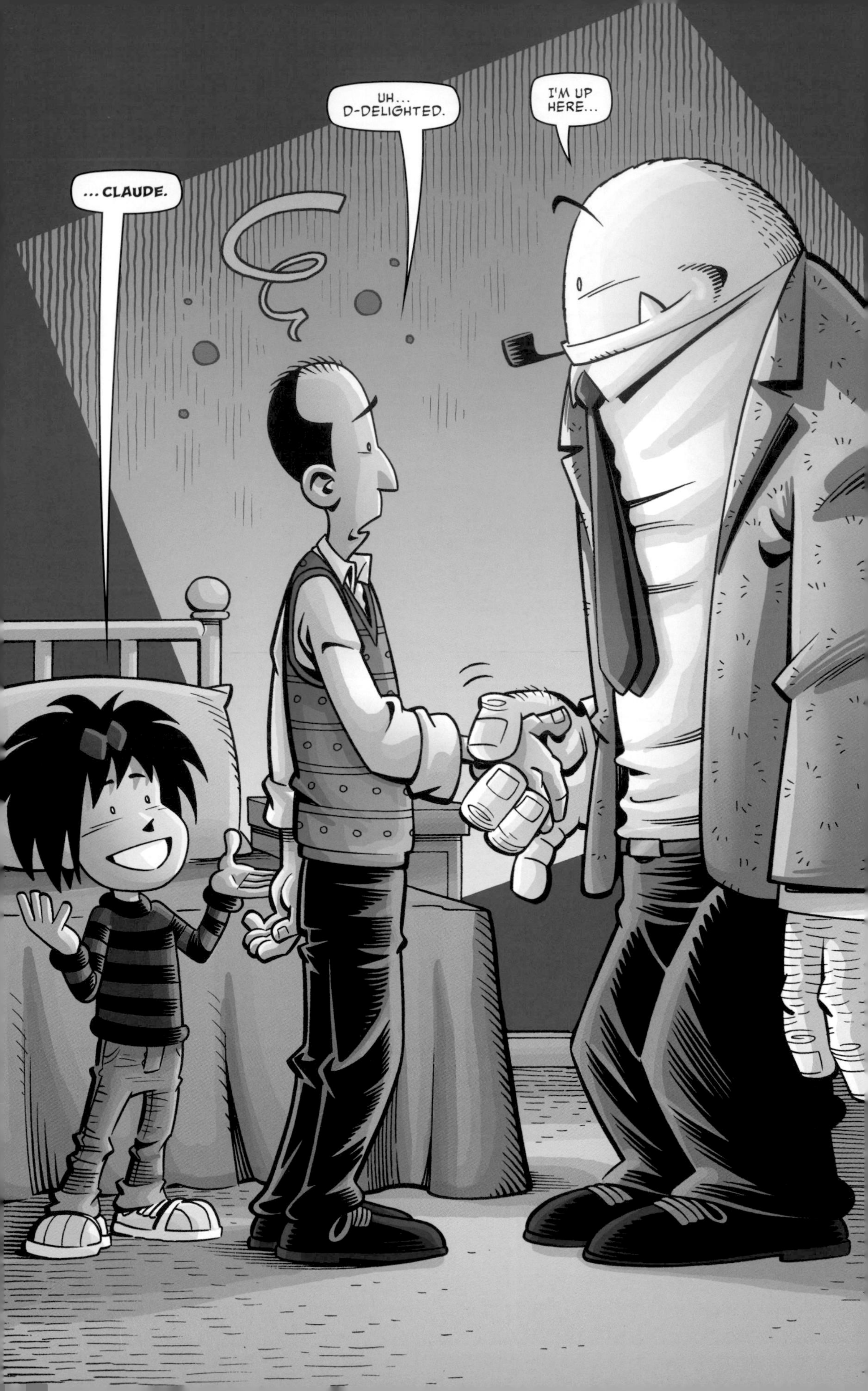
...CLAUDE.
UH... D-DELIGHTED.
I'M UP HERE...

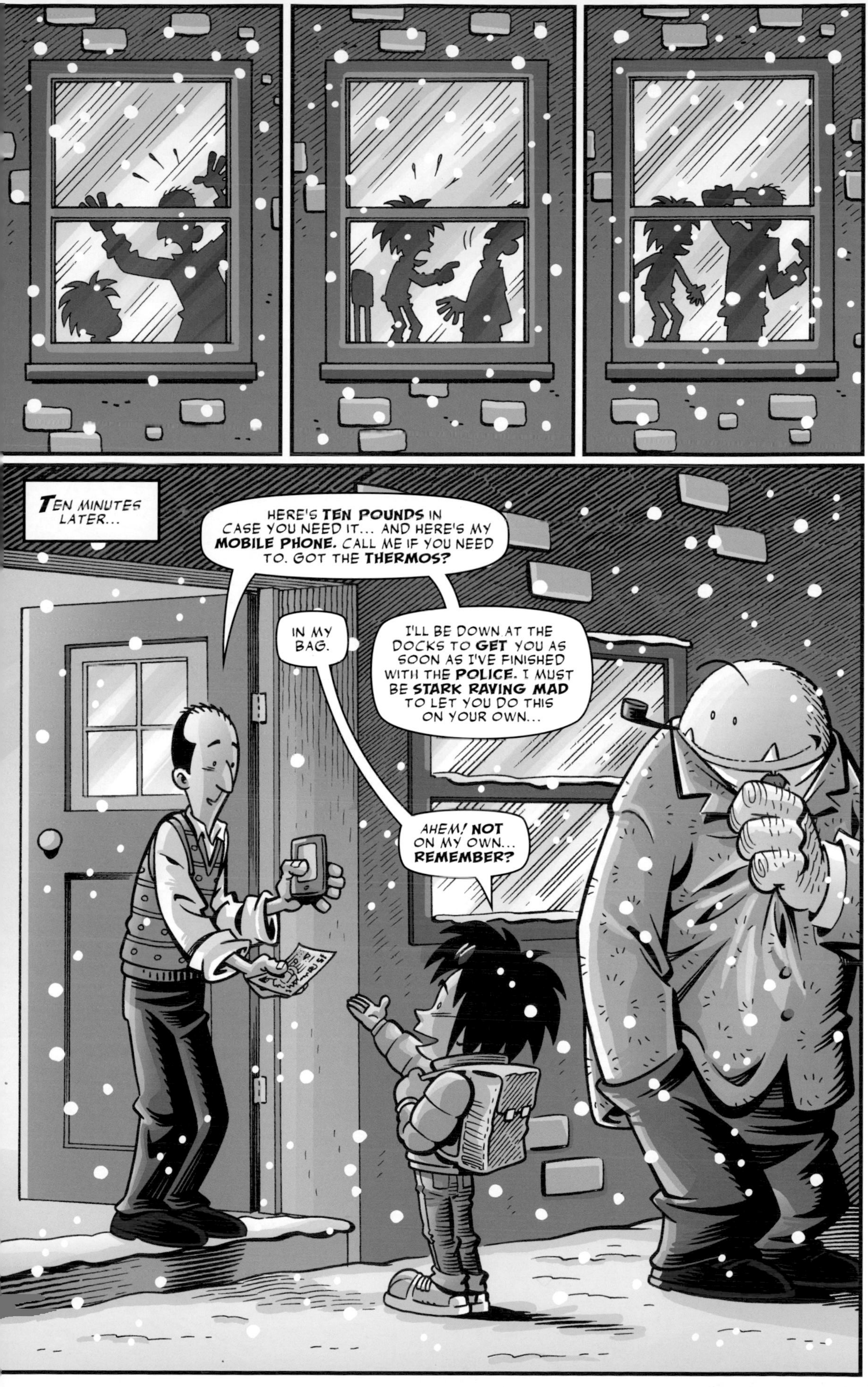
TEN MINUTES LATER...
HERE'S TEN POUNDS IN CASE YOU NEED IT... AND HERE'S MY MOBILE PHONE. CALL ME IF YOU NEED TO. GOT THE THERMOS?
IN MY BAG.
I'LL BE DOWN AT THE DOCKS TO GET YOU AS SOON AS I'VE FINISHED WITH THE POLICE. I MUST BE STARK RAVING MAD TO LET YOU DO THIS ON YOUR OWN...
AHEM! NOT ON MY OWN... REMEMBER?

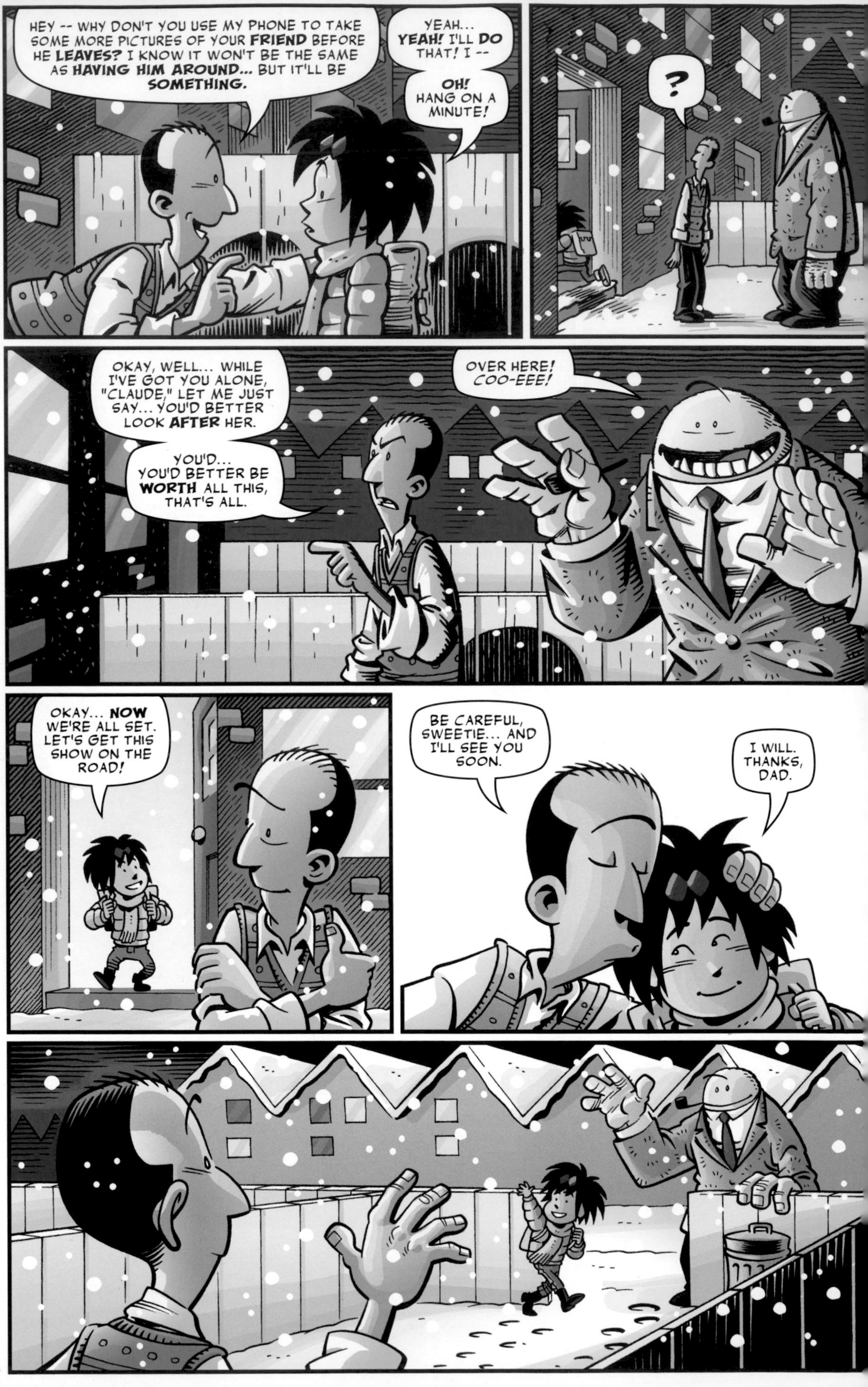
HEY -- WHY DON'T YOU USE MY PHONE TO TAKE SOME MORE PICTURES OF YOUR FRIEND BEFORE HE LEAVES? I KNOW IT WON'T BE THE SAME AS HAVING HIM AROUND... BUT IT'LL BE SOMETHING.
YEAH... YEAH! I'LL DO THAT! I --
OH! HANG ON A MINUTE!
?
OKAY, WELL... WHILE I'VE GOT YOU ALONE, "CLAUDE," LET ME JUST SAY... YOU'D BETTER LOOK AFTER HER.
YOU'D... YOU'D BETTER BE WORTH ALL THIS, THAT'S ALL.
OVER HERE! COO-EEE!
OKAY... NOW WE'RE ALL SET. LET'S GET THIS SHOW ON THE ROAD!
BE CAREFUL, SWEETIE... AND I'LL SEE YOU SOON.
I WILL. THANKS, DAD.

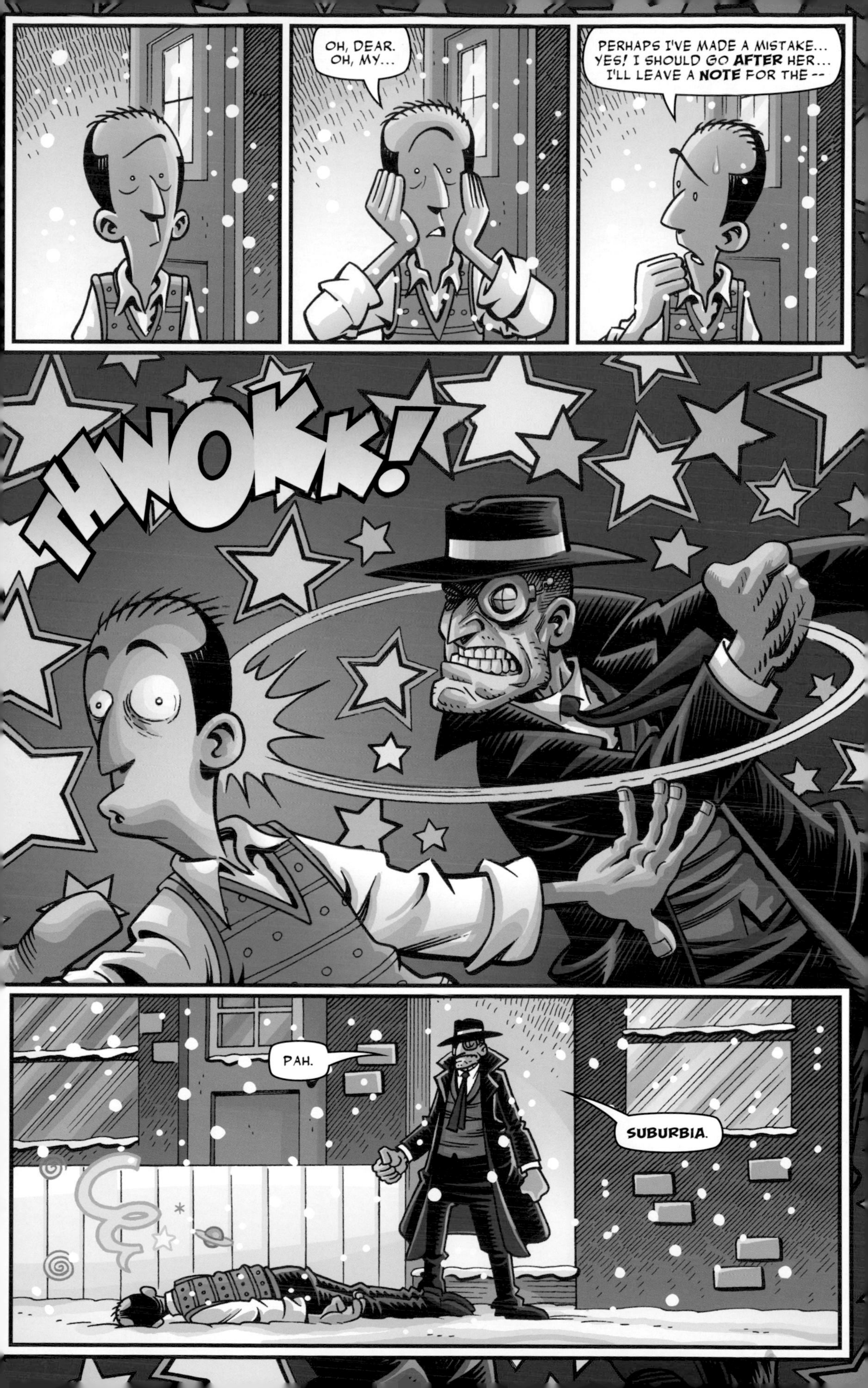
OH, DEAR. OH, MY...
PERHAPS I'VE MADE A MISTAKE... YES! I SHOULD GO AFTER HER... I'LL LEAVE A NOTE FOR THE --
THWOKK!
PAH.
SUBURBIA.

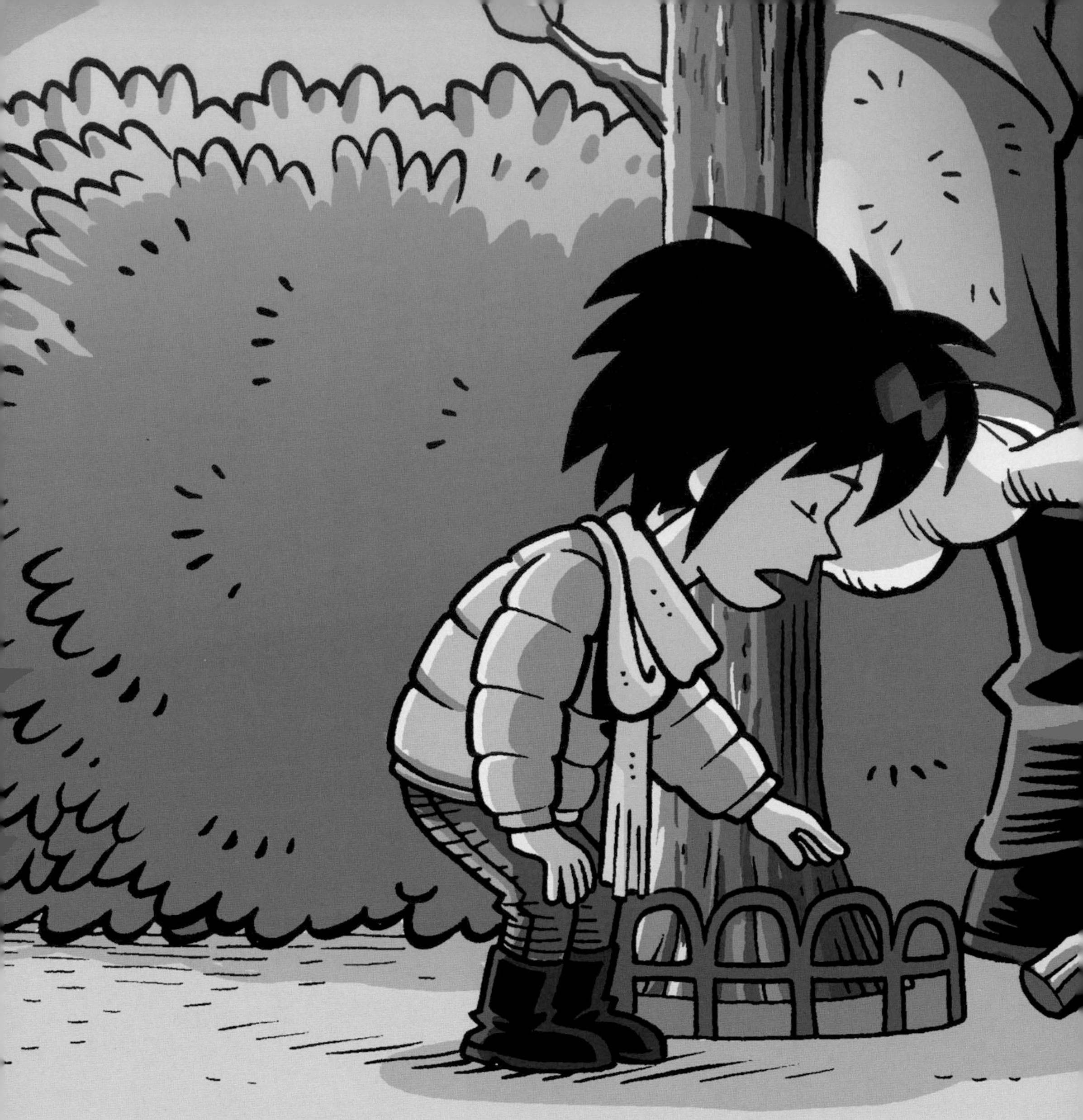

chapter four

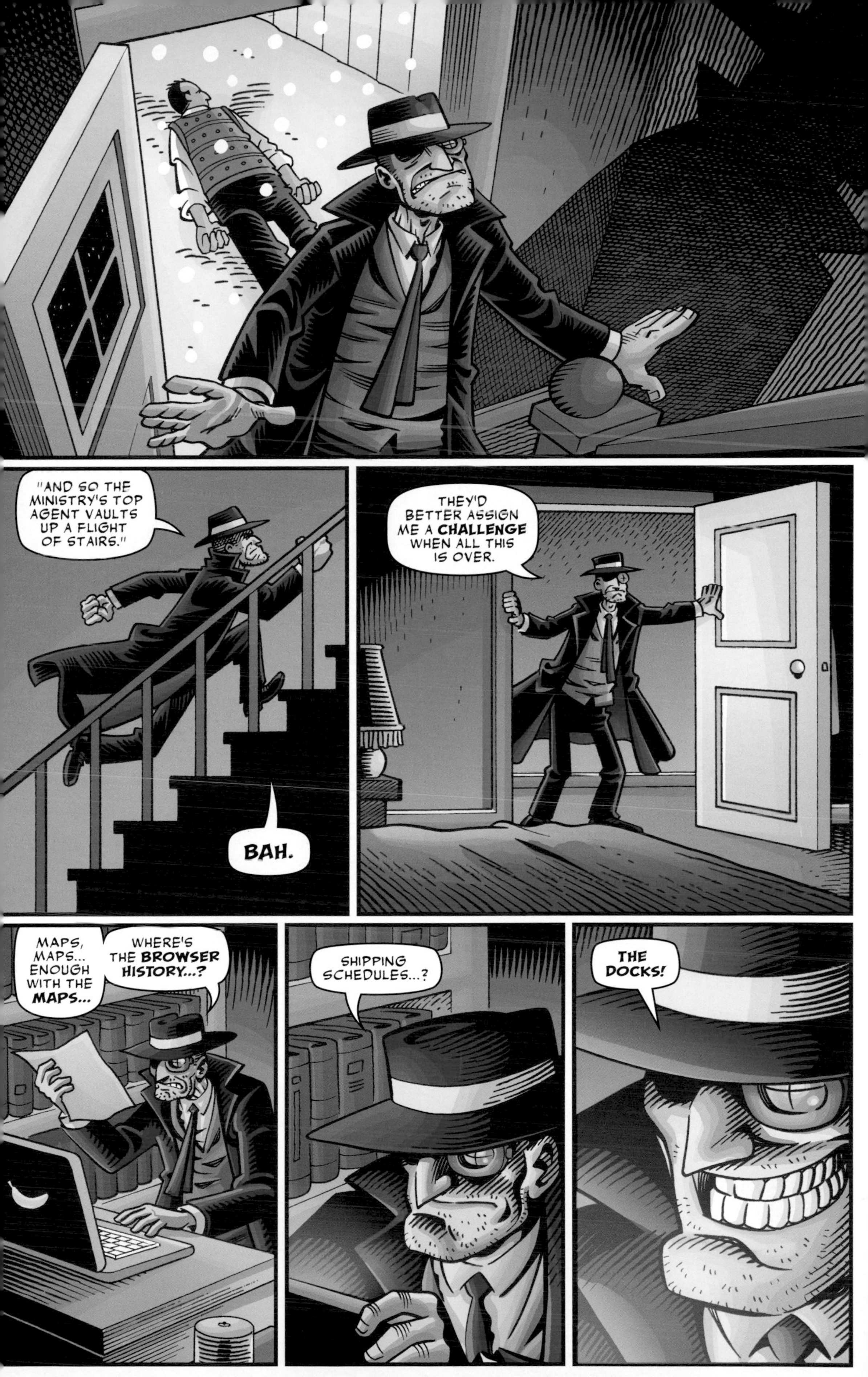
"AND SO THE MINISTRY'S TOP AGENT VAULTS UP A FLIGHT OF STAIRS."
BAH.
THEY'D BETTER ASSIGN ME A CHALLENGE WHEN ALL THIS IS OVER.
MAPS, MAPS... ENOUGH WITH THE MAPS...
WHERE'S THE BROWSER HISTORY...?
SHIPPING SCHEDULES...?
THE DOCKS!

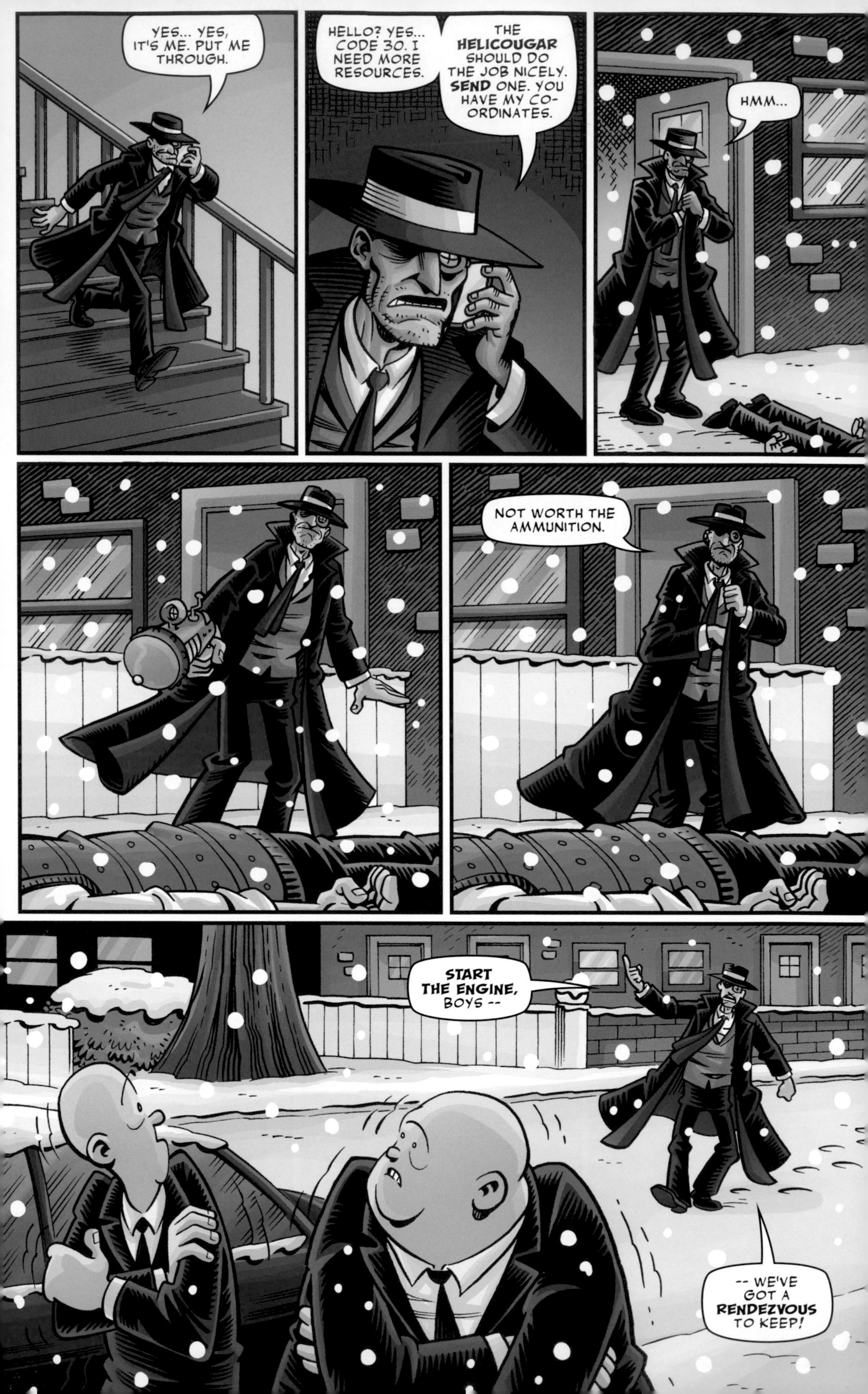
YES... YES, IT'S ME. PUT ME THROUGH.
HELLO? YES... CODE 30. I NEED MORE RESOURCES.
THE **HELICOUGAR** SHOULD DO THE JOB NICELY. **SEND** ONE. YOU HAVE MY CO-ORDINATES.
HMM...
NOT WORTH THE AMMUNITION.
START THE ENGINE, BOYS --
-- WE'VE GOT A **RENDEZVOUS** TO KEEP!

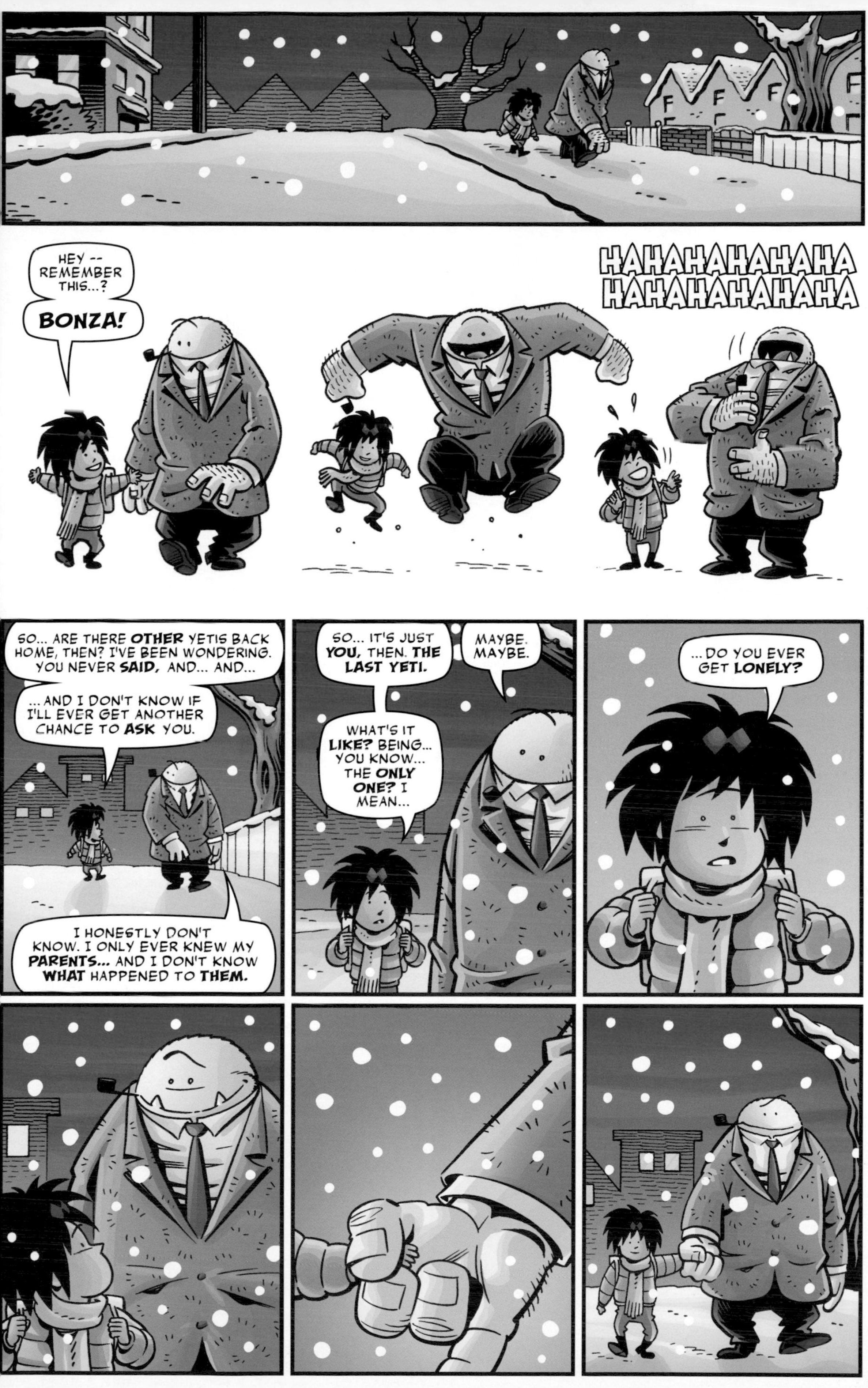
HEY -- REMEMBER THIS...?
BONZA!
HAHAHAHAHAHAHA HAHAHAHAHAHAHA
SO... ARE THERE OTHER YETIS BACK HOME, THEN? I'VE BEEN WONDERING. YOU NEVER SAID, AND... AND...
...AND I DON'T KNOW IF I'LL EVER GET ANOTHER CHANCE TO ASK YOU.
I HONESTLY DON'T KNOW. I ONLY EVER KNEW MY PARENTS... AND I DON'T KNOW WHAT HAPPENED TO THEM.
SO... IT'S JUST YOU, THEN. THE LAST YETI.
MAYBE. MAYBE.
WHAT'S IT LIKE? BEING... YOU KNOW... THE ONLY ONE? I MEAN...
...DO YOU EVER GET LONELY?

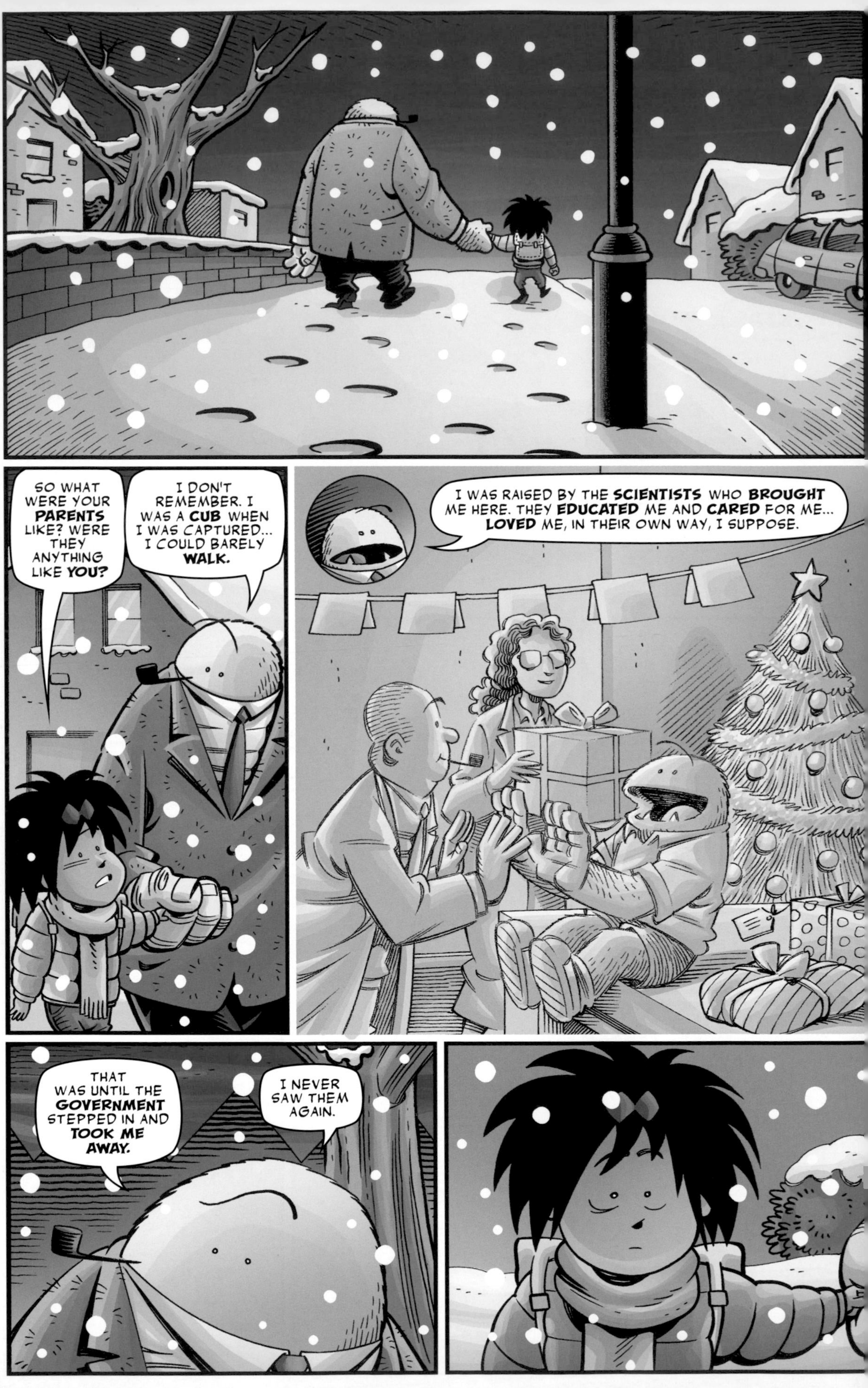
SO WHAT WERE YOUR PARENTS LIKE? WERE THEY ANYTHING LIKE YOU?
I DON'T REMEMBER. I WAS A CUB WHEN I WAS CAPTURED... I COULD BARELY WALK.
I WAS RAISED BY THE SCIENTISTS WHO BROUGHT ME HERE. THEY EDUCATED ME AND CARED FOR ME... LOVED ME, IN THEIR OWN WAY, I SUPPOSE.
THAT WAS UNTIL THE GOVERNMENT STEPPED IN AND TOOK ME AWAY.
I NEVER SAW THEM AGAIN.

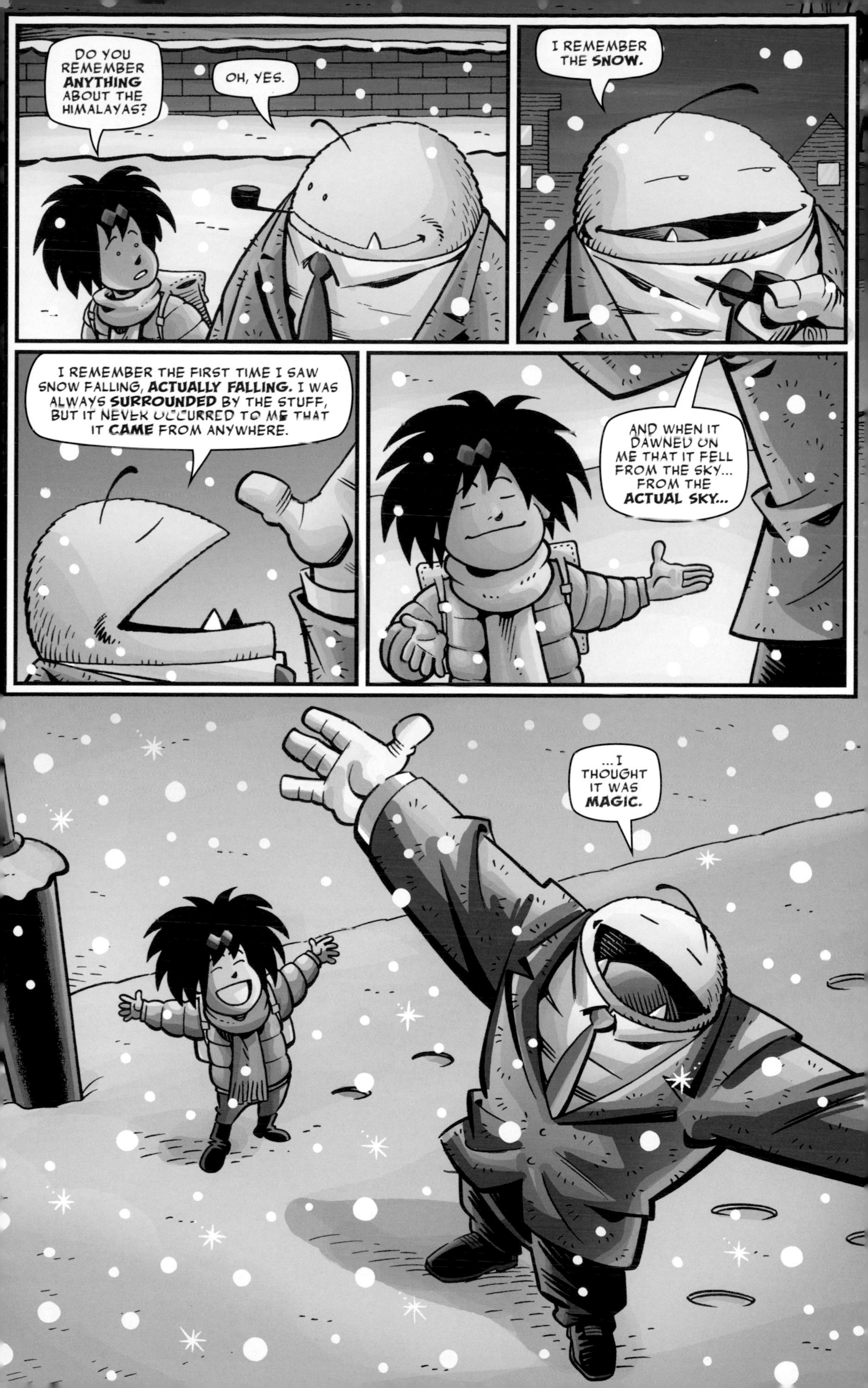
DO YOU REMEMBER ANYTHING ABOUT THE HIMALAYAS?
OH, YES.
I REMEMBER THE SNOW.
I REMEMBER THE FIRST TIME I SAW SNOW FALLING, ACTUALLY FALLING. I WAS ALWAYS SURROUNDED BY THE STUFF, BUT IT NEVER OCCURRED TO ME THAT IT CAME FROM ANYWHERE.
AND WHEN IT DAWNED ON ME THAT IT FELL FROM THE SKY... FROM THE ACTUAL SKY...
...I THOUGHT IT WAS MAGIC.

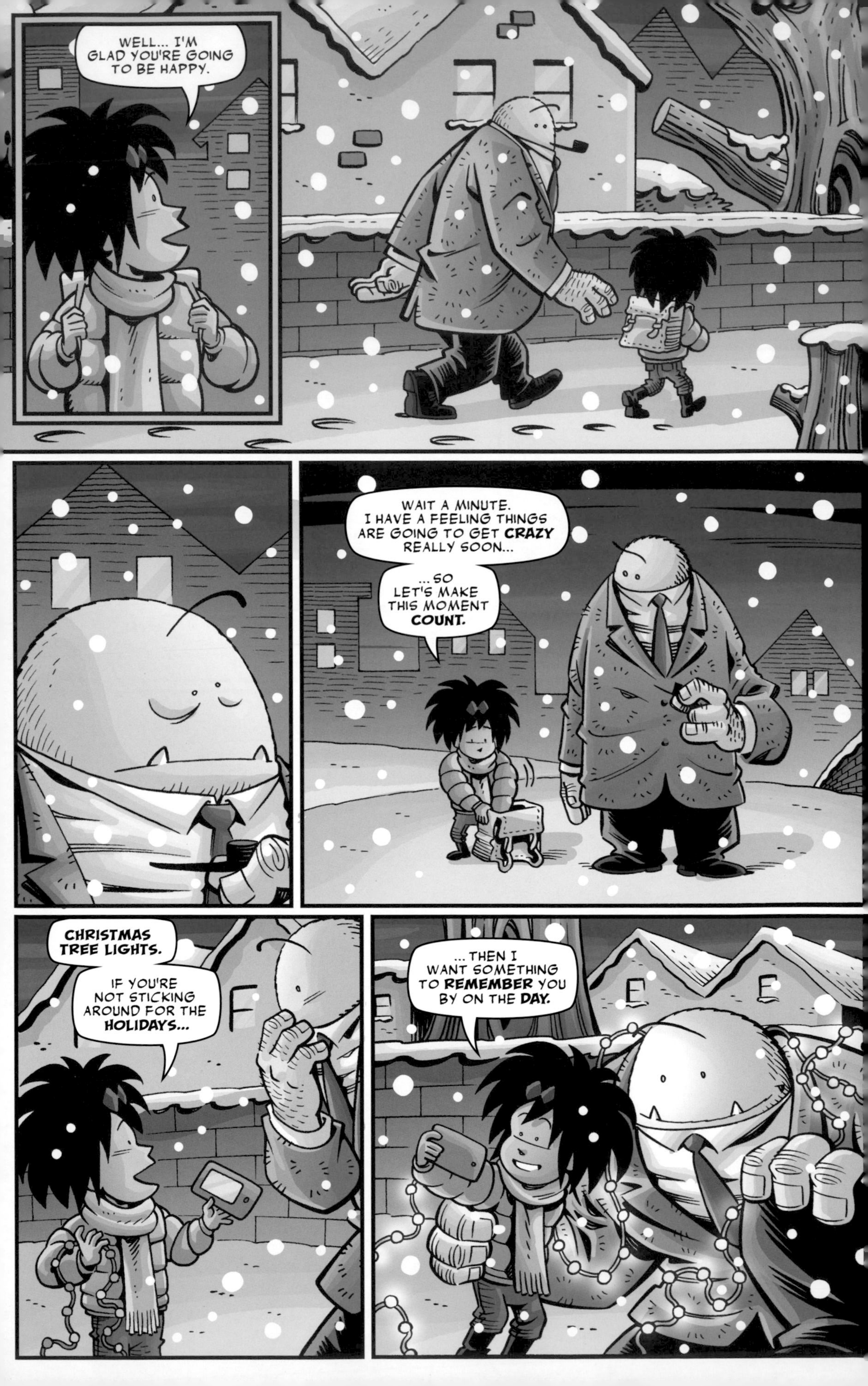

WELL... I'M GLAD YOU'RE GOING TO BE HAPPY.
WAIT A MINUTE. I HAVE A FEELING THINGS ARE GOING TO GET **CRAZY** REALLY SOON...
... SO LET'S MAKE THIS MOMENT **COUNT.**
CHRISTMAS TREE LIGHTS.
IF YOU'RE NOT STICKING AROUND FOR THE **HOLIDAYS...**
... THEN I WANT SOMETHING TO **REMEMBER** YOU BY ON THE **DAY.**

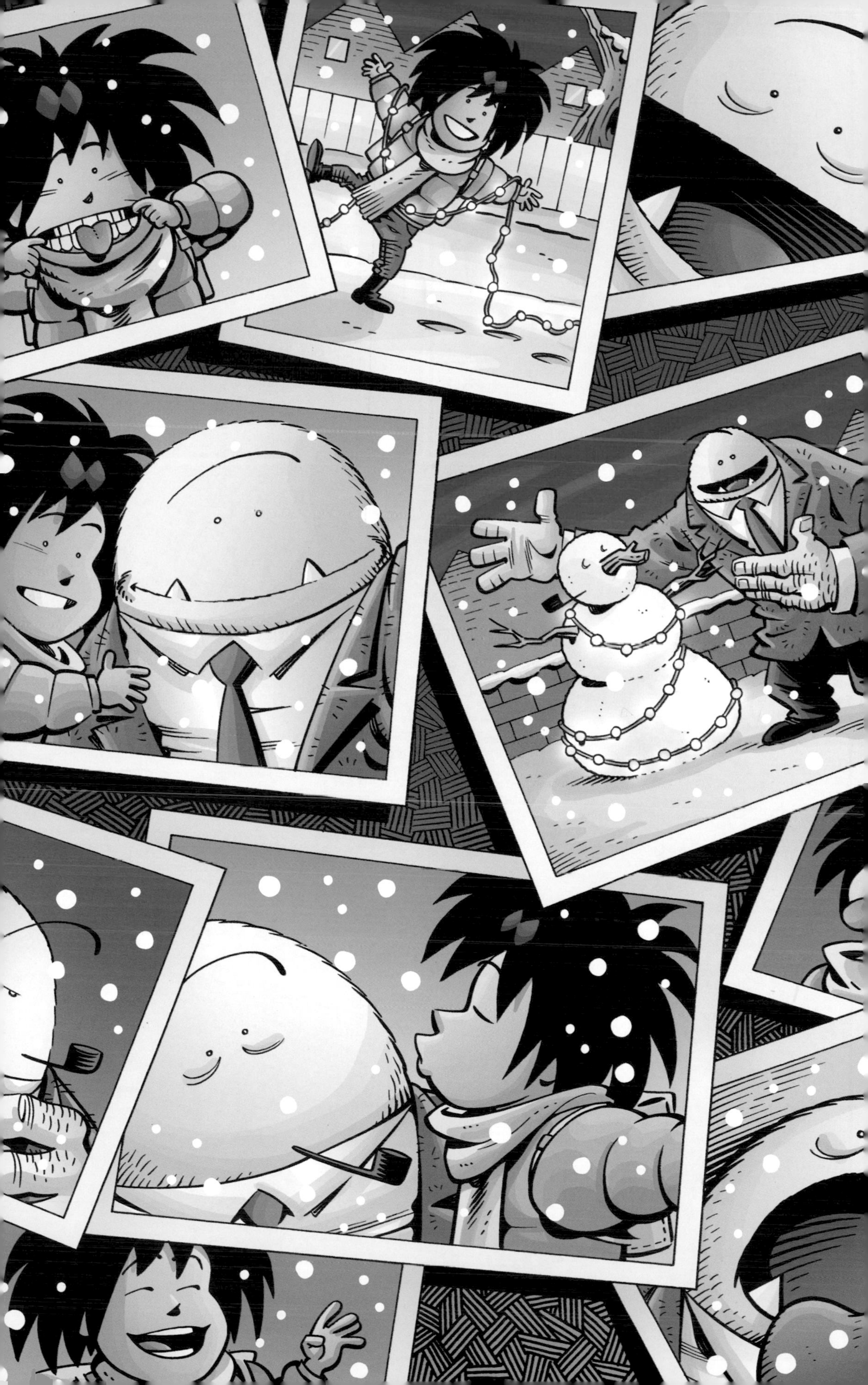

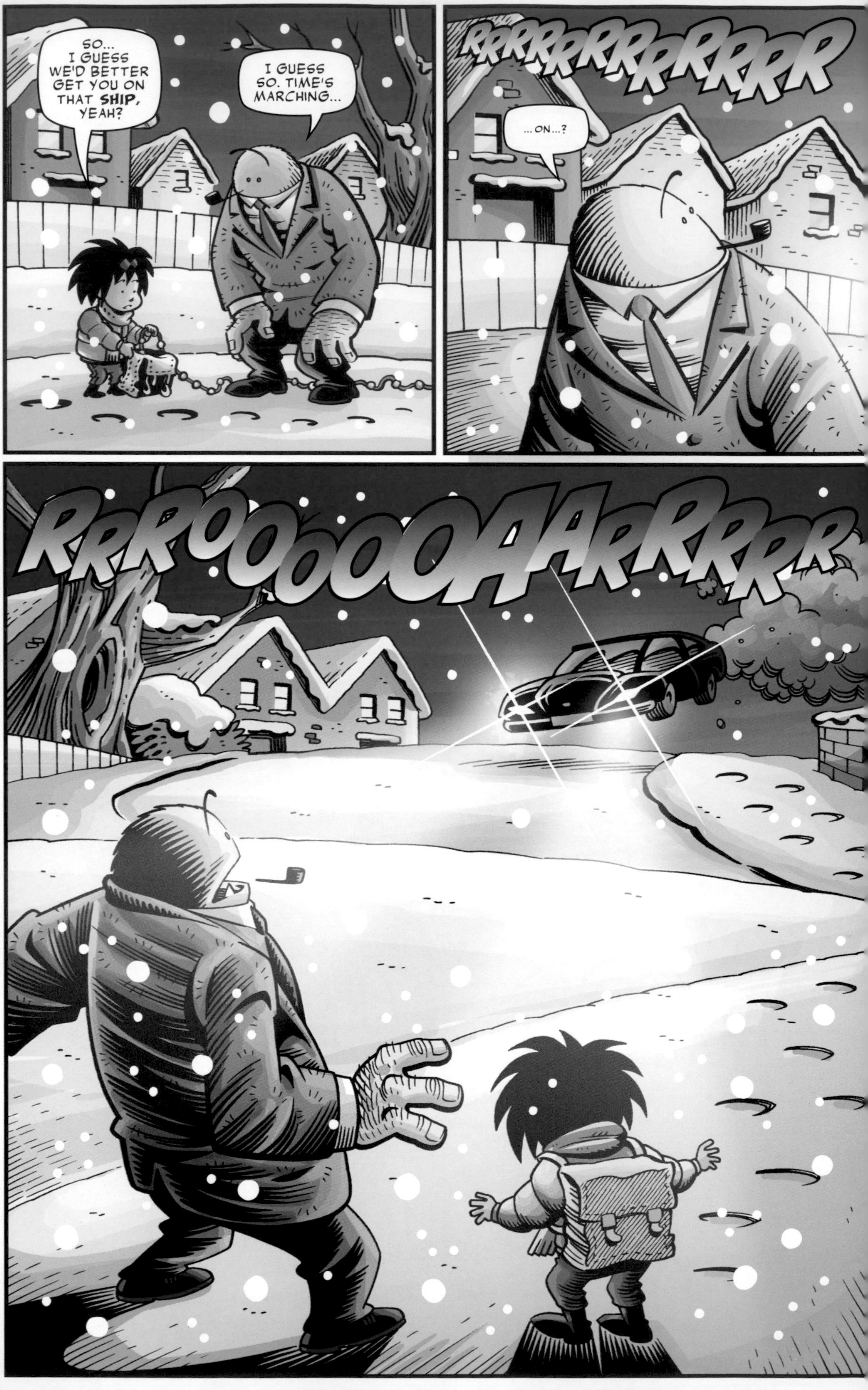
SO... I GUESS WE'D BETTER GET YOU ON THAT **SHIP**, YEAH?
I GUESS SO. TIME'S MARCHING...
RRRRRRRRRRRRRR
...ON...?
RRROOOOOOAARRRRR

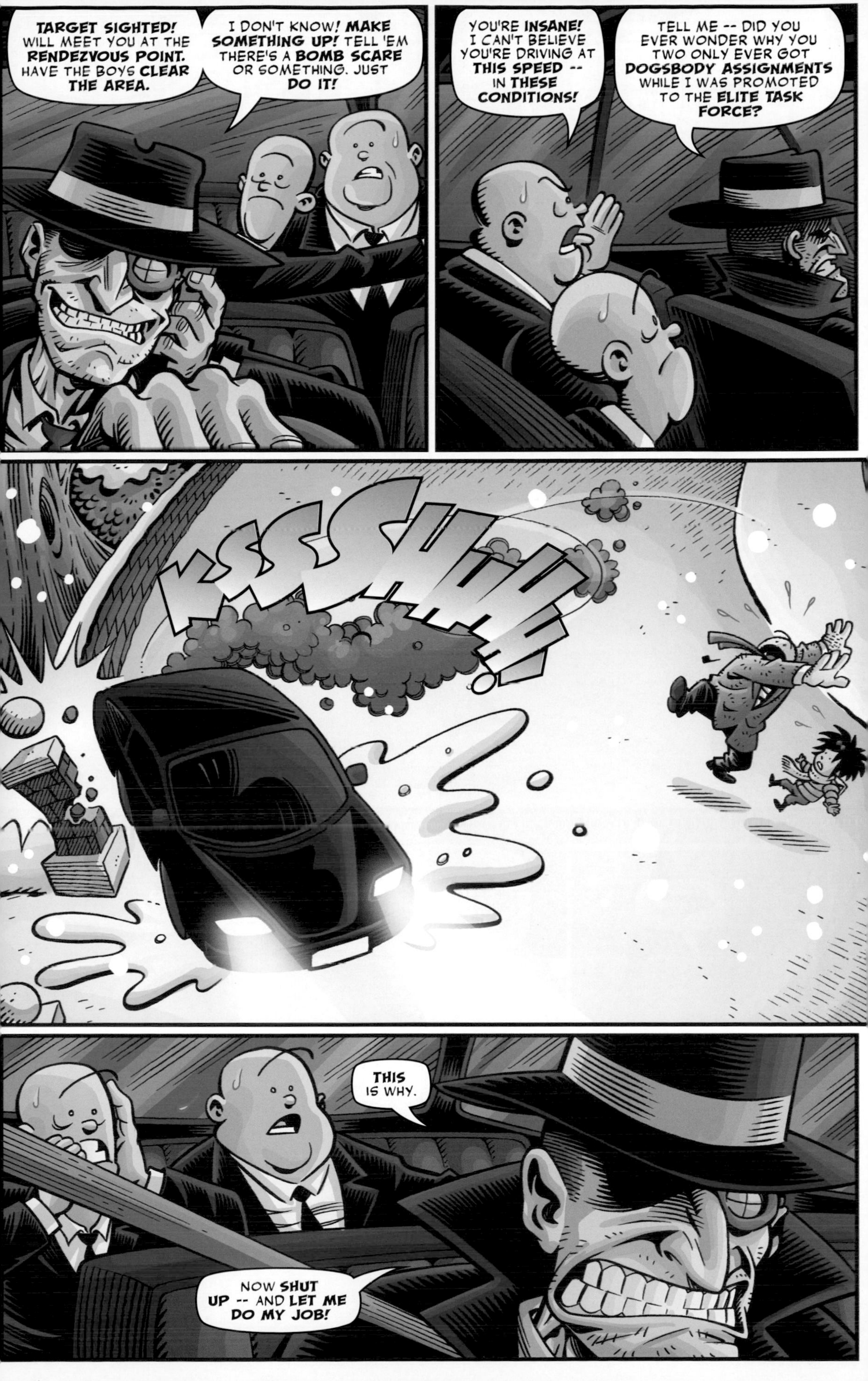
TARGET SIGHTED! WILL MEET YOU AT THE RENDEZVOUS POINT. HAVE THE BOYS CLEAR THE AREA.
I DON'T KNOW! MAKE SOMETHING UP! TELL 'EM THERE'S A BOMB SCARE OR SOMETHING. JUST DO IT!
YOU'RE INSANE! I CAN'T BELIEVE YOU'RE DRIVING AT THIS SPEED -- IN THESE CONDITIONS!
TELL ME -- DID YOU EVER WONDER WHY YOU TWO ONLY EVER GOT DOGSBODY ASSIGNMENTS WHILE I WAS PROMOTED TO THE ELITE TASK FORCE?
KSSSHHH!!
THIS IS WHY.
NOW SHUT UP -- AND LET ME DO MY JOB!

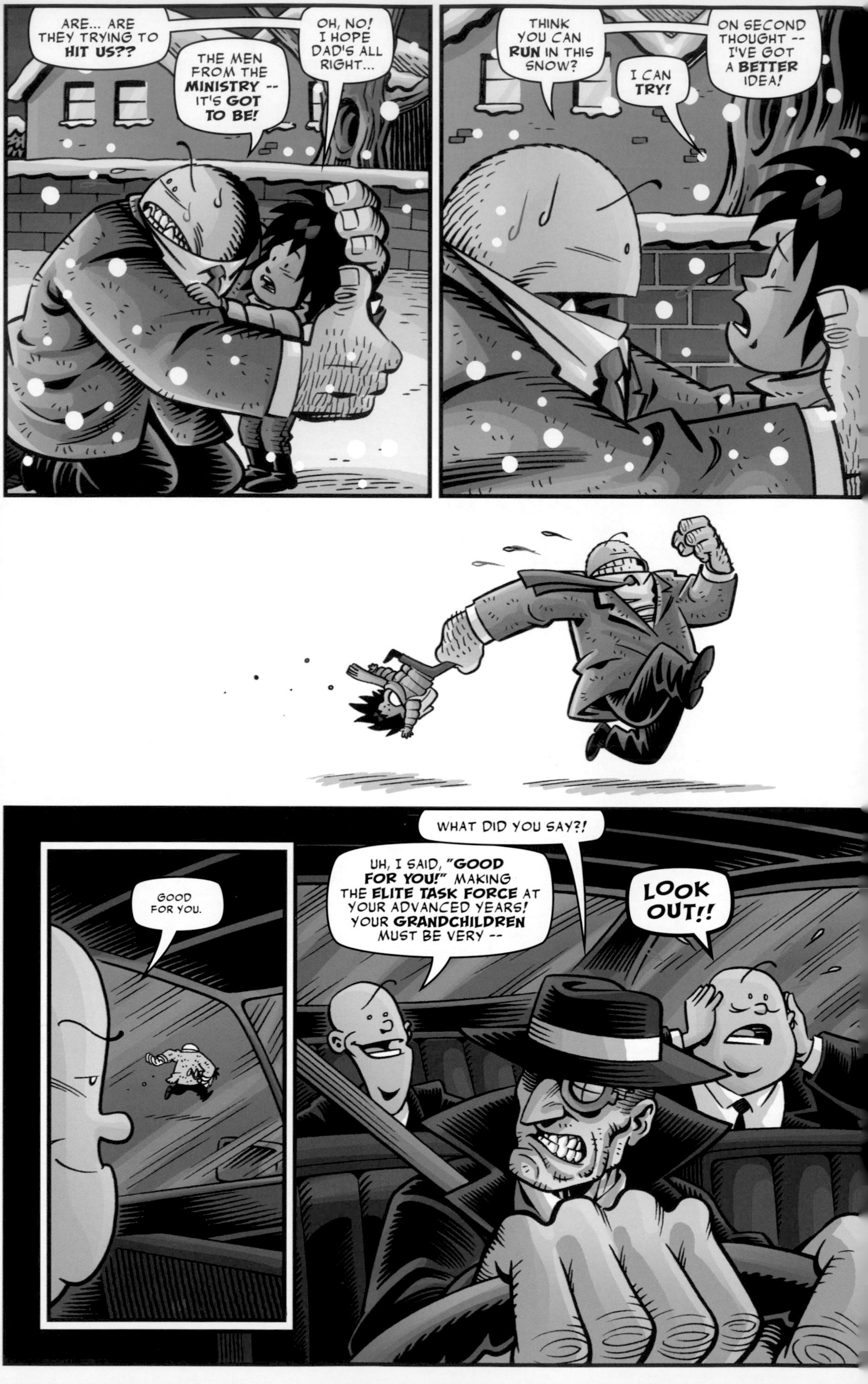
ARE... ARE THEY TRYING TO **HIT US??**
THE MEN FROM THE **MINISTRY** -- IT'S **GOT TO BE!**
OH, NO! I HOPE DAD'S ALL RIGHT...
THINK YOU CAN **RUN** IN THIS SNOW?
I CAN **TRY!**
ON SECOND THOUGHT -- I'VE GOT A **BETTER** IDEA!
GOOD FOR YOU.
WHAT DID YOU SAY?!
UH, I SAID, **"GOOD FOR YOU!"** MAKING THE **ELITE TASK FORCE** AT YOUR ADVANCED YEARS! YOUR **GRANDCHILDREN** MUST BE VERY --
LOOK OUT!!

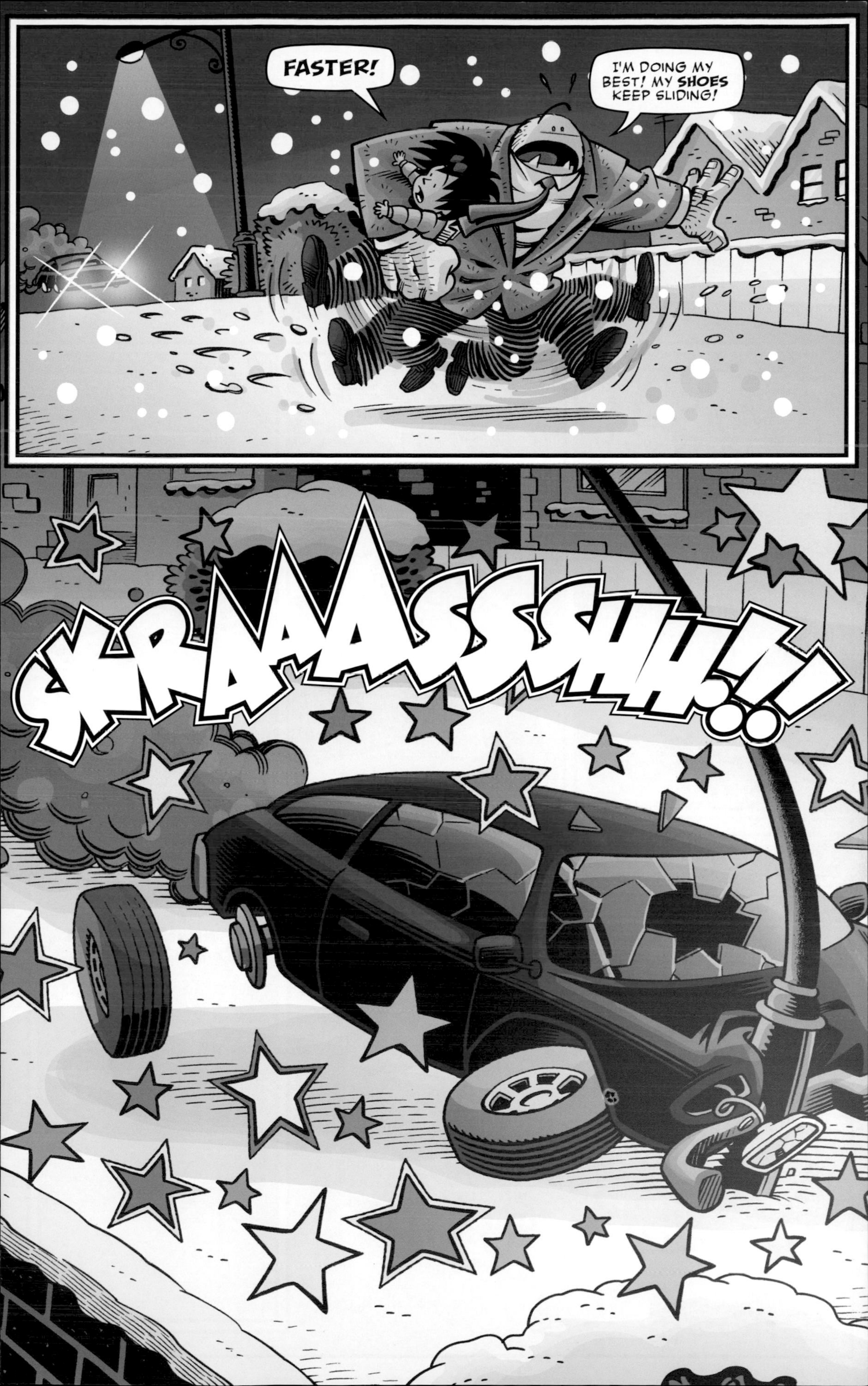
FASTER!
I'M DOING MY BEST! MY SHOES KEEP SLIDING!
SKRAAASSSHH!!!

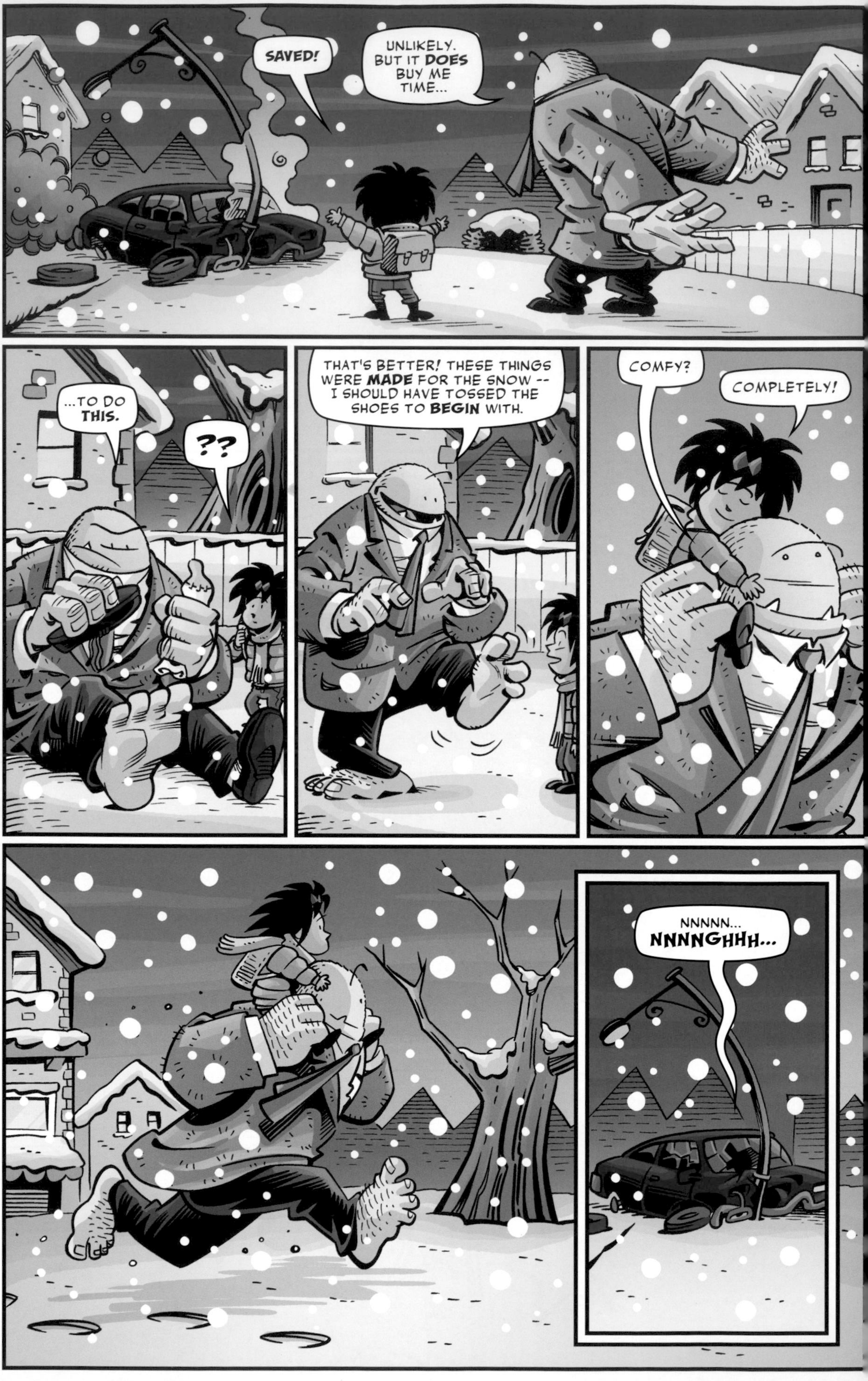
SAVED!
UNLIKELY. BUT IT DOES BUY ME TIME...
...TO DO THIS.
??
THAT'S BETTER! THESE THINGS WERE MADE FOR THE SNOW -- I SHOULD HAVE TOSSED THE SHOES TO BEGIN WITH.
COMFY?
COMPLETELY!
NNNNN... NNNNGHHH...

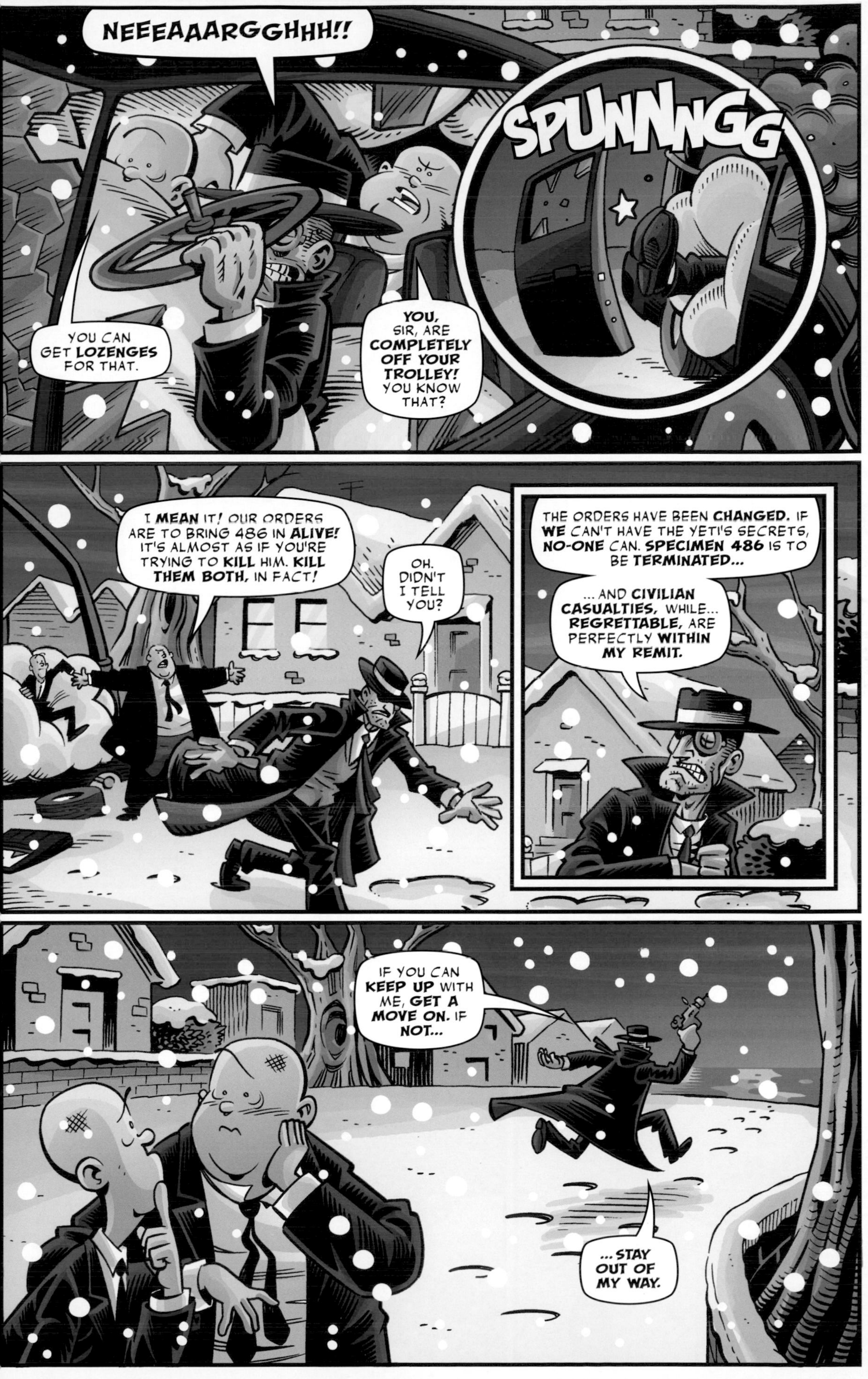
NEEEAAARGGHHH!!
YOU CAN GET LOZENGES FOR THAT.
YOU, SIR, ARE COMPLETELY OFF YOUR TROLLEY! YOU KNOW THAT?
SPUNNNGG
I MEAN IT! OUR ORDERS ARE TO BRING 486 IN ALIVE! IT'S ALMOST AS IF YOU'RE TRYING TO KILL HIM. KILL THEM BOTH, IN FACT!
OH. DIDN'T I TELL YOU?
THE ORDERS HAVE BEEN CHANGED. IF WE CAN'T HAVE THE YETI'S SECRETS, NO-ONE CAN. SPECIMEN 486 IS TO BE TERMINATED...
... AND CIVILIAN CASUALTIES, WHILE... REGRETTABLE, ARE PERFECTLY WITHIN MY REMIT.
IF YOU CAN KEEP UP WITH ME, GET A MOVE ON. IF NOT...
...STAY OUT OF MY WAY.

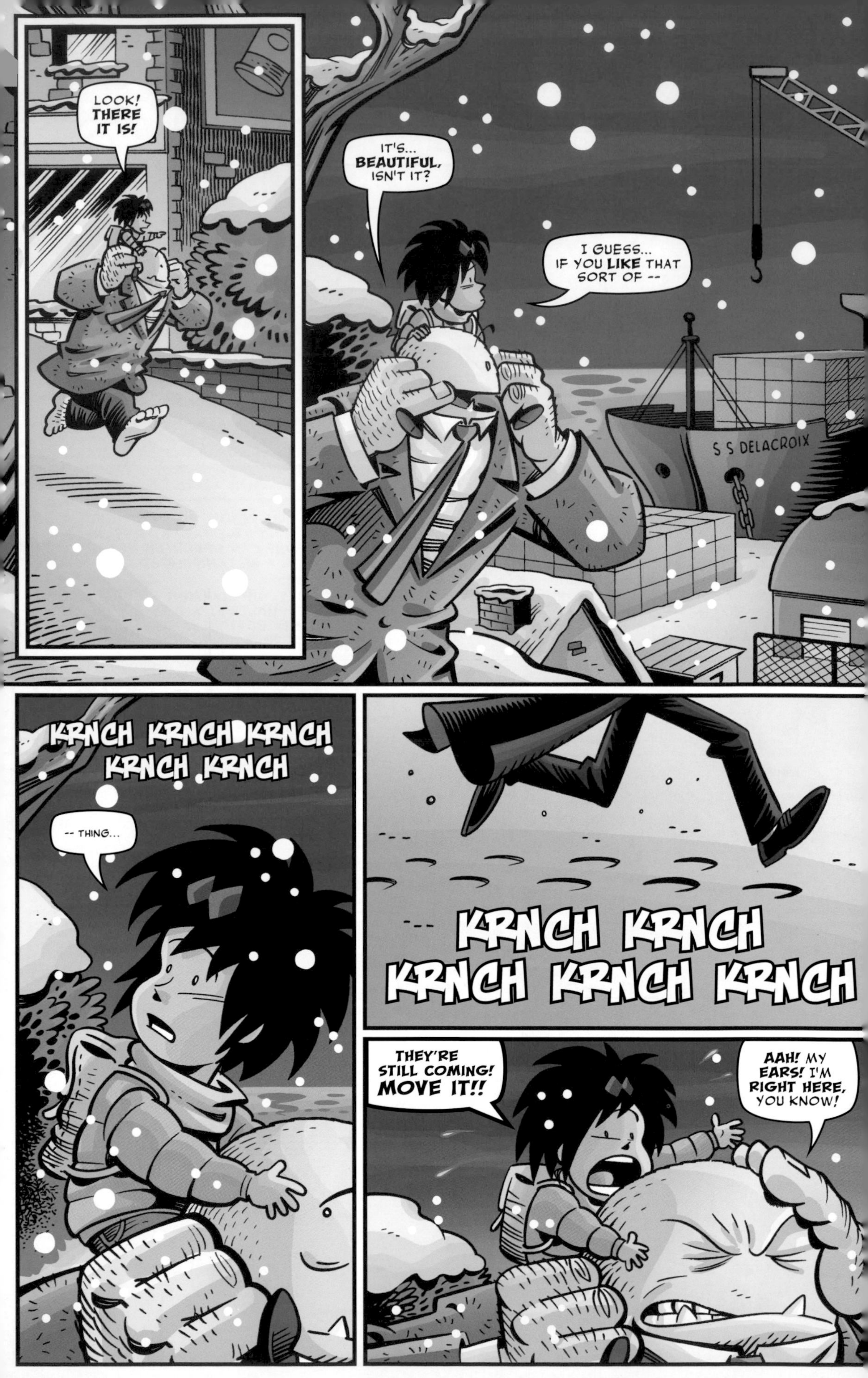
LOOK! THERE IT IS!
IT'S... BEAUTIFUL, ISN'T IT?
I GUESS... IF YOU LIKE THAT SORT OF --
S S DELACROIX
KRNCH KRNCH KRNCH KRNCH KRNCH
-- THING...
KRNCH KRNCH KRNCH KRNCH KRNCH
THEY'RE STILL COMING! MOVE IT!!
AAH! MY EARS! I'M RIGHT HERE, YOU KNOW!

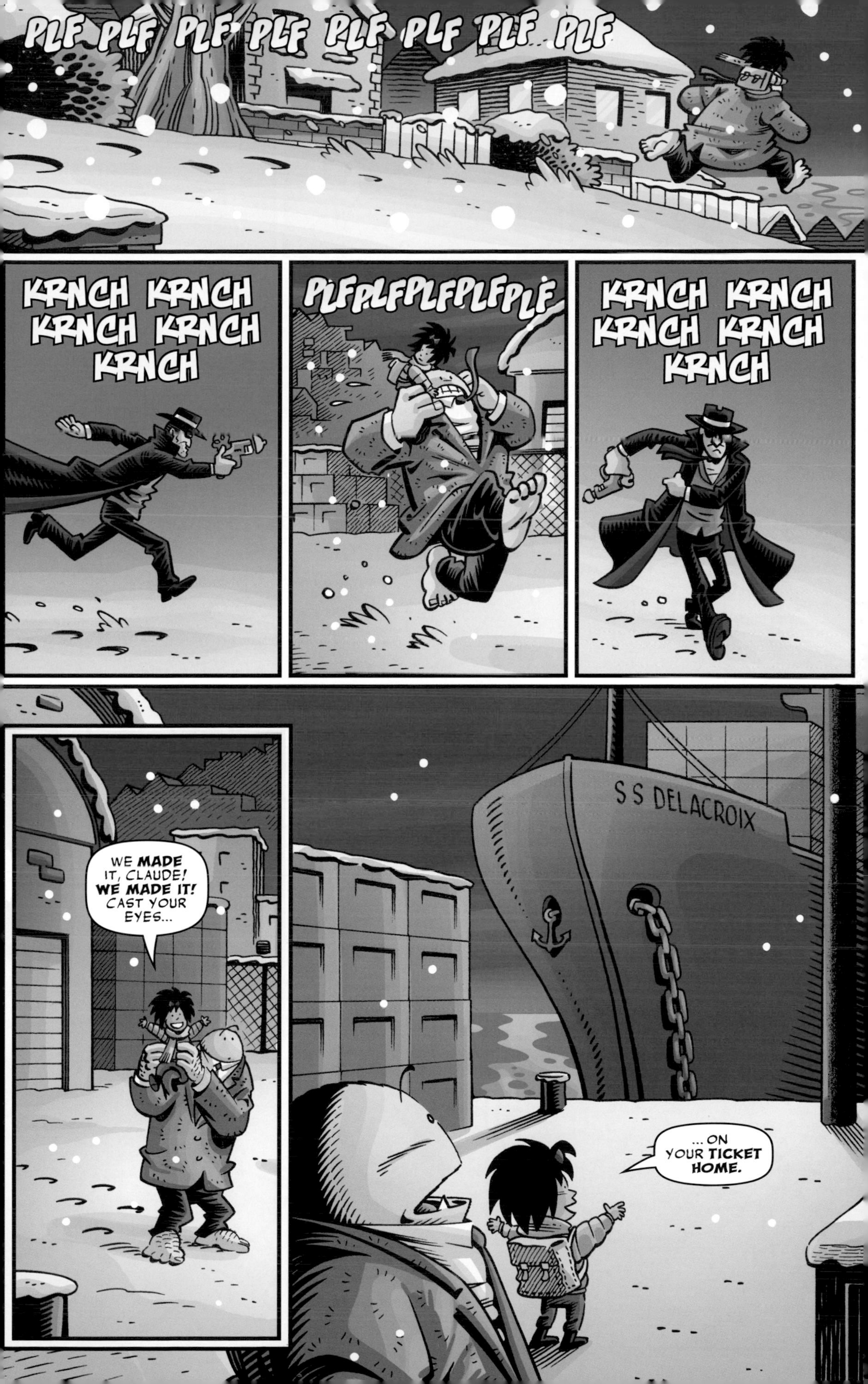
PLF PLF PLF PLF PLF PLF PLF PLF
KRNCH KRNCH KRNCH KRNCH KRNCH
PLFPLFPLFPLFPLF
KRNCH KRNCH KRNCH KRNCH KRNCH
WE MADE IT, CLAUDE! WE MADE IT! CAST YOUR EYES...
S S DELACROIX
...ON YOUR TICKET HOME.

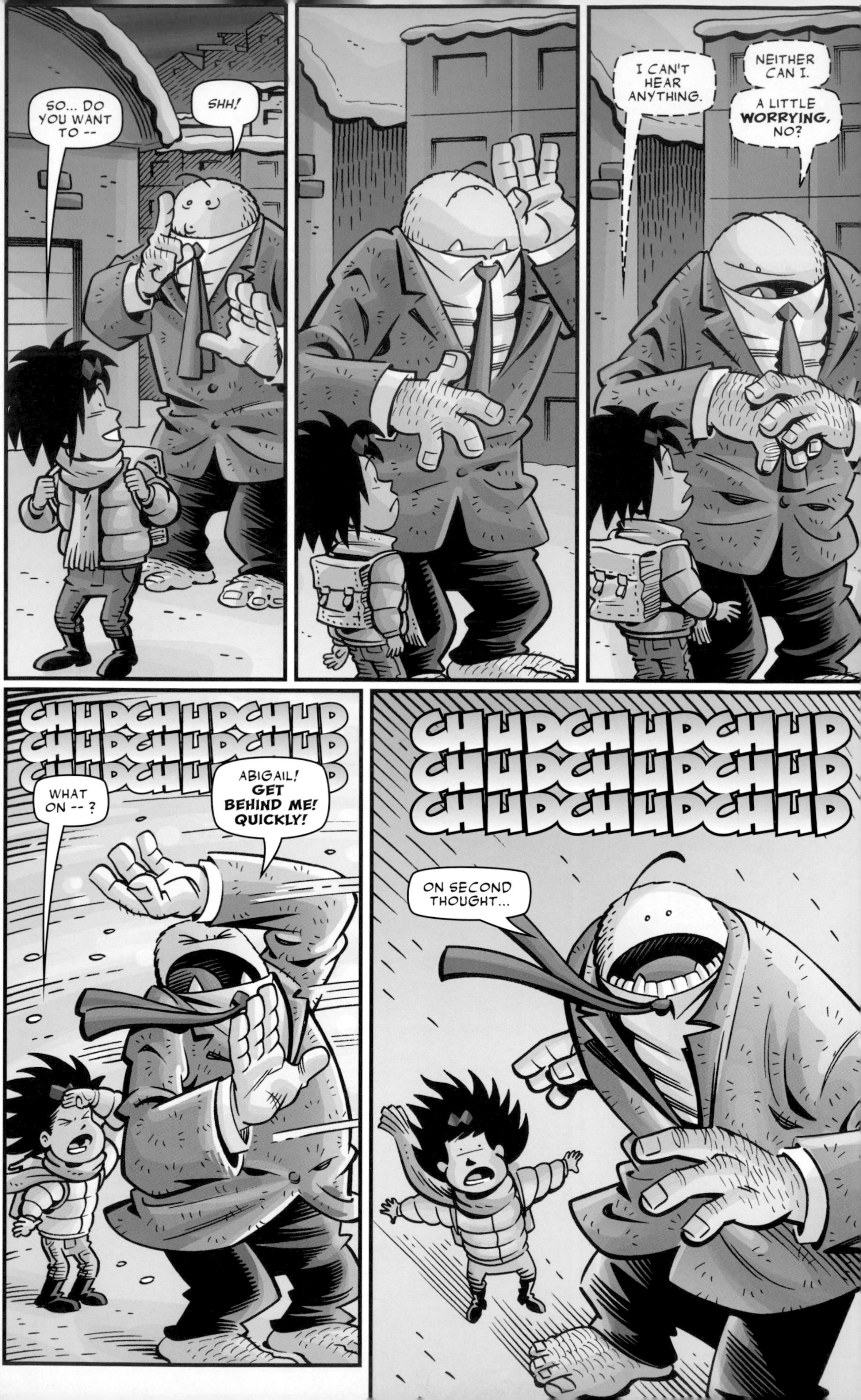
SO... DO YOU WANT TO --
SHH!
I CAN'T HEAR ANYTHING.
NEITHER CAN I.
A LITTLE WORRYING, NO?
CHUDCHUDCHUD CHUDCHUDCHUD CHUDCHUDCHUD
WHAT ON -- ?
ABIGAIL! GET BEHIND ME! QUICKLY!
CHUDCHUDCHUD CHUDCHUDCHUD CHUDCHUDCHUD
ON SECOND THOUGHT...

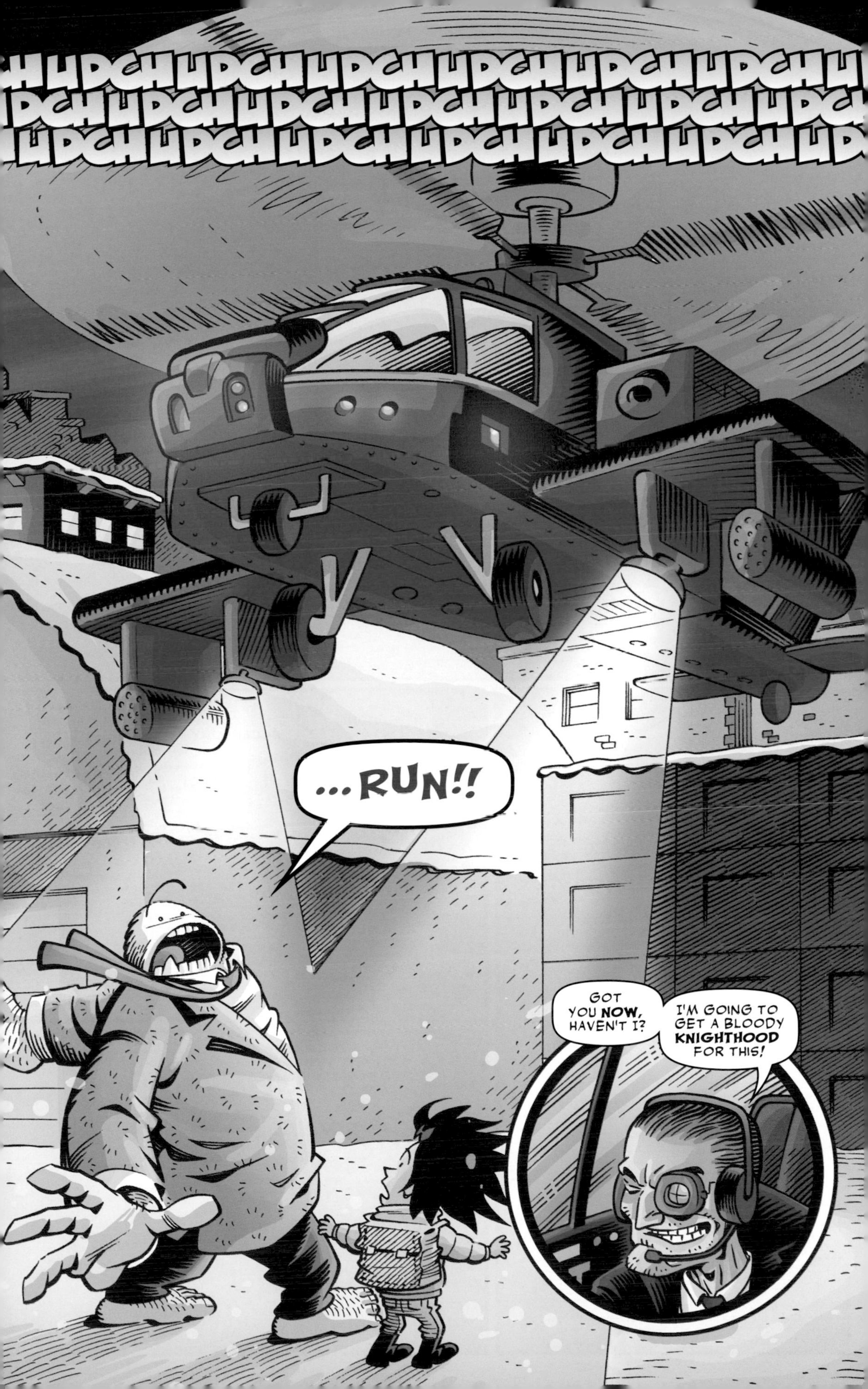

CHUDCHUDCHUDCHUDCHUDCHUDCHUDCHU
DCHUDCHUDCHUDCHUDCHUDCHUDCHUDCH
UDCHUDCHUDCHUDCHUDCHUDCHUDCHUD
...RUN!!
GOT YOU NOW, HAVEN'T I?
I'M GOING TO GET A BLOODY KNIGHTHOOD FOR THIS!

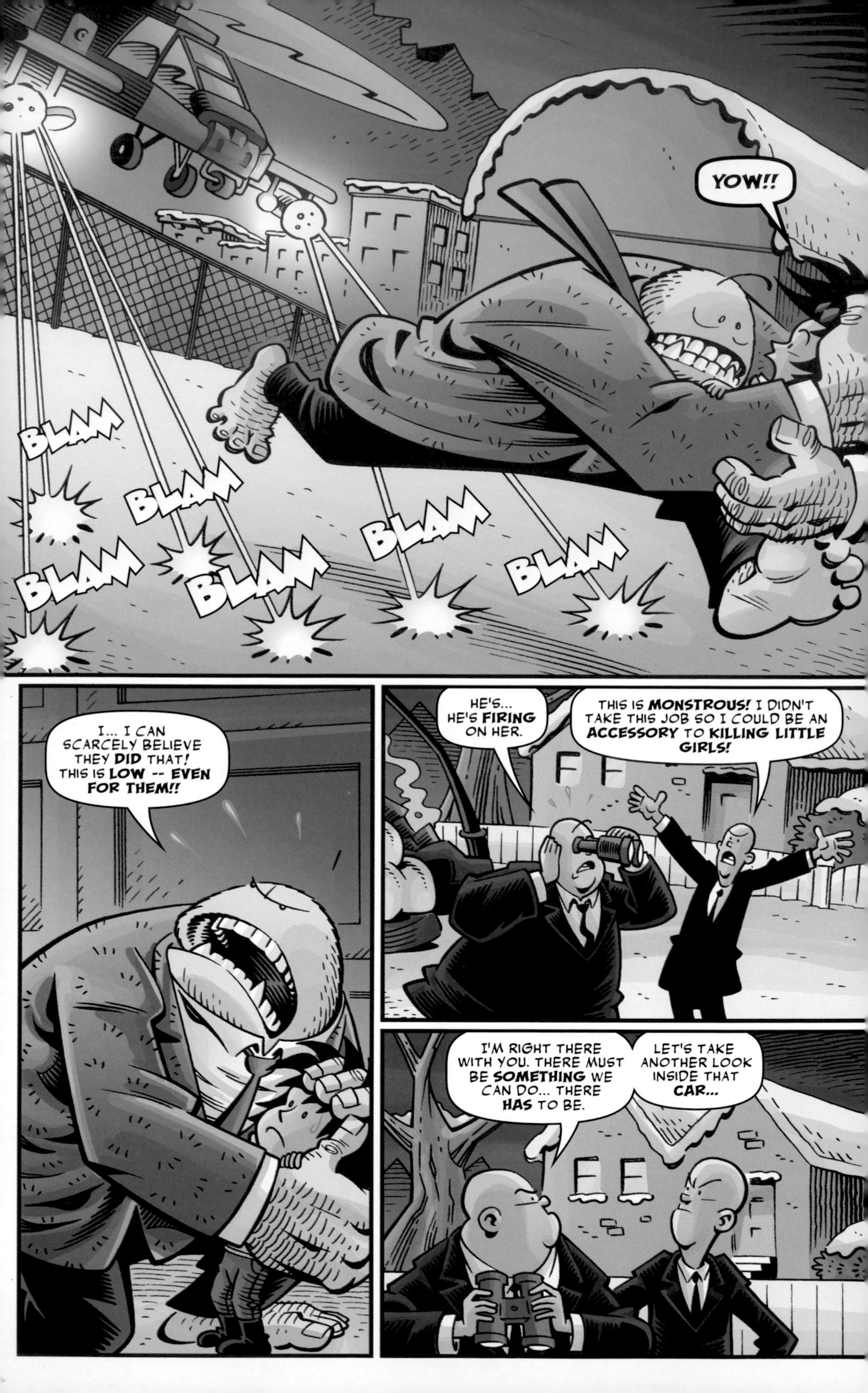
YOW!!
BLAM
BLAM
BLAM
BLAM
BLAM
BLAM
I... I CAN SCARCELY BELIEVE THEY DID THAT! THIS IS LOW -- EVEN FOR THEM!!
HE'S... HE'S FIRING ON HER.
THIS IS MONSTROUS! I DIDN'T TAKE THIS JOB SO I COULD BE AN ACCESSORY TO KILLING LITTLE GIRLS!
I'M RIGHT THERE WITH YOU. THERE MUST BE SOMETHING WE CAN DO... THERE HAS TO BE.
LET'S TAKE ANOTHER LOOK INSIDE THAT CAR...

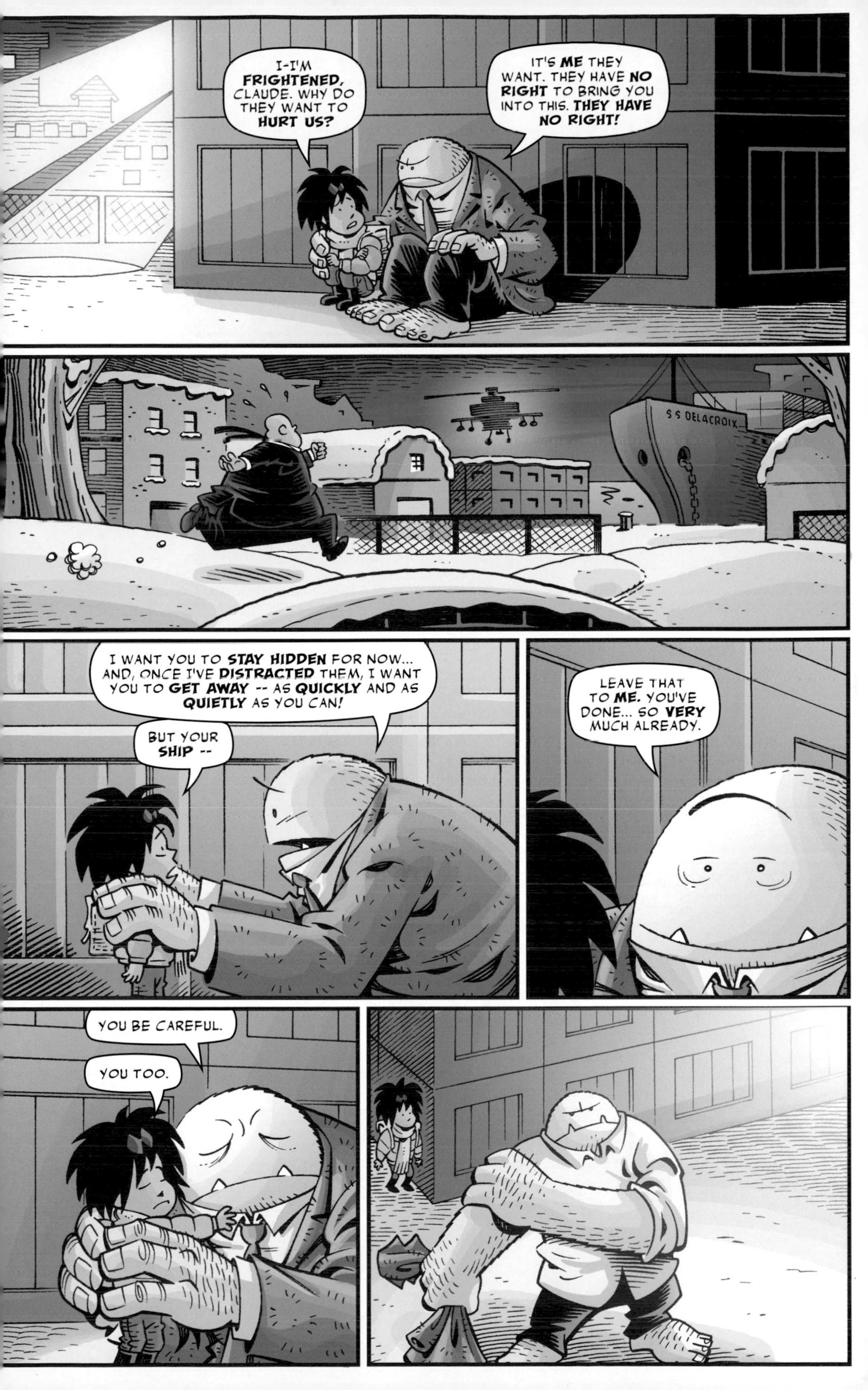

I-I'M **FRIGHTENED,** CLAUDE. WHY DO THEY WANT TO **HURT US?**
IT'S **ME** THEY WANT. THEY HAVE **NO RIGHT** TO BRING YOU INTO THIS. **THEY HAVE NO RIGHT!**
S S DELACROIX
I WANT YOU TO **STAY HIDDEN** FOR NOW... AND, ONCE I'VE **DISTRACTED** THEM, I WANT YOU TO **GET AWAY** -- AS **QUICKLY** AND AS **QUIETLY** AS YOU CAN!
BUT YOUR **SHIP** --
LEAVE THAT TO **ME.** YOU'VE DONE... SO **VERY** MUCH ALREADY.
YOU BE CAREFUL.
YOU TOO.

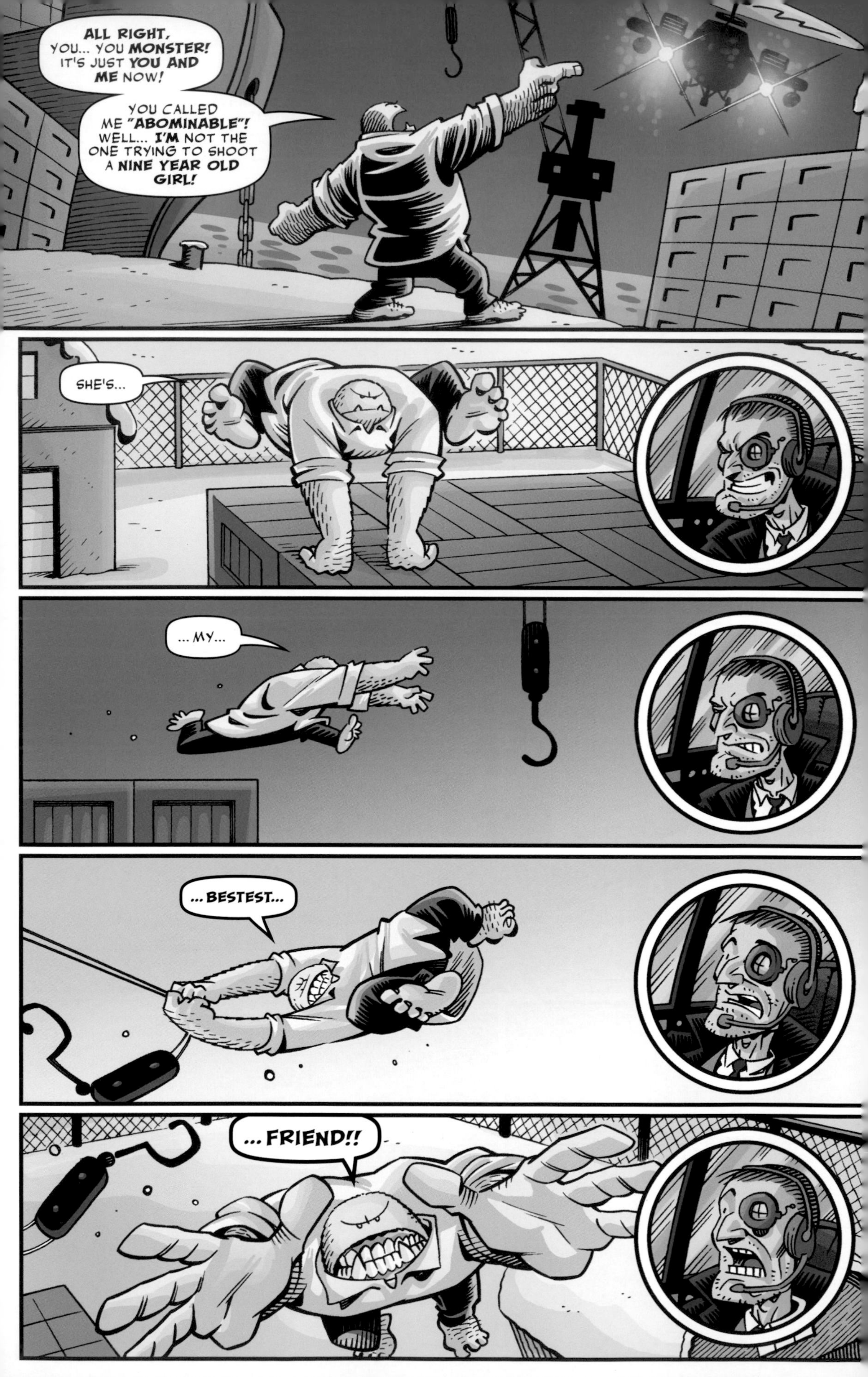
ALL RIGHT, YOU... YOU MONSTER! IT'S JUST YOU AND ME NOW!
YOU CALLED ME "ABOMINABLE"! WELL... I'M NOT THE ONE TRYING TO SHOOT A NINE YEAR OLD GIRL!
SHE'S...
... MY...
... BESTEST...
... FRIEND!!

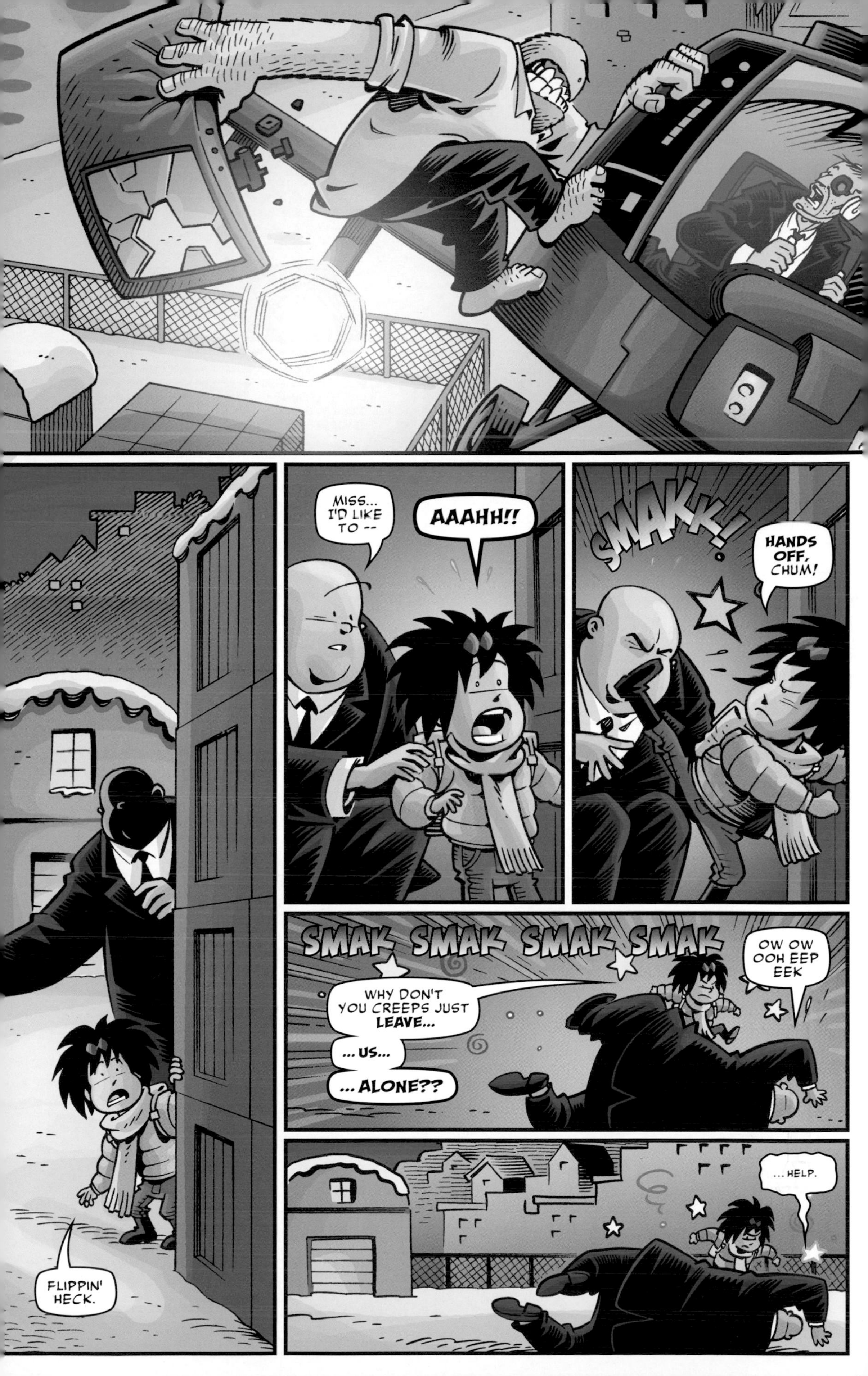
MISS... I'D LIKE TO --
AAAHH!!
SMAKK!
HANDS OFF, CHUM!
FLIPPIN' HECK.
SMAK SMAK SMAK SMAK
WHY DON'T YOU CREEPS JUST LEAVE...
... US...
... ALONE??
OW OW OOH EEP EEK
... HELP.

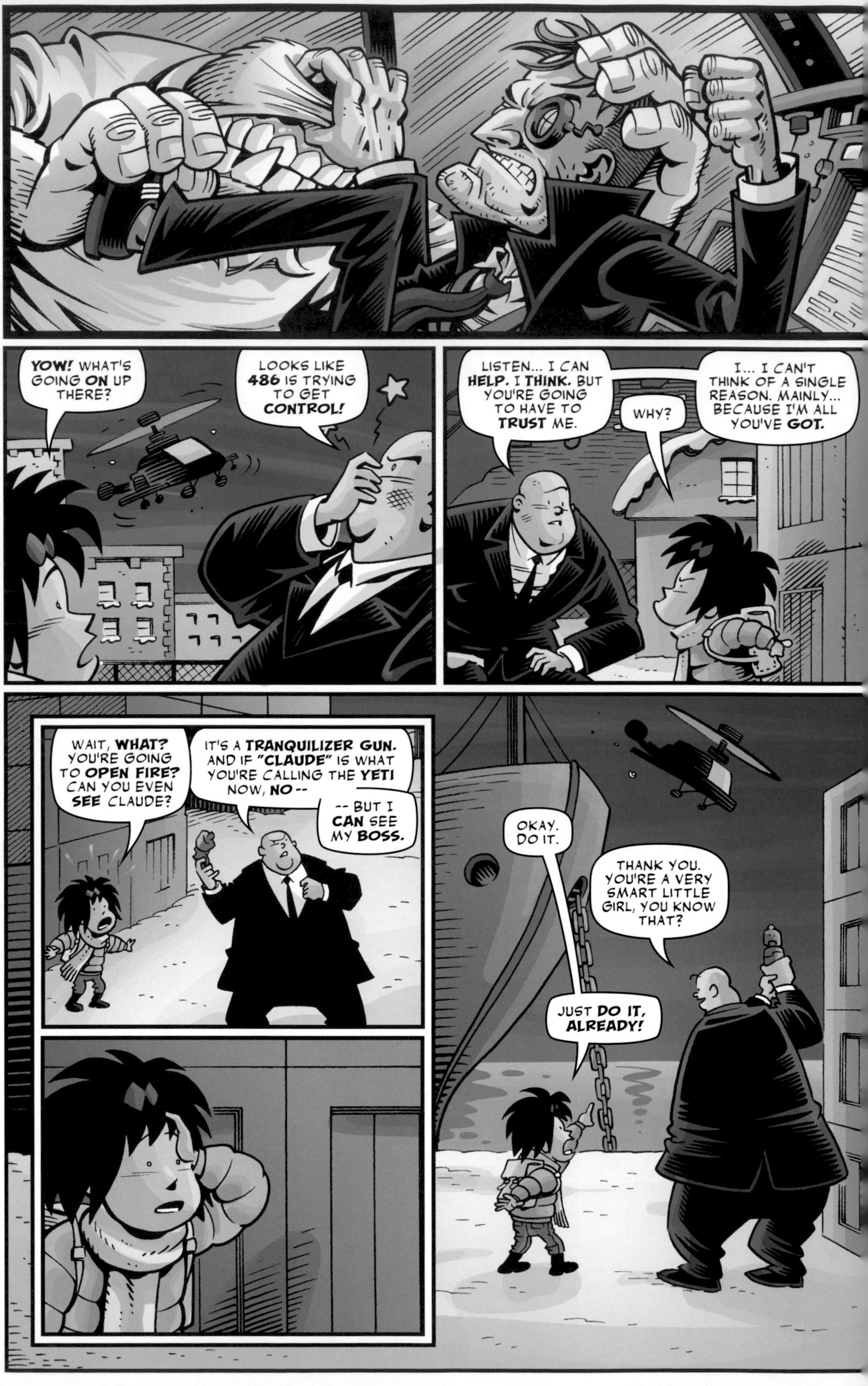
YOW! WHAT'S GOING ON UP THERE?
LOOKS LIKE 486 IS TRYING TO GET CONTROL!
LISTEN... I CAN HELP. I THINK. BUT YOU'RE GOING TO HAVE TO TRUST ME.
WHY?
I... I CAN'T THINK OF A SINGLE REASON. MAINLY... BECAUSE I'M ALL YOU'VE GOT.
WAIT, WHAT? YOU'RE GOING TO OPEN FIRE? CAN YOU EVEN SEE CLAUDE?
IT'S A TRANQUILIZER GUN. AND IF "CLAUDE" IS WHAT YOU'RE CALLING THE YETI NOW, NO --
-- BUT I CAN SEE MY BOSS.
OKAY. DO IT.
THANK YOU. YOU'RE A VERY SMART LITTLE GIRL, YOU KNOW THAT?
JUST DO IT, ALREADY!

FOOP

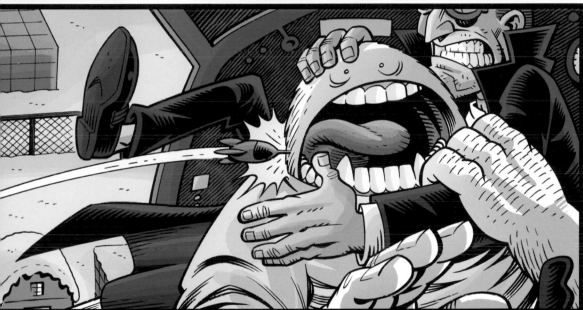

YOU... YOU **NINNY!** **YOU SHOT CLAUDE!!**

WHOOPS.

I JUST HOPE YOU GOT THE **DOSE** WRONG... OR CLAUDE'S **ANGER** IS ENOUGH TO **SEE HIM THROUGH**... OR SOMETHING...

"... OTHERWISE WE'RE **ALL** UP THE CREEK."

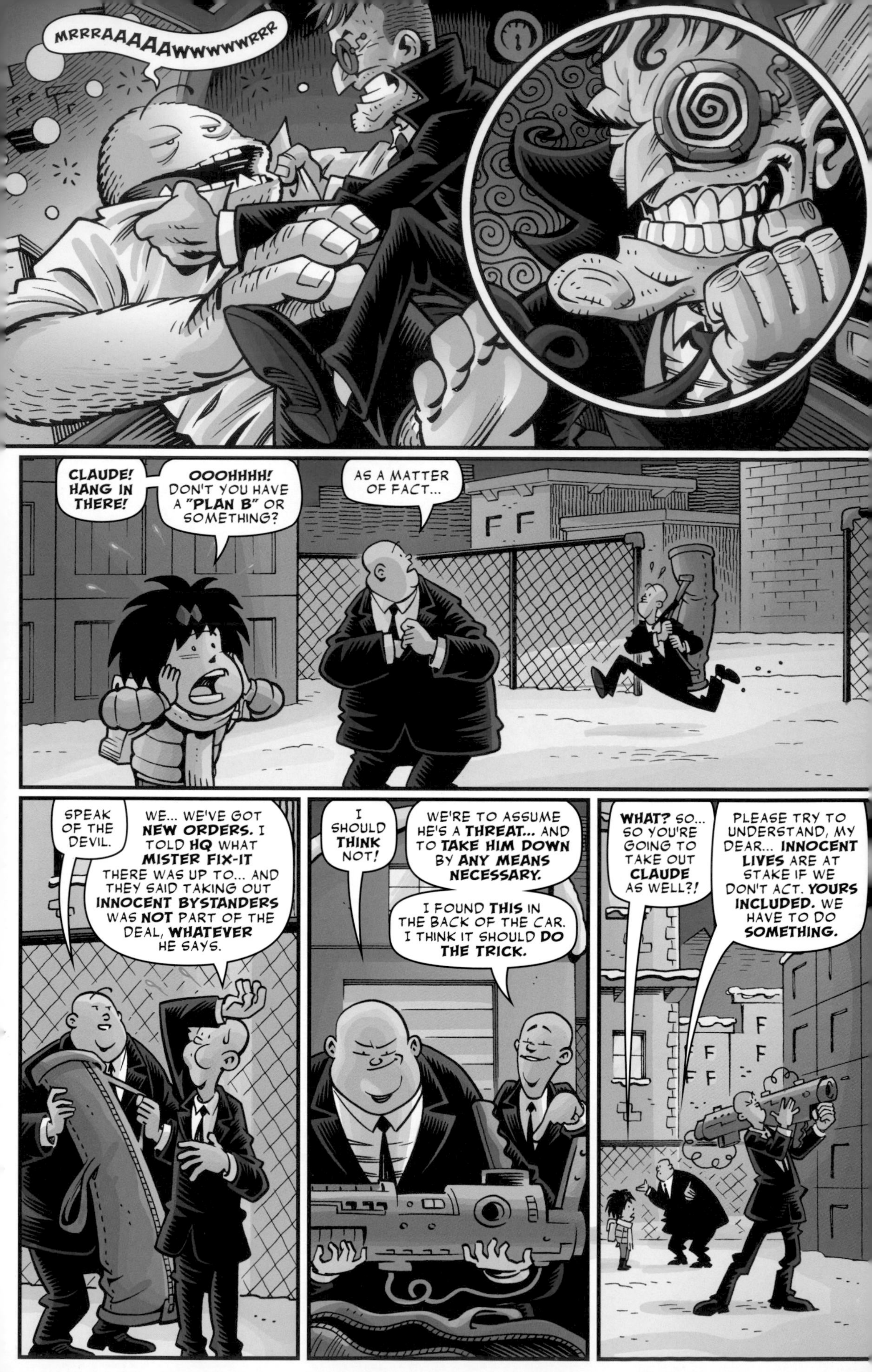
MRRRAAAAAWWWWWRRR
CLAUDE! HANG IN THERE!
OOOHHHH! DON'T YOU HAVE A "PLAN B" OR SOMETHING?
AS A MATTER OF FACT...
SPEAK OF THE DEVIL.
WE... WE'VE GOT NEW ORDERS. I TOLD HQ WHAT MISTER FIX-IT THERE WAS UP TO... AND THEY SAID TAKING OUT INNOCENT BYSTANDERS WAS NOT PART OF THE DEAL, WHATEVER HE SAYS.
I SHOULD THINK NOT!
WE'RE TO ASSUME HE'S A THREAT... AND TO TAKE HIM DOWN BY ANY MEANS NECESSARY.
I FOUND THIS IN THE BACK OF THE CAR. I THINK IT SHOULD DO THE TRICK.
WHAT? SO... SO YOU'RE GOING TO TAKE OUT CLAUDE AS WELL?!
PLEASE TRY TO UNDERSTAND, MY DEAR... INNOCENT LIVES ARE AT STAKE IF WE DON'T ACT. YOURS INCLUDED. WE HAVE TO DO SOMETHING.

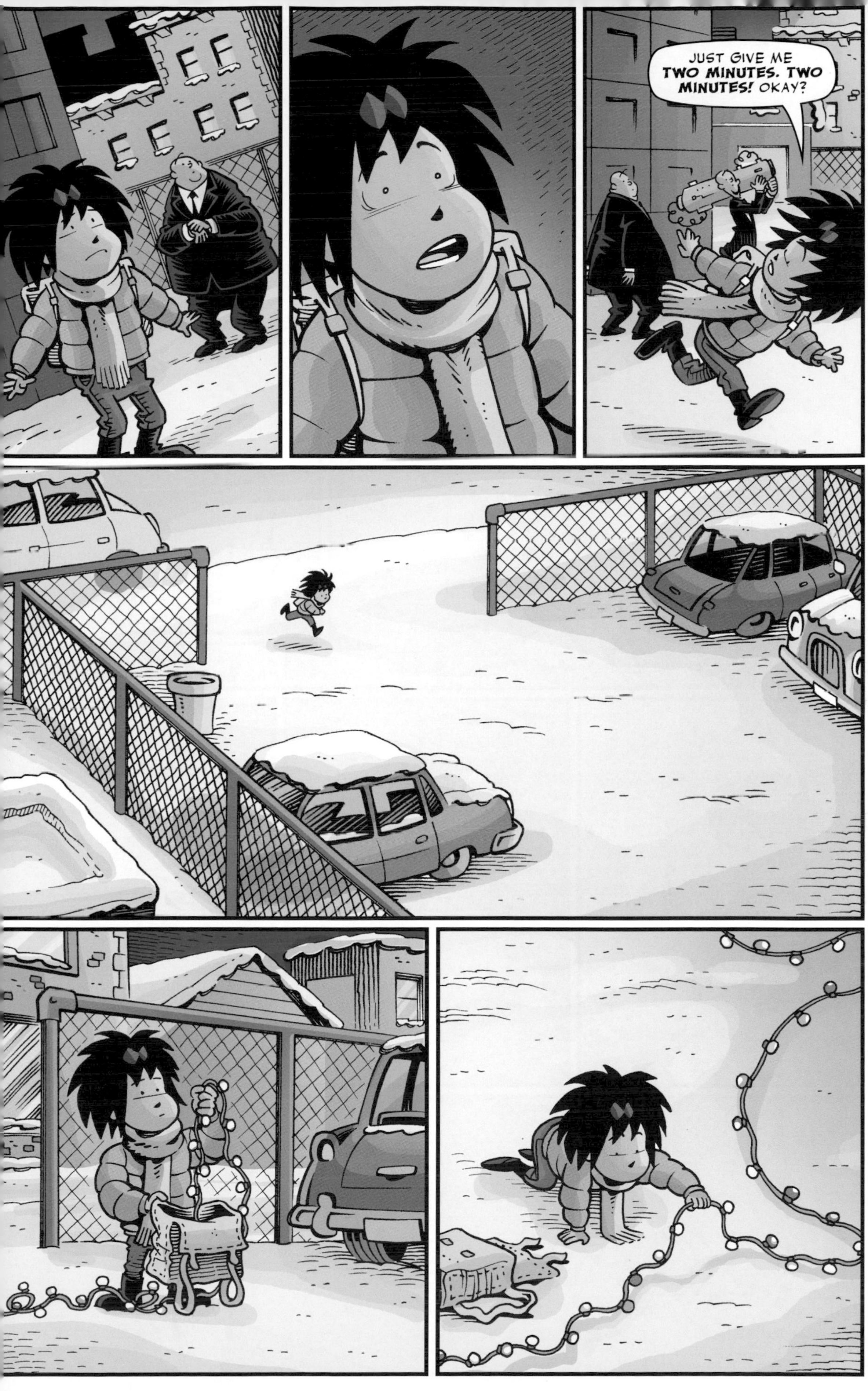
JUST GIVE ME **TWO MINUTES. TWO MINUTES!** OKAY?

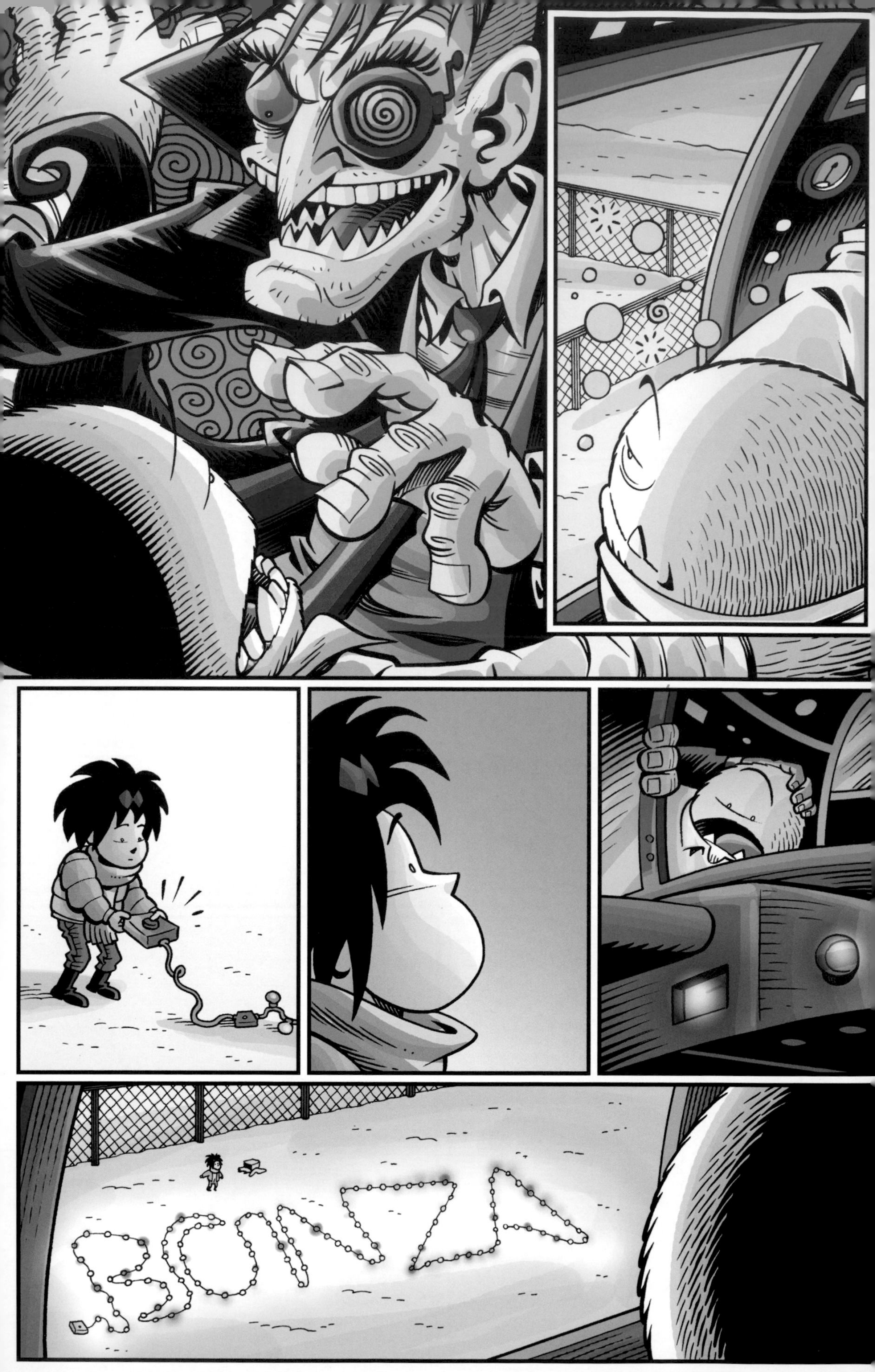
BONZA

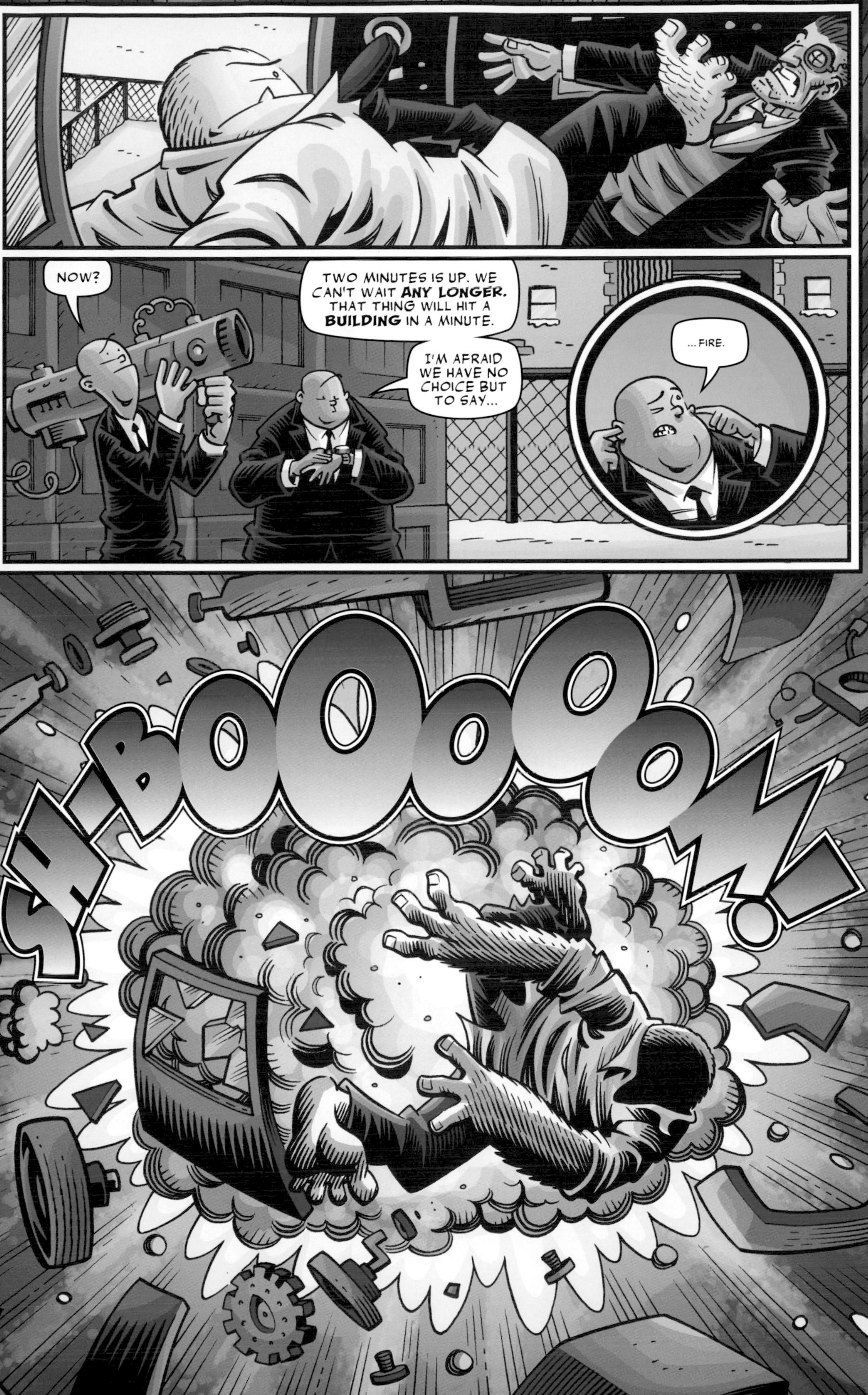
NOW?
TWO MINUTES IS UP. WE CAN'T WAIT **ANY LONGER.** THAT THING WILL HIT A **BUILDING** IN A MINUTE.
I'M AFRAID WE HAVE NO CHOICE BUT TO SAY...
...FIRE.
SH-BOOOOOM!!

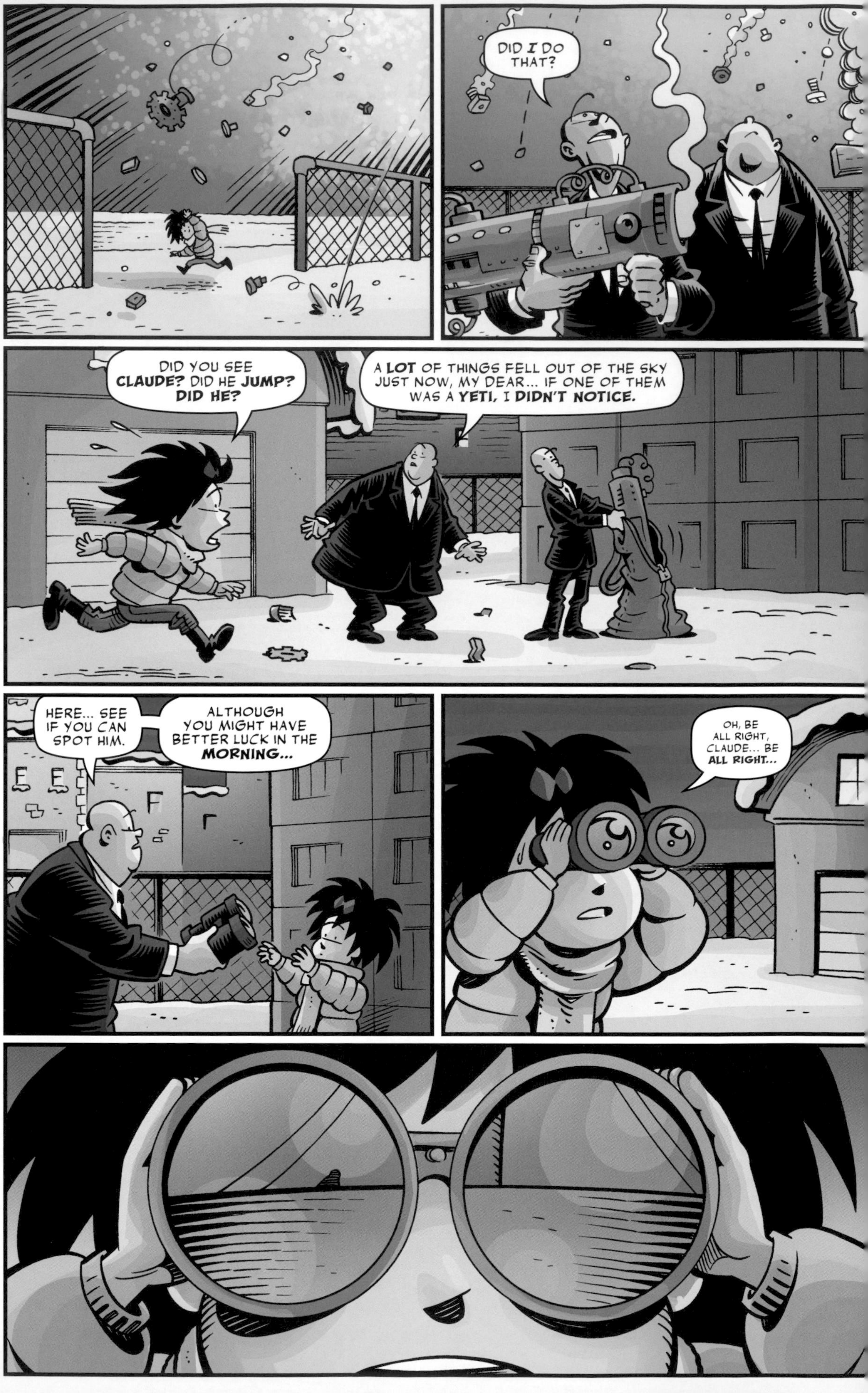

DID I DO THAT?
DID YOU SEE CLAUDE? DID HE JUMP? DID HE?
A LOT OF THINGS FELL OUT OF THE SKY JUST NOW, MY DEAR... IF ONE OF THEM WAS A YETI, I DIDN'T NOTICE.
HERE... SEE IF YOU CAN SPOT HIM.
ALTHOUGH YOU MIGHT HAVE BETTER LUCK IN THE MORNING...
OH, BE ALL RIGHT, CLAUDE... BE ALL RIGHT...

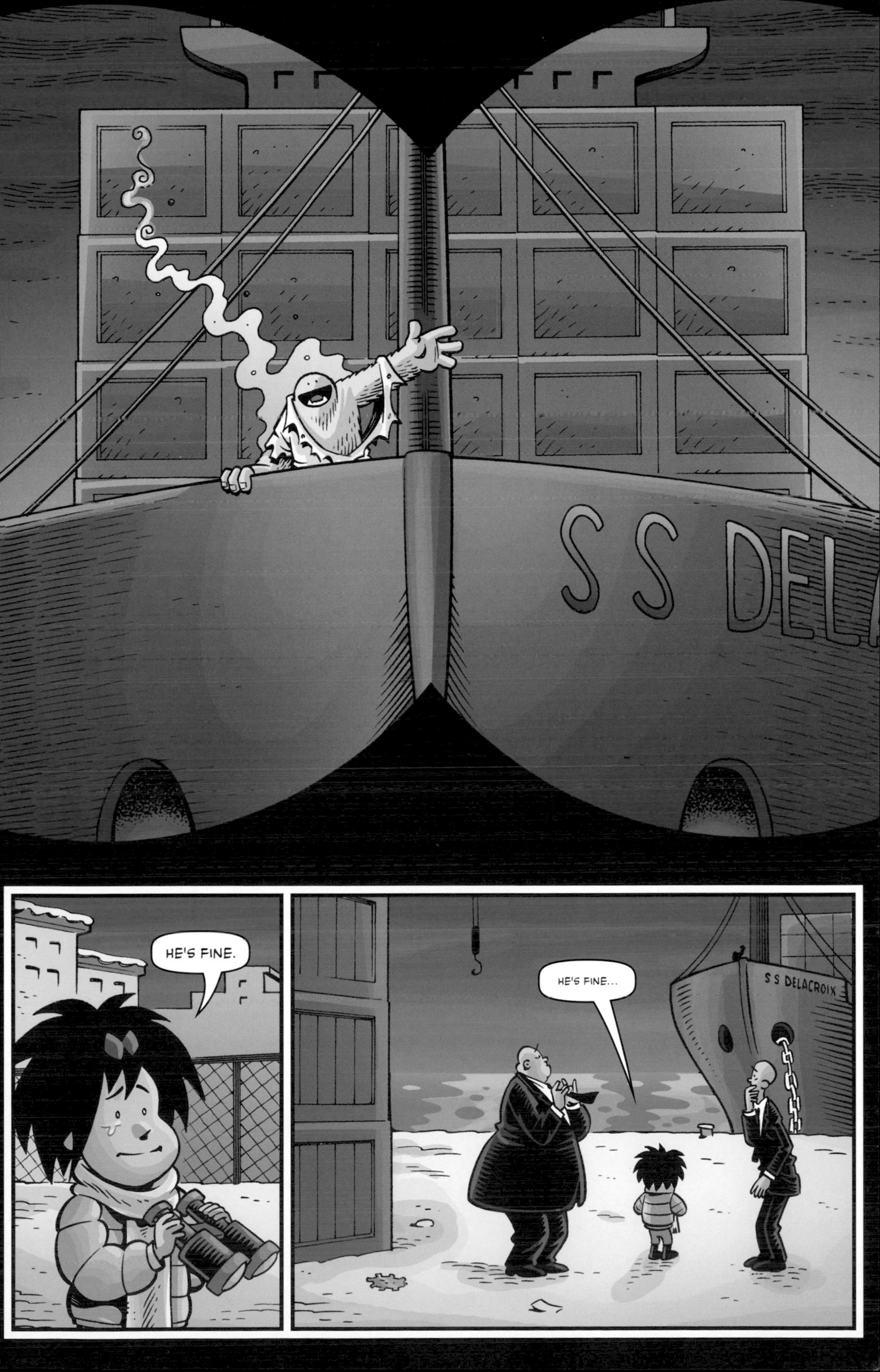
S S DEL
HE'S FINE.
HE'S FINE...
S S DELACROIX

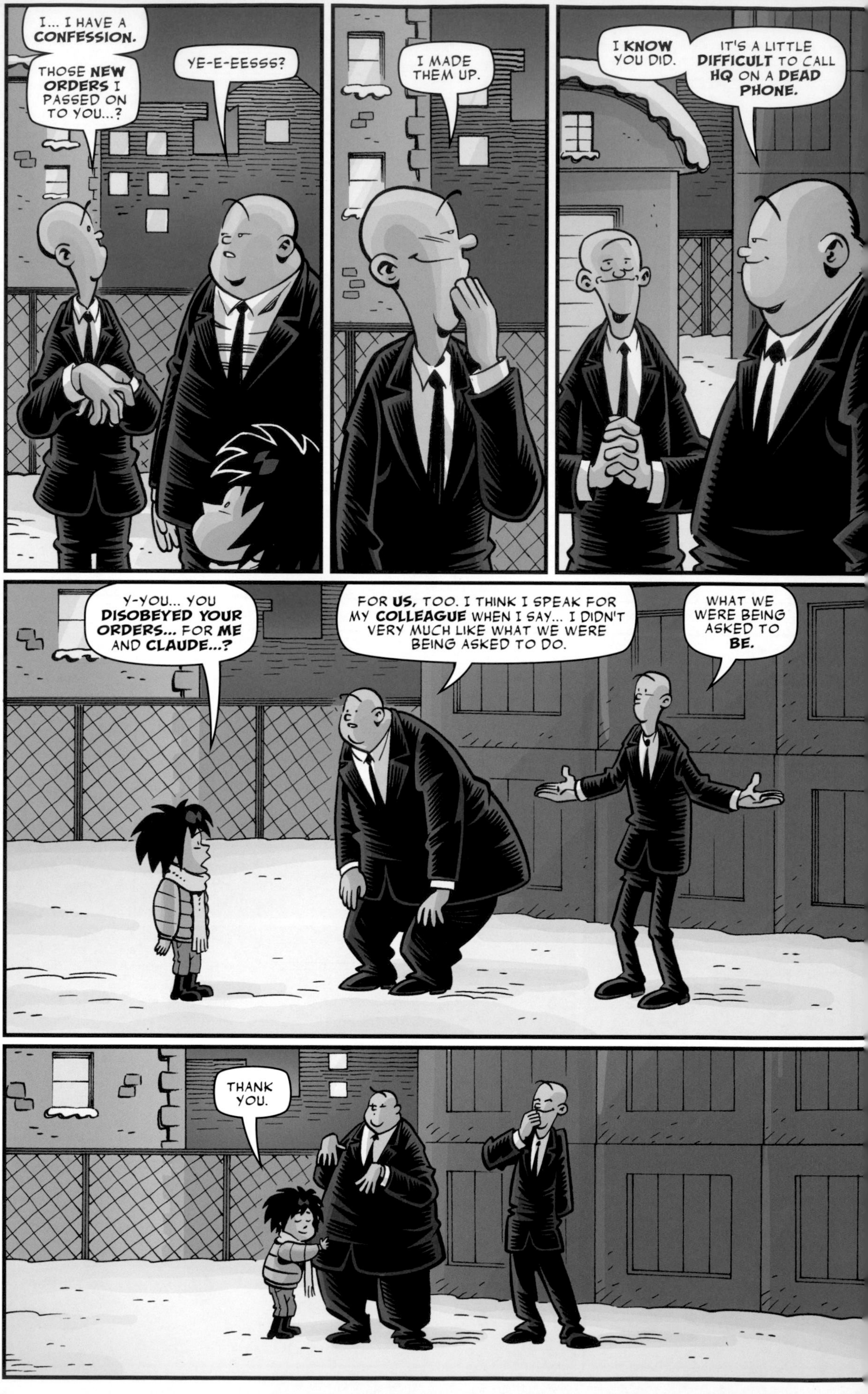
I... I HAVE A CONFESSION.
THOSE NEW ORDERS I PASSED ON TO YOU...?
YE-E-EESSS?
I MADE THEM UP.
I KNOW YOU DID.
IT'S A LITTLE DIFFICULT TO CALL HQ ON A DEAD PHONE.
Y-YOU... YOU DISOBEYED YOUR ORDERS... FOR ME AND CLAUDE...?
FOR US, TOO. I THINK I SPEAK FOR MY COLLEAGUE WHEN I SAY... I DIDN'T VERY MUCH LIKE WHAT WE WERE BEING ASKED TO DO.
WHAT WE WERE BEING ASKED TO BE.
THANK YOU.

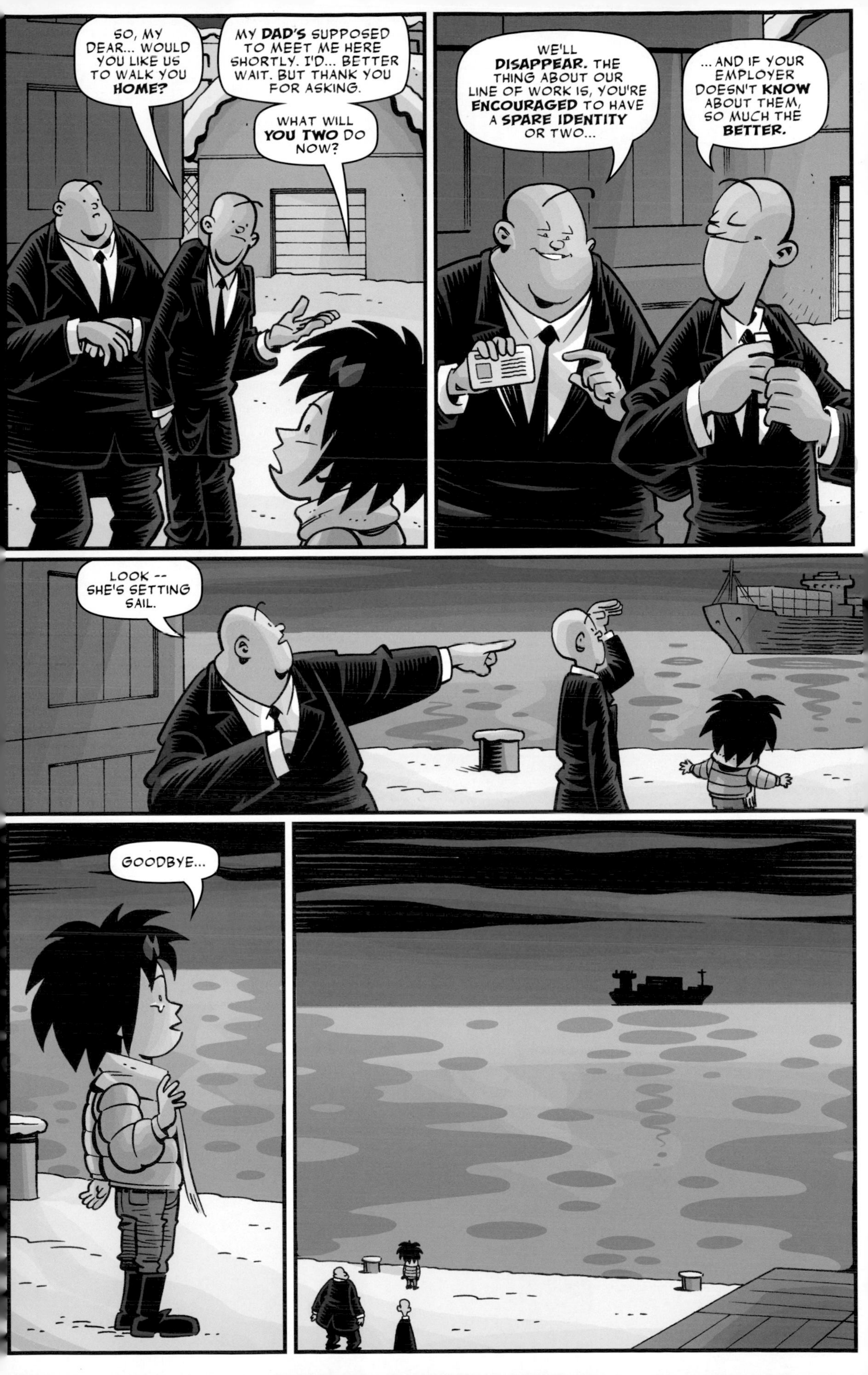
SO, MY DEAR... WOULD YOU LIKE US TO WALK YOU **HOME?**
MY **DAD'S** SUPPOSED TO MEET ME HERE SHORTLY. I'D... BETTER WAIT. BUT THANK YOU FOR ASKING.
WHAT WILL **YOU TWO** DO NOW?
WE'LL **DISAPPEAR.** THE THING ABOUT OUR LINE OF WORK IS, YOU'RE **ENCOURAGED** TO HAVE A **SPARE IDENTITY** OR TWO...
...AND IF YOUR EMPLOYER DOESN'T **KNOW** ABOUT THEM, SO MUCH THE **BETTER.**
LOOK -- SHE'S SETTING SAIL.
GOODBYE...

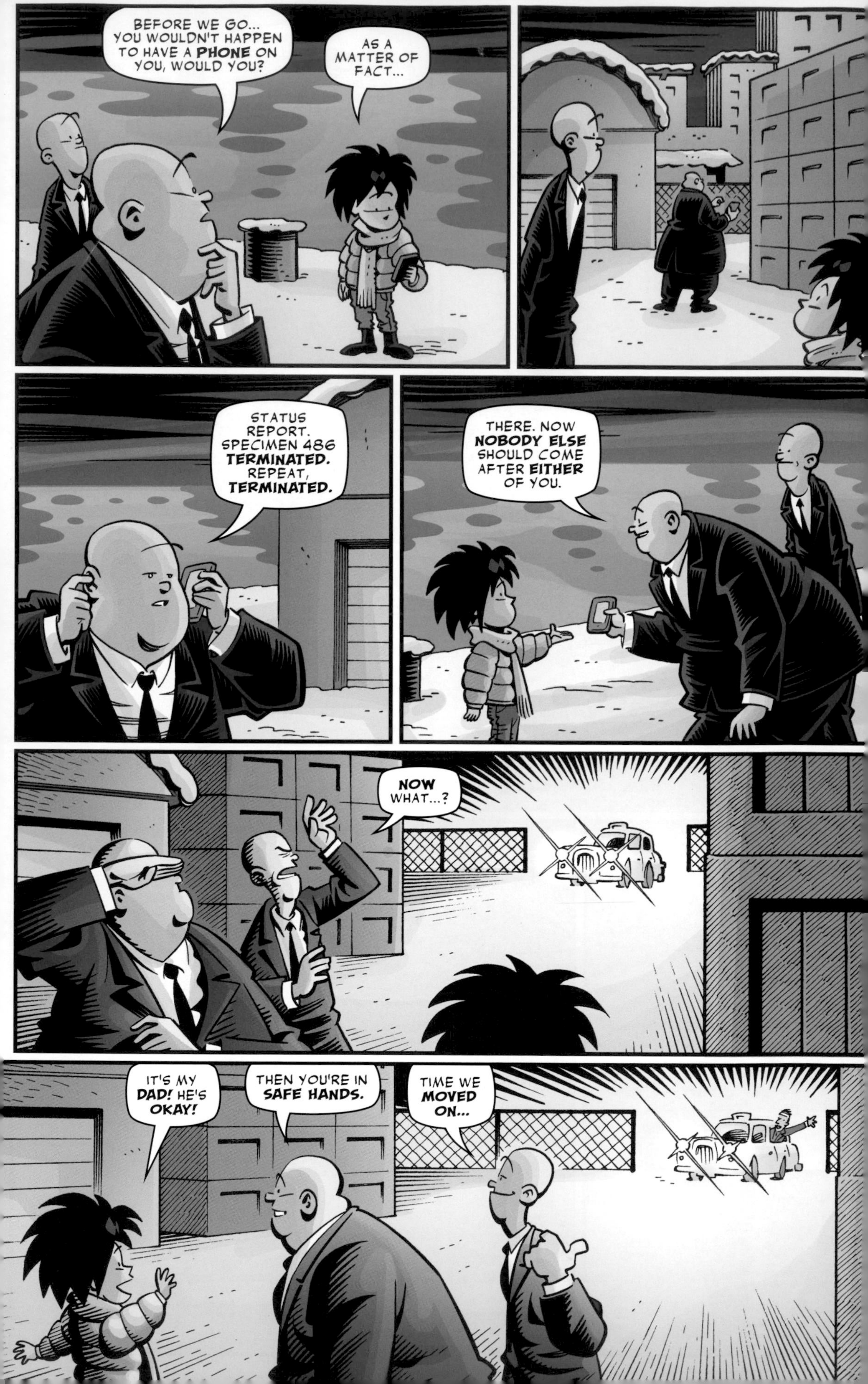
BEFORE WE GO... YOU WOULDN'T HAPPEN TO HAVE A **PHONE** ON YOU, WOULD YOU?
AS A MATTER OF FACT...
STATUS REPORT. SPECIMEN 486 **TERMINATED.** REPEAT, **TERMINATED.**
THERE. NOW **NOBODY ELSE** SHOULD COME AFTER **EITHER** OF YOU.
NOW WHAT...?
IT'S MY **DAD!** HE'S **OKAY!**
THEN YOU'RE IN **SAFE HANDS.**
TIME WE **MOVED ON...**

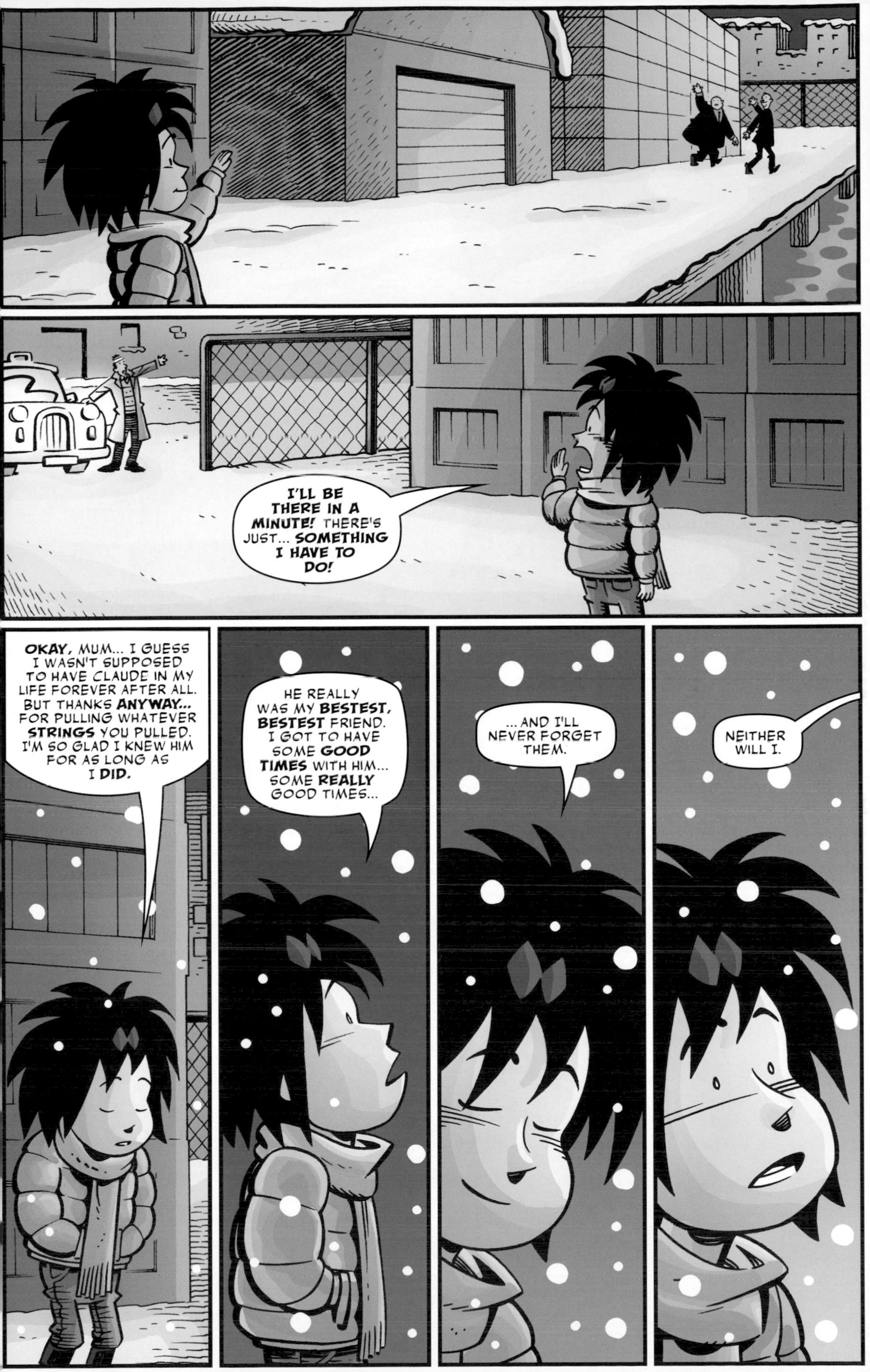
I'LL BE THERE IN A MINUTE! THERE'S JUST... SOMETHING I HAVE TO DO!
OKAY, MUM... I GUESS I WASN'T SUPPOSED TO HAVE CLAUDE IN MY LIFE FOREVER AFTER ALL. BUT THANKS ANYWAY... FOR PULLING WHATEVER STRINGS YOU PULLED. I'M SO GLAD I KNEW HIM FOR AS LONG AS I DID.
HE REALLY WAS MY BESTEST, BESTEST FRIEND. I GOT TO HAVE SOME GOOD TIMES WITH HIM... SOME REALLY GOOD TIMES...
...AND I'LL NEVER FORGET THEM.
NEITHER WILL I.

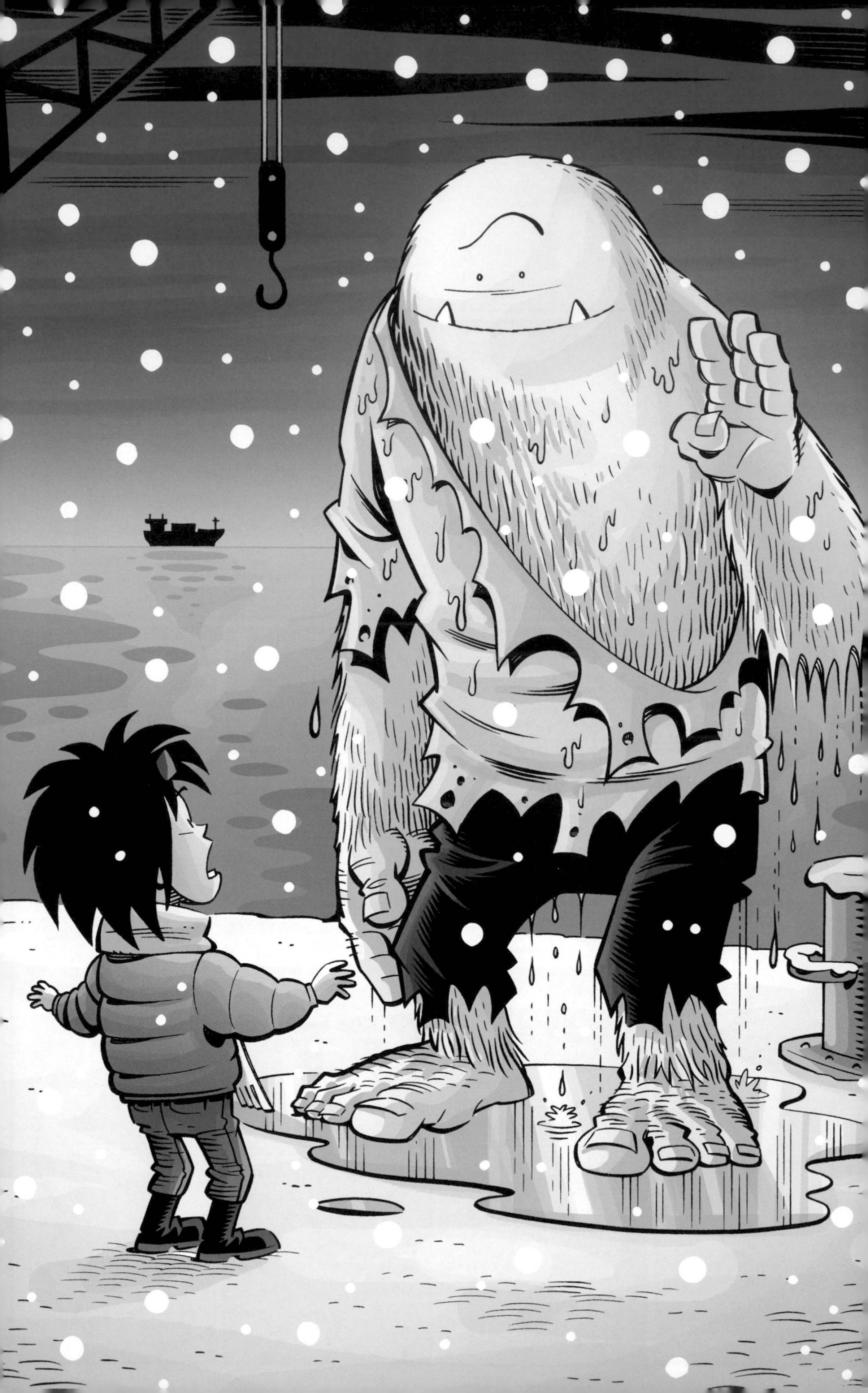

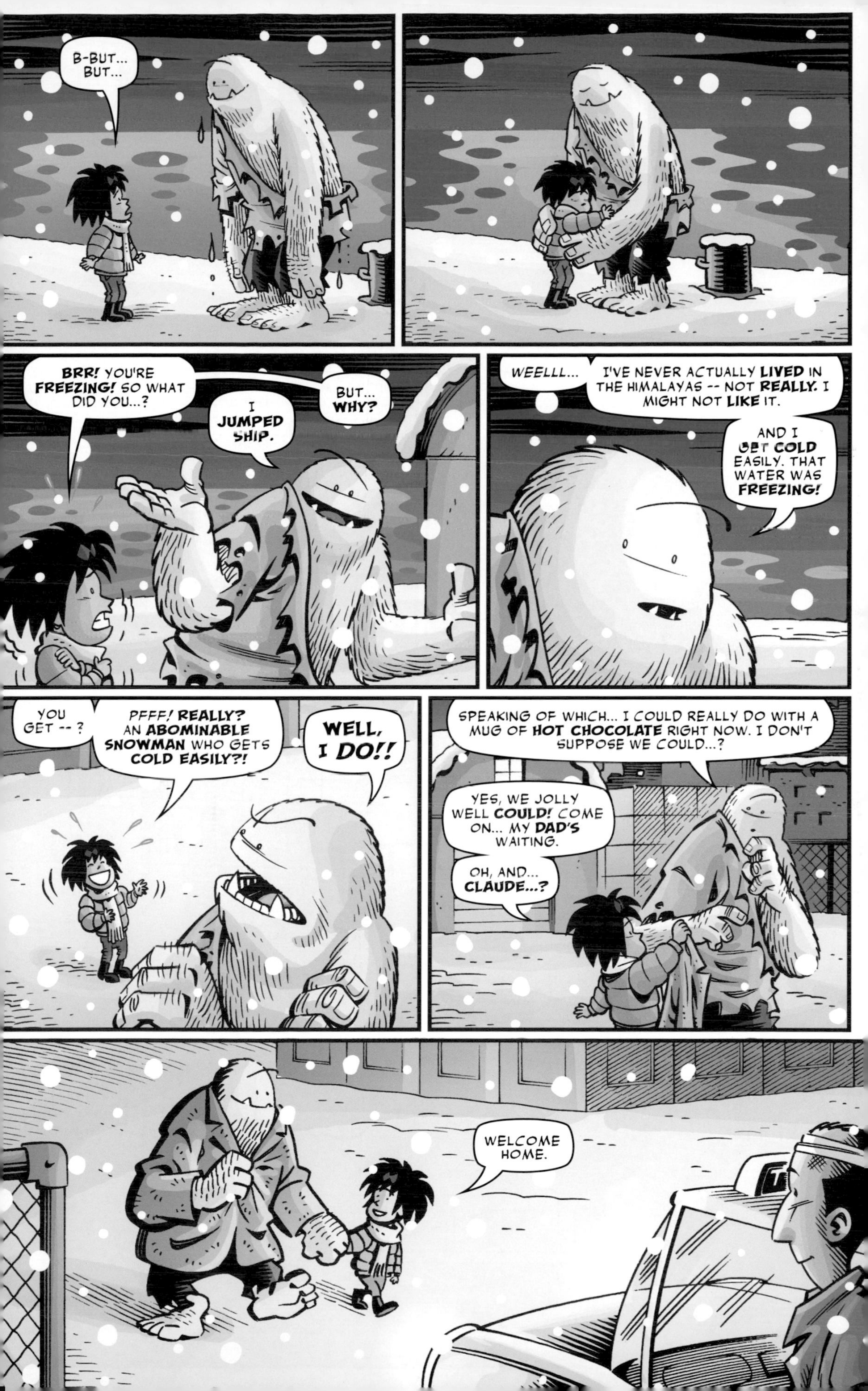
B-BUT... BUT...
BRR! YOU'RE FREEZING! SO WHAT DID YOU...?
I JUMPED SHIP.
BUT... WHY?
WEELLL...
I'VE NEVER ACTUALLY LIVED IN THE HIMALAYAS -- NOT REALLY. I MIGHT NOT LIKE IT.
AND I GET COLD EASILY. THAT WATER WAS FREEZING!
YOU GET -- ?
PFFF! REALLY? AN ABOMINABLE SNOWMAN WHO GETS COLD EASILY?!
WELL, I DO!!
SPEAKING OF WHICH... I COULD REALLY DO WITH A MUG OF HOT CHOCOLATE RIGHT NOW. I DON'T SUPPOSE WE COULD...?
YES, WE JOLLY WELL COULD! COME ON... MY DAD'S WAITING.
OH, AND... CLAUDE...?
WELCOME HOME.

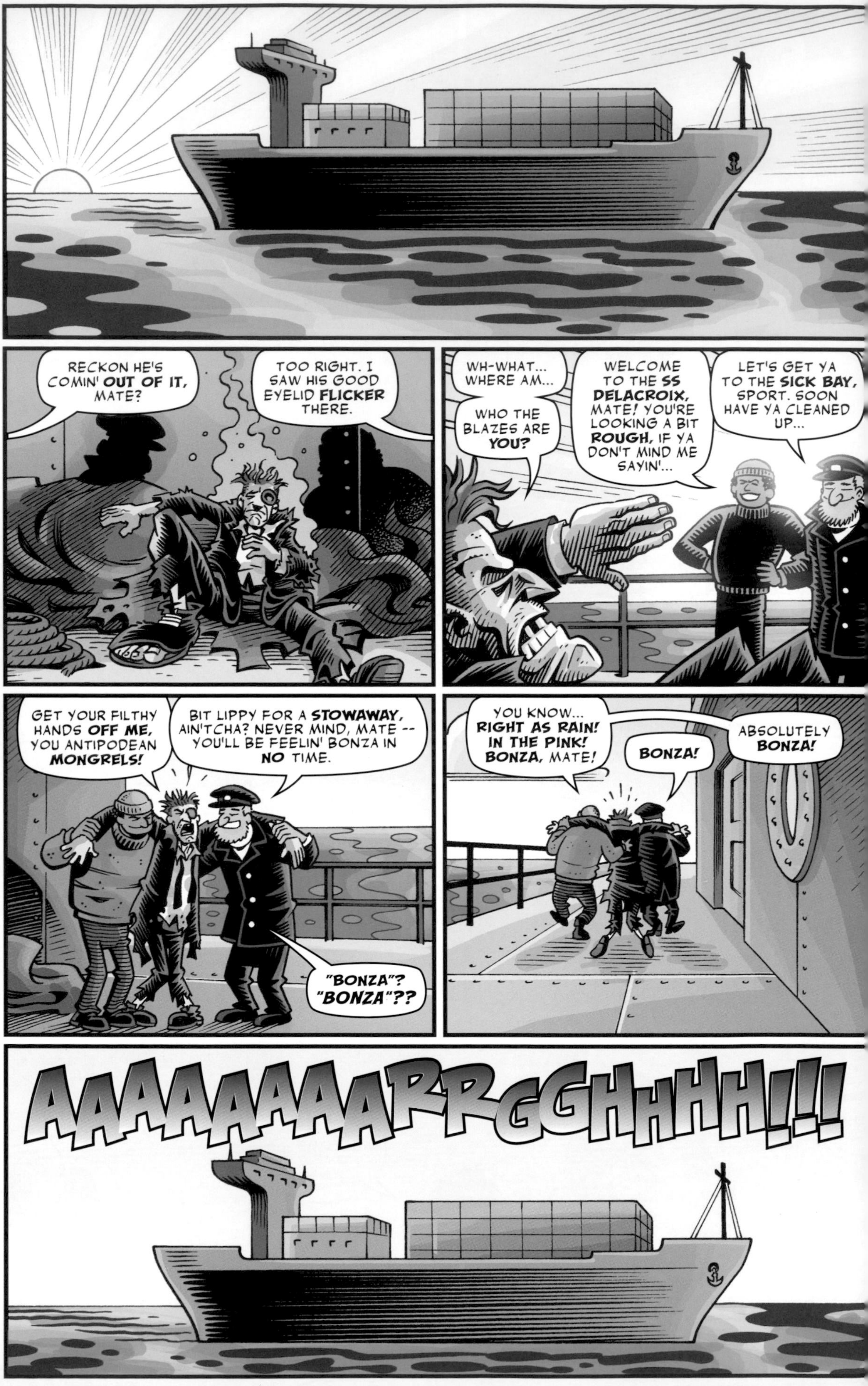
RECKON HE'S COMIN' OUT OF IT, MATE?
TOO RIGHT. I SAW HIS GOOD EYELID FLICKER THERE.
WH-WHAT... WHERE AM...
WHO THE BLAZES ARE YOU?
WELCOME TO THE SS DELACROIX, MATE! YOU'RE LOOKING A BIT ROUGH, IF YA DON'T MIND ME SAYIN'...
LET'S GET YA TO THE SICK BAY, SPORT. SOON HAVE YA CLEANED UP...
GET YOUR FILTHY HANDS OFF ME, YOU ANTIPODEAN MONGRELS!
BIT LIPPY FOR A STOWAWAY, AIN'TCHA? NEVER MIND, MATE -- YOU'LL BE FEELIN' BONZA IN NO TIME.
"BONZA"? "BONZA"??
YOU KNOW... RIGHT AS RAIN! IN THE PINK! BONZA, MATE!
BONZA!
ABSOLUTELY BONZA!
AAAAAAAARRGGHHHH!!!

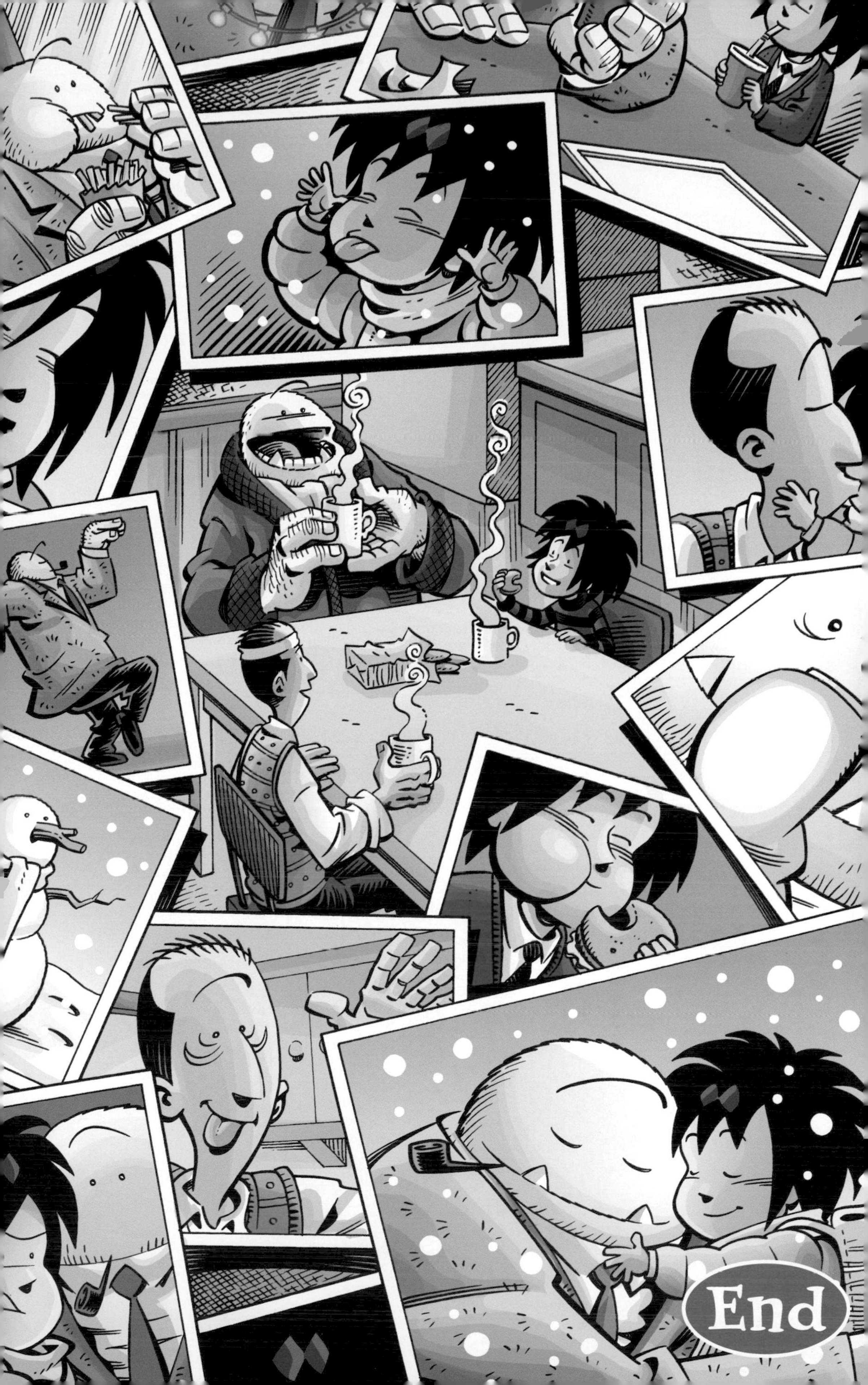
End

cover gallery

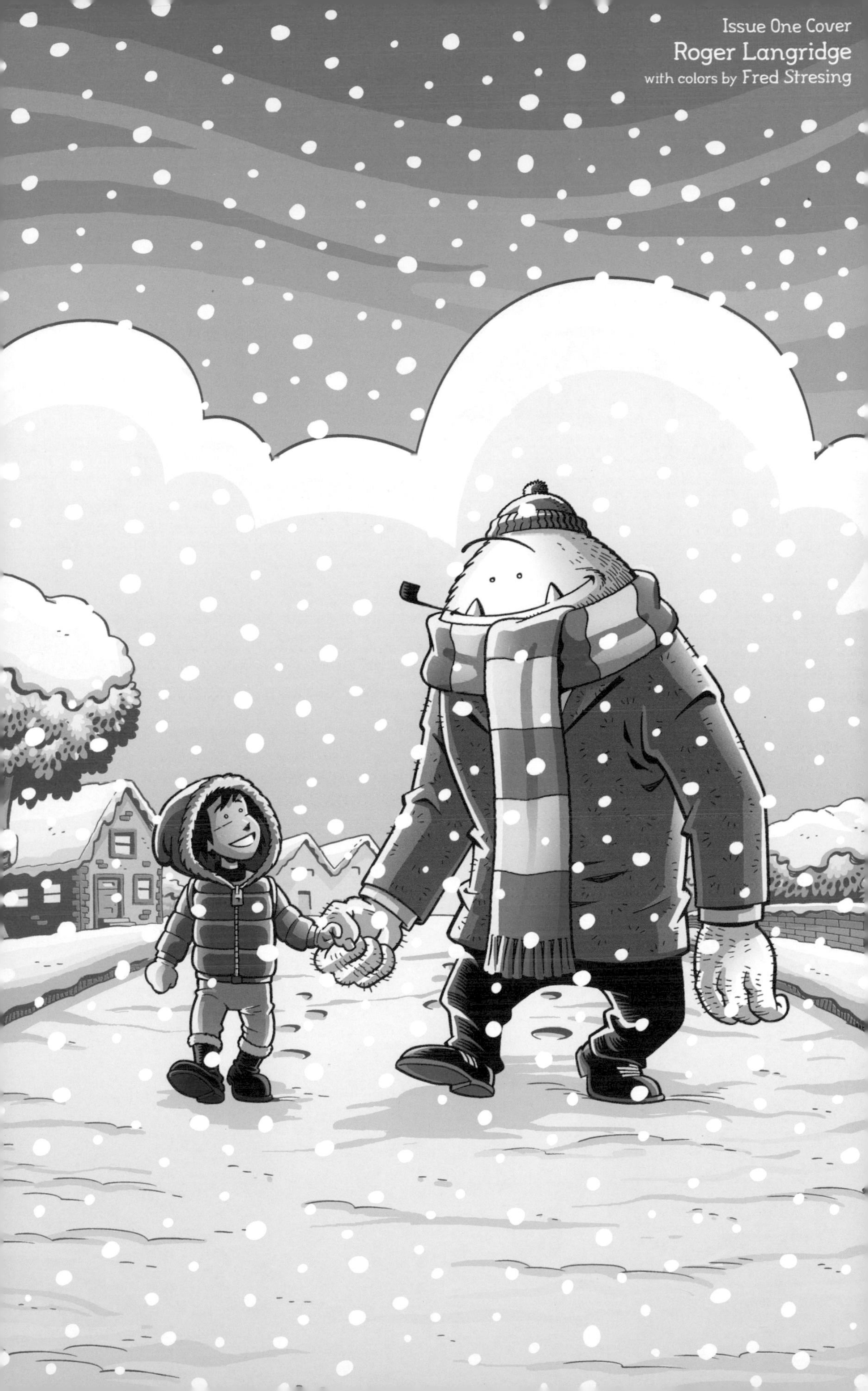

Issue One Cover
Roger Langridge
with colors by Fred Stresing

Issue One Variant Cover

Sonny Liew

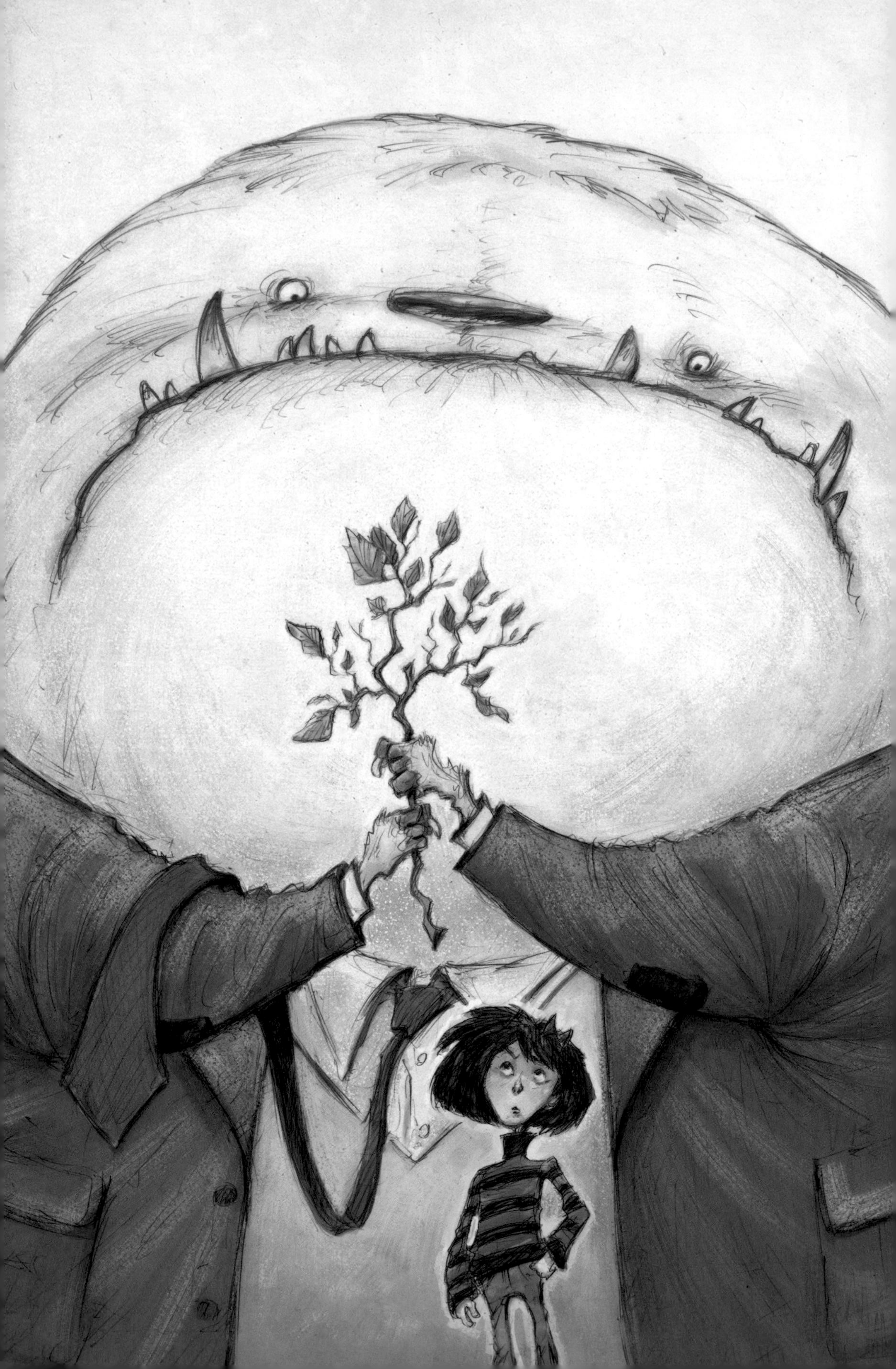

Issue Two Cover
Roger Langridge
with colors by Fred Stresing

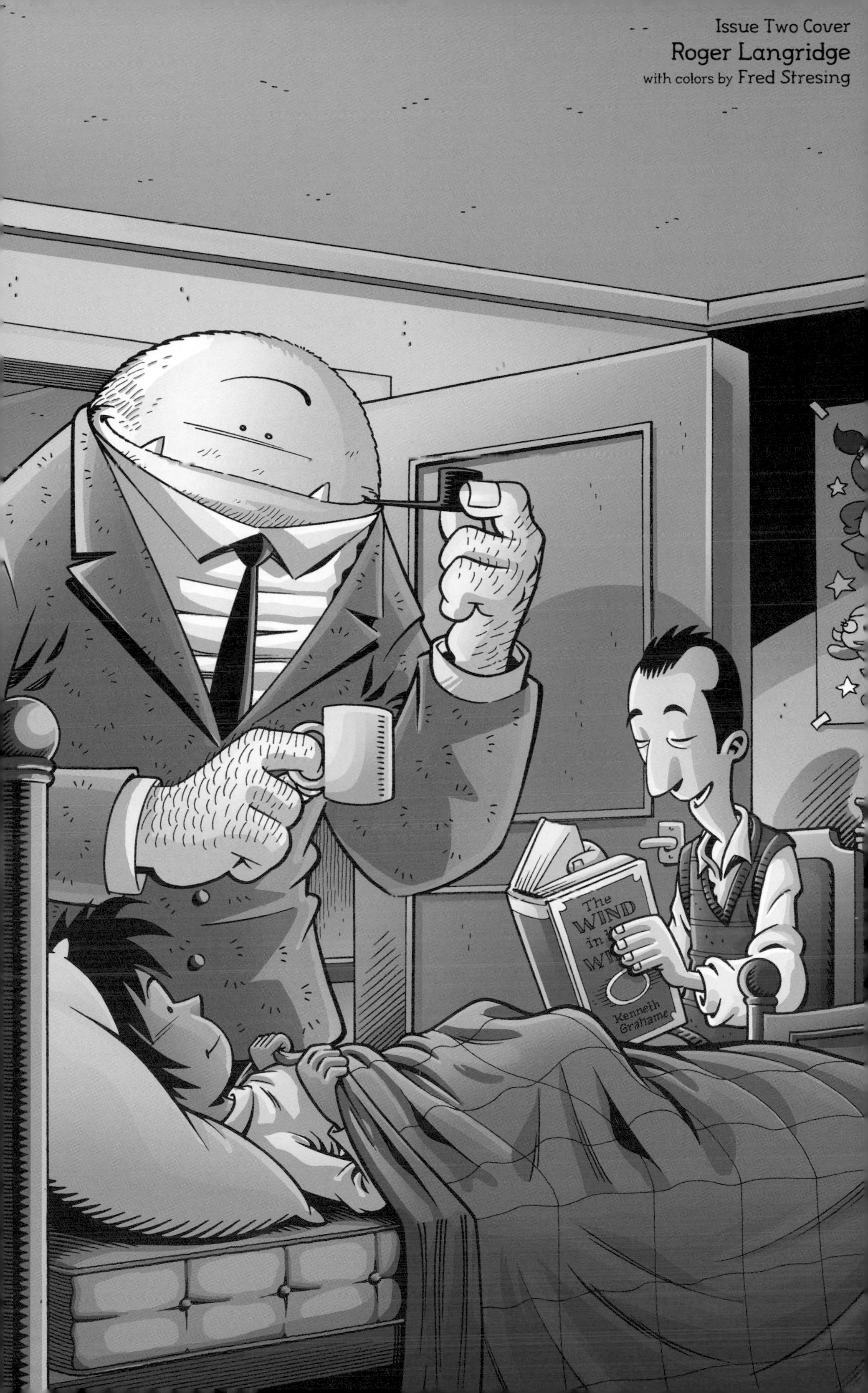
The WIND in
Kenneth Grahame

Issue Three Cover
Roger Langridge
with colors by Fred Stresing

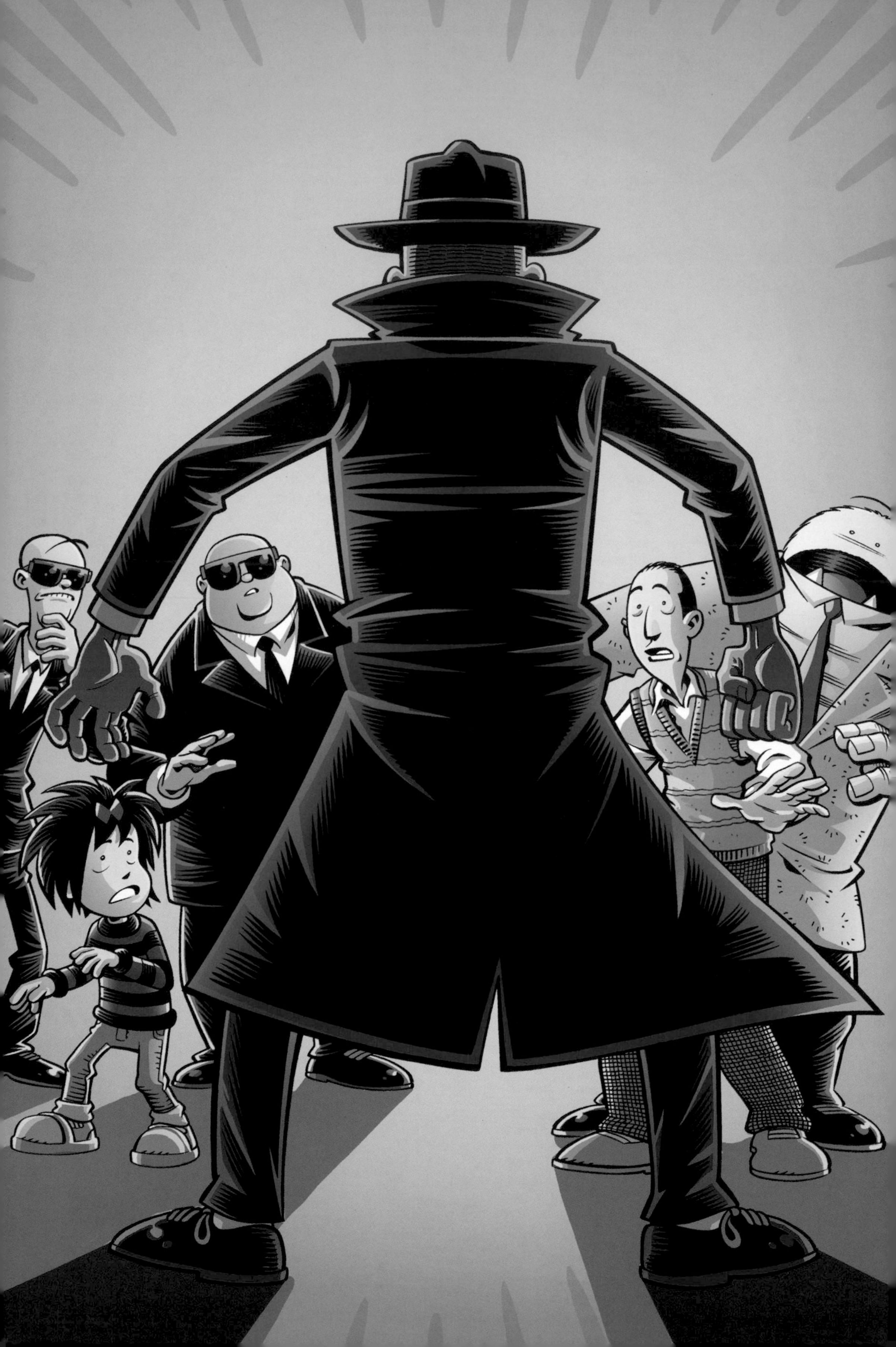

Issue Four Cover

Roger Langridge

with colors by Fred Stresing

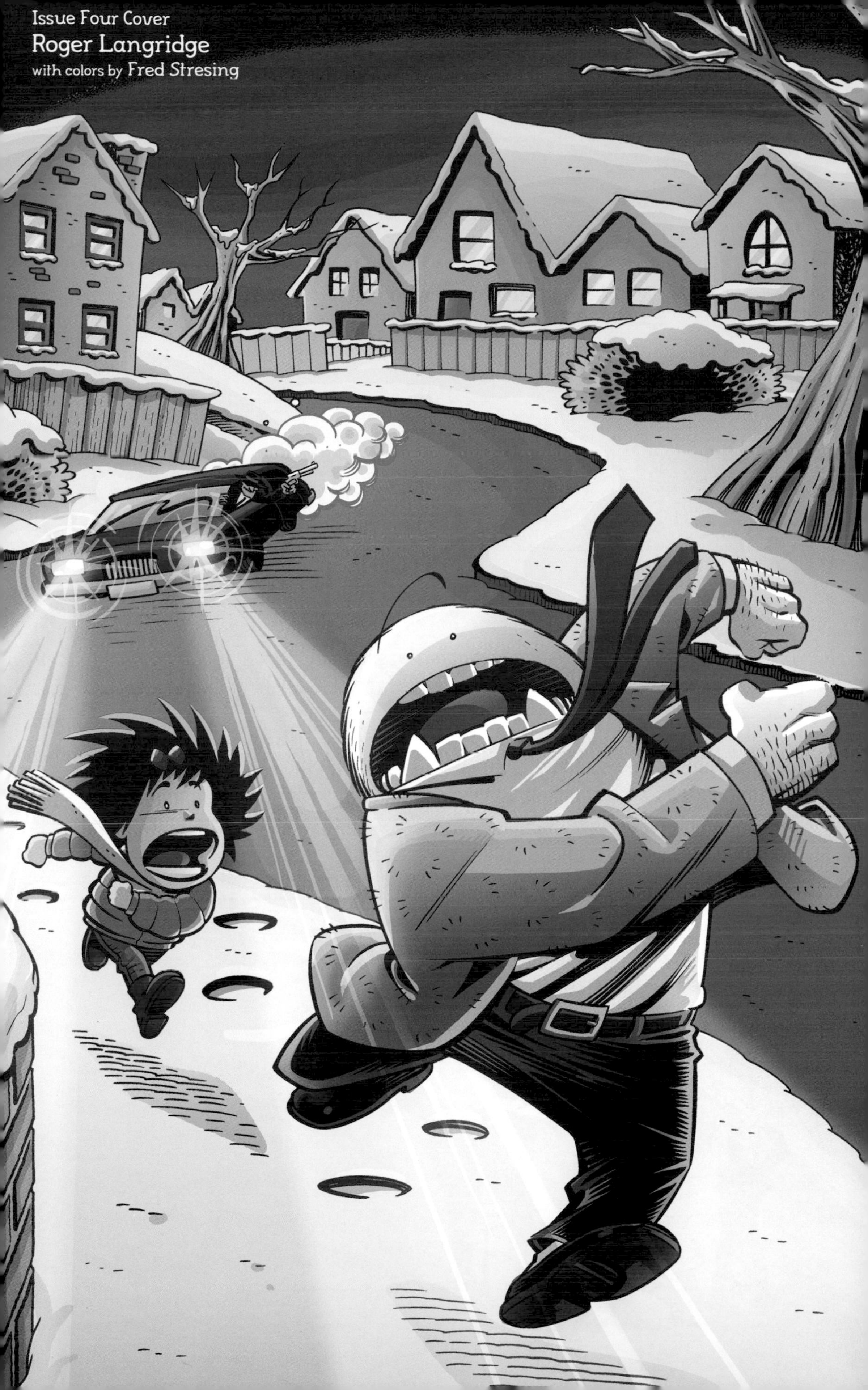

The ZOOKEEPERS

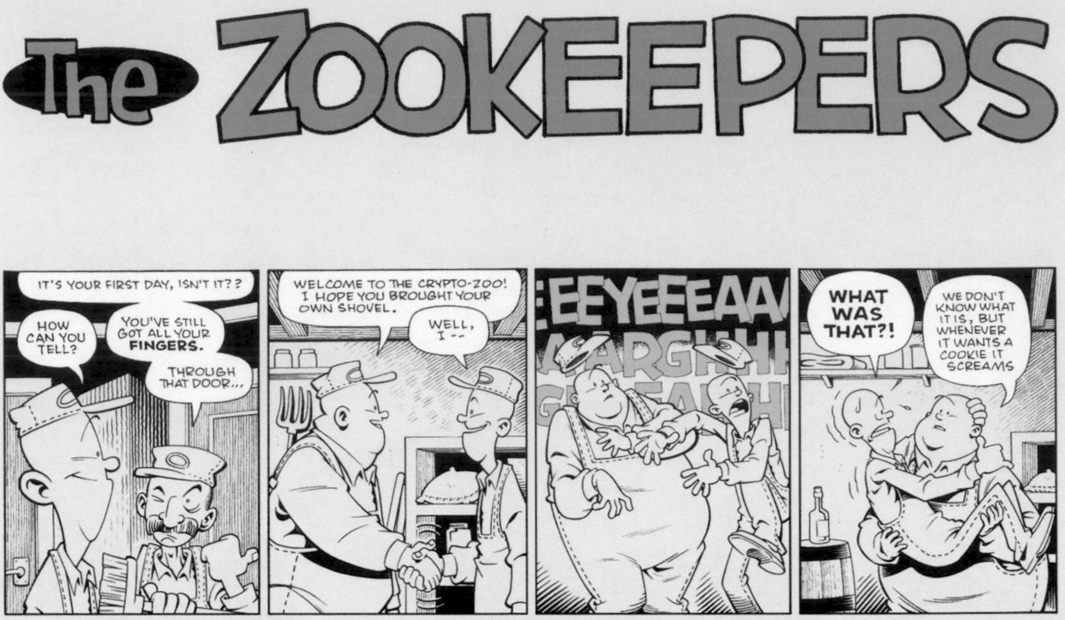
IT'S YOUR FIRST DAY, ISN'T IT??
HOW CAN YOU TELL?
YOU'VE STILL GOT ALL YOUR **FINGERS.**
THROUGH THAT DOOR...
WELCOME TO THE CRYPTO-ZOO! I HOPE YOU BROUGHT YOUR OWN SHOVEL.
WELL, I --
EEYEEEAA
ARGHHH
WHAT WAS THAT?!
WE DON'T KNOW WHAT IT IS, BUT WHENEVER IT WANTS A COOKIE IT SCREAMS

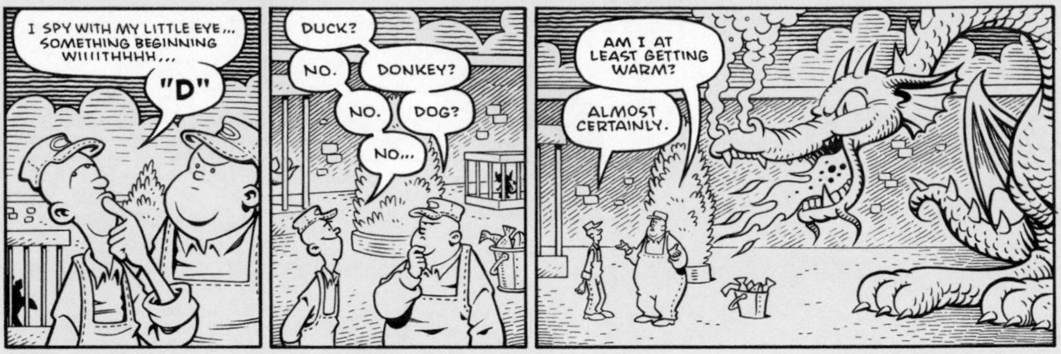
I SPY WITH MY LITTLE EYE... SOMETHING BEGINNING WIIIITHHHH...
"D"
DUCK?
NO.
DONKEY?
NO.
DOG?
NO...
AM I AT LEAST GETTING WARM?
ALMOST CERTAINLY.

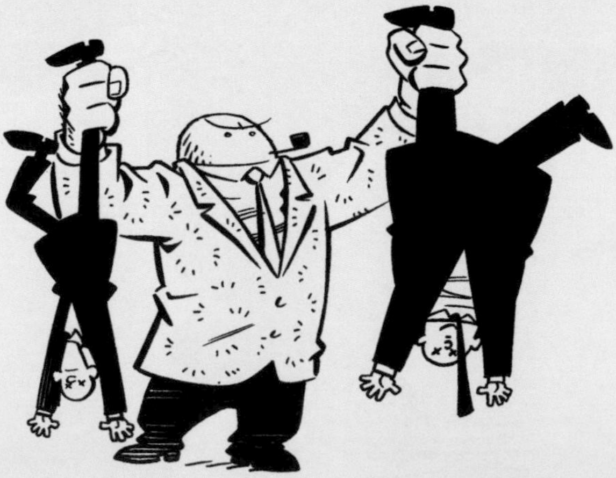

by Roger Langridge

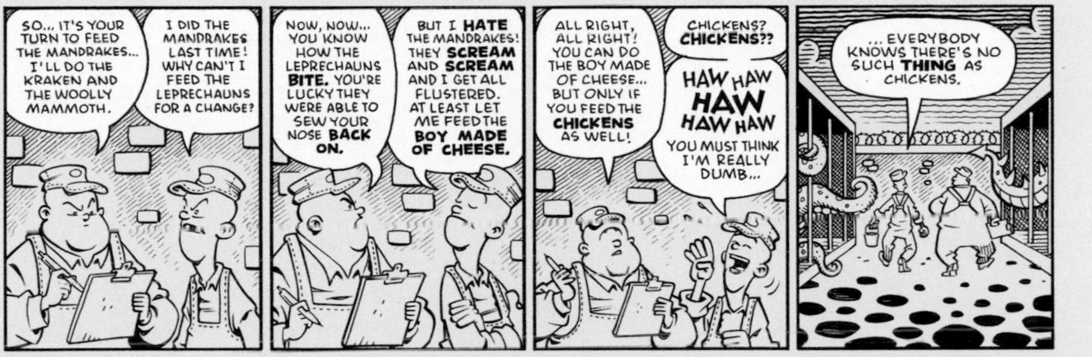
SO... IT'S YOUR TURN TO FEED THE MANDRAKES... I'LL DO THE KRAKEN AND THE WOOLLY MAMMOTH.
I DID THE MANDRAKES LAST TIME! WHY CAN'T I FEED THE LEPRECHAUNS FOR A CHANGE?
NOW, NOW... YOU KNOW HOW THE LEPRECHAUNS BITE. YOU'RE LUCKY THEY WERE ABLE TO SEW YOUR NOSE BACK ON.
BUT I HATE THE MANDRAKES! THEY SCREAM AND SCREAM AND I GET ALL FLUSTERED. AT LEAST LET ME FEED THE BOY MADE OF CHEESE.
ALL RIGHT, ALL RIGHT! YOU CAN DO THE BOY MADE OF CHEESE... BUT ONLY IF YOU FEED THE CHICKENS AS WELL!
CHICKENS? CHICKENS??
HAW HAW HAW HAW HAW
YOU MUST THINK I'M REALLY DUMB...
... EVERYBODY KNOWS THERE'S NO SUCH THING AS CHICKENS.

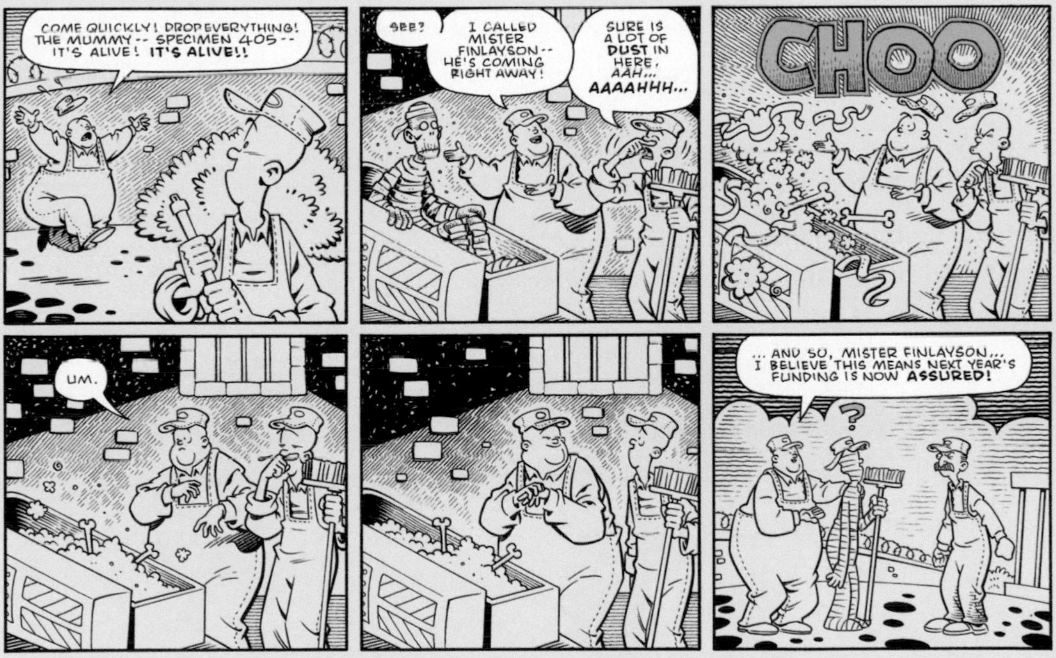
COME QUICKLY! DROP EVERYTHING! THE MUMMY -- SPECIMEN 405 -- IT'S ALIVE! IT'S ALIVE!!
SEE?
I CALLED MISTER FINLAYSON -- HE'S COMING RIGHT AWAY!
SURE IS A LOT OF DUST IN HERE. AAH... AAAAHHH...
CHOO
UM.
?
... AND SO, MISTER FINLAYSON... I BELIEVE THIS MEANS NEXT YEAR'S FUNDING IS NOW ASSURED!

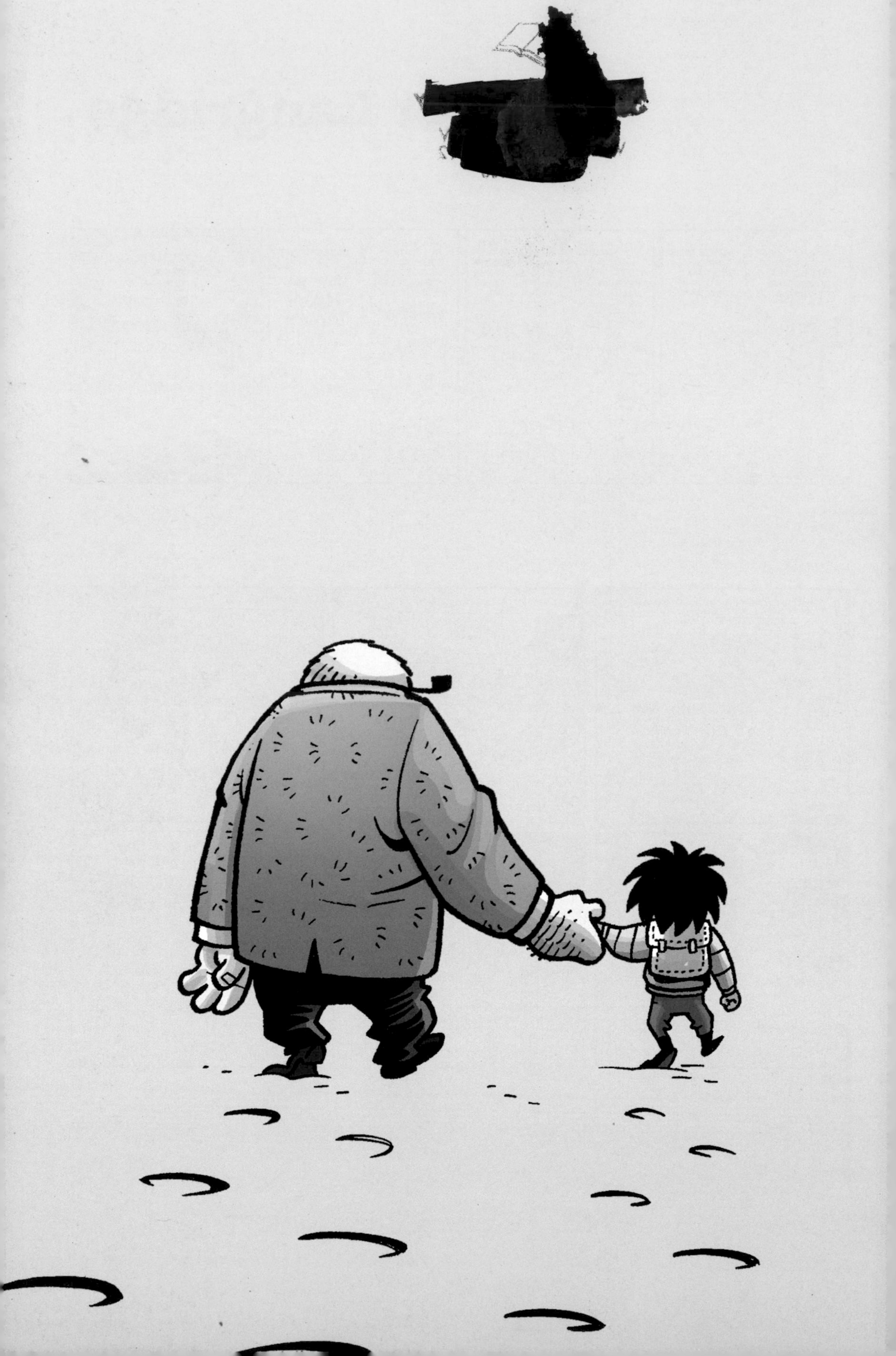